TITLES BY PATRICIA CORNWELL

food to Die for

Secrets from

FOOD T

Kay Scarpetta's Kitchen

Patricia Cornwell

and Marlene Brown

TO DIE F

BERKLEY BOOKS, NEW YORK
PRODUCED BY THE PHILIP LIEF GROUP, INC.

The recipes contained in this book are to be followed exactly as written. Neither the publisher nor the author is responsible for specific health or allergy needs that may require medical supervision, or for any adverse reactions to the recipes contained in this book.

A Berkley Book
Published by The Berkley Publishing Group
A division of Penguin Group (USA) Inc.
375 Hudson Street
New York, New York 10014

Copyright © 2001 by Cornwell Enterprises, Inc.
Produced by The Philip Lief Group, Inc.

Front cover photograph of Patricia Cornwell by Irene Shulgin.
Back cover and spine photographs by Harry Chamberlain.
Cover design by Rich Hasselberger.
Interior photography by Harry Chamberlain.
Food styling by Marlene Brown. Prop styling by Kim Wong.
Interior book design by BTDnyc.

The following titles from Patricia Cornwell: *Postmortem*, copyright © 1990; *Body of Evidence*, copyright © 1991; *All That Remains*, copyright © 1992; *Cruel & Unusual,* copyright © 1993; *The Body Farm*, copyright © 1994; and *From Potter's Field*, copyright © 1995. Used by permission of Scribner, a division of Simon & Schuster, Inc. *Cause of Death*, copyright © 1996; *Unnatural Exposure*, copyright © 1997; *Point of Origin*, copyright © 1998; *Black Notice*, copyright © 1999; and *The Last Precinct*, copyright © 2000. Used by permission of G. P. Putnam's Sons, a division of Penguin Group (USA) Inc.

PRINTING HISTORY
G. P. Putnam's Sons hardcover edition / October 2001
Berkley trade paperback edition / October 2003

Berkley trade paperback ISBN: 0-425-19362-4

The Library of Congress has catalogued the G. P. Putnam's Sons hardcover as follows:

Cornwell, Patricia Daniels.
Food to die for: secrets from Kay Scarpetta's kitchen/
Patricia Cornwell and Marlene Brown.
p. cm.
ISBN 0-399-14799-3
1. Cookery. 2. Literary cookbooks. 3. Scarpetta, Kay (Fictitious character).
I. Brown, Marlene.   II. Title.
TX714.C6912   2001   2001019057
641.5—dc21

PRINTED IN THE UNITED STATES OF AMERICA
10 9 8 7 6 5 4 3 2 1

To

Cindy and Ed Booker,
who gave me my first cooking job—
at the Peregrine House
in Davidson, North Carolina

Acknowledgments

Thank you, Jamie Saxon of The Philip Lief Group, for your clever book concept that brought Patricia and me together, along with your amazing vision and guidance through the entire project. To Patricia Cornwell, my heartiest thanks for sharing with me your warm hospitality, your mouthwatering words in a dozen novels' worth of Kay Scarpetta's cooking adventures, and also your most treasured stew and barbecued steak recipes! I was also privileged to be part of an extraordinary photographic team, with my friend and photographer Harry Chamberlain, prop stylist Kim Wong, and food styling assistant Carolyn Styler. Last but not least, many thanks to my husband and chief taster, John Oliphant, and to my mother, Lorraine Brown, who has always been my best editor.

—*Marlene Brown*

CONTENTS

Point of Origin

Black Notice

The Last Precinct

KILLER INGREDIENTS

COURSES

Appetizers

Funghi e Carciofi *(Mushroom and Artichoke Appetizer)*	92	From Potter's Field
Jumbo Shrimp with Bev's Kicked by a Horse Cocktail Sauce	174	Unnatural Exposure
Crostini di Polenta con Funghi Trifolati *(Grilled Polenta Topped with Sautéed Assorted Mushrooms)*	212	The Last Precinct

Soups

Miami-Style Chili with Beer	58	All That Remains
Zuppa di Aglio Fresco *(Fresh Garlic Soup)*	78	The Body Farm
French Onion Soup	134	From Potter's Field
Rose's Vegetable Soup with Italian Herbs	194	Black Notice

Salads and Side Dishes

Wild Rice Salad with Cashews	62	Cruel and Unusual
Marinated Slaw with Apple Cider Vinaigrette	69	Cruel and Unusual
Linguine with Olive Oil, Parmesan, and Onion	139	From Potter's Field
Fig, Melon, and Prosciutto Salad	160	Cause of Death
Greek Salad with Red Wine Vinaigrette	186	Point of Origin
Salade de Gruyère *(Swiss Cheese Salad)*	198	Black Notice
Giardinetto al Profumo di Erbe *(Grilled Garden Vegetables)*	215	The Last Precinct

Breads

Mrs. McTigue's Cheddar Cheese Biscuits	36	Body of Evidence
Hearty Seven-Grain Bread	66	Cruel and Unusual
Braided Country Bread	152	Cause of Death

Dinner Entrees

Pasta and Pizza

Italian Sausage Pizza with Peppers, Mushrooms, and Onions	28	Postmortem
Le Pappardelle del Cantunzein (*Yellow and Green Broad Noodles with Sweet Peppers and Sausage*)	50	All That Remains
Kay's Fresh Pasta	52	All That Remains
Ravioli with Squash and Chestnut Filling	80	The Body Farm
Rigatoni con Broccolo (*Rigatoni with Broccoli*)	129	From Potter's Field
Tortellini Verdi (*Spinach Tortellini*)	136	From Potter's Field
Lasagne with Marinara Sauce and Porcini Mushrooms	146	Cause of Death
Kay's Marinara Sauce	150	Cause of Death
Lasagne coi Carciofi (*Lasagne with Artichokes and Béchamel Sauce*)	154	Cause of Death
Kay's Grilled Pizza with Sausage, Pepperoni, and Three Cheeses	190	Black Notice

Fish and Seafood

Grilled Grouper with Butter and Key Lime Juice	64	Cruel and Unusual
Shrimp Sauté with Garlic and Lemon	90	From Potter's Field
Bev's Lump Crab Cakes	176	Unnatural Exposure
Lila's Clam Stew	178	Unnatural Exposure

Poultry

Pollo al Limone *(Lemon Chicken)*   94   From Potter's Field
Grilled Chicken Caesar Salad   184   Point of Origin

Meat

Grilled Marinated Rib-Eye Steaks	32	Postmortem
New York Steaks with Red Wine Marinade	42	All That Remains
Veal Breast Stuffed with Spinach Pistou	44	All That Remains
Pork Loin with Fig and Prosciutto Stuffing	47	All That Remains
Fruit-Marinated Lamb Kabobs	76	The Body Farm
Barbecued Baby Back Ribs	84	The Body Farm
Kay's Stew with Red Wine and Garlic	168	Unnatural Exposure
Costolette di Agnello alle Sette Erbe *(Lamb Chops Seasoned with Seven Herbs)*	217	The Last Precinct

Breakfast and Lunch Dishes

Omelet with Sweet Peppers and Onions	38	Body of Evidence
Fresh Fruit Salad with Blood Orange Dressing	162	Cause of Death
Classic English Breakfast *(Bacon and Eggs with Tomatoes and Mushrooms)*	164	Cause of Death
Marino's Breakfast Bagel Sandwich	182	Point of Origin
Marino's BLT on Rye	196	Black Notice

Desserts

Jack Daniel's Chocolate-Pecan Pie	86	The Body Farm
Madame Dugat's Mousse au Chocolat *(Chocolate Mousse)*	202	The Last Precinct
Lucy's Favorite Chocolate Chip Surprise Cookies	204	The Last Precinct
Peanut Butter–Chocolate Pie	206	The Last Precinct
Key Lime Meringue Pie	208	The Last Precinct

Introduction

Food has many meanings for me. It is comfort, love, warmth, and friendship. The essence of good cooking is generosity—not necessarily in the size of the portion served, but in the giving of self to fill spaces in the lives of others. When I cook for friends and family and occasionally when I concoct something special just for myself, I'm trying to supply the hungry spots—in both body and soul. When I invite people into my home, I want them to feel happy and tended to. I mean it as a special gift when I say, "Come over and I'll make pizza." When I return from a book-signing tour or a research trip, I don't feel at home until my refrigerator is full and friends are on their way over.

Using food to connect with others began when I was a child. The cookies I made then for my neighbors are the ones that inspired the cookies Lucy bakes in my novel *The Last Precinct*. I am warmed by recollections of homemade soups before the fire in the split-log house that Ruth Graham built. I treasure memories of Italian Christmas feasts at the home of Dr. Marcella Fierro, the intrepid forensic pathologist who has always been my mentor. When I sent homemade stew to my good friend Senator Orrin Hatch, he called me and said it was the most wonderful thing he'd ever had in his life. I knew it was my gesture—as much as the stew—that had fed a deep emotional need in his exhausting, stressful life. It doesn't matter whether every dish is a gourmet one; its true taste comes from the emotion of the heart that inspired it and the effort of the hands that made it.

Many of the dishes I prepare for others as well as include in my novels are related to healing and comfort. Of course, pasta is a fine medicine, and you'll see many of my favorite pasta recipes in this book, including two lasagnes. I call my Pappardelle del Cantunzein in *All That Remains* "mood food." Pasta is also love food. When you make fresh pasta, you're using your hands. Fresh pasta is light, warmth, and goodness all rolled together and created by touch. I included a Key lime pie for the Christmas dinner scene in *The Last Precinct* because I was inspired by memories of my grandmother, who had a Key lime tree that she allowed me to raid when I visited her in Florida. I would bootleg the limes back home, hoard the juice in the freezer, and make pies on special occasions. Even though I don't really like sweets and rarely eat them, I never turn down a pie made of real Key limes.

As I developed the character of Scarpetta, it was a natural and logical choice for me to decide that she loves to cook. I wanted her to be Italian because such a rich heritage adds a lushness to what for her is otherwise a stark, hard life. After Scarpetta puts her hands on death all day, she needs to come home to abundant beauty, wine, and delicious food with family and friends.

Her philosophy of cooking, like mine, is a blend of the diagnostic and generous. She cooks according to need, whether it is to create a mood or to supply energy or to cure what ails you. She "doctors" whatever she is putting together, and there are no rules. The final outcome justifies the means. Creative cook that she is, she can make do and make it special.

Like Scarpetta, I cook intuitively and sometimes whimsically. For example, I use olive oil and honey in my pizza crust. I didn't discover that combination in a recipe somewhere; I got the idea when I worked my way through college as the chief pizza maker in the Peregrine House deli. One night when things were slow, I tried a little honey on a pizza crust because I had a hunch that it would be good. I have always had an instinct for knowing which ingredients will combine in a wonderful way: I imagine which ones will like each other, and the dish evolves in its own way.

I believe people should approach cooking with the heart and not as technicians. Become part of what you are creating instead of working to control it. Let it teach you instead of your telling it what to do. This is my philosophy of writing, and I learned long ago that if you let go, all that you lose are your limitations.

Many of my signature dishes, such as my Scarpetta Stew, never come out the same way twice. Each one has its own distinct personality, its own unique subtleties. The same is true of good wine, which speaks softly in a harmony of the distinctive tones that compose it. When I make stew, I begin with a huge pot and spend most of the day adding this and that, these and those. When I am really industrious, I pack containers of the finished product, homemade bread, and a nice Bordeaux or Burgundy into baskets that I give to special friends.

Many of my readers think I am Scarpetta. But I am all of my characters. So I can cook like Lucy and Marino, too. If you're not in the mood for homemade chicken soup with bay leaves and lots of sherry, then how about a breakfast bagel loaded with prosciutto, Swiss cheese, and slices of Vidalia onion? What about a Reuben sandwich that is so sinful you need a bib?

Let me make one final and very important point before I turn you loose on my recipes. Just as a case is only as good as the evidence brought in, whatever you cook will either succeed or fail because of the ingredients you use. Be diligent about searching for cold-pressed extra-virgin olive oil and whole milk Buffalo mozzarella. Don't clear the scene until you've found fresh tomatoes, fresh garlic, and fresh herbs like basil and oregano. Don't let bad weather, fatigue, or distractions goad you into buying what's convenient or on special unless you are eating only to refuel. If you are cooking as a gift, spend a little extra money and take your time. Because what you offer others is also what you will receive.

In this book, which was initially conceived by Jamie Saxon and Marlene Brown, you will find recipes for all my favorite dishes as well as several from the restaurants that appear in my novels. I hope you will be inspired to cook from the heart and that you will enjoy both the process and the outcome. Bon appétit!

R. Cornwell

PAGE 78

Zuppa di Aglio Fresco (Fresh Garlic Soup)

(PRECEDING PAGE) PAGE 168

Kay's Stew with Red Wine and Garlic

PAGE 136

Tortellini Verdi (Spinach Tortellini)

PAGE 28

Italian Sausage Pizza with
Peppers, Mushrooms, and Onions

PAGE 36

Mrs. McTigue's Cheddar Cheese Biscuits

(OVERLEAF) PAGE 162

Fresh Fruit Salad with Blood Orange Dressing

Food to Die for

When all else fails, I cook.

Some people go out after a god-awful day and slam a tennis ball around or jog their joints to pieces on a fitness course. I had a friend in Coral Gables who would escape to the beach with her folding chair and burn off her stress with sun and a slightly pornographic romance she wouldn't have been caught dead reading in her professional world—she was a district court judge. Many of the cops I know wash away their miseries with beer at the FOP lounge.

I've never been particularly athletic, and there wasn't a decent beach within reasonable driving distance. Getting drunk never solved anything. Cooking was an indulgence I didn't have time for most days, and though Italian cuisine isn't my only love, it has always been what I do best.

"Use the finest side of the grater," I was saying to Lucy over the noise of water running in the sink.

"But it's so hard," she complained, blowing in frustration.

"Aged Parmigiano-Reggiano is hard. And watch your knuckles, okay?"

I finished rinsing green peppers, mushrooms, and onions, patted them dry, and placed them on the cutting board. Simmering on the stove was sauce made last summer from fresh Hanover tomatoes, basil, oregano, and several cloves of crushed garlic. I always kept a good supply in the freezer for times like these. Luganega sausage was draining on paper towels near other towels of browned lean beef. High-gluten dough was on the counter rising beneath a damp dish towel, and crumbled in a bowl was whole-milk mozzarella imported from New York and still packed in its brine when I'd bought it at my favorite deli on West Avenue. At room temperature the cheese is soft like butter, when melted is wonderfully stringy.

"Mom always gets the boxed kind and adds a bunch of junk to it," Lucy said breathlessly. "Or she buys the kind already made in the grocery store."

"That's deplorable," I retorted, and I meant it. "How can she eat such a thing?" I began to chop. "Your grandmother would have let us starve first."

My sister has never liked cooking. I've never understood why. Some of the happiest times when we were growing up were spent around the dinner table. When our father was well, he would sit at the head of the table and ceremoniously serve our plates with great mounds of steaming spaghetti or fettuccine or—on Fridays—frittata. No matter how poor we were, there was always plenty of food and wine, and it was always a joy when I came home from school and was greeted by delicious smells and promising sounds coming from the kitchen.

It was sad and a violation of tradition that Lucy knew nothing of these things. I assumed when she came home from school most days she walked into a quiet, indifferent house where dinner was a drudgery to be put off until the last minute. My sister should never have been a mother. My sister should never have been Italian.

Greasing my hands with olive oil, I began to knead the dough, working it hard until the small muscles in my arms hurt.

Italian Sausage Pizza with Peppers, Mushrooms, and Onions

When all else fails, I cook," says Kay, well into the pages of *Postmortem*, *in reference to her personal coping strategies on a "god-awful" day. She doesn't consider herself much of an athlete, so she's not apt to go out jogging or dig out her tennis racket to shake off the day. But she does know Italian cuisine, and cooking is a head-clearing indulgence. What better way could there be to work out her frustrations than by greasing up her hands with olive oil and kneading her knuckles into a dough that is destined to become a pizza?*

Teaching a frustrated young Lucy how to grate the hard, well-aged Parmigiano-Reggiano cheese for the topping, Kay advises, "Use the finest side of the grater. . . . And watch the knuckles, okay?" Her other favorite cheese, fresh whole-milk buffalo mozzarella, small balls of butter-soft cheese that float in liquid, is a New York import that Kay buys from her favorite Richmond deli on West Avenue. When she's in New York, she goes to Grace's Marketplace on the Upper East Side, at 1237 Third Avenue (71st Street). The mozzarella must be fully drained before using it to keep it from "weeping" into the pizza toppings. Kay tears the mozzarella into small, tantalizing bits that will melt like silk in the oven and become "wonderfully stringy" when a slice of just-baked pizza is put on the plate. If you've always gone for the hermetically sealed hunk of mozzarella from the deli section of the supermarket, try the fresh—it will be a revelation.

For the sausage, Kay favors the sweet Italian Luganega, but your favorite sweet or spicy sausage will also do. Sometimes she also combines the sausage with well-browned, very lean beef. Bring out your extra-virgin olive oil, if you have it, to use in this recipe, and drizzle a little bit of it over the pizzas just before you bake them, à la Kay.

I worked in a pizza restaurant during my college years and one day hit on the idea of putting honey in my pizza dough. As it is for Kay, pizza is my great emergency food, and I always keep a stash of it in the freezer for quick meals. You can tightly wrap individual slices of the leftover pizza in foil, then place them in a tightly covered freezer container or self-sealing bag.

3/4 pound whole-milk mozzarella cheese (preferably fresh) or 3 cups
    pre-shredded mozzarella cheese

Pizza Crust:

3½ to 3¾ cups high-gluten flour or bread flour (see Note on page 31)

1 package rapid-rise active dry yeast

½ teaspoon salt

1½ cups very warm water (120° to 130°F)

1 tablespoon honey

1 tablespoon olive oil

Toppings:

2 tablespoons olive oil

2 green, red, or yellow bell peppers, cut into 1-inch pieces

1½ cups fresh shiitake mushrooms, stems removed and caps chopped
    or 1 large portobello mushroom cap, chopped

2 cups sliced Vidalia or yellow onions

4 cloves garlic, minced

2 tablespoons olive oil

2 tablespoons chopped fresh basil

2 tablespoons chopped fresh oregano

Salt and freshly ground pepper

$^3/_4$ pound sweet Italian sausage

2 cups Kay's Marinara Sauce (page 150), prepared marinara sauce, or
   Quick Marinara Sauce (below)

$^1/_2$ cup freshly grated Parmigiano-Reggiano

1. At least 4 hours ahead or up to overnight, drain the liquid from the fresh mozzarella cheese, if using. Place the cheese in a strainer lined with a clean kitchen towel or a triple layer of paper towels, set over a large bowl, and place in the refrigerator to drain. Pat the cheese dry, then tear into small bits. Cover and refrigerate until needed.

2. For the crust: In a medium bowl, combine 3 cups of the flour, the yeast, and salt. Stir in the very warm water, honey, and olive oil, stirring until mixture begins to leave the sides of the bowl. Turn the dough out onto a lightly floured surface and gather it into a ball. Knead the dough for about 10 minutes, until it is soft, smooth, and elastic, adding enough of the remaining flour to keep the dough from sticking.

3. Place the dough in a large greased bowl and turn to coat evenly. Cover the dough with plastic wrap or a damp, clean kitchen towel and place on the lowest oven rack. Turn the oven on to the lowest setting for 1 minute, then immediately turn the oven off. Let the dough rise for 30 to 40 minutes, or until doubled in size.

4. Punch the dough down. On a lightly floured surface, knead the dough ten times to release the air bubbles. Cut the dough in half and shape each piece into a ball. Cover the dough and let it rest while preparing the toppings.

5. For the toppings: In a large skillet, heat the olive oil over medium-high heat.

Add the bell peppers, mushrooms, onions, and garlic and cook, stirring frequently, for about 5 minutes, or until the vegetables are tender. Stir in the basil and oregano; season with salt and pepper. Transfer the vegetable mixture to a large strainer set over a bowl to drain. Wipe the skillet dry. In the same skillet, crumble the sausage and cook over medium-high heat for about 8 minutes, or until browned. Transfer to paper towels to drain.

6. To assemble the pizzas: Preheat oven to 450°F. On a lightly floured surface, roll out or pat each piece of the dough into a 12-inch round. Place each round on a lightly oiled baking sheet, pizza pan, or pizza baking stone. Spread half of the marinara sauce on each dough round; then sprinkle with half of the vegetable mixture, sausage, and Parmigiano-Reggiano. Top with the mozzarella.

7. Bake the pizzas (set the baking sheet or pizza pan on the lowest oven rack; set the pizza stone on the highest oven rack) for 10 to 13 minutes, or until the crust is golden brown and the cheese is beginning to brown. Cut into wedges and serve.

| MAKES TWO 12-INCH PIZZAS |

NOTE: *To make high-gluten flour: Place 3 cups all-purpose flour in a large bowl. Add vital gluten powder (available in health food and specialty food stores) according to the package directions. Continue as directed in recipe.*

Variation

QUICK MARINARA SAUCE: In a medium bowl, combine 2 cups pureed tomatoes, 2 tablespoons chopped fresh basil, 1 tablespoon chopped fresh oregano, 1 teaspoon crushed fennel seeds, and salt and freshly ground pepper to taste.

Grilled Marinated Rib-Eye Steaks

Kay Scarpetta could never be a vegetarian, because she simply loves good meat, and she knows how to bring out all of its succulence over a flaming grill. For her grilled marinated steaks, she buys prime-grade beef rib-eye from her favorite butcher. Almost always the health-conscious cook, however, she carefully trims off all of the outside fat from the meat.

This unusual marinade, one of Kay's favorites, has a sweet flavor from honey. A range for the amount of honey has been given for cooks who prefer a little less sweetness and more of a barbecue flavor. Your favorite bottled barbecue sauce serves as the base for this marinade, and extra-virgin olive oil helps to round out the flavor. Because the recipe calls for top-quality steaks, just a short bath in the marinade, as little as 30 minutes, is necessary to imbue them with the honey-barbecue flavors. Avoid marinating longer than a couple of hours, or the meat will have a mushy texture when grilled.

Perhaps because she faces life-and-death situations daily, it's no surprise that Kay's grilling style involves pouring the marinade and the olive oil from an outstretched arm held high over the steaks while they are grilling. This method results in plenty of dramatic flames that require her to be quick on her feet (and can be dangerous to a less experienced grill master). The reward is steaks that cook up with beautifully charred crusts on the outside and are juicy pink on the inside. You can achieve the same sizzling results, with smaller and safer flames, by generously brushing the marinade and the olive oil directly onto the steaks with a long-handled barbecue brush. Kay serves these steaks with a red Bordeaux, a Burgundy, or a pinot noir.

4 beef rib-eye steaks (1 inch thick, 10 ounces each), trimmed of fat

2 cups bottled barbecue sauce

½ to 1 cup honey

3 tablespoons extra-virgin olive oil plus additional for grilling

3 cloves garlic, minced

1. Arrange the steaks in a shallow glass or ceramic dish. In a large bowl, whisk together the barbecue sauce, honey (depending on desired sweetness), olive oil, and garlic until blended. Pour half of the mixture over the steaks, turning them over in the marinade to coat completely. Cover and refrigerate the steaks along with the remaining marinade (to be used later for basting the steaks), for at least 30 minutes or up to 2 hours.

2. To grill: Preheat the grill to medium-hot or preheat the broiler. Drain the marinade from the steaks and discard. Pat the steaks dry with paper towels. Arrange the steaks on the grill directly over the hot coals, then generously baste the meat with the reserved marinade and some olive oil. Grill the steaks for 16 to 20 minutes for medium-rare doneness (20 to 24 minutes for medium), brushing frequently with the marinade and olive oil, and turning the steaks once after 8 minutes. (Or place the steaks on the rack of a broiler pan. Broil 4 inches from the heat source, 9 to 10 minutes for medium-rare, turning them after 5 minutes.) The steaks will be charred on the outside and pink on the inside. Serve immediately on a warm platter.

SERVES 4

M rs. McTigue's apartment was halfway down on the left, and my knock was promptly answered by a wizened woman with scanty hair tightly curled and yellowed like old paper. Her face was dabbed with rouge, and she was bundled in an oversize white cardigan sweater. I smelled floral-scented toilet water and the aroma of baking cheese.

"I'm Kay Scarpetta," I said.

"Oh, it's so nice of you to come," she said, lightly patting my offered hand. "Will you have tea or something a little stronger? Whatever you like, I have it. I'm drinking port."

All this as she led me into the small living room and showed me to a wing chair. Switching off the

BODY

television, she turned on another lamp. The living room was as overwhelming as the set of the opera *Aïda*. On every available space of the faded Persian rug were heavy pieces of mahogany furniture: chairs, drum tables, a curio table, crowded bookcases, corner cupboards jammed with bone china and stemware. Closely spaced on the walls were dark paintings, bell pulls, and several brass rubbings.

She returned with a small silver tray bearing a Waterford decanter of port, two matching pieces of stemware, and a small plate arranged with homemade cheese biscuits. Filling our glasses, she offered me the plate and lacy linen napkins that looked old and freshly ironed. It was a ritual that took quite a long time.

Mrs. McTigue's Cheddar Cheese Biscuits

I n this scene from Body of Evidence, *Kay pays a visit to Mrs. J.R. McTigue, who was in charge of reservations for the Daughters of the American Revolution, where murder victim Beryl Madison spoke some months earlier. Mrs. McTigue serves Kay her freshly baked cheddar cheese biscuits, elegantly arranged on a silver tray with lace-rimmed linen napkins and cut-glass stemware filled with port.*

These miniature biscuits bake up with slightly crunchy edges and a flaky, butter-layered interior redolent of cheddar cheese. Keep in mind these secrets for mixing up light, flaky biscuits: When the butter is "cut in" (incorporated into the flour), make sure to cut the butter into successively smaller pieces, until no larger than small peas (a long-standing culinary phrase where pastry is concerned). The butter pieces must still be large enough to melt between the layers of dough during baking. You can use a pastry blender in a back-and-forth chopping motion in the mixing bowl, or two table knives scissor fashion.

Another secret is not to overwork the dough, because it is based on baking powder, not yeast, and therefore more delicate than bread dough. Knead the dough gently just a few times on a lightly floured surface, and roll it out with a few strokes of the rolling pin.

These biscuits bake up quickly and go well with a dinner or brunch menu, or with a salad lunch. If you prefer larger biscuits, simply use a 2-inch biscuit cutter, and increase the baking time by 2 to 3 minutes.

2 cups all-purpose flour

4 teaspoons baking powder

1 tablespoon sugar

1 teaspoon salt

$\frac{1}{2}$ teaspoon cream of tartar

6 tablespoons cold unsalted butter, cut into pieces

$\frac{2}{3}$ cup finely shredded sharp cheddar cheese

$\frac{3}{4}$ cup milk

1. Preheat the oven to 425°F. In a medium bowl, stir together the flour, baking powder, sugar, salt, and cream of tartar. Using a pastry blender or two knives scissor fashion, cut in the butter until the mixture resembles small peas.

2. Stir in the cheddar cheese. Add the milk all at once; stir the mixture until it is completely moistened.

3. Turn the dough out onto a generously floured board and gather it into a ball; knead about twelve times. With a rolling pin, roll the dough $\frac{1}{2}$ inch thick. With a biscuit or cookie cutter, cut the dough into $1\frac{1}{2}$-inch rounds. Place the rounds 1 inch apart on a greased baking sheet.

4. Bake the biscuits for 10 to 12 minutes, or just until light golden brown. Serve hot.

| MAKES 3 DOZEN BISCUITS |

Omelet with Sweet Peppers and Onions

As the plot thickens in Body of Evidence, Kay decides to cook a simple dinner for herself. As the story goes, it is an omelet that, unfortunately, she isn't destined to eat. But the great thing about omelets is that they can be whipped up in no time—Kay often eats them for supper when she's beat from a day at the morgue. She fills them with vegetables, cheese, and even fruit. (At a restaurant once, I had an omelet filled with cream cheese and fig preserves for brunch, and it was wonderful.)

An omelet pan, a small skillet about six to ten inches in diameter, is a worthwhile investment for making delicious omelets, especially if it is coated with a nonstick surface. Omelet pans have sloped sides that make it easy to move the omelet mixture around, and eventually, to flip it over its filling and slide it out of the pan.

Because omelets cook so quickly, it's important to get the filling ready first. Then heat the oil in the pan until it is just hot enough to sizzle a drop of water. Kay prefers her omelets well done, so she adds an extra flip: before spooning on the filling, she flips the cooked omelet over like a pancake to cook the other side until it's well done.

2 tablespoons olive oil

¼ cup chopped red, yellow, or green bell pepper

¼ cup chopped Vidalia or yellow onion

1 clove garlic, minced

1 tablespoon chopped fresh basil

Salt and freshly ground pepper

2 extra-large eggs

2 tablespoons water

1/3 cup coarsely shredded extra-sharp cheddar, Swiss, provolone, mozzarella, or white cheddar cheese, preferably Vermont

1. In an omelet pan or a small skillet, heat 1 tablespoon of the oil over medium-high heat. Add the bell pepper, onion, and garlic, and cook, stirring frequently, for 3 to 5 minutes, until very tender. Stir in the basil and season with salt and pepper. Transfer the vegetables to a plate; cover and set aside.

2. In a small bowl, whisk together the eggs and water; season with salt and pepper. Heat the remaining 1 tablespoon olive oil in the same skillet over medium-high heat until hot. Pour in the egg mixture all at once.

3. With a metal spatula, gently push the cooked parts of the omelet toward the center of the pan, allowing the uncooked portion of egg to flow underneath. Tilt the pan and continue moving the cooked portion of egg as necessary, until the egg thickens and no liquid remains.

4. When the underside of the omelet begins to brown (use a table knife or narrow metal spatula to lift the edge of the omelet to check it), spoon the vegetable mixture onto one half of the omelet. Sprinkle with half of the cheddar cheese. With a spatula, fold the omelet in half or roll one side of the omelet over the filling.

5. To serve, invert the omelet onto a dinner plate or slide it onto the plate by tilting the pan. Sprinkle the omelet with the remaining cheese and serve immediately.

SERVES 1

S pring lamb with white wine, breast of veal, or roast pork would be perfect." I filled a pot with water and set it on the stove. "I'm pretty amazing with lamb, but I'll have to give you a rain check."

"Maybe you ought to forget cutting up dead bodies and open a restaurant."

"I'll assume you mean that as a compliment."

"Oh, yeah." His face was expressionless, and he was lighting a cigarette. "So what do you call this?" He nodded at the stove.

"I call it yellow and green broad noodles with sweet peppers and sausage," I replied, adding the sausage to the sauce. "But if I really wanted to impress you, I would call it *le pappardelle del Cantunzein.*"

"Don't worry. I'm impressed."

"Marino." I glanced over at him. "What happened this morning?"

He replied with a question, "You mention to anyone what Vessey told you about the hack mark's being made with a serrated blade?"

"So far, you're the only person I've told."

"Hard to figure how Hilda Ozimek came up with that, with the hunting knife with a serrated edge she claims popped into her mind when Pat Harvey took her to the rest stop."

"It is hard to understand," I agreed, placing pasta in the boiling water. "There are some things in life that can't be reasoned away or explained, Marino."

Fresh pasta takes only seconds to cook, and I drained it and transferred it to a bowl kept warm in the oven. Adding the sauce, I tossed in butter and grated fresh Parmesan, then told Marino we were ready to eat.

"I've got artichoke hearts in the refrigerator." I served our plates. "But no salad. I do have bread in the freezer."

"This is all I need," he said, his mouth full. "It's good. Real good."

New York Steaks with Red Wine Marinade

When Washington Post *police reporter Abby Turnbull comes to Richmond, Kay invites her for dinner. It's a great excuse to escape her office at the morgue and head out to her favorite market to plan the menu. Selecting two perfect steaks, she decides that even these choice morsels can be improved greatly by one of her own special marinades. A simple mix of dry red wine, extra-virgin olive oil, and crushed fresh garlic works its magic on the meat, while Kay scrubs down the grill. Kay prefers her steaks medium-rare, with a lot of pink inside, so timings are given for both medium-rare and medium doneness. Add a couple of minutes to the grilling time if you prefer to see only a hint of pink inside the meat.*

For a crisp accompaniment, Kay's favorite choice is a side salad composed of Boston lettuce leaves, mushrooms, sweet Vidalia onions, and locally grown Hanover tomatoes, tossed together with a bottled blue cheese dressing.

4 New York strip steaks (1 inch thick, 10 ounces each), trimmed of fat

1½ cups dry red wine

¼ cup extra-virgin olive oil plus additional for grilling

4 cloves garlic, smashed

2 bay leaves

Salt and freshly ground pepper

1. Arrange the strip steaks in a shallow glass or ceramic dish. In a medium bowl, whisk together the red wine, olive oil, garlic, bay leaves, and salt and pepper to taste. Pour the mixture over the steaks and turn the steaks over to coat them with the marinade. Cover and refrigerate for at least 1 hour or up to 4 hours.

2. To grill the steaks: Preheat the grill to medium-hot or preheat the broiler. Pour off the marinade from the meat and discard. Pat the steaks dry with paper towels. Lightly brush the steaks on both sides with some olive oil. Place them directly over the hot coals and grill for 18 to 22 minutes for medium-rare doneness (20 to 24 minutes for medium), turning them once and brushing with additional olive oil. (Or place the steaks on the rack of a broiler pan. Broil 4 inches from the heat source for 8 to 10 minutes for medium-rare doneness; 12 to 14 minutes for medium doneness.)

3. Season with salt and pepper. Serve immediately on a warm platter.

SERVES 4

Veal Breast Stuffed with Spinach Pistou

An elegant breast of veal, rolled and sliced to display a pinwheel of fragrant basil and spinach stuffing, is a special entree for cooks who want something extra special for their dinner guests. A veal breast is unusual enough to warrant ordering one from your favorite butcher. Ask to have the breast boned, and have the butcher make a "pocket" in the meat for you. The pocket will be a deep slit in the long side of the breast, which makes it easy to stuff the meat.

The French word *pistou actually refers to a version of Italian pesto, made without the traditional pine nuts. Kay's is a combination of a French-style pistou of basil, garlic, and olive oil puree, mixed with sautéed mushrooms, Vidalia onions, spinach, and bread crumbs for a stuffing that promises to wind its way deliciously through the meat. Slathered inside the veal pocket, the stuffing can be corralled by sewing up the opening with a standard needle and thread, using large loose stitches that can easily be seen after roasting for quick removal. (Sterilize a household sewing needle with a flaming match.) Not surprisingly, Kay is good at this.*

Bake the veal roast uncovered at first to give it some color. If desired, you can also brush a meat colorant, such as Kitchen Bouquet, over the roast while it bakes to give it an extra brown glazing. Avoid making the red wine sauce overly salty by opting for canned low-sodium beef broth, and season the sauce with salt and pepper.

Spinach Pistou Stuffing:

1 cup loosely packed fresh basil plus leaves for garnish

2 tablespoons snipped fresh chives

6 cloves garlic, minced

1 extra-large egg

4 tablespoons olive oil

1 teaspoon salt

1/4 teaspoon freshly ground pepper

1 cup chopped fresh mushrooms

1/2 cup chopped Vidalia or yellow onion

1 cup fresh bread crumbs

1 package (10 ounces) frozen chopped spinach, thawed and
   squeezed dry

Veal and Sauce:

1 (3 1/2 to 4-pound) veal breast, boned and with a pocket

Salt and freshly ground pepper

1 1/2 cups dry red or white wine

2 cups homemade beef stock or canned low-sodium beef broth

1 cup minced Vidalia or yellow onions

3 tablespoons cornstarch

1 tablespoon tomato paste

1. To make the pistou: In a food processor or blender, combine the basil, chives, garlic, egg, 2 tablespoons of the oil, salt, and pepper. Purée the mixture until it is smooth.

2. In a small skillet, heat the remaining 2 tablespoons oil over medium-high heat. Add the mushrooms and onion and cook, stirring frequently, for 3 to 5 minutes, until the vegetables are tender but not browned. In a large bowl,

toss together the bread crumbs, spinach, mushroom mixture, and basil puree until combined.

3. Preheat the oven to 325°F. On a large work surface, place the veal breast with the pocket side facing you. Spoon the stuffing into the pocket, spreading it evenly along the length of the meat and keeping it away from the cut edge. Close the pocket by sewing it up with large loose stitches with a standard sewing needle and white thread. Starting at one of the short ends of the meat, roll up the roast, as tightly as you can, and place it seam side down. Tie up the roast with kitchen string.

4. Transfer the roast to a large shallow roasting pan. Season with salt and pepper. Pour the red wine and $1\frac{1}{2}$ cups of the beef stock over the roast. Sprinkle the onions around the meat.

5. Bake, uncovered, for 40 minutes. Cover the roasting pan tightly with aluminum foil. Bake for 1 to $1\frac{1}{2}$ hours longer, or until the meat is tender when pierced with a fork, basting the meat occasionally with the pan drippings.

6. Transfer the meat to a cutting board; cover and keep warm. Strain the pan drippings into a measuring cup; spoon off the fat. Add enough water to the pan drippings to equal $2\frac{1}{2}$ cups, if needed. Stir the cornstarch into the remaining $\frac{1}{2}$ cup beef stock. In a 2-quart saucepan, stir together the pan drippings, beef stock mixture, $\frac{1}{2}$ cup water, and the tomato paste. Bring the mixture to a boil over medium-high heat, stirring constantly. Reduce the heat and simmer, stirring frequently, for 1 to 2 minutes until the mixture thickens. Cook 2 minutes longer; taste and season with salt and pepper, if desired.

7. Untie the roast and remove the stitches. Cut the meat into $\frac{1}{2}$-inch-thick slices and arrange on a warm platter. Garnish with some fresh basil leaves and serve the sauce alongside.

SERVES 8

Pork Loin with Fig and Prosciutto Stuffing

I f you're intimidated by the prospect of cooking a roast, you will find that a boneless pork loin is perhaps the easiest cut of all. It actually consists of two sides of the loin that have been boned and tied with their flat sides slapped together in one neat package. The result is a neat cylinder of pork that, once roasted, can be easily sliced from one end. There is very little fat on this roast.

Kay loves this savory stuffing of dried figs, sautéed prosciutto, and sweet Vidalia onions. Slices of the finished roast reveal ribbons of the filling.

During roasting, watch that the top crust of the roast does not become too dark. Cover the roast loosely with a piece of aluminum foil when it gets to a nice golden brown stage. Pork is very lean and prone to drying out easily when overcooked, so use a meat thermometer, inserting it into the center of the roast. Pork is done at 160°F, but it continues to cook for a few minutes after roasting. So remove it at 150° to 155°F, and the temperature will catch up while you are preparing the sauce.

The glistening port wine sauce gets its stunning looks and flavor from the pan drippings and port wine. Since all of the alcohol cooks away in the saucepan, everyone at your table should be able to enjoy it. Kay's guests always do.

Fig and Prosciutto Stuffing:

1 tablespoon olive oil

¼ cup chopped Vidalia or yellow onion

½ cup chopped dried figs or prunes

½ cup chopped prosciutto (3 ounces)

Roast:

1 tablespoon chopped fresh sage

1 tablespoon chopped fresh thyme

1 teaspoon salt

¼ teaspoon ground allspice

1 (4 to 4½-pound) boneless pork loin roast, tied

Sauce:

3 tablespoons cornstarch

2 cups homemade beef stock or canned beef broth

¼ cup dry port

2 teaspoons chopped fresh thyme

Salt and freshly ground pepper

1. For the Stuffing: In a medium skillet, heat the oil over medium-high heat. Add the onion and cook for 3 to 5 minutes, or until tender and translucent. Stir in the figs and prosciutto; cook for 2 minutes longer. Remove from the heat.

2. Preheat the oven to 350°F. In a small bowl, stir together the sage, thyme, salt, and allspice. Set aside.

3. Place the pork roast, with a long side facing you, on a cutting board. (Do not untie the roast.) With a sharp knife, make vertical cuts about 4 inches long and 3 inches deep, at ½-inch intervals across the top of the roast. Spoon 1 tablespoon of the stuffing mixture into each slit, packing it in with the back of a teaspoon.

4. Place the roast on a rack in a shallow roasting pan. Rub the sage mixture generously over the roast. Roast the pork, uncovered, for 1 hour. Cover the

roast loosely with aluminum foil and roast for 20 to 40 minutes longer, or until the juices run clear when the meat is pierced and a meat thermometer inserted into the center of the meat registers 150° to 155°F (temperature will increase to 160°F during standing).

5. Transfer the meat to a carving board; cover and keep warm.

6. For the Port Wine Sauce: Pour the pan drippings into a strainer set over a measuring cup, scraping up the crusty browned bits from the bottom of the pan. Skim off the fat. Add enough water to the drippings to equal $\frac{2}{3}$ cup liquid, if necessary. Pour into a 2-quart saucepan. Whisk the cornstarch into the beef stock to avoid lumps; stir into the pan drippings with the port and thyme. Bring the mixture to a boil over medium-high heat. Reduce the heat to low and simmer, uncovered, for 2 minutes. Season with salt and pepper.

7. To serve, untie the roast and carefully slice it crosswise between the stuffing pockets into $\frac{1}{2}$-inch-thick slices, to retain some of the stuffing in each slice. Arrange the slices on a warm platter. Serve with the sauce.

SERVES 8 TO 10

Le Pappardelle del Cantunzein

(Yellow and Green Broad Noodles with Sweet Peppers and Sausage)

Kay prepares this colorful Italian dish for Marino, serving it with a bottle of Mondavi red. Pappardelle, $3/4$-inch-wide Italian noodles, can easily be made from Kay's Fresh Pasta.

SHORTCUT TIP: *No time to make homemade pasta? Purchase sheets of fresh spinach and egg pasta, or a high-quality dried pasta from an Italian deli or specialty food store.*

$1/2$ recipe Kay's Fresh Spinach Pasta (page 55), 12 ounces
    store-bought fresh spinach pasta sheets, or 8 ounces dried
    wide spinach noodles

$1/2$ recipe Kay's Fresh Pasta (page 52), 12 ounces store-bought fresh
    egg pasta sheets, or 8 ounces dried plain wide noodles

1 to $1 1/4$ pounds sweet Italian sausage

2 to 3 tablespoons olive oil

1 red bell pepper, julienned

1 yellow bell pepper, julienned

1 cup sliced Vidalia or yellow onions

3 cloves garlic, minced

2 cups peeled (if desired), seeded, and coarsely chopped tomatoes

2 tablespoons chopped fresh basil plus leaves for garnish

$1/2$ teaspoon salt

¼ teaspoon freshly ground pepper

1 tablespoon butter (optional)

⅓ cup freshly grated Parmigiano-Reggiano plus additional for serving

1. *If making Kay's Fresh Pasta:* Roll out 2 balls (½ of recipe) of spinach pasta dough and 2 balls of plain pasta dough as directed in the recipe. Dry the pasta sheets for 30 minutes. Put the pasta sheets on a cutting board and cut into ¾-inch-wide noodles. Separate the noodles and allow to dry for 2 hours. (Or cover noodles with plastic wrap or a clean kitchen towel and let dry up to 24 hours.) Set aside. *If using store-bought fresh pasta sheets:* Place each pasta sheet on a lightly floured cutting board. Cut into ¾-inch-wide strips and allow to dry as directed above.

2. In a large skillet, crumble and cook the Italian sausage over medium-high heat for about 8 minutes or until browned and thoroughly cooked. Drain the sausage well; place a double layer of paper towels over sausage and press out excess fat. Wipe out the skillet. In the same pan, heat 2 tablespoons of the olive oil over medium-high heat; add the red and yellow peppers, onions, and garlic and cook, stirring frequently, for about 5 minutes, until tender.

3. Stir in the sausage, tomatoes, basil, salt, and pepper; cover and simmer over medium-low heat for 10 minutes. Keep hot.

4. Meanwhile, cook pasta. *For Kay's noodles or store-bought fresh pasta sheets:* In a large pot, bring 4 quarts of salted water to a boil. Add the noodles and cook for 2 to 3 minutes, or until *al dente* (tender but still firm to the bite). Drain. *For packaged dry pasta:* Cook according to the package directions; drain.

5. To serve, transfer the noodles to a large platter. Toss the pasta with the butter, if desired. Spoon the hot sausage mixture over the pasta. Sprinkle with the Parmigiano-Reggiano and garnish with basil leaves.

| SERVES 4 |

Kay's Fresh Pasta

When Kay has the time, she uses it wisely—to make her own pasta. This recipe gives you two options: a hand-rolling and cutting method, and a pasta-machine method. Is making fresh pasta really worth it? Think about the difference between store-bought and homemade bread. What do you think Kay would say?

3 cups unbleached or all-purpose flour

3 extra-large eggs, lightly beaten

⅓ cup water

2 teaspoons olive oil

1. Put 2½ cups of the flour into a large bowl; make a well in the center with the back of a spoon. Pour the eggs, water, and olive oil into the well. Stir until all the flour is moistened, and it leaves the side of the bowl.

2. Turn the dough out onto a lightly floured surface and gather it into a ball. Knead the dough for about 10 minutes, until it is smooth and elastic, adding as much of the remaining flour as needed to keep the dough from sticking. (Too much added flour will result in a more brittle pasta when it dries.)

3. Shape the dough into a ball, then cut it into quarters. Shape each quarter into a ball; place each in a self-sealing plastic bag or wrap each one tightly in plastic. Allow the dough to rest for 30 minutes or refrigerate for up to 24 hours.

4. Roll and cut the pasta using the Hand-Rolling or Pasta-Machine Method (below). Dry the cut noodles as directed.

5. To cook the pasta: In a large pot, bring 4 quarts salted water to a boil. Cook freshly made pasta for 2 minutes; cook pasta that has been stored for more than a few days for 5 to 6 minutes, until *al dente* (tender but still firm to the bite). Drain, but do not rinse.

MAKES ABOUT 1⅓ POUNDS FRESH PASTA,
ENOUGH FOR 8 SIDE-DISH OR 4 MAIN-DISH SERVINGS

HAND-ROLLING AND CUTTING METHOD:
Working with one ball (one-quarter) of the pasta dough at a time, place the dough on a lightly floured surface and flatten it into a round with the palm of your hand. With a rolling pin, roll the dough into a 15x10-inch rectangle, frequently lifting the dough, turning it over, and lightly flouring the surface to prevent the dough from sticking. The dough should be ⅛- to 1/16-inch thick (the thinner the dough, the more tender the pasta). If the dough is very elastic and difficult to roll, cover it and allow it to rest for 10 minutes, then continue rolling.

Spread several large pieces of brown paper or a few clean kitchen towels on a work surface. Transfer the pasta sheet to the paper. Roll out the remaining pieces of dough. Allow the pasta to air dry for 30 minutes. With a sharp knife or pizza cutter, cut the dough into ⅛-inch-wide strips for linguine, ¼-inch-wide strips for fettuccine, 2-inch-wide strips for lasagne noodles, or as desired. Separate the noodles and allow them to dry on the brown paper or kitchen towels for at least 30 minutes or up to 2 hours. (To hold the pasta longer, cover it with plastic wrap and dry at room temperature for up to 24 hours.)

HAND-CRANKED PASTA-MACHINE METHOD:

Working with one ball (one-quarter) of the pasta dough at a time, place the dough on a lightly floured surface. Flatten the dough into a round with the palm of your hand. Lightly flour the top of the dough. Set the rollers of the machine at their widest opening. Run dough through the machine two times. Cut the dough crosswise in half; set one piece aside.

Adjust the rollers to the next setting. Run one piece of the dough through the machine two times, catching the dough as it passes through (be careful not to allow the dough to fold back on itself), and lightly flouring the dough on both sides as necessary. Repeat, adjusting the rollers to successively smaller openings. (If the dough becomes too long and cumbersome to handle, cut it crosswise in half.) When the rollers are set to their smallest opening, run the dough through only one time.

Spread several large pieces of brown paper or clean kitchen towels on a work surface. Transfer the pasta sheet to the paper. Allow the pasta to dry for 30 minutes. Select the desired pasta cutter on the machine and cut the pasta according to the manufacturer's directions. Separate the noodles and allow them to dry on the paper or on a standing pasta dryer for at least 30 minutes, or up to 2 hours. (To hold the pasta longer, cover it with plastic wrap and dry at room temperature for up to 24 hours.)

TO STORE PASTA DOUGH:

Place each ball of pasta dough in a separate self-sealing plastic bag or wrap individually in plastic and refrigerate until needed, up to 1 day. To freeze, wrap each pasta ball in plastic and pack into airtight freezer containers; freeze for up to 1 month. Thaw overnight in the refrigerator before using.

TO STORE ROLLED PASTA SHEETS:

For pasta that has been dried for 2 hours, stack the sheets between layers of waxed paper on a baking sheet and wrap airtight in plastic. Store at room temperature for up to several days. Completely dried, cut pasta can be stored in an airtight container at room temperature for up to 2 days.

Variation

KAY'S FRESH SPINACH PASTA: This dough is a little sticky, so be sure to keep the dough lightly sprinkled with flour during the rolling and cutting.

1 cup coarsely chopped fresh spinach leaves

2 extra-large eggs

3 cups all-purpose flour

6 to 7 tablespoons water

1 teaspoon olive oil

In a blender or food processor, combine the spinach and 1 egg; cover and blend until pureed. Put 2½ cups of the flour into a large bowl; make a well in the center with the back of a spoon. Add the spinach puree, the remaining egg, 6 tablespoons of the water, and the olive oil. Stir until the mixture is well blended. If it seems dry, add the remaining 1 tablespoon water and mix until the dough leaves the side of the bowl. Continue with Step 2 of Kay's Fresh Pasta (page 52).

The Quintessential Ingredient of Italian Cooking

Drizzled over fresh oven-baked crusty bread, whisked into the perfect vinaigrette, mingling with sweet onions and peppers in a sauté—oh, the taste, the aroma! There is no question about it, good olive oil imparts a distinct flavor that defines Italian cuisine. How has olive oil come to be equated with great Italian cooking? About 98 percent of the world's olive oil is produced in the Mediterranean region in and around Italy.

Like wine, olive oils vary considerably in flavor and quality. Climate and soil conditions, as well as the method of processing the oils, are factors that impart distinctive flavors, ranging from delicate to semi-fruity to a full-blown olive flavor. Colors vary from palest yellow to vivid dark green. Some olive oils are actually masterful blends of several varieties, so it becomes impossible to generalize about flavor when it comes to a dark-colored oil vs. a light-colored oil, for example.

Types of Olive Oils

Olive oil is made from pressed olives, and most of it comes from a single pressing. Some processors use heat and/or solvents to make the process more efficient. Kay Scarpetta prefers "cold-pressed" olive oils made in the age-old Italian tradition, without the use of heat or solvents. As you experiment with cooking Italian dishes, try a variety of these olive oils:

EXTRA-VIRGIN: The best olive oil you can buy and also the priciest. Made from the highest-grade olives, the oil comes from a single cold pressing. Natural sediments are carefully filtered out. By law, the acidity level must be less than 1 percent. Use extra-virgin oils when the flavor will be most prominent, as in pasta dishes, marinades and sauces, salad dressings, and for basting meats, poultry, and fish or for dipping crusty breads. You'll savor every bite.

FINE VIRGIN: The next best thing to extra-virgin, with an allowable acidity level of

1.5 percent. Fine virgin olive oil has a superior flavor and aroma and is an excellent choice for all of the same uses as extra-virgin oil.

VIRGIN: Still superior in quality and smooth in flavor. The allowed acidity level is 3.3 percent. A good-quality virgin olive oil is for any recipe, especially where a lighter taste is desired, and it can also be used for sautéing and stir-frying.

PURE: Sometimes called "classic," this is a good general-purpose olive oil that is well suited to everything from salad dressings and sauces to sautéing and stir-frying. Pure olive oils have been refined to remove most of the impurities, which also removes some of the flavor and color. The better pure olive oils have some extra-virgin or virgin oils blended in to add back some of the flavor.

LIGHT OR EXTRA LIGHT: These terms have nothing to do with calories; these are highly refined oils with a very mild flavor, color, and aroma. Use as you would any plain vegetable oil, but don't look for this in Kay's kitchen.

POMACE: This is the least expensive olive oil, made by extracting additional oil from the pomace, the portion of the olive that is left after the mechanical pressing. This oil may be blended with a small amount of virgin olive oil, but don't let that impress you. This oil is lowest in terms of the grand order of quality olive oil.

Storing Olive Oil

A very good quality olive oil stores well when it's kept in a cool dark place. Extra-virgin oils keep well up to two years if properly stored, but use pure oil within one year. If the weather is hot or humid, olive oils can be stored in the refrigerator, but once opened should be used within a few months. Some clouding of the oil might occur in the fridge, but neither the flavor nor the quality will be affected. The oil will clear up once it's brought to room temperature—a good idea before using oils that have been chilled. Check your oil after it has been stored for a while. An off-odor or taste or a change in color will tell you it's past its prime.

Miami-Style Chili with Beer

nna, a friend of Kay's, invites Kay over to her house for dinner. Anna cooks up this chili with cans of chiles and garlic-spiked tomatoes that Kay brought home from her last visit to Miami. This chili has the consistency of soup and is pleasantly spicy, since Kay uses the tame green (Anaheim) variety of chiles. However, you can crank up the heat by adding more chili powder and by passing a bottle of hot pepper sauce around the table.

Corona and Dos Equis are popular Mexican beers that will lend great flavor to this chili. If you have leftover chili, it freezes very well. Use airtight freezer containers, leaving $1/2$ inch headspace at the top for expansion.

1 pound lean ground turkey or extra-lean ground beef

3 tablespoons olive oil

$1\frac{1}{2}$ cups trimmed and sliced white mushrooms

$1\frac{1}{2}$ cups chopped green, red, or yellow bell peppers

1 cup chopped Vidalia or yellow onions

2 cloves garlic, minced

2 cans (28 ounces each) chopped tomatoes with diced green chiles

2 cans (16 ounces each) red kidney beans, rinsed and well drained

1 can (16 ounces) black beans, rinsed and well drained

1 bottle (12 ounces) Mexican beer

3 tablespoons red wine vinegar

2 tablespoons chopped fresh oregano or marjoram

2 tablespoons chopped fresh basil

2 bay leaves

1 $\frac{1}{2}$ tablespoons chili powder

2 teaspoons salt

1 $\frac{1}{2}$ teaspoons ground cumin

Coarsely shredded extra-sharp cheddar cheese for garnish

1. In a large Dutch oven or 4-quart saucepan, cook the ground turkey in 1 tablespoon of the olive oil over medium-high heat for about 5 minutes, or until browned, breaking up the meat with the side of a spoon. Drain the turkey well. Transfer to a double layer of paper towels and press out the excess fat. Wipe out the pan.

2. In the same pan, heat the remaining 2 tablespoons olive oil over medium-high heat. Add the mushrooms, bell peppers, onions, and garlic and cook, stirring frequently, for 5 minutes, until the bell peppers are tender. Stir in the turkey, tomatoes with their juices, the kidney and black beans, beer, vinegar, oregano, basil, bay leaves, chili powder, salt, and cumin. Bring the mixture to a boil. Reduce the heat to medium-low and simmer, partially covered, for 1$\frac{1}{2}$ hours, stirring occasionally.

3. Taste the chili for seasoning. Remove the bay leaves. To serve, ladle the chili into bowls and top each serving with cheddar cheese.

SERVES 8 TO 10

She pushed back her chair and got up. "I hope you're hungry. We've got chicken breasts and a chilled wild rice salad made with cashews, peppers, sesame oil. And there's bread. Is your grill in working order?"

"It's after eleven and snowing outside."

"I didn't suggest that we eat outside. I simply would like to cook the chicken on the grill."

"Where did you learn to cook?"

We were walking to the kitchen.

"Not from Mother. Why do you think I was such a little fatso? From eating the junk she bought. Snacks, sodas, and pizza that tastes like cardboard. I have fat cells that will scream for the rest of my life because of Mother. I'll never forgive her."

"We need to talk about this afternoon, Lucy. If you hadn't come home when you did, the police would have been looking for you."

CRUEL

"I worked out for an hour and a half, then took a shower."

"You were gone four and half hours."

"I had groceries to buy and a few other errands."

"Why didn't you answer the car phone?"

"I assumed it was someone trying to reach you. Plus, I've never used a car phone. I'm not twelve years old, Aunt Kay."

"I know you're not. But you don't live here and have never driven here before. I was worried."

"I'm sorry," she said.

We ate by firelight, both of us sitting on the floor around the butler's table. I had turned off lamps. Flames jumped and shadows danced as if celebrating a magic moment in the lives of my niece and me.

"What do you want for Christmas?" I asked, reaching for my wine.

"Shooting lessons," she said.

Wild Rice Salad with Cashews

hile staying with her Aunt Kay, Lucy works up her appetite by tapping into Kay's downtown office computer system to try to learn who has been accessing Kay's work computer. By the time her aunt gets home from a long day and evening, Lucy has prepared a feast of chicken breasts in marinated olive oil, garlic, and lemon juice ready for the grill, a chilled salad of wild rice with cashews, bell peppers, and sesame oil, and bread. "Where did you learn to cook?" Kay asks. "Not from Mother," Lucy replies.

1 cup (6 ounces) wild rice

4 cups chicken broth

3 tablespoons olive oil

1 1/2 cups chopped red or green bell peppers

3/4 cup cashews, coarsely chopped

2 green onions, sliced

Dressing:

3 tablespoons seasoned rice vinegar or apple cider vinegar

2 tablespoons olive oil

1 tablespoon Asian sesame oil

1 clove garlic, minced

1/4 teaspoon salt

Dash freshly ground pepper

Lettuce leaves for serving

1. In a strainer, rinse the wild rice under cool running water; drain well. Into a 3-quart saucepan, put the wild rice and chicken broth; bring to a boil over high heat. Reduce the heat and simmer, covered, for 45 to 50 minutes, until tender. Drain off any excess liquid; set aside.

2. Meanwhile, in a medium skillet, heat the olive oil over medium-high heat; add the bell peppers and cook for 3 to 5 minutes, or until tender. Add the cashews and green onions; cook for 2 to 3 minutes longer, or until the nuts begin to brown. Remove from the heat.

3. In a large bowl, toss together the wild rice and bell pepper mixture.

4. For the dressing: In a jar with a tight-fitting lid, combine the vinegar, olive and sesame oils, garlic, salt, and pepper. Cover and shake until blended; pour the dressing over the salad and toss until evenly coated. Cover and refrigerate salad for at least 2 hours or up to overnight to allow the flavors to blend.

5. To serve the salad, spoon it onto a lettuce-lined platter.

MAKES 6 TO 8 SIDE-DISH SERVINGS

Grilled Grouper with Butter and Key Lime Juice

*T*he sea bass family of fish includes more than 300 species of small to large fish, including grouper. Also known as rock cod or jewfish, grouper thrives in the warm waters surrounding the reefs along the Atlantic coast from North Carolina to Florida, and along the Gulf and Mexican coasts as well. Favored for its lean white meat and mildly sweet flavor, grouper is most often used in chowders or served as simply cooked fillets.

Both grouper and sea bass are great on the grill. Willie Travers, Jennifer Deighton's former husband, prepares fresh grouper for Kay in *Cruel & Unusual* by marinating the fillets in Key lime juice, butter, and olive oil at his cottage in Fort Myers Beach. Then he grills the fish quickly and serves it with his Hearty Seven-Grain Bread (page 66), Marinated Slaw with Apple Cider Vinaigrette (page 69), and Dos Equis Mexican beer. Even Kay couldn't improve on that.

SHORTCUT TIP: *If you don't have time to wait for 30 minutes of marinating, just 10 minutes will do.*

1¼ to 1½ pounds grouper or sea bass fillets (1 inch thick)

¼ cup (½ stick) butter, melted

¼ cup Key lime juice (see Note) or fresh lime juice

1 tablespoon olive oil

Finely grated zest of 1 lime

½ teaspoon salt

¼ teaspoon freshly ground pepper

Lime wedges for serving

1 tablespoon chopped fresh chives

1. In a shallow glass or ceramic dish, place the fish fillets. Stir together the melted butter, lime juice, olive oil, lime zest, salt, and pepper; pour over the fish. Cover and refrigerate for 30 minutes.

2. Meanwhile, preheat the grill to medium-hot or preheat the broiler. Remove the fish from the marinade and arrange the fillets on a lightly oiled grilling tray (or on the lightly oiled rack of the broiler pan). Generously brush the fish with the marinade. Grill the fish for 9 to 12 minutes, until opaque throughout, turning the fish after 5 minutes and basting it several times with the butter mixture. (Or broil the fish 4 inches from heat source for 6 to 8 minutes, turning after 3 minutes.)

3. To serve, arrange the fish and lime wedges on a platter and sprinkle the fish with the chives.

SERVES 4

NOTE: *See page 208 for a mail-order source if you can't find Key lime juice in your local supermarket or specialty food market.*

Hearty Seven-Grain Bread

This rustic bread is filled with high-fiber ingredients, whole grains, and honey for sweetness. Because of all the different grains used, this is a heavier bread that needs a longer time to rise to its full potential. Don't use a rapid-rise yeast; give this dough the benefit of regular active dry yeast. Whole-grain flours, such as rye, contain less gluten, so do not let the dough rise until it's fully doubled in size, or it may collapse before baking. Let it rise three-quarters of the way toward doubling in size—that's enough.

No one sifts flour anymore, except cake flour. Instead, measure flour by spooning it lightly into a metal measuring cup, not the kind used for liquid ingredients, which have a pouring lip, then level off the top with the back of a table knife. Check the temperature of the water with a thermometer, or test it on the inside of your wrist. If it feels very warm but not hot enough to be uncomfortable, it's ready to use.

Kay hardly ever uses butter—and prefers to serve bread brushed with olive oil or dipped in olive oil.

½ cup rye flour

½ cup finely chopped walnuts or pecans, toasted

½ cup oats (old-fashioned or quick-cooking)

¼ cup sunflower seeds

¼ cup toasted wheat germ

3 tablespoons sesame seeds, toasted if desired

3 to 3½ cups bread flour

2 packages active dry yeast

1 tablespoon salt

1¾ cups milk

¼ cup honey

¼ cup (½ stick) butter

1½ to 1¾ cups whole-wheat flour

For Crust:

1 lightly beaten egg white

1 tablespoon water

Sesame seeds or sunflower seeds for sprinkling

1. In a medium bowl, stir together the rye flour, nuts, oats, sunflower seeds, wheat germ, and sesame seeds. Set aside.

2. In a large bowl, stir together 2½ cups of the bread flour, the yeast, and salt. In a medium saucepan, heat the milk, honey, and butter over medium heat, stirring, until it is very warm (120° to 130°F). Butter does not need to melt. Stir the milk mixture into the flour mixture, stirring until well combined. Stir in the rye-flour mixture until blended. Gradually stir in enough of the whole-wheat flour to make a soft dough that leaves the side of the bowl.

3. Turn the dough out onto a generously floured surface and shape it into a ball. Knead the dough for about 10 minutes, until it is soft, smooth, and elastic, adding enough of the remaining bread flour to keep the dough from sticking. Place the dough into a greased bowl and turn to coat evenly. Cover the dough with a damp clean kitchen towel or plastic wrap. Place the dough on the lowest oven rack. Turn the oven on to the lowest setting for 1 minute; then immediately turn the oven off. Let the dough rise for about 1 hour, until not quite doubled in size.

4. Punch down the dough; on a lightly floured surface, knead the dough 10 times to release the air bubbles. Cover and let rest for 10 minutes.

5. Shape the dough into loaves: Cut the dough in half. Shape each half into a smooth, round ball. Place each ball on one large or two small greased baking sheets and flatten slightly with the palm of your hand.

6. In a small bowl, lightly beat the egg white and water; brush over the loaves. Sprinkle the loaves with the sesame seeds. Cover the loaves and let rise 35 to 45 minutes, until not quite doubled in size.

7. Meanwhile, preheat the oven to 375°F. Bake the loaves for 25 to 30 minutes, or until golden brown and they sound hollow when lightly tapped on the bottom. Transfer the loaves to a wire rack to cool slightly. Serve the bread warm or at room temperature with butter or olive oil.

| MAKES 2 LOAVES |

Marinated Slaw with Apple Cider Vinaigrette

There's nothing more all-American than cole slaw, and there are about as many variations of it as there are ethnic groups in America. Combining both red and green cabbage makes this version both colorful and appealing.

Apple cider vinegar, honey, and celery seed flavor the tangy vinaigrette dressing that is first boiled and then cooled. You might think that a marinated slaw like this one will become limp and uninteresting in the fridge. On the contrary, you will find that, like the live-wire guest who can always be relied upon to jazz up the party, this salad never fails to add a sure-shot of pizzazz to the menu.

SHORTCUT TIPS: *You can substitute 4½ cups of store-bought cole slaw salad mix for the shredded cabbage and carrot. Also, you can halve the recipe to serve four.*

Dressing:
¼ cup apple cider vinegar

¼ cup olive oil

2 tablespoons honey

½ teaspoon celery seeds

½ teaspoon dry mustard

Salt and freshly ground pepper

Salad:

2 cups finely shredded green cabbage plus leaves for garnish

2 cups finely shredded red cabbage

1 red or yellow bell pepper, julienned

½ cup shredded carrot

2 green onions, thinly sliced

1. For the dressing: In a small saucepan, whisk together the vinegar, olive oil, honey, celery seeds, mustard, and salt and pepper to taste. Bring the mixture to a boil over medium-high heat; remove from the heat. Let the dressing cool for 15 minutes.

2. In a large bowl, toss together the green and red cabbage, bell pepper, carrot, and green onions. Pour the dressing over and toss well. Cover and refrigerate the slaw for at least 4 hours or up to overnight to allow the flavors to blend.

3. To serve the slaw, line a serving bowl with cabbage leaves. Use a slotted spoon to spoon the slaw into the bowl.

SERVES 8

WHAT'S IN KAY'S PANTRY?

Kay's overall philosophy about the foods she uses in cooking is simple: Use only the best ingredients. Kay knows that a murder case is only as good as the evidence that can be delivered; she knows equally well that both the final taste and the delectable appearance of the dishes she prepares depend almost entirely on the quality of the ingredients that go into them.

Good cooks, whether they spend a lot of time in the kitchen or not, depend on a well-stocked pantry to save the day. Here's a representative list of most of the pantry staples used in this book, items that you would find in Kay's pantry, should you be lucky enough to visit. Together with the fresh cheeses, fruits, vegetables, meats, and seafood Kay keeps on hand in the fridge and her freezerful of sauces and pastas, she whips up her legendary gourmet meals.

Oils and Vinegars

- Extra-virgin olive oil (Mission Olives Supremo is a good brand)
- Pure olive oil (for deep-frying)
- Truffle oil
- Nonstick cooking spray
- Mayonnaise or salad dressing
- Red and white wine vinegars
- Balsamic vinegar

Seasonings

- Jars of pre-minced and crushed garlic
- Capers
- Dry mustard
- Ground nutmeg

- Saffron threads
- Salt
- Sesame seeds
- Bay leaves
- Peppercorns and coarsely ground pepper
- White pepper

Stocks, Sauces, and Vegetables

- Low-fat beef, vegetable, and chicken stock or broth (canned or cartons)
- Bottled barbecue sauce
- Bottled Italian dressing
- Canned crushed tomatoes in puree
- Canned diced tomatoes with Italian seasonings and with mild green chiles and onion
- Tomato puree (Pomi brand)
- Tomato paste
- Marinara sauce
- V-8 juice
- Clam juice
- Worcestershire sauce
- Spicy yellow deli mustard
- Catsup
- Canned artichoke hearts or bottoms
- Vidalia onions

Baking Supplies

- Bread flour
- Whole-wheat flour

- Rye flour
- Yellow cornmeal
- 5-minute polenta mix
- Cornstarch
- Granola
- Honey
- Vanilla
- Sweetened condensed milk
- Dried figs, raisins
- Active dry yeast, both regular and rapid-rise
- Baking soda, baking powder
- Sugars, granulated and light brown
- Sweet and unsweetened baking chocolate
- Chocolate morsels
- Butterscotch, peanut butter, white chocolate chips
- Pine nuts
- Old-fashioned rolled oats

Miscellaneous

- A variety of good-quality dried pastas
- Bottled Key lime juice
- Bread crumbs
- Wild rice
- Anchovies
- Several types of coffee beans
- Saltine crackers

I got a taxi, and the driver, who was local and called himself Cowboy, told me he wrote songs and played piano when he wasn't in a cab.

By the time he got me to the Hyatt, I knew he went to Chicago once a year to please his wife, and that he regularly drove ladies from Johnson City who came here to shop in the malls. I was reminded of the innocence people like me had lost, and I gave Cowboy an especially generous tip. He waited while I checked into my room, then took me to Calhoun's, which overlooked the Tennessee River and promised the best ribs in the USA.

The restaurant was extremely busy, and I had to wait at the bar. It was the University of Tennessee's homecoming weekend, I discovered, and everywhere I looked I found jackets and sweaters in flaming orange, and alumni of all ages drinking and laughing and obsessing about this afternoon's game. Their raucous instant replays rose from every corner, and if I did not focus on any one conversation, what I heard was a constant roar.

THE B

The Vols had beat the Gamecocks, and it had been a battle as serious as any fought in the history of the world. When men in UT hats on either side occasionally turned my way for agreement, I was very sincere in my nods and affirmations, for to admit in that room that I had not *been there* would surely come across as treason. I was not taken to my table until close to ten P.M., by which time my anxiety level was quite high.

I ate nothing Italian or sensible this night, for I had not eaten well in days and finally I was starving. I ordered baby back ribs, biscuits, and salad, and when the bottle of Tennessee Sunshine Hot Pepper Sauce said "Try Me," I did. Then I tried the Jack Daniel's pie. The meal was wonderful. Throughout it I sat beneath Tiffany lamps in a quiet corner looking out at the river. It was alive with lights reflected from the bridge in varying lengths and intensities, as if the water were measuring electronic levels for music I could not hear.

I tried not to think about crime.

Fruit-Marinated Lamb Kabobs

La Petite France at 2108 Maywill Street is one of my favorite restaurants in Richmond, where you can forget about life as you know it and let yourself be spoiled by Chef Paul Elbling and his wife, Marie-Antoinette. As Kay relates in The Body Farm, *"That night I took Lucy to La Petite France, where I surrendered to Chef Paul, who sentenced us to languid hours of Fruit-Marinated Lamb Kabobs and a bottle of 1986 Château Gruaud Larose."*

Marinate the lamb cubes the night before to let them soak up the spicy fruit flavors. Unless you have six very long barbecue skewers (12 to 14 inches in length), you'll need a dozen metal skewers to spear all of the meat and vegetables. Serve the kabobs with an herbed rice pilaf or couscous. A Beaujolais, pinot noir, or red Bordeaux wine will also help you savor the lamb.

Fruit Marinade:

1 can (6 ounces) apple juice (¾ cup)

1 can (6 ounces) pineapple juice (¾ cup)

2 tablespoons fresh lime juice

2 cloves garlic, minced

1 teaspoon salt

½ teaspoon ground allspice

½ teaspoon ground nutmeg

½ teaspoon ground cloves

¼ teaspoon freshly ground pepper

Kabobs:

1¾ to 2-pound boneless leg of lamb, trimmed of fat and cut
    into 2-inch cubes

12 medium white mushrooms, trimmed

1 large Vidalia or yellow onion, cut into 1½-inch wedges

1 green bell pepper, cut into 1½-inch squares

1 red bell pepper, cut into 1½-inch squares

6 to 12 cherry tomatoes for garnish

Hot cooked rice or couscous

1. In a self-sealing plastic bag or shallow glass or ceramic dish, combine all the marinade ingredients until well blended. Set aside 1/4 cup of the marinade. Add the lamb cubes to the marinade and turn the bag over several times to coat the meat all over (or toss the lamb in the dish). Refrigerate lamb (cover the dish, if used) for 8 to 12 hours or up to overnight, turning the bag over occasionally.

2. To grill the kabobs: Heat the grill to medium-hot or preheat the broiler. Remove the lamb from the marinade and discard the marinade. On 6 long metal barbecue skewers, thread the lamb alternately with the mushrooms, onion wedges, and bell peppers, allowing a little bit of space between each item for even cooking. Arrange the skewers on a lightly oiled grilling tray or in the broiler pan. Brush the skewers with some of the reserved marinade.

3. Grill the kabobs for about 8 minutes for medium-rare doneness, turning the kabobs after 4 minutes and basting several times with reserved marinade. (Or broil 4 inches from the heat source for 8 minutes for medium-rare doneness.) Discard the remaining marinade.

4. To serve, place a cherry tomato on the end of each kabob. Pass the hot cooked rice or couscous separately.

SERVES 6

Zuppa di Aglio Fresco
(Fresh Garlic Soup)

After Lucy's hospital stay from a near-fatal car accident in The Body Farm, her Aunt Kay brings her home for some R & R. Kay "put on a pot of Zuppa di Aglio Fresco, a fresh garlic soup popular in the hills of Brisighella, where it has been fed to babies and the elderly for many years." This wonderful soup is the Italian version of chicken soup, a comforting potage of chicken stock, carrots, thyme, bay leaf, and sherry, thickened with egg yolks and enriched with Parmigiano-Reggiano. Kay serves the soup with Ravioli with Squash and Chestnut Filling (page 80).

The best way to peel and smash garlic is to first pull off the loose papery skin from the whole head, then separate the cloves. Place one or two cloves on a cutting board, and lay the flat side of a wide-bladed knife over them. Punch the flat of the knife with one strike of your fist, and voila! The husk falls away from the cloves and you have smashed garlic.

SHORTCUT TIP: Look for jars of peeled whole garlic cloves in the produce department of your market.

4 tablespoons olive oil

1½ cups finely chopped carrots

10 cloves garlic, peeled and smashed

4 cups homemade chicken stock or canned chicken broth

1 tablespoon chopped fresh thyme

1 bay leaf

¼ cup dry sherry

3 extra-large egg yolks

½ cup freshly grated Parmigiano-Reggiano

2 tablespoons chopped fresh Italian parsley

Salt and freshly ground pepper

4 slices (1 inch thick) day-old sourdough, multi-grain,
   or country-style bread

1. In a 3-quart saucepan, heat 2 tablespoons of the olive oil; add the carrots and garlic. Cook over medium-high heat, stirring frequently, for 3 to 5 minutes, or until tender but not brown.

2. Stir in the chicken stock, thyme, and bay leaf. Bring the mixture to a boil over high heat. Reduce the heat to low and simmer, covered, for 30 minutes.

3. Discard the bay leaf. In a blender or food processor, puree the soup in several batches, transferring the puree to a large bowl. Return the pureed mixture to the saucepan; stir in the sherry.

4. In a small bowl, whisk together the egg yolks and the remaining 2 tablespoons oil; whisk in the Parmigiano-Reggiano until blended. Gradually whisk ¼ cup of the soup into the yolk mixture; whisk mixture into the soup. Heat the soup over medium-low heat, stirring constantly, for 8 to 10 minutes, until the soup thickens (do not boil or the soup will curdle). Stir in the parsley; season to taste with salt and freshly ground pepper. Remove the soup from the heat.

5. To serve the soup, place a slice of bread in each soup bowl. Ladle the soup over the bread and serve immediately.

SERVES 4

Ravioli with Squash and Chestnut Filling

Legend has it that ravioli was first made aboard ships that left Genoa's port for long voyages, in an effort to make use of every bit of food that was brought on board. Bits of leftover meats and vegetables from one day's meal were minced up, combined, and stuffed into pockets of pasta dough to be served the next day. Kay's ravioli features a squash and chestnut puree, a reflection of how far ravioli has come since its humble beginnings. (Look for canned chestnut puree in the gourmet food sections of larger markets or at Italian delis.)

Making ravioli is fun, because it's simple to do and it's easy to make a half dozen servings once you get the hang of it. Remember to start with rolled pasta that has dried for no more than 1 hour, because it needs to be moist enough to hold the filling securely. Picture dividing your sheets of dough into $1^1/_2$-inch squares when you spoon the mounds of filling onto the pasta. (Place a ruler just above your pasta sheet as an easy guide.) Each mound will be at the center of the square, and you'll be cutting around each square to make the ravioli. A ravioli cutter, which has a rolling zigzag edge, will give that pinking-shear look to the edges of the pasta; a sharp knife can also be used.

A ravioli pan is a surefire way to make perfect squares of ravioli. You will have to roll and cut out pasta sheets that fit the pan exactly. Follow the manufacturer's directions for filling the ravioli.

If you have leftover cooked ravioli, you can enjoy it the next day: Add it to 3 or 4 cups of simmering chicken or vegetable broth. Cook just 1 or 2 *minutes until heated through. Sprinkle with lots of grated Parmigiano-Reggiano and serve it with your favorite bread.*

MAKE-AHEAD TIP: You can freeze cooked and well-drained ravioli, layered flat between sheets of waxed paper, in a tightly covered freezer container, for up to a month.

SHORTCUT TIP: A 10-ounce package of thawed, frozen squash can be substituted for the cooked fresh squash. Set aside 1 cup of the squash for this recipe. Instead of Kay's fresh pasta, you can use store-bought fresh pasta sheets.

1 recipe Kay's Fresh Pasta (page 52) or store-bought

1 ½ teaspoons olive oil

¼ cup minced Vidalia or yellow onion

1 cup mashed cooked squash such as butternut, acorn, buttercup,
   kabocha, or Hubbard (about 8 ounces raw squash)

½ cup canned chestnut puree

1 extra-large egg

2 tablespoons honey

¼ teaspoon ground nutmeg

¼ teaspoon salt

1 recipe Béchamel Sauce (page 157)

Freshly grated Parmigiano-Reggiano for sprinkling

Chopped fresh chives or fresh parsley for garnish

1. Mix, knead, and let the pasta dough rest as directed. To roll and cut the pasta: *If hand-rolling the pasta,* roll each piece of the dough into a 16x9-inch rectangle. *If using the pasta-machine method,* roll the sheets about 4 inches wide or a bit wider. Dry the rolled pasta, uncovered, for 30 minutes.

If pasta must be held longer, cover it well with plastic wrap or clean kitchen towels for up to 1 hour.

2. While the pasta is drying, prepare the filling. In a small skillet, heat the olive oil over medium heat. Add the onion and cook, stirring, for 3 to 5 minutes, until tender and golden brown.

3. In a blender or food processor, combine the squash, chestnut puree, and egg; blend the mixture until smooth. Add the onion mixture, honey, nutmeg, and salt; blend until pureed.

4. To cut and fill the ravioli: Cut each sheet of pasta dough into 4-inch-wide rectangles (the length can vary, but trim the edges of each pasta sheet so they are straight). Place one pasta rectangle on a lightly floured cutting board. Keep the remaining dough covered. Drop mounds of the squash filling in 2 lengthwise rows, using a rounded teaspoonful for each mound, placing them $1\frac{1}{2}$ inches apart and leaving a $\frac{1}{2}$-inch border on all sides.

5. Brush the dough around the filling and along the edges with water (this will help the dough seal when the ravioli are cut).

6. Drape a second sheet of pasta on top, carefully pressing around each mound of filling to seal the two sheets and to create ravioli squares. If the bottom rectangle is longer or shorter than the top one, cut the top rectangle at a point halfway between two mounds of filling, then fill in with another rectangle to cover the remaining mounds of filling. Seal the dough all around with wet fingers, pressing the pasta around each mound of filling and along edges to secure.

7. Using a sharp knife, a pizza cutter, or a ravioli cutter, cut the ravioli into squares by cutting lengthwise between the 2 rows of mounds, then cutting crosswise between each pair of mounds. (Makes 54 to 60 ravioli.)

8. To cook the ravioli: In a large pot, bring 4 quarts of salted water to a boil. Add the ravioli, about 10 at a time, by sliding them off a large spoon or spatula into the boiling water. Reduce the heat to a gentle boil, stirring occasionally to keep ravioli separated. Cook the ravioli for about 3 minutes,

or until *al dente* (tender but still firm to the bite). Drain on a paper towel-lined plate.

9. Serve the hot ravioli topped with the béchamel sauce, grated Parmigiano-Reggiano, and chives.

SERVES 6 TO 7

(8 TO 9 RAVIOLI PER PERSON)

Barbecued Baby Back Ribs

*C*alhoun's Restaurant in West Knoxville, located at 400 Neyland Drive, overlooks the Tennessee River on the University of Tennessee campus. In The Body Farm, *Kay dines at the restaurant while staying in Knoxville to gather evidence about the Temple Gault murders. A fixture since the early 1980s, Calhoun's is known for their award-winning "best ribs in America," and they certainly have the "taste of Tennessee" down pat.*

Here they share their recipe for their pride and joy, baby back pork ribs, smoked with Tennessee hickory and slathered with their signature Bar-B-Que Sauce. The barbecue sauce, which boasts 20 secret ingredients, comes from an age-old Smoky Mountain recipe. You can order it directly from the restaurant's Web site, www.calhouns.com, or call (800) 258-RIBS. For a smoky Tennessee flavor, add some pre-soaked hickory chips to your coals. One slab (one pound) of ribs is about right for a hearty serving, since the ribs themselves do not have a lot of meat on them. Guests with smaller appetites will be satisfied with a half slab ($^1/_2$ pound) of the ribs.

Follow Kay's lead and round out your meal with some hot biscuits, tossed salad, and very cold beer, or a dry chardonnay, sauvignon blanc, or a light red wine.

4$^1/_4$ cups water

1 tablespoon liquid smoke (see Note)

1$^1/_2$ teaspoons salt

$^1/_2$ teaspoon garlic powder

> ¼ teaspoon ground white pepper
>
> 4 slabs baby back pork ribs (4 pounds)
>
> 1½ cups Calhoun's BBQ Sauce or other barbecue sauce

1. Preheat the oven to 275°F. In a large shallow roasting pan, stir together 4 cups of the water and liquid smoke. It should come ½ inch up the sides of the pan; add more water, if necessary.

2. In a small bowl, stir together the salt, garlic powder, and white pepper. Sprinkle the mixture evenly over the meaty side of the ribs. Place the ribs, meat side up, in the roasting pan. Cover the pan tightly with aluminum foil.

3. Bake the ribs for 2 hours and 15 minutes. Remove the ribs from the oven and let stand, covered, for 15 minutes.

4. To grill: Preheat the grill to medium or preheat the broiler. In a 1-quart saucepan, combine the barbecue sauce and the remaining water. (This helps prevent the sauce from burning on the grill.) Heat the mixture just until it simmers; remove from the heat. Arrange the ribs on the hot grill. Cook for 10 to 12 minutes, turning and basting with the barbecue sauce mixture every 2 minutes, being careful not to allow the sauce to burn. (Or broil the ribs for 8 to 10 minutes, turning and basting every 2 minutes.)

5. To serve, baste the ribs with the barbecue sauce; cut the racks between the bones into 2-rib portions.

| SERVES 4 TO 6 |

NOTE: *Liquid smoke is available in the sauce section or special condiments section of your supermarket.*

Jack Daniel's Chocolate-Pecan Pie

On the tail end of Calhoun's mouthwatering menu of barbecue specialties are the inevitable desserts. If you've ever played the dinner party game of planning the last menu of your life, here's a to-die-for dessert you will want to consider. This unbelievably delicious pecan pie is studded throughout with chocolate and laced with Tennessee whiskey. Serve it warm, cut into modest-sized pieces, and savor every bite. After that, there's no place to go but straight to heaven.

MAKE-AHEAD TIP: *If you are preparing the pie a day ahead, cool the pie on a rack for 1 hour after baking, then cover and refrigerate. For the best flavor, let the refrigerated pie stand at room temperature for 1 hour before serving.*

SHORTCUT TIP: *If you don't have time to make the pie crust, use a half package of store-bought refrigerated pie crusts. Just unfold one of the crusts into the pie plate, trim, and flute the edge as directed in step 1.*

Pastry dough for one 9-inch pie

3 extra-large eggs

2 extra-large egg yolks

⅔ cup sugar

¾ cup dark corn syrup

5 tablespoons butter, melted

¼ cup Jack Daniel's or whiskey

⅔ cup chopped bittersweet chocolate or semisweet chocolate
   morsels
1¼ cups pecan halves or pieces
Vanilla ice cream for serving

1. Preheat the oven to 350°F. Ease the pastry dough into a 9-inch pie plate. Trim and flute the edge of the dough, if desired, or trim the dough even with the plate edge. Place the pie plate on a baking sheet.

2. In a large bowl, whisk together the eggs, egg yolks, and sugar until well combined. Whisk in the corn syrup, melted butter, and Jack Daniel's until well blended.

3. Sprinkle ⅓ cup of the chocolate pieces over the bottom of the pastry crust. Pour in the pie filling. Sprinkle ½ cup of the pecans over the filling. Sprinkle the remaining chocolate pieces over, then top with the remaining ¾ cup pecans.

4. Bake the pie for 50 to 55 minutes, or until set in the center. Turn off the oven; leave the pie in the oven, with the door closed, for 15 minutes longer to crisp the top. Transfer the pie to a wire rack to cool for at least 2 hours. To serve, cut into small wedges and top with vanilla ice cream.

MAKES ONE 9-INCH PIE

A round the corner of the Museum of Natural History was the snowcapped pink awning of a restaurant called Scaletta, which I was surprised to find lit up and noisy. A couple in fur coats turned in and went downstairs, and I wondered if we shouldn't do the same. I was actually getting hungry, and Wesley didn't need to lose any more weight.

"Are you up for this?" I asked him.

"Absolutely. Is Scaletta a relative of yours?" he teased.

"I think not."

We got as far as the door, where the maître d' informed us that the restaurant was closed.

"You certainly don't look closed," I said, suddenly exhausted and unwilling to walk any more.

"But we are, signora." He was short, balding and wearing a tuxedo with a bright red cummerbund. "This is a private party."

"Who is Scaletta?" Wesley asked him.

"Why do you want to know?"

"It is an interesting name, much like mine," I said.

"And what is yours?"

"Scarpetta."

He looked carefully at Wesley and seemed puzzled. "Yes, of course. But he is not with you this evening?"

I stared blankly at him. "Who is not with me?"

"Signor Scarpetta. He was invited. I'm sorry, I did not realize you were in his party…"

"Invited to what?" I had no idea what he was talking about. My name was rare.

I had never encountered another Scarpetta, not even in Italy.

The maître d' hesitated. "You are not related to Scarpetta who comes here often?"

"What Scarpetta?" I said, getting uneasy.

"A man. He has been here many times recently. A very good customer. He was invited to our Christmas party. So you are not his guests?"

"Tell me more about him," I said.

"A young man. He spends much money." The maître d' smiled.

I could feel Wesley's interest pique. He said, "Can you describe him?"

"I have many people inside. We reopen tomorrow..."

Wesley discreetly displayed his shield. The man regarded it calmly.

"Of course." He was polite but unafraid. "I find you a table."

"No, no," Wesley said. "You don't have to do that. But we need to ask more about this man who said his last name was Scarpetta."

"Come in." He motioned us. "We talk, we may as well sit. You sit, you may as well eat. My name is Eugenio."

He led us to a pink-covered table in a corner far removed from guests in party clothes filling most of the dining room.

They were toasting, eating, talking and laughing with the gestures and cadences of Italians.

"We do not have full menu tonight," Eugenio apologized. "I can bring you *costoletta di vitello alla griglia* or *pollo al limone* with maybe a little *capellini primavera* or *rigatoni con broccolo*."

We said yes to all and added a bottle of Dolcetto D'Alba, which was a favorite of mine and difficult to find.

Shrimp Sauté
with Garlic and Lemon

Kay is invited to dinner at NYPD Commander Frances Penn's light, bright fifteenth-floor apartment on the West Side of Manhattan, to discuss the Temple Gault murder case. The Commander's menu is simple but elegant: sautéed shrimp, warm bread, and steamed asparagus, served with a crisp chardonnay. It takes as little as 10 minutes to marinate the shrimp, for a zing of lemon-garlic flavor.

To steam asparagus, snap off the bottom woody portions of the stalks. Arrange the spears in a steamer basket set over a pan of simmering water. Cook the asparagus, partially covered, for 4 to 8 minutes (depending on the thickness of the stalks) until they are nearly tender. Drizzle the asparagus with a bit of extra-virgin olive oil and season with salt and pepper. Add a healthy grating of Parmigiano-Reggiano or a sprinkling of your favorite chopped fresh herbs.

Marinade:

2 tablespoons olive oil

2 tablespoons fresh lemon juice

2 cloves garlic, minced

¾ pound jumbo shrimp (about 10 to 12 shrimp), peeled and deveined

Sauté:

2 tablespoons olive oil

1 tablespoon butter

2 shallots, chopped

2 large cloves garlic, slivered

1 tablespoon fresh lemon juice

2 tablespoons chopped fresh parsley

Salt and freshly ground pepper

Lemon wedges for serving

1. For the marinade: In a medium nonmetal bowl, combine the oil, lemon juice, and garlic. Add the shrimp, turning to coat with the marinade. Cover and refrigerate for 10 to 30 minutes.

2. With a slotted spoon, remove the shrimp from the marinade; discard the marinade. In a medium skillet, heat the olive oil with the butter over medium-high heat. Add the shrimp and cook, stirring and turning the shrimp frequently, for 2 to 3 minutes, until they just turn pink and opaque throughout. Immediately remove the shrimp from the pan; set aside.

3. In the same pan, add the shallots and garlic. Cook over medium-high heat, stirring frequently, for 3 minutes. Stir in the lemon juice and parsley. Return the shrimp to the pan and cook for 1 minute longer, or until heated through. Season with salt and pepper. Serve immediately with lemon wedges.

| SERVES 2 |

Funghi e Carciofi
(Mushroom and Artichoke Appetizer)

This unusual appetizer from Scaletta's Restaurant in New York is worth going off your low-fat diet for one evening. After all, you'll be using olive oil for the frying, which has no cholesterol, and there is no breading on the artichokes and mushrooms. Share this simple appetizer with five friends, so you'll have just a modest portion to indulge in.

Make certain that your vegetables have been patted dry with paper towels to avoid excess spattering during frying.

In From Potter's Field, *Temple Gault enjoys this dish with a couple of French white wines, such as Château Carbonnieux and Château Olivier. Other appropriate choices would be a crisp California chardonnay, an Italian pinot grigio, or a light red, such as Bordeaux or rosé.*

24 medium white mushrooms (10 to 12 ounces)

1 can (13¾ ounces) artichoke bottoms or hearts, drained

2 cups olive oil

5 to 6 cloves garlic, crushed

3 tablespoons chopped fresh basil plus leaves for garnish

Salt and freshly ground pepper

Freshly grated Parmigiano-Reggiano for sprinkling

1. Cut off the stems from the mushrooms. Cut the mushroom caps into quarters or thirds. Pat the artichoke bottoms (or hearts) dry with paper towels; cut into quarters (or use hearts as is).

2. In a deep skillet or 3-quart saucepan, heat the olive oil with the garlic until the oil reaches 375°F on a deep-fry thermometer. Remove the garlic with a slotted spoon. (Otherwise, the garlic will burn and impart an unpleasant flavor to your vegetables.) Using the slotted spoon, add the mushroom and artichoke pieces, a few at a time, to the hot oil. Cook for 3 to 4 minutes, or until the vegetables are golden brown.

3. Transfer the vegetables to paper towels to drain well. Wait 1 to 2 minutes between each batch to allow the oil to return to the proper temperature.

4. Toss the hot vegetables with the basil and season with salt and pepper. Cool for 2 to 3 minutes. To serve, transfer the hot vegetables to appetizer plates. Sprinkle with Parmigiano-Reggiano and serve immediately.

MAKES 4 TO 6 APPETIZER
OR FIRST-COURSE SERVINGS

Pollo al Limone

(Lemon Chicken)

I t's Christmas, and Kay and Benton Wesley have spent the day in New York City, retracing serial killer Temple Gault's steps in the neighborhood of Central Park West and 81st Street, where he had been spotted in the subway station with his latest victim. Kay is attracted to the pink awning of a restaurant called Scaletta's, where she and Benton have an illuminating discussion with Eugenio, the maître d'. It seems that Gault has practically become a regular at the restaurant in recent days, helping himself to several of their best entrees and white wines, on Kay's stolen American Express Gold card.

I discovered Scaletta's quite by accident. While researching the New York subway system for the book, I came out of the subway one day at the Museum of Natural History and around the corner I saw Scaletta's at 50 West 77th Street. I thought how remarkable it was that its name was so close to Scarpetta. Since then I've dined there several times and am a real fan of Chef Omer Grgurev.

Pollo al Limone is one of the dishes that Eugenio presents to Kay and Benton, along with Rigatoni con Broccolo (page 129). A bottle of Dolcetto D'Alba, 1979, a favorite of Kay's, is their wine of choice this evening. It's very light, like a Beaujolais.

SHORTCUT TIP: In place of the clarified butter, you can use equal parts extra-virgin olive oil and regular butter. The oil keeps the butter from burning, and you will still get plenty of butter flavor.

6 skinless, boneless chicken breast halves (2 pounds total)

⅔ cup all-purpose flour

½ teaspoon salt

¼ teaspoon freshly ground pepper

3 tablespoons clarified butter (see Note)

Sauce:

1½ cups homemade chicken stock or canned chicken broth

½ cup dry white wine

¼ cup fresh lemon juice

½ teaspoon salt

⅛ teaspoon ground white pepper

3 tablespoons chopped fresh parsley

Lemon slices for garnish

Hot cooked pasta

1. Place one chicken breast half between two pieces of waxed paper or inside a self-sealing plastic bag. Pound the chicken with a meat mallet to ¼-inch thickness. Repeat with the remaining chicken. In a small bowl, stir together the flour, salt, and pepper. Coat the chicken with the seasoned flour, shaking off the excess. Arrange the chicken on a waxed paper-lined baking sheet or tray.

2. Pour 2 tablespoons of the clarified butter into a large skillet. Brown the chicken over medium-high heat for about 3 minutes per side. Transfer the chicken to a plate and set aside. Wipe out the pan with paper towels.

3. To make the sauce: In the same skillet, combine the chicken stock, white wine, lemon juice, salt, and white pepper. Bring to a boil over medium-high heat; reduce the heat to low and simmer, uncovered, for 5 to 8 minutes, or until the sauce is reduced by half.

4. Return the chicken pieces to the skillet and spoon the sauce over the chicken. Cover and cook over medium heat for 2 to 3 minutes longer, or until the thickest part of the chicken is no longer pink. Uncover and add the remaining 1 tablespoon butter to the pan. Simmer for 5 minutes longer, stirring frequently.

5. To serve, place a chicken breast half on each plate. Stir the parsley into the sauce and spoon it over the chicken. Garnish with the lemon slices, and serve with the hot pasta.

SERVES 6

NOTE: *To make clarified butter: Start with cut-up unsalted butter. Melt it completely over low heat in a small heavy saucepan without stirring it. Carefully pour the clear yellow liquid that is on top into a container. Discard the milky layer. You can refrigerate or freeze clarified butter, although it tends to become grainy when it solidifies. Use it only for browning or sautéing.*

PAGE 176

Bev's Lump Crab Cakes

(PRECEDING PAGE) PAGE 64

Grilled Grouper with
Butter and Key Lime Juice

PAGE 94

Pollo al Limone (Lemon Chicken)

PAGE 212

Crostini di Polenta con Funghi Trifolati

(Grilled Polenta Topped with Sautéed Assorted Mushrooms)

PAGE 47

Pork Loin with Fig and Prosciutto Stuffing

PAGE 86

Jack Daniel's Chocolate-Pecan Pie

PAGE 44

Veal Breast Stuffed with Spinach Pistou

PAGE 50

Le Pappardelle del Cantunzein

(Yellow and Green Broad Noodles with Sweet Peppers and Sausage)

PAGE 84

Barbecued Baby Back Ribs

PAGE 62

Wild Rice Salad with Cashews

110

PAGE 76

Fruit-Marinated Lamb Kabobs

PAGE 152

Braided Country Bread

PAGE 174

Jumbo Shrimp with Bev's Kicked by a Horse
Cocktail Sauce

PAGE 42

New York Steaks with Red Wine Marinade

PAGE 164

Classic English Breakfast

(Bacon and Eggs with Tomatoes and Mushrooms)

PAGE 38

Omelet with Sweet Peppers and Onions

PAGE 182

Marino's Breakfast Bagel Sandwich

PAGE 129

Rigatoni con Broccolo

(Rigatoni with Broccoli)

PAGE 90

Shrimp Sauté with Garlic and Lemon

Giardinetto al Profumo di Erbe

(Grilled Garden Vegetables)

PAGE 217

Costolette di Agnello alle Sette Erbe

(Lamb Chops Seasoned with Seven Herbs)

PAGE 80

Ravioli with Squash and Chestnut Filling

PAGE 160

Fig, Melon, and Prosciutto Salad

(OVERLEAF) PAGE 139

Linguine with Olive Oil, Parmesan, and Onion

Rigatoni con Broccolo
(Rigatoni with Broccoli)

Chef Omer at Scaletta's Restaurant in New York likes to use sliced garlic in this rigatoni side dish. Cutting the slices into slivers spreads the flavor even further. Extra-virgin olive oil is a must for this dish.

A safety note: Remove the skillet from the heat before pouring the wine into the skillet. Otherwise, you might have a small bonfire on your hands.

MAKE-AHEAD TIP: You can cook the broccoli and prepare the white sauce ahead of time and refrigerate them. Then you can easily whip up the broccoli sauce while the pasta is cooking.

1 ½ pounds broccoli

16 ounces rigatoni

2 tablepoons extra-virgin olive oil

4 cloves garlic, slivered

¼ cup dry white wine

1 cup homemade chicken or veal stock or canned chicken broth

¼ cup Omer's White Sauce (page 130)

1 teaspoon butter

½ teaspoon salt

¼ teaspoon freshly ground pepper

⅓ cup freshly grated Parmigiano-Reggiano plus additional for serving

1. Trim the stems from the broccoli and cut it into small florets. Fill a large bowl with ice water. In a large saucepan, bring 4 quarts of salted water to a boil. Add the broccoli and boil for 2 minutes, just to bring up the color. Drain the broccoli and transfer to the bowl of ice water to stop the cooking. Pour off any water remaining in the pot.

2. In the same pot, bring 4 quarts of fresh salted water to a boil. Cook the rigatoni according to the package directions until *al dente* (tender but still firm to the bite). Drain the pasta well and toss it with 1 tablespoon olive oil; set aside.

3. To make the sauce: In a large skillet, heat the remaining oil over medium heat. Cook the garlic for 3 to 5 minutes until golden brown, being careful not to let it burn. Remove from the heat.

4. Add the white wine to the skillet, then stir in the chicken stock. Return the pan to the heat and whisk in the white sauce. Bring the mixture to a boil over medium-high heat, stirring frequently. Reduce the heat to low and simmer for about 7 minutes, or until it is reduced by half.

5. Stir in the butter, salt, and pepper. Add the broccoli; simmer the mixture for 1 to 2 minutes longer, or until the broccoli is heated through.

6. Return the pasta to the pasta pot; add the broccoli sauce mixture and the Parmigiano-Reggiano; toss to coat well. Serve with extra Parmigiano-Reggiano alongside.

MAKES 6 TO 8 SIDE-DISH SERVINGS

Omer's White Sauce

SHORTCUT TIP: *This recipe yields enough sauce for four batches of Rigatoni con Broccolo. Freeze it in 1 tablespoonfuls by spooning the finished sauce into ice cube trays. When frozen, pop out the cubes and freeze them in a self-sealing freezer bag. You'll have white sauce on hand any time you need it.*

2 tablespoons butter

2 tablespoons all-purpose flour

$\frac{1}{2}$ cup milk

$\frac{1}{2}$ cup homemade chicken or veal stock or canned chicken broth

$\frac{1}{4}$ teaspoon salt

Dash freshly ground pepper

In a 1-quart saucepan, melt the butter over medium heat. Stir in the flour until blended. Add the milk and chicken stock all at once, stirring constantly, until the mixture thickens and bubbles. Cook, stirring, for 2 minutes longer. Stir in the salt and pepper. Makes 1 cup sauce.

Among the array of aromatic ingredients that Italian cooks have to choose from, the venerable garlic holds top culinary status. Its strong, unmistakable aroma and flavor come packaged in a plain papery skin that belies the versatility within.

Chopped into a vegetable sauté, crushed and rubbed over a lamb roast, sliced and stuffed under the skin of a chicken, minced into a vinaigrette, or baked and spread over crusty sourdough bread, no other seasoning can hold a candle to the tantalizing flavor of garlic.

It's interesting to note that although garlic is such an important ingredient today in Italian cooking, it was once snubbed by wealthy Romans, who gave it to their slaves and laborers to give them strength. A veteran of 5,000 years of intriguing history, during which it was used largely for medicinal purposes, garlic has only been welcome in the kitchen for the past couple of hundred years.

Today, this member of the onion family and botanical cousin of the lily is plentiful in markets year-round, coming mainly from California during the summer months and from Mexico during the off-season.

Cooking with Garlic

Kay, the purist, prefers to begin with fresh garlic for all of her recipes. In a pinch, however, pre-minced garlic and even jarred peeled fresh garlic cloves make handy substitutes that compromise the flavor only a little while saving on preparation time. When buying fresh garlic, look for well-shaped bulbs with papery skin, without soft or dented spots or green sprouts. If purchasing processed garlic, check the expiration date on the label.

Fresh garlic has a stronger, more pungent flavor than cooked garlic. When sautéing or browning garlic, take care not to let it burn; cook it just until golden. Burned garlic imparts an off-flavor to food and makes it taste bitter. Stews and soups containing garlic get the benefit of a sweeter garlic flavor because of the longer cooking at moderate to low temperatures. Baking or roasting garlic also softens or sweetens the flavor, because some of the pungent oils are released during cooking. It also softens the texture of garlic, which morphs into a spread with the consistency of thick mayonnaise. That's why roasted cloves of garlic are so coveted as a spread for bread.

Here are some tips on preparing fresh garlic:

PEELING AND CRUSHING GARLIC. You can use a garlic peeler, a gadget available in specialty cookware shops, or use the fist-and-knife method: Place a garlic clove on a cutting board, and lay the flat side of a large, preferably heavy knife over it. Hit the side of the knife once with your fist, and the paper husk will fall away, leaving a crushed clove of garlic.

CHOPPED GARLIC. For more than a few cloves of garlic, store-bought pre-peeled garlic is handy to start with. Or, peel the cloves, place them in a mini-food processor, and chop or mince as needed. For one or two cloves of garlic, see the instructions above for peeling garlic; then remove the peel and chop the crushed garlic.

MINCED GARLIC. This is very finely chopped garlic; simply cut a peeled clove of garlic one way, then slice again the other way into very small pieces.

PRESSED GARLIC. When garlic is required to be very smooth for a recipe, pressed garlic may be needed. The best technique is to use a garlic press, although there will be some waste, because a portion of the clove will be left behind in the press.

Storage Tips

Store fresh garlic or garlic braids at room temperature, out of bright light or sunlight. Keep the bulbs or unpeeled cloves in open containers; never store a garlic bulb in a plastic produce bag—it needs good ventilation. Also, do not refrigerate garlic unless it has been peeled, because it needs to be kept dry. Properly stored, a garlic bulb should last about two months.

French Onion Soup

Kay, Marino, Lucy, and Lucy's companion and FBI cohort, Janet, leave the Quantico Marine Corps Base together and head for the Globe & Laurel at 18418 Jefferson Davis Highway in Triangle, VA for dinner and, of course, some serious conversation. A fixture in the area since 1968, the restaurant is dedicated to the proud history and traditions of the Marine Corps. Amidst the resplendent Highland plaid décor, police shoulder patches donated by the many law enforcement officers who frequent the Globe & Laurel are displayed. The restaurant's patch collection, which represents a number of foreign countries, is thought to be one of the world's largest.

Marine Major Richard T. Spooner, proprietor, has shared his rich, traditional French Onion Soup recipe—perfected over the past thirty years—with countless Marine Corps families, but this is the first time it has appeared in print. Spooner is adamant about using authentic sherry wine in this soup, in place of often poor-quality cooking sherry. And provolone cheese is his first choice for melting over the soup. "We have tried other cheeses, but find that provolone brings far more compliments," says Spooner. "Serve it with pride."

1 ½ tablespoons butter

4 cups sliced Vidalia or yellow onions (3 to 4 medium)

1 tablespoon all-purpose flour

4 cups homemade beef stock or canned beef broth

4 cups homemade chicken stock or canned chicken broth

¼ cup dry sherry

2 medium tomatoes, peeled, seeded, if desired (see Note),
    and chopped

1 to 1½ teaspoons salt

¼ teaspoon freshly ground pepper

1 tablespoon Kitchen Bouquet, Magic Chef, or beef gravy base (optional)

8 slices (½ inch thick) French or sourdough bread, lightly toasted

8 thin slices provolone cheese (about 6 ounces)

1. In a Dutch oven or 4-quart saucepan, melt the butter over medium-low heat. Add the onions and cook slowly for about 10 minutes, stirring frequently, until the onions begin to turn translucent and a nice golden color.

2. Sprinkle the flour over the onions; cook, stirring with a wooden spoon, for 2 to 3 minutes longer. Stir in the beef stock, chicken stock, and sherry, then add the tomatoes. Bring the soup to a boil over medium-high heat. Reduce the heat and simmer, uncovered, for 15 minutes.

3. Stir in the salt and pepper (use the lower amount of salt if you plan to add the Kitchen Bouquet). Add the Kitchen Bouquet or beef gravy base to yield a deeper color and a stronger flavor, if desired. At this point, the soup is ready.

4. To serve, preheat the broiler. Ladle the soup into a 3-quart ovenproof casserole or 8 ovenproof crocks (put the casserole or crocks onto a sturdy rimmed baking sheet for easier handling). Float the toasted bread slices in the soup and top with the provolone. Place the soup about 3 inches from the heat source and broil just about 1 minute, until the cheese melts and browns slightly. Serve immediately.

| SERVES 8 |

NOTE: *To peel and seed tomatoes: Cut an "x" in the bottom of each tomato. Plunge the tomatoes into boiling water for 60 seconds; with a slotted spoon, transfer to a bowl of ice water for 2 minutes. Peel off the skins. Halve the tomatoes and squeeze out the seeds and juice.*

Tortellini Verdi

(Spinach Tortellini)

Benton Wesley drops Kay off at her home and orders her to barricade herself inside with Marino, Lucy, and Janet. After a traumatic day that included seeing a horrifying videotape of Temple Gault's latest murder, both Benton and Marino are concerned for Kay's safety. As Marino prepares Lucy and Janet for the worst, Kay rallies herself by trying to do something normal—and for her that means cooking. She checks the fridge for dinner prospects, trying to ignore the around-the-clock surveillance outside her home.

Tortellini look like funny little Italian hats, perhaps something that a bishop would wear, and they are usually stuffed with cheese or meat fillings. These satisfying little pastas make wonderful comfort food and, with a little time and patience, are easy to make from Kay's Fresh Spinach Pasta recipe. Kay keeps cooked tortellini on hand in her freezer for quick meals.

Only just-made pasta sheets, dried for 30 minutes, are moist enough to be filled and shaped for tortellini. Once shaped, they are ready to cook. Simmer them gently to keep their shape. Tortellini usually float up to the top of the pasta water when they are done.

MAKE-AHEAD TIP: You can refrigerate the cooked tortellini for up to several days, or freeze them on layers of waxed paper or aluminum foil in freezer containers for up to several months.

½ recipe Kay's Fresh Spinach Pasta (page 55)

Filling:

1 cup ricotta cheese (8 ounces)

½ cup shredded mozzarella cheese

¼ cup freshly grated Parmigiano-Reggiano plus additional for serving

2 tablespoons finely chopped fresh basil or oregano

1 tablespoon finely chopped fresh chives

1 egg white, lightly beaten

Sauce:

2 cups Kay's Marinara Sauce (page 150) or other prepared
  marinara sauce

1. Make the pasta dough and roll out the pasta sheets as directed. While the pasta is drying, prepare the tortellini filling. In a bowl, stir together the ricotta, mozzarella, Parmigiano-Reggiano, basil, chives, and egg white until blended.

2. To make the tortellini: Use a 2-inch round cookie or biscuit cutter to cut out as many rounds as possible from the sheets of pasta dough. Discard the dough trimmings.

3. To stuff and shape the tortellini: Place ½ teaspoon of the cheese filling in the center of one round of dough. With your fingers, moisten the bottom edge of the round with water. Fold the circle in half, away from you, pressing the edges together with your fingers to seal tightly. Moisten the corners of the half-circle with water and bring them together toward you, overlapping them and pressing the ends together to seal. (The pasta dough and the filling make 65 to 70 tortellini.)

4. Place the filled and shaped tortellini on a waxed paper-lined baking sheet; keep covered with plastic wrap until all of the tortellini are made.

5. To cook the tortellini: In a large pot, bring 4 quarts of salted water to a boil. Add the tortellini in batches and cook, stirring occasionally, for about 5 minutes, or until *al dente* (tender but still firm to the bite). Drain well, but do not rinse.

6. Serve the tortellini topped with the marinara sauce and sprinkled with Parmigiano-Reggiano.

MAKES 8 FIRST-COURSE SERVINGS
OR 4 MAIN-DISH SERVINGS

Linguine with Olive Oil, Parmesan, and Onion

Cooking for others is one way Kay expresses herself emotionally, and one of her favorite comfort foods is pasta. Preparing this simple, delicious pasta dish laced with olive oil (Kay favors extra-virgin), sautéed sweet Vidalia onions, and freshly grated Parmigiano-Reggiano helps Kay feel she is comforting herself and those she loves. This is an excellent side dish served with grilled meat, fish, or poultry; or serve it as an entree, lavished with the cheese.

Kay's Fresh Pasta, cut into fettuccine (1/4-inch-wide strips),
    or 2 packages (9 ounces each) store-bought fresh fettuccine

4 to 5 tablespoons extra-virgin olive oil

1 cup chopped Vidalia or yellow onions

1/4 cup chopped fresh parsley

2 tablespoons chopped fresh basil

2 tablespoons chopped fresh thyme

1 tablespoon chopped fresh oregano

Salt and freshly ground pepper

1/2 cup freshly grated Parmigiano-Reggiano plus additional for serving

1. If preparing Kay's Fresh Pasta: Roll out the pasta and dry as directed, then cut into fettuccine noodles or linguine noodles. Dry the noodles as directed

in the recipe. In a large pot, bring 4 quarts salted water and 1 tablespoon of the olive oil to a boil.

2. Meanwhile, in a small skillet, heat 1 tablespoon of the olive oil over medium-low heat. Add the onions and cook, stirring frequently, for about 10 minutes until translucent and tender. Stir in the parsley, basil, thyme, and oregano. Remove from the heat and keep warm.

3. Cook the fettuccine in the boiling water for 2 to 5 minutes, until *al dente* (tender but still firm to the bite). Immediately drain well. Do not rinse. (Cook store-bought fettuccine according to the package directions.)

4. Turn the pasta into a large serving bowl. Add the onion-herb mixture and season with salt and pepper. Drizzle generously with the remaining olive oil and sprinkle with $1/2$ cup of the Parmigiano-Reggiano and toss well to combine. Serve at once with additional cheese on the side.

MAKES 8 SIDE-DISH SERVINGS
OR 4 MAIN-DISH SERVINGS

Swimming in a tomato-basil sauce, richly layered with mozzarella, Italian sausage, and sweet peppers, stuffed and shaped into bite-size ravioli pillows or tortellini, or floating sublimely in a savory vegetable soup, pasta is the equivalent of gastronomic pleasure. Whether the Italians invented it (or the Asians or Egyptians) we'll probably never know for sure. But pasta has been around for so long (over 7,000 years, according to pasta experts) that no one really cares exactly whence it came.

Pasta is at once both gourmet and soul food, economical and upscale, a child's delight and yet grand enough for royal fare. Perhaps no other food can deliver pleasure in so many interesting ways. It's amazing to think that a simple mixture of flour, water, and egg can be so versatile, such great food for the hungry soul. Pasta alone complements so many other savory (and yes, sometimes sweet) foods that it would be difficult to name any other food that could serve in its place.

Cooking Tips

No matter which pasta you choose to serve, you need to start with a generous pot of water—at least 4 quarts of rapidly boiling water. Add 1 teaspoon salt to the water, if desired. You may have heard that you should add olive or vegetable oil to the water to keep pasta from sticking together. It's not necessary to do this; simply using enough water and stirring the pot occasionally is enough to keep the pasta separated.

Add pasta gradually to the boiling water so the water continues to boil. Do not break long pastas when adding them to the pot. Instead, grip a handful of the pasta, such as spaghetti, at one end and dip the other end into the boiling water. The pasta will soften almost immediately, so that you can curve it around the bottom of the pot and stir in the entire length of the noodles.

Pasta should be cooked until it is tender but still slightly firm when you bite into it, a quality described by Italians as *al dente*. Begin testing the pasta for doneness a couple of minutes before the end of the suggested cooking time.

Pasta should be well drained the moment it is done. Never rinse pasta, except when it will be used in a cold pasta salad (this stops the cooking and chills the pasta quickly). Never place pasta in a bowl of water to cool; it will soften further and swell.

If you are not tossing the pasta immediately with sauce, 1 tablespoon of extra-virgin olive oil or butter per pound of cooked pasta can be tossed with the pasta after it is drained; this adds a note of flavor and keeps the pasta from sticking together before it is served. You can quickly reheat pasta by dipping it, colander and all, into a pot of boiling water for 30 seconds; drain well and serve.

How Much Pasta to Cook?

DRY PACKAGED PASTA

Thin noodles. A pound of dry packaged noodles makes 6 to 8 side-dish or appetizer servings, or 4 to 5 main-dish servings. One serving, 4 ounces of dry spaghetti or fine noodles held together in a bunch, measures about 1 inch in diameter.

> 4 ounces dry spaghetti or fine noodles = 2 cups cooked spaghetti

Macaroni or small pastas.

> $3\frac{1}{2}$ ounces of dry packaged macaroni or tiny pasta = $2\frac{1}{2}$ cups cooked

Medium-wide noodles.

> 2 ounces of dry packaged medium noodles = $1\frac{1}{2}$ cups cooked

FRESH OR HOMEMADE PASTA

One pound of fresh pasta makes fewer servings than a pound of dried pasta. If a serving size for dried pasta is 2 ounces, the same serving calls for 3 ounces of fresh pasta.

> 1 appetizer serving = 3 ounces fresh pasta = 1 cup cooked pasta
>
> 1 main dish serving = 5 ounces fresh pasta = $1\frac{2}{3}$ cups cooked pasta
>
> 1 pound fresh pasta = about 5 to 6 appetizer servings or 3 main-dish servings
>
> $1\frac{1}{3}$ pounds fresh pasta = 1 pound dried pasta

Pasta Shapes

A pasta name speaks volumes, but what does it say? You don't have to be an Italian to find out. Use this handy guide to expand your pasta horizons!

SMALL SHAPES

Acini di pepe—small dots or
   peppercorns

Alphabet—tiny letter shapes

Anellini—tiny ring macaroni

Conchigliette—tiny shell macaroni

Couscous—tiny round grains that cook
   up like rice

Cravattini—little bow ties

Ditalini—tiny tubes or little thimbles

Farfalletti—little butterflies

Occhi di trota—trout's eyes (half the
   length of ditallini)

Orzo (also called rosamarina)—
   a Greek pasta shaped like rice

Spezziello—tiny tubes

Stellini—tiny star macaroni

Tripolini—tiny bow ties

LARGER SHAPES

Cavatelli—clam shells

Conchiglie—medium shell macaroni

Conchiglioni—large shell macaroni

Farfalle—bow ties

Gemelli—rope macaroni

Mostaccioli—bias-cut tubes, 2 inches
   long and $\frac{1}{2}$ inch wide

Penne—bias-cut tubes, 2 inches long
   and $\frac{1}{4}$ inch wide

Radiatori—little radiators

Rigatoni—ridged hollow tubes,
   2 inches long

Rotelle—corkscrew

Ruote—wagon wheels

NOODLES

Angel hair—fine noodles

Fettuccine—medium-wide noodles

Fusilli—long corkscrew noodles

Lasagne—flat noodles with straight
   or curly edges, 2 to 3 inches wide

Linguine—small tongues; thicker
   than spaghetti

Mafalde—$\frac{1}{2}$-inch-wide noodles with
   a ruffled edge

Pappardelle—$\frac{3}{4}$-inch-wide noodles

Spaghetti—standard long noodles

Verdi—green noodles

Vermicelli—straight fine noodles

Wide noodles—$\frac{1}{2}$ inch wide, usually
   egg pasta

Ziti—long thin tubular pasta

PASTAS USED FOR STUFFING

Agnolotti—half rounds

Cannelloni—large ridged tubes with
   bias-cut ends

Cappelletti—little hats

Cappelli di prete—priests' hats

Lumache—jumbo shells

Manicotti—large tubes

Orecchioni—large ears

Ravioli—little pillows

Tortellini—Italian hat shapes

Cause of Death

At the back was a screened-in porch, and we went in that way and deposited my gear on the wooden floor. Lucy opened the door leading into the kitchen, and we were enveloped by the aroma of tomatoes and garlic. She looked baffled as she stared at Marino and the dive equipment.

"What the hell's going on?" she said.

I could tell she was upset. This had been our night to be alone, and we did not have special nights like this often in our complicated lives.

"It's a long story." I met her eyes.

We followed her inside, where a large pot was simmering on the stove. Nearby on the counter was a cutting board, and Lucy apparently had been slicing peppers and onions when we arrived. She was dressed in FBI sweats and ski socks and looked flawlessly healthy, but I could tell she had not been getting much sleep.

CAUSE

"There's a hose in the pantry, and just off the porch near a spigot is an empty plastic trash can," I said to Marino. "If you'd fill that, we can soak my gear."

"I'll help," Lucy said.

"You most certainly won't." I gave her a hug. "Not until we've visited for a minute."

We waited until Marino was outside, then I pulled her over to the stove and lifted the lid from the pot. A delicious steam rose and I felt happy.

"I can't believe you," I said. "God bless you."

"When you weren't back by four I figured I'd better make the sauce or we weren't going to be eating lasagne tonight."

"It might need a little more red wine. And maybe more basil and a pinch of salt. I was going to use artichokes instead of meat, although Marino won't be happy about that, but he can just eat prosciutto. How does that sound?" I returned the lid to the pot.

Lasagne with Marinara Sauce and Porcini Mushrooms

Kay, Lucy, and Marino find themselves together on a snowy New Year's Eve in a tiny coastal cottage belonging to Dr. Philip Mant, Kay's Deputy Chief Medical Examiner for Virginia's Tidewater district.

Kay's own Italian tradition of cooking a pasta dish, with all of the components prepared from scratch, is carried on this night by Lucy, who has marinara sauce bubbling on the stove when Kay and Marino arrive. While Kay prepares the meal, which will include Braided Country Bread (page 152) and Fig, Melon, and Prosciutto Salad (page 160), she sips a glass of Côte Rôtie. (This was my father's favorite wine. When I went to France in June 1992 to accept the French book award, the Prix du Roman d' Aventures, for Postmortem, I brought several cases back with me.) Lucy enjoys a bottle of Peroni, an Italian beer. With the meal, Kay serves a Chianti.

MAKE-AHEAD TIP: Prepare the lasagne up to the baking step. Cover the pan tightly with two layers of aluminum foil. Freeze. Bake it frozen (do not thaw) and covered for 2 hours in preheated 375°F oven. Uncover and bake 15 to 20 minutes longer, until bubbly.

SHORTCUT TIP: Instead of making your own pasta, purchase fresh pasta sheets from an Italian deli or gourmet shop, as Kay does when she's short on time. The sheets of pre-rolled pasta can be refrigerated for several days or kept in the freezer for future use.

1 pound whole-milk mozzarella cheese (preferably fresh) or 4 cups
    pre-shredded mozzarella cheese

$\frac{1}{2}$ recipe Kay's Fresh Pasta (page 52), 8 ounces store-bought fresh
    pasta sheets, or 9 to 12 dried lasagne noodles (about 9 ounces)

1 ounce dried porcini mushrooms or $1\frac{1}{2}$ cups chopped trimmed
    white mushrooms

2 cups water

1 pound very lean ground beef

2 green, red, or yellow bell peppers, julienned

$1\frac{1}{2}$ cups sliced Vidalia or yellow onions

4 cloves garlic, minced

2 tablespoons olive oil

1 can ($13\frac{3}{4}$ ounces) artichoke hearts, drained and cut into $\frac{1}{2}$-inch
    pieces (do not use marinated artichoke hearts)

2 tablespoons chopped fresh oregano

1 teaspoon crushed fennel seeds

1 teaspoon salt

$\frac{1}{2}$ teaspoon freshly ground pepper

$3\frac{1}{2}$ cups Kay's Marinara Sauce (page 150) or prepared marinara sauce

$\frac{1}{3}$ cup dry red wine

1 container (32 ounces) ricotta cheese

2 extra-large eggs

1 cup freshly grated Parmigiano-Reggiano plus additional for serving

$\frac{1}{4}$ cup chopped fresh basil

$\frac{1}{4}$ cup chopped fresh Italian parsley

1. At least 4 hours ahead or up to overnight, drain the liquid from the fresh
   mozzarella, if using. Place the cheese in a strainer lined with a clean kitchen
   towel or a triple layer of paper towels, set over a large bowl, and place in

the refrigerator to drain. Pat the cheese dry and tear into small bits. Cover and refrigerate until needed.

2. If making Kay's Fresh Pasta, follow the instructions for rolling out the pasta, using 2 balls (one-half) of the dough for the lasagne noodles. Dry the pasta for 30 minutes as directed. Place the rolled-out pasta on a cutting board and cut into 2-inch-wide noodles. Separate the noodles and allow to dry for 2 hours. (If drying the pasta longer, cover with plastic wrap or kitchen towels and set aside up to 24 hours.)

3. In a small saucepan, combine the porcini mushrooms and water. Bring to a boil over medium-high heat; remove from the heat. Cover and let stand 15 minutes. Drain the mushrooms well and rinse under cool water to remove any excess grit. Drain well again and chop. Set aside.

4. In a large deep skillet, brown the ground beef thoroughly over medium heat. Drain the meat well. Transfer to a double layer of paper towels and press out the excess fat. In the same skillet, cook the bell peppers, onions, and garlic in the olive oil for about 5 minutes, until tender.

5. Stir in the ground beef, artichoke hearts, porcini or white mushrooms, oregano, fennel, salt, and pepper. Stir in marinara sauce and red wine; bring the mixture to a boil over medium-high heat. Reduce the heat to low and simmer, stirring occasionally, for 20 minutes.

6. To cook the pasta: *For homemade noodles.* In a large pot, bring 4 quarts of salted water to a boil. Add the noodles and cook for 3 to 5 minutes, or until *al dente* (tender but still firm to the bite). Drain the pasta and transfer to a pan of cold water to stop the cooking. Drain well and pat the noodles dry with paper towels.

   For store-bought fresh pasta sheets. Add the pasta sheets, one at a time, to the boiling water and cook for 2 ½ to 3 minutes, until *al dente* (tender but still firm to the bite). As each sheet is done, carefully remove with tongs and transfer to a large pan of cold water to stop the cooking. Drain well and pat the noodles dry with paper towels. Cut the pasta into 2-inch-wide strips.

For packaged dry pasta. Cook according to the package directions; drain and place in a pan of cold water to stop the cooking. Pat dry with paper towels.

7. In a large bowl, stir together the ricotta cheese, eggs, $\frac{1}{2}$ cup of the Parmesan cheese, and the basil until combined. Put the mozzarella cheese into a separate bowl.

8. Preheat the oven to 375°F. Lightly oil a 13x9x2-inch rectangular baking dish. Arrange one-third of the noodles in the bottom of the dish. Spoon one-third of the ricotta cheese mixture over the noodles, spreading evenly to cover the pasta. Spoon one-third of the marinara sauce mixture over the ricotta layer. Sprinkle with one-third of the mozzarella. Repeat the layers two times. Sprinkle with the remaining Parmesan and the parsley.

9. Place the baking dish on a sturdy rimmed baking sheet to catch any drips. Cover the dish with aluminum foil. Bake for 45 minutes. Uncover and bake for 10 to 15 minutes longer, or until the top is just beginning to brown and the filling is bubbly. Let the lasagne rest for 5 minutes before serving. Cut into 9 or 12 squares, depending on appetites.

SERVES 9 TO 12

Variation

FETTUSAGNE: I discovered this wonderful variation quite by accident when I had only packaged fettuccine noodles on hand. Substitute 2 packages (9 ounces each) store-bought fresh fettuccine noodles for the lasagne. Cook the noodles according to package directions, drain well, and layer the noodles as directed for the lasagne.

Kay's Marinara Sauce

Make this incredible sauce during the summer when tomatoes are at their peak. You will find nothing compares to the fresh, rich flavor of this sauce. It takes some time to make, but remember that all good things come to those who wait. If you are a teetotaler, use chicken or vegetable stock or broth in place of the red wine.

There is one important thing to remember when cooking this sauce: Use a non-aluminum saucepan. The acid in tomatoes reacts with aluminum and produces a discoloration and a metallic off-flavor.

Since Kay lives in Richmond, it's easy for her to visit farm stands in the summer to get the delicious regional variety of tomatoes called Hanover, but you can use any good beefsteak or Roma (plum) tomatoes.

You can use this sauce in recipes like the lasagnes or pizzas in this book, over your own favorite pasta, over a cheese omelet, on steamed fresh vegetables, or in any recipe that calls for a good dose of marinara sauce.

MAKE-AHEAD TIP: This sauce freezes very well—Kay's freezer is stocked with it so she can enjoy it year-round. Just use some good freezer containers with tight-fitting lids. Put one or two cups of sauce in each container, and mark the top. Leave at least 1/2 inch of headspace at the top for expansion.

6 to 7 pounds fresh ripe Hanover, beefsteak, or Roma (plum) tomatoes

2 tablespoons olive oil

2 cups chopped Vidalia or yellow onions

4 cloves garlic, minced

1 can (6 ounces) tomato paste

½ cup chopped fresh basil

2 to 3 tablespoons chopped fresh oregano

1 tablespoon salt

¼ teaspoon freshly ground pepper

2 bay leaves

½ cup dry red wine

1. Peel and seed the tomatoes; set aside. (For how-to, see Note on page 135.)

2. In an 8-quart Dutch oven or stockpot, heat the olive oil over medium heat. Add the onions and garlic and cook for about 3 minutes, or until tender but not brown. (Note: Although the sauce cooks down to 7 cups, the size of the pot allows room for simmering and prevents spattering.) Stir in the chopped tomatoes and all of the remaining ingredients except the red wine; bring to a boil over medium-high heat. Reduce the heat and simmer, covered, stirring frequently, for 20 minutes.

3. Stir in the red wine. Cook for 30 to 35 minutes longer, or until the sauce cooks down to a thick consistency. Remove the bay leaves.

4. Use the sauce as needed, or cool to room temperature, then freeze as directed in the headnote.

MAKES ABOUT 7 CUPS

Braided Country Bread

Part of Kay's lasagne feast includes her homemade bread, a sumptuous braided loaf, enriched with high-gluten flour and flavored with olive oil and honey. You can place the dough in the oven to rise as the recipe directs, or if the oven is already being used, cover the dough and place the bowl on a rack set over a bowl of hot water. Often the top of your range is slightly warm if the oven is going, so it's perfect for rising dough.

You'll find it's easier to make a neat braided loaf if you start braiding in the middle of the three ropes. Braid them together toward one end, seal the ends together, then turn the baking sheet around and braid the other half.

SHORTCUT TIP: *If you don't want to fuss with braiding, divide the dough in half and shape each half into two 18-inch ropes. Twist the two ropes, pressing the ends together to seal. Bake as directed.*

$5\frac{1}{2}$ to 6 cups high-gluten flour (see Note on page 31) or bread flour

2 packages rapid-rise active dry yeast

2 teaspoons salt

$1\frac{1}{2}$ cups milk

$\frac{1}{2}$ cup water

5 tablespoons olive oil

2 tablespoons honey

1 egg, lightly beaten

---

1. In a large bowl, stir together 2½ cups of the flour, the yeast, and the salt. In a medium saucepan, combine the milk, water, 3 tablespoons oil, and honey. Heat the mixture over medium heat, stirring, until it is very warm (120° to 130°F). Stir the liquid into the flour mixture, then stir in 2 more cups of the flour.

2. Stir the flour mixture until it is well combined and the mixture begins to leave the side of the bowl. Turn the dough out onto a generously floured work surface and gather into a ball. Knead for about 10 minutes, until it is soft, smooth, and elastic, adding enough of the remaining flour to keep the dough from sticking.

3. Place the dough in a large greased bowl and turn the dough to coat evenly. Cover the dough with plastic wrap or a damp clean kitchen towel. Place the bowl on the lowest oven rack. Turn the oven on to the lowest setting for 1 minute; immediately turn the oven off. Let the dough rise for 30 to 40 minutes or until doubled in size.

4. Punch down the dough; on a lightly floured surface, knead the dough 10 times to release the air bubbles. Cover the dough; let rest for 10 minutes.

5. To shape the dough: On a lightly floured surface, divide the dough in half. Set aside half the dough. Divide the remaining half of the dough into thirds; shape each third into a 14-inch rope. Place the three ropes, side by side, on a greased large baking sheet. Braid the ropes together, pinching the ends together to seal. Repeat with the remaining half of the dough. Brush the loaf with the beaten egg, then with olive oil. Cover the loaves and let rise 20 to 25 minutes, or until doubled.

6. Meanwhile, preheat the oven to 375°F. Bake the loaves for 20 to 25 minutes, or until golden brown and loaves sound hollow when lightly tapped on the bottom. Transfer the loaves to a wire rack to cool slightly. Serve the bread warm or at room temperature with butter or olive oil for dipping.

| MAKES TWO LOAVES |

Lasagne coi Carciofi

(Lasagne with Artichokes and Béchamel Sauce)

Kay promises to make Lucy this unforgettable green noodle and white sauce lasagne, with its mild, delicate flavor. The béchamel sauce and artichokes make this a sophisticated twist on the traditional—and perfect for a holiday meal or dinner party. Even though béchamel sauce sounds intimidating, it is merely a simple white sauce. This is one recipe, like Kay's other lasagne (page 146), where it's definitely worthwhile to use fresh mozzarella.

As Kay does, you will want to reserve this extraordinary lasagne for special times when you have the afternoon to spend in the kitchen cooking for those you love. One bite of this heavenly lasagne will tell you that it was well worth the effort.

MAKE-AHEAD TIP: *See Make-Ahead Tip for Lasagne with Marinara Sauce and Porcini Mushrooms (page 146).*

1 pound whole-milk mozzarella cheese (preferably fresh) or 4 cups
    pre-shredded mozzarella cheese

½ recipe Kay's Fresh Spinach Pasta (page 55), or 8 ounces
    store-bought fresh spinach pasta sheets, or 9 to 12 dried lasagne
    noodles (about 9 ounces)

1 pound sweet Italian sausage, casings removed

2 tablespoons olive oil

2 cups stemmed and sliced shiitake mushrooms or trimmed and sliced
    white mushrooms

1 cup chopped Vidalia or yellow onions

3 cloves garlic, minced

1 jar (12 ounces) roasted red peppers, well drained and julienned
(1½ cups)

1 can (13¾ ounces) artichoke bottoms or hearts, drained and cut
into ½-inch pieces

¼ cup chopped fresh basil

Salt and freshly ground pepper

1 recipe Béchamel Sauce (page 157)

1 cup freshly grated Parmigiano-Reggiano

¼ cup chopped fresh Italian parsley

1. At least 4 hours ahead or up to overnight, drain the liquid from the fresh mozzarella, if using. Place the cheese in a strainer lined with a clean kitchen towel or a triple layer of paper towels, set over a large bowl, and place in the refrigerator to drain. Pat the cheese dry and tear into bits. Cover and re-frigerate until needed.

2. If making Kay's Fresh Spinach Pasta, follow the instructions for rolling out the pasta, using 2 balls (one-half) of the dough for the lasagne noodles. Dry the pasta for 30 minutes as directed. Place the rolled-out pasta on a cutting board and cut into 2-inch-wide noodles. Separate the noodles and allow to dry for 2 hours. (If drying the pasta longer, cover with plastic wrap or kitchen towels and dry up to 24 hours.)

3. To cook the pasta: *For homemade noodles.* In a large pot, bring 4 quarts of salted water to a boil. Add the noodles and cook for 3 to 5 minutes, or until *al dente* (tender but still firm to the bite). Drain the pasta and transfer to a pan of cold water to stop the cooking. Drain well and pat the noodles dry with paper towels.

For store-bought purchased fresh pasta sheets. Add the pasta sheets, one at a time, to the boiling water and cook for 2½ to 3 minutes, until *al dente* (tender but still firm to the bite). As each sheet is done, carefully remove it with tongs and transfer to a large pan of cold water to stop the cooking. Drain well and pat the noodles dry with paper towels. Cut into 2-inch-wide strips.

For packaged dry pasta. Cook according to the package directions, drain, and place in a pan of cold water to stop the cooking. Pat dry with paper towels.

4. In a large skillet, crumble the sausage and cook over medium-high heat, for about 8 minutes, until browned. Drain well. Transfer the sausage to a double layer of paper towels and press out the excess fat. Wipe out the skillet.

5. In the same skillet, heat the olive oil over medium-high heat. Add the mushrooms, onions, and garlic and cook for about 5 minutes, or until the vegetables are tender. Stir in the roasted peppers, artichokes, sausage, and basil; season with salt and pepper. Remove from the heat. Transfer the mixture to a colander and drain off all the excess liquid. Cover and set aside.

6. Prepare the béchamel sauce (page 157). Cover and remove from the heat. Preheat the oven to 350°F. Lightly oil a 13x9x2-inch rectangular baking dish.

7. Spread ½ cup of the béchamel sauce over the bottom of the dish. Arrange one-third of the noodles over the sauce, spreading evenly to cover. Top with half of the sausage and all of vegetable mixture; sprinkle with 1 cup of the mozzarella and ⅓ cup of the Parmigiano-Reggiano. Arrange another layer of noodles over the cheese, then top with the remaining sausage mixture, 1 cup mozzarella, and ⅓ cup of the Parmigiano-Reggiano. Arrange remaining noodles on top. Spread with the remaining béchamel sauce. Sprinkle the remaining 2 cups mozzarella and ⅓ cup Parmigiano-Reggiano evenly over the top. Sprinkle with parsley.

8. Place the baking dish on a sturdy rimmed baking sheet to catch any drips. Bake for 45 to 50 minutes, until the top is browned and the filling is bubbly.

9. To serve, let the lasagne rest, covered, for 5 minutes before cutting. Cut into 9 to 12 squares, depending on appetites.

SERVES 9 TO 12

Béchamel Sauce

Béchamel is classic French white sauce. This version is a bit unusual because both half-and-half and chicken broth are added. Use this recipe to make the Lasagne coi Carciofi, or you can jazz up Kay's lasagne (page 146) by substituting this sauce for half of the marinara sauce in the recipe. It's also an elegant drape for steamed fresh asparagus or broccoli.

5 tablespoons butter

5 tablespoons all-purpose flour

1½ cups half-and-half or light cream

1 cup chicken broth

¼ teaspoon salt

¼ teaspoon ground nutmeg

⅛ teaspoon ground white pepper

1. In a medium saucepan, melt the butter over medium-low heat; stir in the flour. Cook, stirring constantly, for about 3 minutes, until the mixture thickens and becomes golden in color.

2. Stir in the half-and-half and chicken broth all at once, whisking the mixture until smooth. Cook over medium heat, stirring constantly, for about 5 minutes, until the mixture comes to a boil. Reduce the heat to low and simmer for 2 minutes longer. Stir in the salt, nutmeg, and pepper.

3. Remove from the heat. Press a piece of waxed paper directly onto the surface to prevent a skin from forming.

| MAKES 2½ CUPS |

Kay's freezer provides her with a wonderful backup for long work days and times when she has unexpected guests, such as Marino or Lucy. For cooks like Kay, who prepare food in generous amounts when time allows, freezing the leftovers is a great way to save time. And freezing, done correctly and promptly after food is prepared, won't alter the texture or taste of the food.

Start with good-quality freezer containers with tight-fitting lids or self-sealing freezer bags to preserve your bounty. Leave at least $\frac{1}{2}$ to 1 inch of headspace at the top of the containers to allow for expansion during freezing, or fill freezer bags only three-quarters full for the same reason. If you are freezing a casserole in a baking dish, wrap the dish in heavy-duty aluminum foil (use two layers) and seal the edges securely with freezer tape (available in gourmet food and cookware shops). Always be sure to label the containers, freezer bags, and packages with the date and the contents; the number of servings is also helpful.

Be sure food is cool before placing it in your freezer (a casserole hot from the oven will disrupt the operation of your freezer and delay freezing long enough to endanger the quality of your food). Don't overfill your freezer by stacking it to the top; leave enough room for the air to circulate. The food will freeze faster and the freezer temperature will be maintained. Here's a little-known tip: Freezers operate more efficiently when they are filled to at least half-capacity. Your freezer should be set at 0°F.

Thawing Tips

Food safety experts recommend three ways to defrost frozen foods. Use the one that is most convenient for you.

> ◆ Place the frozen food in the refrigerator. Allow it to thaw at least overnight or up to several days for larger items. To defrost a turkey, here's an easy guide: Allow one day for every five pounds. (A twenty-pound turkey will take about four days to thaw.)

- Place the food in a leakproof bag, and place the bag in the sink or in a large bowl of very cold water. Replace the water at least every 30 minutes to maintain the temperature; then refrigerate the food as soon as it thaws.

- Thaw the frozen food using your microwave oven. Refer to the manual for specific instructions. Plan to cook microwave-thawed food immediately after micro-thawing, as some portions of the food may have begun cooking during the defrosting.

Foods for the Freezer

Below is a list of foods that freeze very well, many of which you would find if you were to look in Kay's freezer. (Foods that don't freeze well include canned foods, foods that are tossed in mayonnaise or cream dressings, lettuce, custard-type puddings and desserts, and cream sauces.)

- Breads, rolls, biscuits, bagels, pizza
- Cookies, cakes, cheesecakes, coffee cakes, fruit pies
- Fresh pasta dough, rolled pasta sheets, cooked pasta in casseroles, such as lasagne, filled pastas (cooked or uncooked), such as ravioli and tortellini
- Sauces, including marinara, bolognese, vegetable-based sauces
- Stews, soups, chili, and strained chicken, beef, fish, or vegetable stocks
- Fresh fruit, except for kiwi fruit, bananas
- Fish, poultry, or meat casseroles
- Chopped or sliced fresh vegetables, such as summer squash, beans, peas, eggplant, onions, bell peppers, broccoli, cauliflower, carrots

Fig, Melon, and Prosciutto Salad

This salad is an Italian classic, often served as a separate course as part of a pasta meal. However, there's no reason this salad couldn't be a meal in itself, if arranged on a large platter with some extra prosciutto and served with a crusty loaf of bread and a chilled chardonnay or white Burgundy wine. It's a special treat for dining al fresco and reason enough to go on a romantic picnic.

In Cause of Death, Kay prepares this appetizer to serve with the New Year's Eve dinner she's sharing with Lucy and Marino at Dr. Mant's house.

Try to find a good source for the prosciutto. Have it freshly sliced at the deli in your market, or seek out a great gourmet store or Italian deli, where you'll have a variety of prosciuttos to choose from. (At Kay's house, Marino always gets extra prosciutto on his salad.)

Fresh figs, such as Calimyrna, Black Mission, Kadota, or Brown Turkey, are in season during the summer months and then again from November through January. They may be dark purple, reddish brown, bright green, or greenish yellow, depending on the variety. When fresh figs are not to be had, you can substitute dried brown or mission figs, quartered.

MAKE-AHEAD TIP: This salad can be made up to a day ahead; assemble it on a pretty serving platter, then cover and chill for up to 24 hours before serving.

6 to 8 fresh figs

½ of a large ripe cantaloupe, seeded

Lettuce leaves

12 slices prosciutto (about 4½ ounces)

Dijon mustard for serving

1. Remove the stems from the figs and cut them into quarters. Cut the melon into quarters and cut off the rind. Cut each quarter into two wedges, then cut crosswise in half.

2. To serve, line four salad plates with lettuce leaves. Arrange the figs and melon slices decoratively over the lettuce. Separate the prosciutto slices and fold each slice in half or roll up. Arrange three slices on each salad. Serve with the Dijon mustard.

SERVES 4

Fresh Fruit Salad
with Blood Orange Dressing

In one of her frequent attempts to prod Marino into improving his diet, Kay devises this beautiful fruit salad for his breakfast one morning. When Marino says with disgust, "This ain't food. And what the hell are these little green slices with black things?" Kay patiently replies, "The kiwi fruit I told you to get. I'm sure you must have had it before." Marino brightens up when Kay produces bagels from her freezer and cream cheese. As usual, he's had a long night, so he is relieved when Kay pours caffeine-laden Guatemalan coffee, just the way he likes it. You might choose café au lait or a flavored tea instead.

Blood oranges are an exotic variety of orange with a raspberry red interior and a reddish orange blush on the skin. Their flavor is rich and intense, like raspberry and orange combined, and they make a very attractive addition to salads and fruit compotes. Look for them in better markets that carry exotic produce.

4 blood oranges or navel oranges

¾ cup red or green seedless grapes, halved

3 kiwi fruit, peeled, halved crosswise, and sliced

1 cup sliced strawberries, blueberries, or raspberries

Blood Orange Dressing:

2 tablespoons blood orange juice or orange juice

1 tablespoon olive oil

1 teaspoon grated blood orange or navel orange zest

1 teaspoon honey

Fresh mint leaves for garnish

1. Reserve one of the oranges for the dressing. Peel the remaining oranges and slice thinly. Arrange the orange slices on 4 salad plates. Top with the grapes, kiwi fruit, and berries.

2. For the dressing: In a jar with a tight-fitting lid, combine the orange juice, olive oil, orange zest, and honey; shake well. Drizzle the dressing over the salads and garnish with mint leaves.

SERVES 4

Classic English Breakfast
(Bacon and Eggs with Tomatoes and Mushrooms)

The far-reaching case of Temple Gault takes Kay and Benton Wesley to London. Jet lag, lack of sleep, and raging appetites lead them further to breakfast at Richoux, a small, pretty restaurant at 41a South Audley Street in Mayfair. For the past ninety-odd years, Richoux has been famous for its all-day breakfast and traditional afternoon tea. (I discovered Richoux's beautiful French pastries and chocolates when I had a flat in London several years ago.)

This recipe for Classic English Breakfast is a hearty plateful of British Cumberland sausages, bacon, eggs, mushrooms, tomatoes, and toasted bread. The delectable sausages hail from Cumberland County in northern England. If you live in a city that has a shop that sells English food, you might find them there. Or, call Myers of Keswick in New York at (212) 691-4194; you can have the sausages shipped to you via overnight mail. However, your favorite fresh link pork sausage is a very acceptable substitute.

Though Richoux toasts the bread for this breakfast, traditional Brits fry their bread in the same pan after cooking their bacon and eggs. Consider this breakfast a Marino special gone English, and you'll get the idea.

1 tablespoon butter

1 cup small white mushrooms, trimmed

4 slices thick-cut bacon

2 Cumberland or link breakfast sausages

2 Roma (plum) tomatoes, halved or 1 medium tomato, cut into
    4 thick slices

4 extra-large eggs

2 thick slices white or French bread, halved diagonally

1. In a large skillet, melt the butter over medium-high heat. Add the mushrooms and cook for about 3 minutes, or until browned. Transfer the mushrooms to a plate; keep warm.

2. In the same pan, fry the bacon for about 5 minutes, until crisp and brown; transfer to a paper towel-lined plate to drain. Pour off the pan drippings; add the sausages to the pan and cook over medium heat for about 8 minutes, or until cooked through. Transfer the sausages to a plate to drain.

3. Pour the fat from the skillet into a separate dish; return 1 teaspoon of the bacon fat to the skillet and fry the tomatoes for 3 minutes per side. Arrange the tomatoes on 2 breakfast plates.

4. Add 1 tablespoon bacon fat to the skillet; fry the eggs over medium-low heat to the desired doneness. Arrange the eggs on the plates.

5. In the same pan, quickly fry the bread slices for 1 to 2 minutes, until golden brown, adding more bacon fat if necessary. Arrange the hot bread slices, bacon, sausage, and mushrooms on the plates. Serve immediately.

SERVES 2

Unnatural Exposure

A shadow passed over her face as she opened a jar of horseradish. "I'm afraid I can imagine what you've been doing," she said. "Been hearing it on the news." She shook her head. "You must be plumb worn out. I don't know how you sleep. Let me tell you what to do for yourself tonight."

She walked over to a case of chilled blue crabs. Without asking, she selected a pound of meat in a carton.

"Fresh from Tangier Island. Hand-picked it myself, and you tell me if you find even a trace of cartilage or shell. You're not eating alone, are you?" she said.

"No."

"That's good to hear."

She winked at me. I had brought Wesley in here before.

She picked out six jumbo shrimp, peeled and deveined, and wrapped them. Then she set a jar of her homemade cocktail sauce on the counter by the cash register.

UNNAT

"I got a little carried away with the horseradish," she said, "so it will make your eyes water, but it's good." She began ringing up my purchases. "You sauté the shrimp so quick their butts barely hit the pan, got it? Chill 'em, and have that as an appetizer. By the way, those and the sauce are on the house."

"You don't need to . . ."

She waved me off. "As for the crab, honey, listen up. One egg slightly beaten, one-half teaspoon dry mustard, a dash or two of Worcestershire sauce, four unsalted soda crackers, crushed. Chop up an onion, a Vidalia if you're still hoarding any from summer. One green pepper, chop that. A teaspoon or two of parsley, salt and pepper to taste."

"Sounds fabulous," I gratefully said. "Bev, what would I do without you?"

"Now you gently mix all that together and shape it into patties." She made the motion with her hands. "Sauté in oil over medium heat until lightly browned. Maybe fix him a salad or get some of my slaw," she said. "And that's as much as I would fuss over any man."

TURAL

Kay's Stew with Red Wine and Garlic

On a balmy Halloween day, Kay puts on a pot of her homemade stew, which simmers through the afternoon in anticipation of a dinner with Marino. This is actually an adaptation of one of my own signature dishes—a rich, generous stew of vegetables, veal or beef chunks, garlic, Italian seasonings, and a lot of Gallo red Burgundy wine. I say adaptation because my stew never turns out exactly the same way twice, since the choice of meat and vegetables is different every time. I love to make a pot of this richly satisfying stew for friends, often creating a gift basket with a loaf of homemade bread and a bottle of good French Burgundy. To me, nothing is more special than a gift made with your own hands—it's a direct expression of the heart. I've even flown this stew, packed in dry ice, in my helicopter to friends, including Ruth and Billy Graham and Senator Orrin Hatch. (It didn't make it past Senate security initially, and when it did, Senator Hatch called and said, "I only got one bite—my staff ate it all.")

The secret to the deep, earthy flavors that develop in this stew comes from the careful browning of the meat cubes and the vegetables. Dredging the meat in flour encourages a nice brown crust and also helps thicken the stew later on. So don't skimp on the browning steps; keep cooking and stirring until you have achieved a nice deep golden brown color on the meat and the vegetables.

Allow yourself a leisurely afternoon to make this stew, and you will be rewarded with a highly soul-satisfying meal in a bowl. The ingredient list for this wonderful stew may seem daunting, but all of the elements of this stew are simple to prepare. In preparation for this dish, spend a quick half hour *doing the ingredient chopping at the beginning; then it's a simple matter of adding everything at the appropriate time. As Kay does on this Indian summer day, you may want to serve the stew with Braided Country Bread (page 152).*

2 pounds boneless veal shoulder or boneless beef round, trimmed
    of fat and cut into 1-inch cubes

4 tablespoons all-purpose flour

4 tablespoons olive oil

1 large Vidalia or yellow onion, cut into 1-inch wedges

4 cloves garlic, minced

1 cup chopped carrots

1 cup sliced celery

2 cups red Burgundy wine

2 cups homemade beef stock or canned beef broth

1 cup V-8 juice

1 cup tomato sauce

2 tablespoons chopped fresh basil

1 tablespoon chopped fresh oregano

1 tablespoon chopped fresh thyme

2 bay leaves

1½ teaspoons salt

¼ teaspoon freshly ground pepper

8 ounces white mushrooms, trimmed and sliced (3 cups)

1 can (13¾ ounces) artichoke hearts, drained and halved

8 ounces asparagus, trimmed and cut into 1-inch lengths

1 cup diced peeled potato

1 cup shelled fresh peas or frozen peas

3 tablespoons chopped fresh parsley for garnish

1. Place the veal cubes in a large self-sealing bag with the flour. Seal the bag and shake well to coat the meat with the flour. In a 6-quart saucepan or Dutch oven, heat 2 tablespoons of the oil over medium-high heat. Brown the meat cubes on all sides, turning frequently, for about 10 minutes, or until meat is a deep golden brown. Make sure that the pan is always hot enough to sizzle the meat and the vegetables, but not so hot that they burn and stick to the pan. Remove meat from the pan.

2. Add 1 tablespoon oil to the pan. Add the onion and garlic and cook over medium-high heat, stirring frequently, for about 8 minutes, or until deep golden brown. Transfer the onion mixture to a dish. Add the remaining 1 tablespoon oil to the pan; add the carrots and celery and cook over medium-high heat, stirring frequently, for about 8 minutes, until deep golden brown.

3. Return the meat and onion mixture to the pan. Add 1 cup of the red wine, the beef stock, and V-8 juice, scraping up the crusty browned bits of meat and vegetables from the bottom of the pan so they can meld with the liquid. Stir in the tomato sauce, basil, oregano, thyme, bay leaves, salt, and pepper until well blended. Bring the mixture to a boil over high heat, then reduce heat to low and simmer gently, uncovered, stirring occasionally, for 1½ hours.

4. Stir in the remaining 1 cup wine, the mushrooms, artichoke hearts, asparagus, potato, and peas. Simmer for 1 to 1½ hours longer, or until the meat is very tender.

5. Taste for seasoning and remove the bay leaves. Ladle the stew into shallow serving bowls and sprinkle with the parsley.

SERVES 8

What would great Italian cooking be without the tomato? Chopped up for a fresh pasta sauce, simmered in a creamy soup, pureed and spread over a pizza crust, nestled with garlic and herbs for a killer bruschetta, or layered with fresh mozzarella cheese and doused with balsamic vinegar—the culinary opportunities are endless! Hot or cold, fresh off the vine, pureed, crushed, stewed, stuffed, or dried, there is hardly a more versatile vegetable than the tomato.

Tomato Varieties

Take your pick from the harvest of tomatoes available in food markets, farmers' markets, gourmet catalogs, or at your local nursery.

BEEFSTEAK—a large tomato with broad "shoulders" or knobs near the stem; perfect for sandwiches, salads, and flavorful sauces.

ROMA—a small, oval or pear-shaped tomato that is very meaty. Ideal for cutting into wedges or slices, chopping for vegetable mixtures, or for sauces.

CHERRY— miniature round tomatoes, available in both golden and red varieties. Great for salads, appetizers, vegetable platters.

GOLDEN—"yellow" tomato with a golden yellow skin and flesh, available as large tomatoes, cherry tomatoes, or as a grape or pear tomato. It has a sweet flavor and is as versatile as the red tomato.

GRAPE—smaller than cherry tomatoes, with an elongated round shape like a grape; available in red and golden varieties. Use as substitute for cherry tomatoes.

GREEN—an unripe red tomato. Coat and batter-fry or use in sauces.

ORANGE—a tomato hybrid with orange skin and flesh; sweet in flavor. Use as you would a red tomato.

PEAR—or "teardrop" tomato; a small cherry tomato with a pear shape. In yellow and red varieties. Use as substitute for cherry tomatoes.

ROUND RED—more medium sized and rounder than a beefsteak tomato, most common variety available. A good slicing and all-purpose tomato.

VINE-RIPENED—medium-sized red tomatoes with the vine and stems still attached. These tomatoes have tender skins and should be used within a couple of days for best flavor. As versatile as any tomato.

Buying and Storing Fresh Tomatoes

Buy tomatoes with smooth rich red (or gold or orange) skins that have a subtle sweet scent and yield slightly with gentle pressure when held between your palms. Avoid bruised or split tomatoes, or hard, pale pink-skinned winter tomatoes; if that's all you see in your market's produce aisle, then do as Kay does in a pinch—look for hothouse tomatoes (sometimes called Holland tomatoes or tomatoes-on-the-vine), or opt for a canned product, instead.

MEASUREMENT EQUIVALENTS:

2 large or 3 medium tomatoes = 1 pound

8 to 9 Roma tomatoes or 24 cherry tomatoes = 1 pound

1 medium tomato or 6 cherry tomatoes = 1 serving

There are two things to remember when storing tomatoes: Never ripen tomatoes in sunlight (which only makes them mushy), and never refrigerate tomatoes unless they are very ripe and you don't plan to use them for several days (chilling them does nothing to develop the flavor). Tomatoes ripen naturally and develop their flavor when kept out of sunlight in temperatures between 50° and 60°F. Rotate your tomato supply and use the ripest ones first, as you do bananas. You can speed up the ripening by placing the tomatoes in a fruit-ripening bowl (available in specialty cooking stores and catalogs) or in a brown paper bag, but be sure to check their progress daily.

Tomatoes for Your Pantry

During the winter season, it's perfectly fine to rely on canned and packaged tomato puree and sauces, which are processed when tomatoes are at their peak. These are also very convenient products to use when time is too short to cook fresh tomatoes. Here's a condensed list of what you'll find on your supermarket shelf:

- crushed tomatoes in tomato puree
- diced tomatoes
- whole peeled tomatoes
- stewed tomatoes
- Italian-style tomatoes with herbs and garlic
- Mexican tomatoes with chiles
- Cajun-style tomatoes
- chunky-style or "pasta ready" tomatoes
- low-sodium tomato products
- tomato puree, tomato paste
- tomato sauce
- dried tomatoes, packed dry or in oil

Jumbo Shrimp with Bev's Kicked by a Horse Cocktail Sauce

Kay heads for home in a heavy rain, anticipating dinner at her house with Wesley. She takes the turnoff to Carytown, a shopping district in Richmond, to buy some shrimp and fresh crabmeat at P. T. Hasting's Famous Seafood. This seafood shop, with two Richmond locations at 3545 West Cary Street and 8128 West Broad Street, offers an abundance of top-quality local fish and seafood.

Bev, the kind lady behind the counter, picks out six jumbo shrimp for Kay's tête-à-tête with Wesley. Kay also picks up a jar of Bev's Kicked by a Horse Cocktail Sauce to accompany the shrimp. Both Bev's character and the cocktail sauce were fictional when Unnatural Exposure was published, but after P. T. Hasting, Jr., the proprietor, and his staff received so many inquiries about the nonexistent sauce, they started making and selling it.

Bev's cooking advice for the shrimp is summed up succinctly this way: "You sauté the shrimp so quick their butts barely hit the pan, got it? Chill 'em and have that as an appetizer." Enough said.

6 jumbo shrimp, peeled and deveined
1 tablespoon olive oil

Cocktail Sauce:

½ cup catsup

2 tablespoons prepared horseradish

½ teaspoon Worcestershire sauce

Few dashes hot pepper sauce

1 teaspoon fresh lemon juice

Lettuce leaves and/or crushed ice for serving

Lemon or lime wedges for garnish

1. Rinse the shrimp and pat dry. In a small skillet, heat the oil over medium-high heat. Add the shrimp and cook, turning frequently, for about 3 minutes, or until they turn pink and opaque throughout. Immediately remove the pan from the heat and transfer the shrimp to a plate. Cover and chill at least 1 hour or up to 24 hours before serving.

2. For the cocktail sauce: In a small bowl, stir together the catsup, horseradish, Worcestershire, hot pepper sauce, and lemon juice. Cover and chill until serving time.

3. To serve, arrange the shrimp over lettuce leaves and/or crushed ice with lemon or lime wedges. Serve along with the cocktail sauce for dipping.

| MAKES 2 APPETIZER SERVINGS |

Bev's Lump Crab Cakes

These delicate crab cakes are an adaptation of the off-the-cuff recipe that counter clerk Bev gives Kay at P. T. Hasting's seafood shop in Carytown. If fresh lump crabmeat is expensive in your area, you can substitute canned lump crabmeat—be sure to pick through for any small pieces of cartilage.

On Bev's recommendation, Kay likes to serve the crab cakes with cole slaw (you might try the Marinated Slaw with Apple Cider Vinaigrette on page 69) or a simple tossed salad. For an elegant touch, wrap lemon or lime halves in gauze wrappers (available in specialty food and cookware shops) to decorate each plate. When the juice is squirted over the crab cakes, the wrappers act as a nifty catch-all for the citrus seeds and pulp.

Benton Wesley brings along a Cakebread chardonnay to drink that evening, but you could also try a white Burgundy.

3 large eggs, lightly beaten

2 tablespoons milk

1 teaspoon Worcestershire sauce

½ teaspoon dry mustard

1 pound lump crabmeat or 4 cans (6 ounces each) lump crabmeat, drained and picked over

1½ cups crushed saltine crackers (about 16 crackers)

1 cup chopped green bell pepper

½ cup chopped Vidalia or yellow onion

1 tablespoon chopped fresh parsley

½ teaspoon salt

¼ teaspoon freshly ground pepper

2 tablespoons olive oil

Lemon or lime wedges for serving

1. In a large bowl, whisk together the eggs, milk, Worcestershire sauce, and dry mustard. Stir in the crabmeat, crackers, green pepper, onion, parsley, salt, and pepper and toss well to combine. Cover and chill for 30 minutes to allow the crab mixture to absorb the eggs and the milk so the patties hold together.

2. With your hands, shape the crab mixture into nine round cakes, about 3 inches wide and ½ inch thick.

3. In a large skillet, heat the oil over medium-high heat. Add the crab cakes and cook for about 5 minutes per side, or until golden brown, turning the cakes carefully with a wide spatula to preserve their shape.

4. Serve the crab cakes hot with lemon or lime wedges.

MAKES 2 TO 3 MAIN-DISH SERVINGS
OR 4 APPETIZER SERVINGS

Lila's Clam Stew

ay finds a handwritten recipe for this stew on a discarded scrap of paper during her search of Lila Pruitt's house on Tangier Island, off the Virginia coast. Before her tragic death from smallpox, Lila made her living selling recipes on the sidewalk for a quarter each. This recipe for a wonderful clam and fish stew with an authentic island flavor might have been a bestseller for a character like Lila.

Though the ingredient list looks long and complicated, this is actually a very simple dump-in-the-pot stew that you can assemble in half an hour, and the cooking time totals only about 45 minutes. The blend of herbs, wine, and saffron flavors is reminiscent of bouillabaisse, but you'll find that the ingredients for this hearty concoction are much easier to come by. Serve the stew with slices of warm, crusty bread, a simple mesclun or mixed-lettuce salad, and a spicy gewürtztraminer, California chardonnay, or pinot gris wine.

3 tablespoons olive oil

8 ounces white mushrooms, trimmed and sliced (3 cups)

1½ cups chopped celery

1½ cups chopped carrots

1 cup chopped Vidalia or yellow onions

3 cloves garlic, minced

1 can (28 ounces) crushed tomatoes in puree

2 bottles (8 ounces each) clam juice

½ cup dry white wine

2 tablespoons chopped fresh basil

1 tablespoon chopped fresh thyme

2 bay leaves

$\frac{1}{2}$ teaspoon salt

$\frac{1}{4}$ teaspoon crushed saffron threads

$\frac{1}{8}$ to $\frac{1}{4}$ teaspoon crushed red pepper flakes

1 pound fish fillets (such as grouper, red snapper, halibut, white fish, or cod), cut into $\frac{1}{2}$-inch chunks

1$\frac{1}{2}$ to 2 dozen littleneck clams, scrubbed

1. In a 4-quart saucepan, heat the oil over medium-high heat; add the mushrooms, celery, carrots, onions, and garlic and cook for 5 to 8 minutes, or until the vegetables are tender. Stir in the tomatoes with their puree, clam juice, white wine, basil, thyme, bay leaves, salt, saffron, and crushed red pepper. Bring the mixture to a boil. Reduce the heat to low and simmer, uncovered, stirring occasionally, for 30 minutes.

2. Add the fish chunks to the stew; cook 5 minutes. Add the clams and cover the pan tightly. Simmer for 3 to 5 minutes, or until shells open, discarding any clams that do not open.

3. To serve, remove the bay leaves. Ladle the stew into large pasta or soup bowls.

| SERVES 6 TO 7 |

Well, I think you look pretty cool, as Lucy would say. I've got coffee and granola."

"How many times do I got to tell you that I don't eat friggin' birdseed," he grumbled as he followed me through the house.

"And I don't cook steak-egg biscuits."

"Well, maybe if you did, you wouldn't spend so many evenings alone."

"I hadn't thought about that."

"Did the Smithsonian tell you where we was going to park up there? Because there's no parking in D.C."

"Nowhere in the entire district? The President should do something about that."

We were inside my kitchen, and the sun was gold on windows facing it, while the southern exposure caught the river glinting through trees. I had slept better last night, although I had no idea why, unless my brain had been so overloaded it simply had died. I remembered no dreams, and was grateful.

"I got a couple of VIP parking passes from the last time Clinton was in town," Marino said, helping himself to coffee. "Issued by the mayor's office."

He poured coffee for me, too, and slid the mug my way, like a mug of beer on the bar.

"I figured with your Benz and those, maybe the cops would think we have diplomatic immunity or something," he went on.

"I'm supposing you've seen the boots they put on cars up there."

I sliced a poppyseed bagel, then opened the refrigerator door to take an inventory.

"I've got Swiss, Vermont cheddar, prosciutto."

I opened another plastic drawer.

"And Parmigiano-Reggiano—that wouldn't be very good. No cream cheese. Sorry. But I think I've got honey, if you'd rather have that."

"What about a Vidalia onion?" he asked, looking over my shoulder.

"That I have."

"Swiss, proscuitto, and a slice of onion is just what the doctor ordered," Marino happily said. "Now that's what I call a breakfast."

"No butter," I told him. "I have to draw the line somewhere so I don't feel responsible for your sudden death."

"Deli mustard would be good," he said.

I spread spicy yellow mustard, then added prosciutto and onion with the cheese on top, and by the time the toaster oven had heated up, I was consumed by cravings. I fixed the same concoction for myself and poured my granola back into its tin. We sat at my kitchen table and drank Colombian coffee and ate while sunlight painted the flowers in my yard in vibrant hues, and the sky turned a brilliant blue.

Marino's Breakfast Bagel Sandwich

Before making a drive to Washington, D.C., with Marino, Kay offers him her standard-issue coffee and granola breakfast. When Marino announces to Kay that he simply won't eat "friggin' birdseed," Kay switches gears and produces a breakfast on a bagel that makes him much happier. "Now that's what I call a breakfast," says Marino with enthusiasm.

Kay admits, ". . . by the time the toaster oven had heated up, I was consumed by cravings. I fixed the same concoction for myself and poured my granola back into its tin." I often tell people I'm a mix of my characters—I'm mostly healthy like Kay, but sometimes I indulge in awfully fattening foods like Marino's favorites and the cookies that Lucy loves to bake so much. This bagel recipe, as Marino says, is just what the doctor ordered. Brew up some Colombian coffee to sip alongside.

1 poppyseed bagel, split and toasted

Butter or mayonnaise

6 slices prosciutto

2 slices (¼ inch thick) Vidalia or yellow onion

2 slices Swiss cheese

Spicy yellow deli mustard

1. Spread the toasted bagel halves with butter or mayonnaise. Arrange the bagel halves, cut side up, on a toaster oven tray. Layer the prosciutto slices on top of one bagel half; top with onion and cheese slices.

2. Slide the cheese-topped bagel half into a toaster oven, and heat on the "top brown" or toast setting until cheese melts. (Or place the bagel half on a broiler pan under preheated broiler, 4 inches from the heat source, for about 1 to $1\frac{1}{2}$ minutes, or just until cheese melts.) Top with second bagel half. Serve the sandwich immediately with deli mustard.

| SERVES 1 |

Grilled Chicken Caesar Salad

Kay treats Marino to dinner at the Old Ebbitt Grill, a Washington, D.C., institution that was founded in 1856. Known as the oldest saloon in the city, the restaurant actually began as a boarding house on the other side of town, purchased by innkeeper William E. Ebbitt. Many a distinguished name in history either lived there or tipped a few at the stand-up bar, including Presidents McKinley, Grant, Andrew Johnson, Cleveland, Teddy Roosevelt, and Warren G. Harding.

The Old Ebbitt Grill has occupied various locations in its lifetime, finally moving to its current address, a renovated theater, at 675 15th Street NW. Its Victorian décor is punctuated by relics from the past, including beer steins, animal heads bagged by Teddy Roosevelt, and even some of Alexander Hamilton's wooden bears, which he is rumored to have brought in for his own private bar.

Of course, Marino can't resist indulging in several pints of Samuel Adams brew along with his Swiss cheese burger. Kay opts for the healthier Chicken Caesar Salad, a recipe that chef Tom Myer graciously shared with us. The Old Ebbitt serves large portions—this salad comes with a sliced double chicken breast on it. If Kay were to make this at home, she would use just one chicken breast per serving. If you don't wish to use raw egg in the dressing, you can substitute a hard-cooked egg, finely chopped.

Caesar Dressing:

1 large egg yolk or 1 hard-cooked egg, peeled and finely chopped

1 tablespoon Dijon mustard

2 anchovy fillets, drained and mashed

2 cloves garlic, minced

²⁄₃ cup olive oil

¹⁄₄ cup fresh lemon juice

1 tablespoon white vinegar

Salad:

4 skinless, boneless chicken breast halves (about 1 ¹⁄₂ pounds total)

1 cup bottled Italian dressing

1 large head romaine, trimmed and chopped

¹⁄₂ cup freshly grated Parmigiano-Reggiano

1. For the Caesar Dressing: In a bowl, whisk together the egg yolk (or hard-cooked egg) and mustard. Mix in the anchovy and garlic. While whisking, slowly pour in the olive oil in a thin stream, until blended. Whisk in the lemon juice and vinegar until the dressing is thick and well blended. Cover and refrigerate until needed.

2. In a shallow glass or ceramic dish, marinate the chicken breasts in Italian salad dressing for at least 1 hour or up to overnight. Drain the marinade from the chicken and discard.

3. To cook the chicken: Preheat the grill to medium hot or preheat the broiler. Grill the chicken for 13 to 15 minutes, until the thickest part is no longer pink, turning once. (Or place chicken pieces on the oiled rack of a pan; broil 4 inches from the heat source for 10 to 12 minutes, turning once.) Set the chicken aside to cool slightly.

4. Whisk the dressing and reserve ¹⁄₄ cup. In a large bowl, toss together the romaine, Parmigiano-Reggiano, and the remaining dressing. Divide the salad among four large dinner plates. Thinly slice each chicken breast and arrange the slices, overlapping, on the top of the salad. Drizzle the reserved dressing over the chicken. Serve immediately.

| SERVES 4 |

Greek Salad
with Red Wine Vinaigrette

On their way to meet Lucy and her companion, Janet, at their apartment just off Dupont Circle in Washington, D.C., Kay and Marino stop to pick up some take-out. In the 2000 block of P Street, D.C. Café, a twenty-four-hour self-serve restaurant, seems to be just the ticket. On the menu are Greek and Mediterranean specialties, including gyros, pita sandwiches, baklava, and Lebanese beer.

D.C. Café's owner, Ayman Almoualem, shares his version of Greek salad—a colorful mix of cucumbers, tomatoes, calamata olives, and feta cheese, laced with a minted red wine vinaigrette, a side dish that never fails to please customers. To make this an entree salad, double the amount of feta cheese and/or add some slices of roasted lamb or beef.

MAKE-AHEAD TIP: *Make the salad ahead, if you prefer, by refrigerating the salad mixture and the dressing separately for up to several hours. Toss the salad with the dressing just before serving.*

Red Wine Vinaigrette:

3/4 cup olive oil

1/2 cup red wine vinegar

1/2 cup fresh lemon juice

1 teaspoon crushed dried mint

1/2 teaspoon salt

1/4 teaspoon cracked black pepper

Salad:

3 cups torn romaine lettuce

2 cups mixed torn lettuce or mesclun mix

1 cup shredded red cabbage

1½ cups sliced cucumbers (1 medium)

2 medium tomatoes, cut into thin wedges

1 cup sliced red onions

1 cup trimmed and sliced white mushrooms

1 red bell pepper, julienned

1 cup crumbled feta cheese (4 ounces)

½ cup pitted and sliced calamata olives

1. For the Red Wine Vinaigrette: In a large jar with a tight-fitting lid, combine the oil, vinegar, lemon juice, mint, salt, and pepper. Cover and shake well; set aside.

2. For the salad: In a large salad bowl, toss together the romaine, lettuce mix, and cabbage. Add all the remaining ingredients and toss gently.

3. To serve the salad, shake the dressing, drizzle over the salad, and toss well. Serve immediately.

MAKES 6 TO 8 SIDE-DISH SERVINGS

We turned off the Boulevard des Italiens onto the Rue Favard. "I shouldn't be bitter when I was *sent* here to solve problems—when I've been a pawn in some scheme I knew nothing about?"

"I'm sorry you look at it that way," he said.

"We're bad for each other," I said.

Café Runtz was small and quiet, with green checked cloths and green glassware. Red lamps glowed and the chandelier was red. Odette was making a drink at the bar when we walked in. Her way of greeting Talley was to throw her hands up in despair and chastise him.

BLACK

"She's accusing me of staying away two months and then not calling before I come in," he translated for me.

He leaned over the bar and kissed her on both cheeks to make amends. Regardless of how crowded the café was, she managed to fit us into a choice corner table because Talley had that effect on people. He was used to getting what he wanted. He picked out a Santenay red burgundy since he remembered I'd told him how much I like burgundies, although I didn't recall when I'd said that or if I really had. By now I wasn't sure what he already knew and what he'd gotten directly from me.

"Let's see," he said, scanning the menu. "I highly recommend the Alsacienne specialities. But to start? The *salade de gruyère*—shaved gruyère that looks like pasta on lettuce and tomato. It's filling, though."

NOT

Kay's Grilled Pizza
with Sausage, Pepperoni, and Three Cheeses

For this grilled version of pizza, it's imperative that you control the temperature of the grill. If the gas is turned up too high or the coals are too hot, the crust will burn on the bottom before the toppings warm up and the cheese melts. It's a simple matter to turn down the gas, but for a charcoal grill, use indirect heat. Before you arrange the coals, use a disposable foil drip pan placed in the center of the firebox, just under where you will place the pizza on the grate. Then using long tongs, arrange the coals in mounds around the drip pan. For this type of indirect-heat cooking, you'll need hot coals for a medium-hot effect. You can tell you have hot coals if, by holding your hand palm side down just above the grate, you need to remove your hand in the time it takes you to say, "one-thousand one, one-thousand-two."

If you prefer a crispy crust, turn the crust once after the first grilling before adding the topping ingredients. Also see Kay's recipe for baked pizza on page 28.

¾ pound whole-milk mozzarella cheese (preferably fresh) or 3 cups pre-shredded mozzarella cheese

Pizza Dough:

1 teaspoon rapid-rise active dry yeast

½ cup warm water (110° to 115°F)

1 tablespoon honey

2⅓ to 2⅔ cups high-gluten flour (see Note on page 31)

    or bread flour

1 tablespoon olive oil

1 teaspoon salt

Topping:

3 tablespoons olive oil

1 green, red, or yellow bell pepper, julienned

1 portobello mushroom, stem removed, quartered and thinly sliced

    or 1½ cups trimmed and sliced white mushrooms

1 cup sliced Vidalia or yellow onions

3 cloves garlic, minced

Salt and freshly ground pepper

½ pound sweet Italian sausage, crumbled

1½ cups Kay's Marinara Sauce (page 150) prepared marinara sauce,

    or Quick Marinara Sauce (page 31)

½ pound sliced turkey pepperoni

¼ cup chopped fresh basil

½ cup shredded fontina cheese

½ cup freshly grated Parmigiano-Reggiano

1. At least 4 hours ahead or up to overnight, drain the liquid from the fresh mozzarella, if using. Place the cheese in a strainer lined with a clean kitchen towel or a triple layer of paper towels, set over a large bowl, and place in the refrigerator to drain. Pat the cheese dry and tear into bits. Cover and refrigerate until needed.

2. For the pizza dough: In a large bowl, dissolve the yeast in the warm water; stir in the honey. Stir in 2 cups of the flour, the oil, and salt until moistened. Stir in enough additional flour so the mixture leaves the side of the bowl. Turn the dough out onto a lightly floured surface and gather it into a ball. Knead the dough for about 10 minutes, until the dough is soft, smooth, and elastic, adding enough of the remaining flour to keep the dough from sticking.

3. Place the dough in a large greased bowl and turn the dough to coat evenly. Cover the dough with plastic wrap or a damp clean kitchen towel. Place the bowl on the lowest oven rack. Turn the oven on to the lowest setting for 1 minute; immediately turn the oven off. Let the dough rise for about 30 minutes, or until doubled in size.

4. Punch down the dough; on a lightly floured surface, knead the dough 10 times to release the air bubbles. Cover the dough and let it rest while making the topping.

5. For the topping: In a large skillet, heat 2 tablespoons of the olive oil over medium-high heat; add the bell pepper, mushroom, onions, and garlic and cook for about 5 minutes, or until very tender. Transfer the vegetables to a colander to drain well. Season with salt and pepper. Wipe the skillet dry. In the same skillet, crumble the sausage and cook over medium-high heat for about 8 minutes, or until browned. Transfer to paper towels to drain.

6. To grill the pizzas: Oil the grill grate. Preheat the grill to medium. Cut the pizza dough in half; shape each half into a ball. Flatten each dough ball with the palm of your hand; roll or pat into a 12-inch round. Lightly brush the top of the dough with olive oil. Place each crust on a separate large rimless baking sheet. Using the baking sheet like a large spatula, slide one of the crusts onto the grill; cook for 2 to 3 minutes, or until the bottom of the crust is lightly browned and the top of the crust begins to puff. Remove from the grill; repeat with the second crust.

7. If the crusts are still puffed on the top, flatten them with a metal spatula. Spread the marinara sauce evenly over the crusts. Top with the sausage, pepperoni, and vegetable mixture, dividing them evenly. Sprinkle with the basil, then top with the mozzarella, fontina, and Parmigiano-Reggiano.

8. Return the pizzas to the grill and close the grill lid or cover the pizzas loosely with aluminum foil. Grill for 4 to 6 minutes longer, or until the toppings are hot and the cheeses melt. Using a large spatula, transfer the pizzas to the baking sheets. Serve immediately, cut into wedges.

MAKES TWO 12-INCH PIZZAS

Rose's Vegetable Soup
with Italian Herbs

Kay's loyal secretary, Rose, about whom we know very little until this revealing scene in Black Notice, *turns out to have a dynamite recipe for vegetable soup. She shares a frozen container of the soup with her tired boss, knowing that this Christmas is an exceptionally difficult one for Kay.*

This soup has an old-fashioned flavor that is intended to warm the cockles of your heart, as it did Kay's. If you have never used leeks before, they resemble giant green onions, with a fat white end and long green leaves. It's very important to remove all the sand and grit before slicing them. Trim off a slice from the root, then trim off the green leaves to within 2 inches of the white part of the leeks. Split the leaves apart down to the white portion of the leek, and wash the leaves and the white part under cold running water until you have rinsed away all of the dirt. Cut off the green leaves down to the white and discard them. Then thinly slice the white portion.

Choose a combination of your favorite vegetables to make the soup. It cooks in just under an hour.

MAKE-AHEAD TIP: *Like Rose, you can freeze the soup after it cools, in meal-sized portions; just use freezer-safe containers.*

SHORTCUT TIP: *You can substitute frozen loose-pack vegetables for most of the fresh vegetables listed, except the cabbage, celery, and mushrooms.*

3 tablespoons olive oil

1 cup chopped green, red, or yellow bell pepper

2 leeks, sliced (white part only)

3 cloves garlic, minced

7 cups homemade vegetable stock or canned vegetable broth

1 can (14 ½ ounces) Italian-style diced tomatoes in juice

8 to 9 cups fresh vegetables in any combination (broccoli or
    cauliflower florets; shredded cabbage; yellow or green beans or
    asparagus cut into 1-inch lengths; julienned carrots, fennel, or
    parsnips; niblet corn; sliced celery; trimmed and sliced button
    mushrooms; or fresh or frozen peas)

¼ cup chopped fresh basil

1 tablespoon chopped fresh thyme

1 tablespoon chopped fresh sage

2 bay leaves

1 teaspoon salt

¼ teaspoon freshly ground pepper

Freshly grated Parmigiano-Reggiano for garnish

1. In a 4-quart saucepan or Dutch oven, heat the olive oil over medium-high heat. Add the bell pepper, leeks, and garlic and cook for 5 minutes, stirring frequently so garlic does not brown. Stir in the vegetable stock, tomatoes with their juices, vegetables, basil, thyme, sage, bay leaves, salt, and pepper.

2. Bring the mixture to a boil over high heat. Reduce heat to low, cover, and simmer for 30 minutes.

3. Uncover the soup and simmer for 15 to 20 minutes longer, or until the soup is of the desired consistency. To serve, remove the bay leaves and ladle the soup into bowls. Sprinkle Parmigiano-Reggiano over each serving.

SERVES 8

Marino's BLT on Rye

There are times in life when only a Marino-style sandwich will do. Marino's version, bacon and sweet Vidalia onion paired together with a perfectly ripe tomato, is accented with a quick Russian dressing concoction of Miracle Whip and catsup. You be the judge. My personal recommendation is, if you can find Mrs. Fanning's Bread & Butter Pickles to serve on the side, so much the better.

Kay's desire to make this healthier for Marino only results in her deciding to microwave the bacon instead of frying it. This is practically a guilt-free method for enjoying bacon without all the grease. Arrange the bacon slices on a stack of three paper towels on a microwaveable plate. Cover the bacon with another paper towel. Microwave on HIGH power for 2 1/2 to 4 minutes, or until the bacon is browned and crisp.

Russian Dressing:

1 tablespoon mayonnaise or salad dressing

1 tablespoon catsup

1 teaspoon pickle relish

Sandwich:

2 large slices rye bread, toasted and kept warm

Butter

Lettuce leaves

4 slices thick-cut bacon, cooked crisp and well drained

2 slices beefsteak tomatoes

Salt

2 slices (¼ inch thick) Vidalia or yellow onion

1. For the Russian Dressing: In a small bowl, stir together the mayonnaise, catsup, and pickle relish until blended.

2. To make the sandwich: Place the toasted rye bread on a cutting board. Spread with butter, then top one of the slices with a layer of lettuce leaves. Spread half of the Russian Dressing over the lettuce. Top with the bacon and tomato slices; sprinkle the tomatoes with salt, if desired. Add the onion slices and another layer of lettuce leaves. Spread with the remaining dressing. Top with the second slice of rye bread. Cut the sandwich in half and serve.

| SERVES 1 |

Salade de Gruyère

(Swiss Cheese Salad)

Walking on the streets of Paris, Kay and Jay Talley, an ATF agent at Interpol, wind up at the charming Café Runtz at 16 Rue Favart (which I discovered while researching Black Notice in Paris, one of many Parisian bistros recommended by my friend Paul Elbling, the chef at La Petite France in Richmond). The bistro, which features Alsatian dishes like this Salade de Gruyère, was recently given a total makeover by star decorator Jacques Grange. Since the menu is in French, Jay, who speaks fluent French, suggests starting off with the Salade de Gruyère. The Gruyère, or Swiss cheese, on the salad looks like pasta, because it's cut into long narrow strips.

The interesting thing about this salad is that the cheese is first marinated in a white wine vinaigrette dressing, then the salad is assembled with the cheese placed on the top and the dressing spooned over. Jay chooses a Santenay red Burgundy to drink, but a Beaujolais would also be a great choice.

Dressing:

4 ounces sliced Gruyère or Swiss cheese

1/3 cup olive oil

1/3 cup white wine vinegar

2 tablespoons minced fresh parsley

2 teaspoons Dijon mustard

½ teaspoon salt

¼ teaspoon freshly ground pepper

½ cup finely chopped Vidalia or yellow onion

Salad:

6 cups torn mixed salad greens

1. For the dressing: Cut the Gruyère cheese into strips that are 2 inches long and ¼ inch wide. Arrange the cheese in a shallow bowl. In a jar with a tight-fitting lid, combine the olive oil, vinegar, parsley, mustard, salt, and pepper. Shake well to combine. Add the onion to the dressing and pour over the cheese. Cover and refrigerate for at least 1 hour or up to several hours.

2. To serve the salad, arrange the salad greens on salad plates. Using a slotted spoon, arrange the marinated cheese strips over the salads. Stir the dressing remaining from the cheese and drizzle it over each salad. Serve immediately.

SERVES 6

In the kitchen, I set the oven and cook pasta. I mix grated cheeses with ricotta and begin layering it and meat sauce between noodles in a deep dish. Anna stuffs dates with cream cheese and fills a bowl with salted nuts while Marino, Lucy and McGovern pour beer and wine or mix whatever holiday potion they want, which in Marino's case is a spicy Bloody Mary made with his moonshine.

He is in a weird mood and well on his way to getting drunk. The Tlip file is a black hole, still in the bag of presents, ironically under the Christmas tree. Marino knows what's in that file, but I don't ask him. Nobody does. Lucy begins getting out ingredients for chocolate chip cookies and two pies—one peanut butter, the other Key lime—as if we are feeding the entire city. McGovern uncorks a Chambertin Grand Cru red Burgundy while Anna sets the table, and the file pulls silently and with great force. It is as if all of us have made an unspoken agreement

THE L

to at least drink a toast and get dinner going before we start talking about murder.

"Anybody else want a Bloody?" Marino talks loudly and hangs out in the kitchen doing nothing helpful. "Hey, Doc, how 'bout I mix up a pitcher?" He yanks open the refrigerator and grabs a handful of Spicy Hot V8 juices and starts popping open the small cans. I wonder how much Marino had to drink before he got here and the safety comes off my anger. In the first place, I am insulted that he put the file under the tree, as if this is his idea of a tasteless, morbid joke. What is he implying? This is my Christmas present? Or is he so callous it didn't even occur to him that when he rather unceremoniously stuck the bag under the tree the file was still in it? He bumps past me and starts pressing lemon halves into the electric juicer and tosses the rinds in the sink.

"Well, I guess nobody's gonna help me so I'll just help myself," he mutters. "Hey!" he calls out as if we aren't in the same room with him. "Anybody think to buy horseradish?"

Madame Dugat's Mousse au Chocolat

(Chocolate Mousse)

Kay reminisces wistfully with her friend Anna about a trip to France that she and Benton made, remembering the wine tasting from the casks of Dugat and Drouhin. *When I was doing research for* The Last Precinct, *I traveled extensively through the French wine country. My French publisher and I had lunch with Monsieur and Madame Dugat after touring their vineyard and wine cellar. It was an authentic French country repast, a sausage and cheese platter with, of course, different wines for sampling. For dessert, Madame Dugat presented us with her Mousse au Chocolat, a heavenly chocolate creation that I will never forget.*

Here is an American adaptation of that dessert, which calls for readily accessible sweet baking chocolate—Baker's German Sweet Chocolate is a good one for this recipe. The whipping cream helps provide the proper texture for this delectable mousse. Caution: If you cannot eat foods that contain uncooked eggs, skip this dessert.

The Dugats recommend a red dessert wine, such as a Banyuls or a Maury, both made in Roussillon, France, but any light, mildly sweet red wine or red Bordeaux will do.

8 ounces sweet baking chocolate (not chocolate morsels)

¼ cup water

6 extra-large eggs, separated

½ cup heavy whipping cream

Fresh raspberries and mint leaves for garnish

1. Break the chocolate into small pieces and place in a heavy 1-quart saucepan with the water. Melt the chocolate over low heat, stirring constantly, until it is completely melted and smooth. Remove from the heat; cool for 10 minutes.

2. In a large bowl, beat the egg yolks with an electric mixer on high speed for about 5 minutes, until thick and lemon-colored. Beat in the chocolate mixture until blended; set aside.

3. Wash the beaters thoroughly with hot soapy water (any fat remaining on beaters will prevent the egg whites from whipping). In a large bowl, beat the egg whites on high speed until stiff peaks form. In a third bowl, beat the heavy cream on high speed until stiff (no need to wash the beaters again).

4. With a rubber spatula, gently fold the beaten egg whites and whipped cream into the chocolate mixture with an up-and-over motion, until the mixture is thoroughly blended and no traces of white remain. Do not stir.

5. Spoon the mousse into six to eight individual dessert dishes or long-stemmed goblets, or turn the mixture into a large serving bowl. Cover and refrigerate the mousse several hours or up to overnight, until firm. To serve, garnish each serving with fresh raspberries and mint leaves.

| SERVES 6 TO 8 |

Lucy's Favorite Chocolate Chip Surprise Cookies

I n this Christmas scene from The Last Precinct, "Lucy begins getting out ingredients for chocolate chip cookies and two pies—one peanut butter, the other Key lime—as if we are feeding the entire city." Lucy has learned the art of intuitive cooking from her Aunt Kay, who knows that cooking at its core is an emotion. It's a way to show affection and love. And we should never get caught up in exactly how to do it, only in the fact that we should do it. (As a child growing up in Florida, I used to make cookies for all my neighbors—this recipe uses all my favorite ingredients.)

These chewy cookies are irresistible morsels for the soul. They can be made with your favorite lavish combination of chocolate and butterscotch, peanut butter, or white chocolate chips, or English toffee bits (your choice is the surprise) and any of four kinds of nuts. Rich in oats, brown sugar, and butter, they can be made into giant-size cookies for gifts or into smaller rounds to fill up the cookie jar.

If you are tempted to double this recipe, you will get better results if you make two batches at the same time in separate bowls. Otherwise when all the ingredients are doubled, the cookies tend to spread too much on the baking sheet.

1 cup (2 sticks) butter, softened

1 cup packed light brown sugar

1/2 cup granulated sugar

2 extra-large eggs

1 tablespoon vanilla extract

2 1/2 cups all-purpose flour

1½ cups old-fashioned rolled oats

1 teaspoon baking soda

½ teaspoon salt

1½ cups semisweet chocolate morsels

1 cup butterscotch, peanut butter, or white chocolate morsels,
  or English toffee bits

1 cup chopped nuts, such as pecans, walnuts, peanuts, or macadamia nuts

1. Preheat the oven to 375°F. In a large bowl, beat together the butter, light brown sugar, and granulated sugar with an electric mixer on low speed until blended. Beat in the eggs and vanilla until well mixed. Set aside.

2. In a medium bowl, stir together the flour, oats, baking soda, and salt. Stir the flour mixture into the butter mixture until well blended.

3. Stir in the chocolate morsels, chips of choice, and nuts until combined. Drop the dough by rounded tablespoonfuls, 2 inches apart, onto greased baking sheets.

4. Bake the cookies on the middle oven rack for 9 to 11 minutes, or until the cookies are golden brown and set in the center. Allow the cookies to rest on the baking sheets for 1 minute, then transfer to wire racks. When the cookies have cooled completely, store in a tightly covered container.

MAKES ABOUT 4 DOZEN COOKIES

Variation

CHOCOLATE CHIP COOKIE GIANTS: Prepare the cookie dough as directed. Drop the dough by ¼ cupfuls onto baking sheets, placing the mounds 3 inches apart. Bake for 13 to 15 minutes, or until golden brown. Makes about 28 large cookies.

Peanut Butter-Chocolate Pie

Kay cleverly puts chocolate in her peanut butter pie to avoid that pesky problem of peanut butter sticking to the roof of your mouth. She crushes chocolate wafers into the butter-crumb crust and melts some chocolate to weave into the peanut butter-honey filling. The whole creation is topped with a whipped-cream layer, sweetened with brown sugar, and dotted with chopped peanuts.

Cut the pie into small wedges to delight your dinner guests (and so they won't feel so guilty asking for seconds).

MAKE-AHEAD TIP: You can make this pie up to two days ahead, and if you have a very strong character, you may be able to forget it's in the fridge for that length of time.

SHORTCUT TIP: Purchase a 9-inch chocolate crumb crust to use in place of the crust recipe. Begin making the pie at step 2.

Crust:

1½ cups crushed chocolate wafers (about 32 cookies)

6 tablespoons butter, melted

Filling:

3 tablespoons cornstarch

Dash salt

3 extra-large egg yolks

1¼ cups milk

½ cup honey

½ cup creamy peanut butter

2 squares (2 ounces) unsweetened baking chocolate, chopped

Topping:

1 cup heavy whipping cream

3 tablespoons packed brown sugar

½ cup chopped peanuts

1. For the crust: In a medium bowl, stir together the crumbs and melted butter until moistened. With clean hands or the back of a spoon, press the mixture onto the bottom and sides of a 9-inch pie plate. Refrigerate the crust while preparing the filling.

2. For the filling: In a medium saucepan, stir together the cornstarch and salt. In a small bowl, whisk together the egg yolks, milk, and honey; gradually whisk into the cornstarch mixture until blended. Cook over medium heat, stirring constantly, for 3 to 5 minutes, until the mixture thickens and boils; stir constantly for 1 minute.

3. Remove the pan from the heat. Stir in the peanut butter and chocolate until the mixture is well combined and the chocolate is melted and smooth. Press a piece of waxed paper directly over the filling to prevent a skin from forming. Cool the mixture for 15 minutes.

4. Pour the filling into the chilled pie shell. Cover the pie with aluminum foil or plastic wrap and refrigerate it for several hours or overnight, until firm.

5. For the topping: In a large bowl, beat the cream with an electric mixer on high speed until stiff. Sprinkle the brown sugar over the whipped cream and beat it in until blended. Spread the cream mixture over the pie. Sprinkle the peanuts over the top. Cover the pie loosely and refrigerate at least 2 hours or until ready to serve. Cut into small wedges.

| MAKES ONE 9-INCH PIE |

Key Lime Meringue Pie

Key lime pie is a signature dessert for many a south Florida restaurant and throughout the West Indies where Key limes, or the bottled juice, are available. Key limes are a specific hybrid of lime that's different from the common green Persian limes that are the most familiar. Small golf ball-size Key limes have yellowish green rinds and distinctively flavored juice. (You can make this pie with fresh regular lime juice; it will simply have a different flavor.) One caveat: Be sure to use regular limes for the grated zest, since the zest of Key limes can be quite bitter.

It can be difficult to find Key limes outside of Florida, but, fortunately, the juice is available bottled. One good source comes from Key West, a product called Nellie & Joe's Famous Key West Lime Juice. Call them at 1-800-LIME-PIE, go to their Web site at www.keylimejuice.com, or check larger supermarkets and specialty food markets in your area.

This sublime Key Lime Meringue Pie is an ethereal dessert, topped with a billowy meringue that has about as much substance as Kay's love life does most of the time. And though Kay is typically not a dessert eater, she always cleans her plate with this one. (In Miami, where I grew up, my grandmother had Key lime trees and we would squeeze the juice, freeze it, and enjoy fresh Key lime pies year-round.)

I like to serve this pie at Christmas, which gave me the idea to include it in the Christmas scene in The Last Precinct. With the pie, I always pass around Belgian chocolates. A few years ago, I had two hours off during a Belgian book tour and where did I go? I hopped in a cab to find the best Belgian chocolates—Wittamer. Founded in 1910 by Henri Wittamer in the Grand Sablon, the fashionable quarter of art and antique shops in Brussels, Wittamer Chocolates to this day is world renowned for its stringent quality requirements and time-honored traditional methods. (You can order Wittamer Chocolates, shipped directly from Belgium, at www.chocolatepicture.com.)

Making a meringue is an easy matter of knowing how long to beat the egg whites. First, separate the whites carefully; even a trace of egg yolk in them is fat that will prevent the whites from billowing up in your mixing bowl. Use a glass or metal bowl, never plastic, and squeaky-clean beaters. If possible, allow the whites to stand at room temperature while you are making the crust and filling for the pie; that encourages better volume when you beat them. Beat the whites, adding the sugar gradually by tablespoonfuls so that it dissolves, until the whites become thick and snow white. At intervals, turn off the beaters and lift them out of the meringue—if the peaks of meringue stand up straight, the meringue is ready to use. If you see peaks, but the tips of them curl over, keep beating and testing the meringue until they stand up and salute!

Allow the pie to cool for a minimum of four hours before cutting it.

MAKE-AHEAD TIP: Cool the pie and chill it, uncovered, until the next day.

SHORTCUT TIP: In place of the homemade Butter Crust, you can substitute a half package of refrigerated pie crusts. Follow the package directions for pre-baking a single 9-inch crust. Then continue the recipe with step 4.

Butter Crust:

1 1/2 cups all-purpose flour

2 teaspoons sugar

1/4 teaspoon salt

½ cup (1 stick) cold butter, cut up

5 to 6 tablespoons ice water

Filling:

1 can (14 ounces) sweetened condensed milk

4 extra-large egg yolks

½ cup Key lime or fresh regular lime juice

Grated zest of 2 limes (not Key limes)

Dash salt

Meringue:

4 extra-large egg whites

¼ teaspoon cream of tartar

½ cup sugar

1. For the crust: In a medium bowl, stir together the flour, sugar, and salt. With a pastry blender or two knives, cut in the butter until it resembles small peas. (For helpful hints on cutting in butter, see the headnote for Mrs. McTigue's Cheddar Cheese Biscuits, page 36.) Sprinkle the water over the dough one tablespoon at a time, stirring it in until the dough comes together and leaves the side of the bowl. Turn the dough out onto a lightly floured surface or pastry board and gather it into a ball. Wrap the dough in plastic and place it in the freezer for 20 to 30 minutes, or until well chilled, but not frozen.

2. Preheat the oven to 400°F. Knead the chilled dough about 5 times on a lightly floured surface. Flatten the dough into a disk with the palm of your hand. With a lightly floured rolling pin, roll the dough into an 11-inch round. Gently fold the dough into quarters, and transfer it to a 9-inch pie plate or a tart pan. Carefully unfold the dough and ease it into the pan with-

out stretching it. Turn the edges under and flute them, if desired or, if using a tart pan, trim the dough all around the edge of the pan.

3. To bake the crust: Loosely line the pastry crust with a 12x12-inch piece of aluminum foil; fill it with 1 cup of dry beans to prevent shrinkage. Bake the crust for 10 minutes. Remove the beans with the foil; bake for 6 to 8 minutes longer, or until golden brown. Transfer to a wire rack to cool.

4. For the filling: Reduce the oven temperature to 325°F. In a medium bowl, stir together the sweetened condensed milk, egg yolks, lime juice, lime zest, and salt until well combined. Pour the mixture into the crust. Bake for 10 minutes (the filling will be soft-set on top). Leave the oven on.

5. For the meringue: In a large bowl, beat the egg whites and cream of tartar with an electric mixer on medium speed until foamy. Beating on high speed, add the sugar, one tablespoon at a time, until the mixture forms stiff peaks.

6. With a rubber spatula, spread the meringue over the hot pie, sealing it to the edges of the crust so that there are no gaps between the crust and the meringue (this prevents "weeping" and shrinkage later). Bake the meringue for 15 to 20 minutes, or until golden brown.

7. Transfer the pie to a wire rack; cool at least 4 hours before cutting and serving. If not serving it right after cooling, refrigerate the pie and serve it the next day.

MAKES ONE 9-INCH PIE

Crostini di Polenta con Funghi Trifolati
(Grilled Polenta Topped with Sautéed Assorted Mushrooms)

Polenta is the Italian version of cornmeal mush, a mixture of yellow cornmeal cooked with water until it makes a thick batter. Spread in a shallow pan and then baked, fried, or grilled, the bright yellow triangles, squares, or sticks of polenta are a delightful substitute for bread or pasta in any menu.

Lumi Restaurant, an elegant, romantic regional Italian restaurant housed in a two-story brownstone at 963 Lexington Avenue (70th Street) in New York City, is first described in a deposition scene in The Last Precinct. The former private residence is filled with comfortable tables, a fireplace, bay windows, antique mirrors, and candlelight. Chef Hido Holli likes to use fresh seasonal ingredients in his ever-changing Italian menu.

An alleged serial killer named Jean-Baptiste Chandonne is questioned about an attractive woman he met at the restaurant. In perfect Italian, he describes the polenta crostini he was enjoying, topped with assorted sautéed mushrooms and a drizzle of truffle oil. It was complemented by a 1993 Massolino Barolo, a red Italian Burgundy wine, which happens to be Kay's favorite. Any good red French Burgundy or merlot could be served with the polenta.

Chef Hido Holli and his wife, Lumi, proprietors of Lumi, were kind enough to share this recipe, along with the next two to follow. The combination of mushrooms gives the topping a mix of meaty, rich flavors. The truffle *oil, available at specialty food shops, adds a subtle, earthy flavor when drizzled over the finished dish.*

SHORTCUT TIP: *Instead of making the polenta recipe as directed in step 1, purchase a box of 5-minute polenta. Follow the package directions for making the polenta, then continue with step 2 and the Mushroom Topping.*

Polenta:

6 cups water

1 teaspoon sea salt or table salt

1½ cups yellow cornmeal

2 tablespoons olive oil

Mushroom Topping:

3 tablespoons olive oil

4 cups trimmed and chopped fresh mushrooms such as oyster, chanterelle, portobello, or shiitake (if using portobellos or shiitakes, remove the stems)

2 cloves garlic, minced

1 tablespoon chopped fresh rosemary plus sprigs for garnish

1 tablespoon chopped fresh parsley

¼ teaspoon salt

Dash freshly ground pepper

1 tablespoon truffle oil or extra-virgin olive oil

Freshly grated Parmigiano-Reggiano for sprinkling

1. For the polenta: In a heavy 2-quart saucepan, bring the water and salt to a boil over high heat. Gradually add the cornmeal by handfuls in a thin stream into the boiling water, stirring constantly to prevent lumps, until all

of the cornmeal has been added. Reduce the heat to low and cook the mixture, stirring constantly, for 20 to 25 minutes, until it becomes very thick and leaves the side of the pan. Remove from the heat; stir in the olive oil.

2. Line a 13x9x2-inch baking pan or dish with aluminum foil; spray the foil with nonstick cooking spray or oil it lightly. Spread the cooked polenta evenly in the pan, smoothing the top with a rubber spatula. Cool for 30 minutes.

3. Twenty minutes before serving, prepare the Mushroom Topping: In a large skillet, heat 2 tablespoons of the olive oil over medium-high heat. Add the mushrooms and garlic and cook, stirring frequently, for 5 minutes. Stir in the rosemary, parsley, salt, and pepper. Cook, stirring frequently, for 3 to 5 minutes longer, or until the mushrooms are deep golden brown and tender. Remove from the heat; cover and keep warm.

4. Preheat the grill to medium-hot or preheat the broiler. Holding both ends of the foil, carefully lift the polenta from the pan onto a cutting surface. Cut the polenta into 12 to 16 triangles or rectangles (for either 6 or 8 servings); transfer the polenta to a lightly oiled grilling tray or the rack of the broiler pan. Brush the polenta with the remaining 1 tablespoon of olive oil.

5. Grill the polenta for 8 to 10 minutes, until the slices are heated through and beginning to brown around the edges, turning once halfway through the grilling time. (Or broil the polenta 4 inches from the heat source for 6 to 8 minutes, turning once.)

6. To serve, arrange 2 pieces of polenta on 6 or 8 salad or first-course plates. Spoon the warm mushroom mixture over the polenta, dividing it evenly. Drizzle the truffle oil over each serving, if desired, and garnish with rosemary sprigs. Serve with Parmigiano-Reggiano for sprinkling on top.

SERVES 6 TO 8

Giardinetto al Profumo di Erbe

(Grilled Garden Vegetables)

*I*n this scene from The Last Precinct, *Susan Pless orders this delicious appetizer/side dish while dining with Chandonne at Lumi. This dish is made from a seasonal selection of vegetables quickly grilled in a light bath of extra-virgin olive oil and fragrant fresh herbs. Choose a variety of your favorite vegetables or use whatever you have on hand. Firm vegetables, such as carrots and fennel, should be boiled or steamed first for 2 to 3 minutes to soften them a bit before finishing them off on the grill.*

It's amazing how grilling brings out the sweet, subtle flavors of different vegetables. This simple dish is the perfect accompaniment to grilled or roasted meats, salmon, or chicken. If you don't have a large grill, grill the vegetables in batches, then grill your entree. It's fine if the vegetables are served just warm or at room temperature. Any cold leftovers, if you are lucky enough to have them, are excellent the next day, tossed into a salad.

4 cups assorted vegetables, cut into $1/4$-inch-thick slices or sticks
   (peeled eggplant; blanched, trimmed fennel; blanched, peeled
   carrot, zucchini, or summer squash; shiitake mushroom caps;
   portobello mushroom caps; Belgian endive; yellow, red, or green
   bell pepper; or trimmed asparagus spears)

2 plum tomatoes, quartered lengthwise

4 green onions, roots trimmed

¼ cup olive oil

1 tablespoon chopped fresh thyme

1 teaspoon chopped fresh rosemary

1 teaspoon chopped fresh sage

1 teaspoon chopped fresh oregano

1 teaspoon salt

1½ teaspoons freshly ground pepper

Freshly grated Parmigiano-Reggiano for sprinkling

1. Preheat the grill to medium-hot or preheat the broiler. On a lightly oiled grilling tray or broiler pan arrange the vegetables in a single layer. Whisk together olive oil, herbs, salt, and pepper. Drizzle mixture over the vegetables (Or toss the vegetables with the oil mixture and grill them in batches, if necessary.)

2. Grill for 5 to 8 minutes, or until the vegetables are nearly tender. (Or broil 4 inches from the heat for 5 to 7 minutes.) Serve hot or at room temperature, sprinkled with Parmigiano-Reggiano.

SERVES 4

Costolette di Agnello alle Sette Erbe

(Lamb Chops Seasoned with Seven Herbs)

This roasted rack of lamb from Lumi is one of the easiest, most elegant dishes you can make in just about an hour from start to finish. To make this dish successfully, it's wisest to order two racks of baby lamb that have been trimmed and Frenched, with the backbone of the rack removed, to make carving them easy.

"Frenching" a rack of lamb means trimming the meat and fat from the rib bones so that they are exposed. Each rack will contain seven to eight ribs. Each lamb chop has only a small nugget of succulent meat on it, allowing for just 2 to 2 $\frac{1}{2}$ servings per rack. Larger racks weighing up to 2 pounds will provide 3 servings per rack. (Increase the roasting time, using 30 minutes per pound as a guide for medium-rare doneness.)

Before roasting, if necessary, trim away everything but a thin layer of the fat that's covering the meaty end of the rack. The seasoning is a simple herb rub composed of seven fresh herbs. If only three or four of the fresh herbs are available, simply double the amount of each herb, and rub the mixture generously over the fat side of the racks.

Chef Hido Holli serves the lamb with three side dishes: eggplant, artichoke, and asparagus. Included here is a simple treatment for a grilled asparagus accompaniment. You can also serve this entree with Hido's polenta (page 212) or add some boiled new potatoes, tossed with melted butter and herbs. Pour a good red Bordeaux or pinot noir wine to drink.

Lamb:

1 teaspoon chopped fresh Italian parsley

1/2 teaspoon chopped fresh rosemary plus leaves for garnish

1/2 teaspoon chopped fresh thyme

1/2 teaspoon chopped fresh oregano, plus leaves for garnish

1/2 teaspoon chopped fresh tarragon

1/2 teaspoon chopped fresh basil

1/2 teaspoon chopped fresh sage

2 racks (7 to 8 ribs each, about 1 1/4 to 1 1/2 pounds each) lamb,
    trimmed of fat and Frenched

Salt and freshly ground pepper

Grilled Asparagus:

1 pound fresh asparagus, trimmed

1 to 2 tablespoons olive oil

Salt and freshly ground pepper

2 tablespoons balsamic vinegar

Grated Parmigiano-Reggiano for sprinkling

1. For the lamb: Preheat the oven to 375°F. In a small bowl, mix together all the herbs. Rub the herb mixture over the meaty side of the lamb; season with salt and pepper. Place the lamb racks, meaty side up, on a rack in a shallow roasting pan. Insert a meat thermometer into the meatiest part of the roast, not touching the bone.

2. Roast for 30 to 40 minutes, or until thermometer registers about 130°F for medium-rare (temperature will rise about 5 degrees after roast is removed from the oven). Cover the roast and let stand for 5 minutes before carving.

3. For the asparagus: While the meat is roasting, preheat the grill to medium-hot or preheat the broiler. Arrange the asparagus on a grilling tray. Brush with the olive oil and sprinkle with salt and pepper. Grill for about 5 min-

utes, until asparagus is nearly tender, turning the spears once after 2 minutes. (Or broil 4 inches from the heat source for about 5 minutes.) Transfer the asparagus to a platter and drizzle the vinegar over it. Sprinkle with Parmigiano-Reggiano.

4. Carve the lamb rack by cutting between the ribs into individual chops. Arrange the chops on each dinner plate and garnish with fresh herb sprigs. Serve immediately with the asparagus.

| SERVES 4 TO 5 |

Index

Resources

Items in the photographs not credited are privately owned.

Page 17, Kay's Stew with Red Wine and Garlic: Vietri Cucina Fresca square casserole and wire basket from Sur La Table, (800) 243-0852. Le Jacquard Francais "Abecedaire" dishtowel from Malibu Colony Company, (310) 317-0177. Wine from Wally's Wine & Spirits, (310) 475-0606.

Page 18, Zuppa di Aglio Fresco: Cottura "Pompeii" bowl and plate from BoDanica, (858) 454-6107.

Page 19, Tortellini Verdi: "Beyrle" plate by Sud & Company from Salutations Home, (626) 577-7460. Sabre flatware from Maison Sud, (310) 207-5669.

Page 20, Salade de Gruyère: "Noisette" pewter flatware, salt and pepper shakers, and French tumbler from Maison Sud, (310) 207-5669. Reidel stemware from Wally's Wine & Spirits, (310) 475-0606.

Page 21, Madame Dugat's Mousse au Chocolat: Antique silver tray courtesy of The Bissell House Bed & Breakfast, (626) 441-3535. Silver filigree Italian compotes from Maison Sud, (310) 207-5669. White hemstitched cocktail napkins from Salutations Home, (626) 577-7460. Dessert wine from Larch-mont Wine & Spirits, (323) 856-8699.

Page 22, Italian Sausage Pizza with Peppers, Mushrooms, and Onions: Cottura "Animali Birds" dinner plate, (800) 348-6608.

Page 23, Mrs. McTigue's Cheddar Cheese Biscuits: Spode "Stafford Flowers" porcelain compote, Nay et Al napkin, Waterford "Lismore" decanter and port wine glasses all from Geary's, (310) 273-4741. Warwick oval tray from Room with a View, (310) 998-5858.

Page 24, Fresh Fruit Salad with Blood Orange Dressing: Mottahedeh "Merian" dinner plate and cup and saucer from Jimmy K's, (805) 379-4775. Kirk & Matz silver tea strainer from Jensen-Young, (805) 449-0079. Sferra Bros. "Madeira" hand-embroidered placemat and napkin from Shaxted, (310) 273-4320. Sferra Bros. "Venice Lace" boudoir pillow from Room with a View, (310) 998-5858. Ives Delorme "Triomphe" quilted sham and blanket cover from Malibu Colony Company, (310) 317-0177. Labrazel antique gold "Classico" bed tray from Linens et Al, (310) 652-7970 or www.Labrazel.com. Italian filigree champagne flute and "Noisette" pewter flatware from Maison Sud, (310) 207-5669.

Page 97, Grilled Grouper with Butter and Key Lime Juice: "Torsade Ivory" flatware by Zrike, (973) 616-1668.

Page 99, Pollo al Limone: Plate and glass from Sur La Table, (800) 243-0852. Vertu "Rooster" tile coasters from Maison Sud, (310) 207-5669. Wine from Wally's Wine & Spirits, (310) 475-0606.

Page 100, Pork Loin with Fig and Prosciutto Stuffing: Hand-painted Italian platter and pewter carving set from Maison Sud, (310) 207-5669. Illume candles from Illume, (323) 782-0342.

Page 101, Crostini di Polenta con Funghi Trifolati: Mottahedeh Italian majolica square tray from The Blue House, (310) 451-2243.

Page 102, Jack Daniel's Chocolate-Pecan Pie: Emile Henry pie plate from Sur La Table, (800) 243-0852.

Page 103, Veal Breast Stuffed with Spinach Pistou: Mottahedeh "Festival Red" charger from Room with a View, (310) 998-5858. Le Jacquard Francais "Palazzo" tablecloth from Malibu Colony Company, (310) 317-0177. Cottura antique reproduction vase, (800) 348-6608.

Page 104, Lasagne with Marinara Sauce and Porcini Mushrooms: Wines from Wally's Wine & Spirits, (310) 475-0606.

Page 105, Greek Salad with Red Wine Vinaigrette: Annieglass "Rock" salad bowl from LG Gallery, (702) 258-1076. Nutmeg pewter salad servers by Sally Richards, (203) 281-6129.

Page 106, Rose's Vegetable Soup with Italian Herbs: Cottura "Garofano" soup tureen, (800) 348-6608. Lace tablecloth courtesy of The Bissell House Bed & Breakfast, (626) 441-3535.

Page 108, Le Pappardelle del Cantunzein: Cottura "Geometrico" platter, (800) 348-6608.

Page 109, Barbecued Baby Back Ribs: Beer mug and denim napkin from Sur La Table, (800) 243-0852.

Page 110, Wild Rice Salad with Cashews: Provence wine glass from Maison Sud, (310) 207-5669. Sferra Bros. hemstitched linen napkin from Shaxted, (310) 273-4320.

Page 111, Fruit-Marinated Lamb Kabobs: Pewter charger and napkin ring from Salutations Home, (626) 577-7460. Rattan vase and wine coaster from Upstairs at Diamond, (323) 933-5551. Sabre flatware from Maison Sud, (310) 207-5669. Pewter salt and pepper shakers from Sur La Table, (800) 243-0852. "Aspen" leaf skewers by Janet Torelli from Tesoro, (310) 273-9890. Reidel stemware and wine from Wally's Wine & Spirits, (310) 475-0606.

Page 112, Lasagne coi Carciofi: Royal Worcester "Contrast" dinner plate from David Orgell, (310) 272-3355. Mottahedeh charcoal "Festival" charger from Panache of La Jolla, (858) 454-4220. "Acropole" flatware by Zrike, (973) 616-1668.

Page 114, Braided Country Bread: Kitchen towel, Terramoto mixing bowls, and decorative bottles from Sur La Table, (800) 243-0852.

Page 115, Jumbo Shrimp with Bev's Kicked by a Horse Cocktail Sauce: Sea motif cocktail picks from Sur La Table, (800) 243-0852.

Page 116, New York Steaks with Red Wine Marinade: Cottura "Quartieri" dinner plate from BoDanica, (858) 454-6107. "Antique Rope" flatware from Pottery Barn, (888) 779-5176.

Page 117, Classic English Breakfast: Rustic French buffet plate and cup and saucer from Salutations Home, (626) 577-7460. Toast rack from Sur La Table, (800) 243-0852. Antique salt and pepper set and flatware courtesy of The Bissell House Bed & Breakfast, (626) 441-3535.

Page 118, Omelet with Sweet Peppers and Onions: BIA "Sienna" dinner plate, (800) 242-2210. Le Jacquard Francais "Ispahan" tablecloth from Malibu Colony Company, (310) 317-0177. Etched grape pattern wine glass from Maison Sud, (310) 207-5669. Wine from Wally's Wine & Spirits, (310) 475-0606.

Page 119, Marino's Breakfast Bagel Sandwich: Spode "Mansard" plate from Janus, (650) 941-6530. Antiques courtesy of The Bissell House Bed & Breakfast, (626) 441-3535.

Page 120, Rigatoni con Broccolo: Annieglass "Tuscan Braid" salad bowl from Geary's, (310) 273-4741.

Page 121, Shrimp Sauté with Garlic and Lemon: Silver charger and martini glasses from Sur La Table, (800) 243-0852. Janet Torelli "Aspen" leaf martini pick and "Gingko Leaf" sterling tongs and "Objects Pointus" flatware by Sasaki from Tesoro, (310) 273-9890.

Page 122, Costolette di Agnello alle Sette Erbe: Plate from Sur La Table, (800) 243-0852. Zrike "Rococo" wood-handled flatware, (973) 616-1668. Reidel stemware from Wally's Wine & Spirits,

(310) 475-0606. Chair courtesy of The Bissell House Bed & Breakfast, (626) 441-3535.

Page 123, Giardinetto al Profumo di Erbe: Janet Torelli "Gingko Leaf" sterling silver tongs from Tesoro, (310) 273-9890.

Page 124, Grilled Chicken Caesar Salad: Nancy Calhoun "Delmar Sand" plate from Pottery Shack, (949) 494-1141. Dransfield & Ross napkin from Statements, (323) 655-4521. Les Etains pewter fork from Maison Sud, (310) 207-5669. Wine glass and pewter salt and pepper shakers from Sur La Table, (800) 243-0852. Table courtesy of The Bissell House Bed & Breakfast, (626) 441-3535.

Page 125, Key Lime Meringue Pie: Antique silver tea service, tiered server, and green glass plates courtesy of The Bissell House Bed & Breakfast, (626) 441-3535. Hobnail cakestand by L.E. Smith, (800) LE-SMITH.

Page 126, Ravioli with Squash and Chestnut Filling: Cottura "Geometrico" pasta bowl, (800) 348-6608.

Page 127, Fig, Melon, and Prosciutto Salad: Le Jacquard Francais "Andalousie" napkin from Malibu Colony Company, (310) 317-0177.

Page 128, Linguine with Olive Oil, Parmesan, and Onion: Riverside glass plate from Soho, (310) 451-7474.

Study Guide
to Accompany

Contemporary Financial Management

FOURTH EDITION

R. Charles Moyer
Wake Forest University

■

James R. McGuigan
JRM Investments

■

William J. Kretlow
University of Houston

■

Prepared by
John D. Stowe
University of Missouri-Columbia

■

West Publishing Company

St. Paul   New York   Los Angeles   San Francisco

ISBN 0-314-68812-9

Contents

Preface

This <u>Study Guide</u> has been developed for use with <u>Contemporary Financial Management</u>, 4th edition, by Moyer, McGuigan and Kretlow. The objective of this Guide is to assist you in learning the basic material in the text. Each chapter (with the exception of Chapter 1) contains the following items:

1.   A detailed outline of the key ideas developed in the chapter of the main text. This outline can be used both before and after reading the entire chapter to provide an overview of the content and a concise review.

2.   A series of true-false statements. If a statement is false, you are asked to modify it to make it correct.

3.   A series of numerical problems covering the key analytical techniques developed in each chapter. Each problem is followed by a detailed solution. You will find these solved problems to be of the most benefit if you attempt to solve them first on your own and <u>then</u> check your solution with the recommended solution.

The <u>Study Guide</u> also includes the solutions to several finance problems using the Lotus 1-2-3 templates available with the textbook. No prior knowledge of Lotus 1-2-3 is required to use the templates. You should try out these Lotus 1-2-3 templates even if your professor is not requiring you to do so for credit.

1

The Finance Function: An Overview

The introductory chapter discusses the important general questions faced in finance. How is finance related to other fields of study? What are the goals and objectives of the financial manager? And how has the finance field evolved and how is it changing today?

I.   Finance is concerned with several important questions which face all business firms. Examples of financial management questions include:

      A.   What assets should be acquired?

      B.   How should the acquisition of assets be financed, i.e., what are the costs and sources of funds?

      C.   What is the proper mix of the various sources of funds used to finance a firm's activities, i.e. what is the optimal capital structure?

      D.   How should the profits from an enterprise be used or distributed, i.e., what is the optimal dividend policy?

      E.   What is the nature of the trade-offs between risk and expected return that have to be made in financial management decisions?

      F.   How much inventory should be held?

      G.   Who should be granted credit?

      H.   Is a merger or acquisition advisable?

> I. How much cash-or access to cash-does the firm need to meet its daily operating needs?

II. The field of financial management has undergone rapid change over the last 50 years and this pace of rapid change promises to continue.

  A. Prior to the 1930s, finance was preoccupied with descriptive discussions of the various financial markets and the securities traded in those markets.

  B. In the 1930s, finance focused on legal matters, such as bankruptcy, reorganization, and regulation. Finance remained descriptive, legalistic, and nonquantitative until well into the 1950s.

  C. In the 1950s, researchers made significant breakthroughs in discounted cash flow techniques for capital budgeting, in the cost of capital area, and in the valuation of financial assets.

  D. In the 1960s, the field became much more quantitative, with the development of significant mathematical and theoretical models for management of cash, accounts receivable, and inventories, for capital budgeting, and for valuation of risky assets.

  E. In the 1970s, more precise theories were developed and applied to investment analysis and valuation.

  F. During the 1980s, there is an increasing emphasis on applying computer (and related) technology to assist in financial decision-making.

  G. In the late 1980s and projected into the 1990s, there is a renewed focus on the goal of shareholder wealth maximization and the creation of structures that enhance the achievement of this goal.

III. In order to understand this book and the real world practice of finance, it is crucial to understand the objective of financial management.

  A. Profit maximization is inadequate for handling many finance decisions.

    1. Profit maximization does not have a time dimension.

    2. The term profit is ambiguous; it has many different definitions.

    3. Profit maximization does not consider risk.

  B. Shareholder wealth maximization is the primary objective guiding financial management decisions.

    1. Wealth maximization means maximizing the present value (value today) of all future benefits to be received by the owners of the firm.

2.   The advantages of wealth maximization are that it is a conceptually clear guide for decisions, that it does consider risk, and that it is impersonal.

C.   Wealth maximization does not deny the existence of social objectives and obligations. In many respects, these other objectives are consistent with shareholder wealth maximization and, in addition, the government may place regulations and laws on businesses (as well as individuals) whenever it feels that private and public goals are in conflict.

D.   Due to a separation of ownership and control in many corporations, a divergence frequently exists between the owners' goals (shareholder wealth maximization) and the managers' goals (such as job security).

E.   Agency relationships occur when one or more individuals (the principals) hire another individual (the agent) to perform a service on behalf of the principals. In an agency relationship, decision-making authority is often delegated to the agent.

1.   An important agency relationship is between stockholders and managers.

2.   Inefficiencies that arise in agency relationships are called agency problems. Agency problems occur when managers maximize their own welfare instead of that of the principals. Examples of agency problems can include a preoccupation by management with their job security, excessive perquisite (perk) consumption, and managerial shirking.

3.   Agency costs are incurred by stockholders to minimize agency problems. Agency costs include:

a.   the cost of management incentives designed to induce managers to act in the shareholders' interests,

b.   expenditures to monitor management's actions and performance,

c.   bonding expenditures to protect shareholders from managerial fraud, and

d.   the opportunity cost of lost profits arising from complex organizational structures that prevent timely responses to opportunities.

4.   Another agency conflict is between stockholders and creditors. If the firm engages in high risk activities, the creditors (because they have fixed claims against the firm) may not share the rewards if the risky venture works out well, but the creditors are left holding the bag if things don't work out well. In order to protect their interests

creditors often insist on certain protective covenants in their contracts with the firm.

5.   Agency problems and agency costs can be reduced when financial markets operate efficiently.

IV.   If the managers accept the goal of profit maximization how should they proceed to achieve this goal?

A.   <u>Profit maximization</u> has too many shortcomings to provide consistent guidance to the practicing manager.

1.   The profit maximization rule is that an economic action should be continued up to the point where marginal revenue (benefit) just equals marginal costs.

2.   While the rule offers excellent insights, it frequently fails because (1) it is static, ignoring the time value of money, (2) it is vague with many differing definitions, and (3) it ignores risk.

B.   Maximization of shareholder wealth is a market concept. Managers should attempt to maximize the market value of the company's shares, not their accounting or book value per share.

C.   The three major factors that determine the market value of a company's stock are (1) the amount of the cash flows expected to be generated for the benefit of stockholders, (2) the timing of these cash flows, and (3) the risk of the cash flows. <u>Management decisions affect these three factors</u>. In addition, <u>economic environment factors</u> and <u>conditions in financial markets</u> outside of management control affect the amount, timing, and risk of expected cash flows and, hence, the market price of the company's stock. Examples of decisions under management control, economic environment factors, and conditions in financial markets that affect stock prices are summarized in the figure on page 5.

Factors Affecting Stock Prices

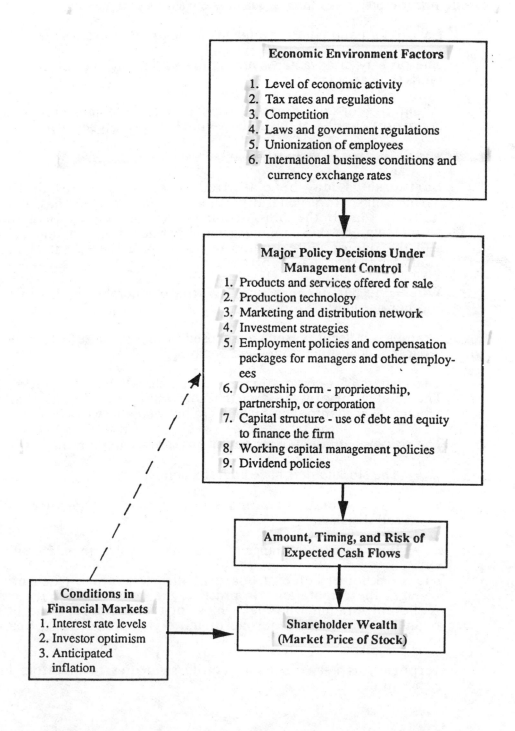

Economic Environment Factors

1. Level of economic activity
2. Tax rates and regulations
3. Competition
4. Laws and government regulations
5. Unionization of employees
6. International business conditions and currency exchange rates

Major Policy Decisions Under Management Control

1. Products and services offered for sale
2. Production technology
3. Marketing and distribution network
4. Investment strategies
5. Employment policies and compensation packages for managers and other employees
6. Ownership form - proprietorship, partnership, or corporation
7. Capital structure - use of debt and equity to finance the firm
8. Working capital management policies
9. Dividend policies

Amount, Timing, and Risk of Expected Cash Flows

Conditions in Financial Markets

1. Interest rate levels
2. Investor optimism
3. Anticipated inflation

Shareholder Wealth (Market Price of Stock)

V.   The three principal forms of business organization are the sole proprietorship, partnership, and corporation.

    A.   A sole proprietorship is simply a business owned by one person.

        1.   Ease of formation is an advantage of sole proprietorships.

        2.   The primary disadvantages are unlimited liability and difficulty raising funds to finance growth.

        3.   About 80% of all businesses are sole proprietorships accounting for approximately 10% of the dollar volume of business activity.

    B.   A partnership is a business organization of two or more persons.

        1.   Partnerships may be classified as either general or limited partnerships. In a general partnership, each partner has unlimited liability for all the obligations of the business. In a limited partnership, the one or more general partners have unlimited liability and the one or more limited partners have the extent of liability limited in the partnership agreement.

        2.   When one partner dies or quits, the partnership is dissolved and another one must be formed.

    C.   A corporation is a "legal person" composed of one or more natural persons and is separate and distinct from these persons.

        1.   The owners of a corporation are called shareholders or stockholders. The money they invested in the corporation is called capital stock which is divided into shares which are individually owned.

        2.   The corporate form of organization has three major advantages.

            a.   The stockholders have limited liability.

            b.   The corporation continues in existence if shareholders die or sell their shares.

            c.   It is very easy to change ownership (compared to partnerships).

        3.   The stockholders elect a board of directors which (theoretically) manages the corporation. In practice, the board chooses the officers of the corporation who make most of the decisions. The officers might include a president, one or more vice presidents, a treasurer, and a secretary.

        4.   Corporations issue debt and equity securities to investors in the corporation.   LEND   OWNERS
                              MONEY   COMMON + PREFERRED

        a.   Debt securities promise periodic interest payments as well as the return of the principal amount of the debt.

        b.   Preferred stockholders have priority over common stockholders with regard to the earnings and assets of the corporation. Creditors have priority over preferred stockholders.

        c.   Common stockholders are the true residual owners of the corporation.

    5.   Common stockholders possess several specific rights including:

        a.   Dividend rights--stockholders share equally on a per share basis in any distribution of dividends.

        b.   Asset rights--in the case of liquidation, stockholders share on a pro-rata basis the assets that remain after satisfying obligations to employees, governments (taxes), debtholders, and preferred stockholders.

        c.   Voting rights--stockholders have the right to vote on stockholder matters, such as the election of the board of directors.

        d.   Preemptive rights--unless they vote otherwise, common stockholders have the right to purchase their proportionate share of any new stock issued.

VI.   In a large corporation, the finance area is headed by a person normally titled the financial vice president or chief financial officer.

    A.   The financial vice president or chief financial officer reports directly to the president.

    B.   The chief financial officer might divide financial management responsibility between the controller and the treasurer.

    C.   The controller normally has responsibility for accounting- related activities. These activities include:

        1.   Financial accounting - the preparation of financial statements,

        2.   Cost accounting - preparing operating budgets and monitoring the performance of units within the firm,

        3.   Taxes - preparing local, state, and federal tax reports, and

        4.   Data processing.

D.   The treasurer is normally concerned with the acquisition, custody, and expenditure of funds. Treasury activities include:

1.   Cash and marketable securities management - forecasting cash needs, obtaining short-term funds and investing short-term funds,

2.   Capital budgeting analysis - evaluating the purchase of long-term assets,

3.   Financial planning - analyzing long-term sources of funds (issuing bonds or stocks),

4.   Credit analysis - evaluating the credit-worthiness of credit customers,

5.   Investor relations - working with institutional investors, bond-rating agencies, and the general financial community, and

6.   Pension fund management - managing the investment of employee pension fund contributions.

E.   There are several professional organizations for practicing financial management.

1.   These include the Financial Executives Institute, the Institute of Chartered Financial Analysts, and the Financial Management Association.

2.   The FMA (Financial Management Association) sponsors student chapters at many universities as well as the FMA National Honor Society. For membership information, contact your professor or the Financial Management Association, c/o College of Business Administration, University of South Florida, Tampa, Florida 33620.

VII.   Finance has drawn heavily from other disciplines, most notably economics and accounting, and financial managers must learn from and communicate with persons from many disciplines.

A.   Accountants develop financial statements such as balance sheets, income statements, and sources and uses of funds statements.

1.   These financial statements assist in evaluating past performance and in making decisions about the future direction of the firm.

2.   The payment of taxes is based on the accounting system.

B.   Finance also draws heavily on economics.

1.   Several macroeconomics topics are relevant to finance, such as the banking system and operation of money and capital markets.

2.   Finance evolved from the theory of the firm in microeconomics.

C.   Marketing, production, and quantitative methods are frequently related to the day-to-day decisions of financial managers.

2

Foundation Concepts for Financial Management

The objective of financial management is to maximize shareholder wealth, as measured by the market price of a firm's common stock. Chapter 2 establishes why cash flows are the source of value, introduces the net present value decision rule, and presents the role of financial markets in the resource allocation and valuation process.

I. The concept of cash flow is a central element in financial analysis, planning, and resource allocation decisions.

   A. The value of common stock, bonds, and preferred stock is based on the present value of the cash flows that these securities are expected to provide to investors. Similarly, the value to a firm of a capital expenditure is equal to the present value of the cash flows that the capital expenditures is expected to produce for the firm.

   B. The two most common cash flow definitions are after-tax operating cash flow and free cash flow.

      1. After-tax operating cash flow (CF) is defined as operating cash flows before tax minus tax payments. Operating cash flows before tax equal total revenues minus total cash operating costs. Depreciation expenses are not a cash expense, although depreciation expenses affect taxes. Thus, CF equals the operating cash flow times one minus the firms tax rate plus non-cash expenses times the tax rate:

$$CF = (R - O)(1 - t) + Dep(t)$$

where:
R = total revenues
O = cash operating expenses
Dep = depreciation
t = marginal tax rate

An equivalent formula is:

$$CF = (R-O-Dep)(1-t) + Dep$$

2. Free cash flow (FCF) is the after-tax operating cash flow (CF) minus some funds that are not available for distribution to the firm's owners. Free cash flow is:

$$FCF = CF - I(1-t) - D_p - P - B - WC - Y$$

where:

I = before-tax interest payments
$I(1-t)$ = after-tax interest payments
D_p = preferred stock dividend payments
P^p = required redemption of preferred stock
B = required redemption of debt
WC = required net investment in working capital (increases in inventories and receivables less increases in non-interest bearing current liabilities)
Y = investment in property, plant and equipment required to maintain cash flows at their current levels.

FCF represents the portion of a firm's total cash flow that is available to invest in other projects, to service additional debt, and to make dividend payments to common stockholders.

C. By emphasizing cash flows, rather than accounting-based measures of performance, a manager is more likely to achieve the goal of shareholder wealth maximization.

II. Many financial decisions involve outlays that result in a stream of benefits over several future time periods. The net present value (NPV) rule is used in these cases.

A. The net present value of an investment is equal to

NPV = Present value of future returns minus Initial outlay

B. The NPV of an investment shows the contribution of that investment to value of the firm and the wealth of shareholders.

C.   The NPV is based on cash flows and the present value of future cash flows depends on their timing and risk.

III. NPVs depend on the investor's required rate of return. Since required rates of return are determined in the financial marketplace, managers must understand the functioning of the U.S. financial system and the factors that influence required rates of return.

A.   The savings-investment cycle is based on net savers, or surplus spending units who supply the investable funds for net investors, or deficit spending units.

B.   The funds flow through financial middlemen and financial intermediaries.

1.   Financial middlemen include brokers (who buy securities for investors), dealers (who sell securities to investors from their own inventory of securities), and investment bankers (who help corporations sell their securities).

2.   Financial intermediaries sell claims against themselves (called secondary claims) to surplus spending units in order to get the funds to buy the obligations of the deficit spending units (called primary claims). Secondary claims frequently possess more liquidity, safety, and divisibility than primary claims.

C.   Financial markets are classed as money or capital markets and as primary or secondary markets.

1.   Money markets deal in securities with a maturity of one year or less. Capital markets deal in securities with maturities exceeding one year.

2.   The market for newly issued securities is the primary market. The market for reselling outstanding securities is the secondary market.

D.   An investment bank and a commercial bank are good examples of a financial middleman and a financial intermediary.

1.   Investment bankers help corporations sell new security issues. For large, secure corporations, the investment bankers may underwrite a security issue by guaranteeing to purchase the whole issue at a fixed price. In other cases, the investment bankers sell on a "best efforts" basis, which does not include a guaranteed price. Investment bankers organize the marketing effort to sell these security issues. Frequently, companies make a private placement of new securities where the securities are sold to large investors (such as insurance companies) rather than selling the securities to the public through an investment banker.

2.   Commercial banks are major suppliers of short-term and intermediate-term loans to businesses for a variety of purposes. Banks also provide many businesses with advice on investments, new projects, and credit-granting decisions.

3.   There are several types of financial intermediaries, including:

   a.   Commercial banks,

   b.   Thrift institutions--savings and loan associations, mutual savings banks,

   c.   Investment companies--mutual funds and real estate investment trusts (REIT's)

   d.   Pension funds, and

   e.   Insurance companies--life insurance companies and property and casualty insurance companies, and finance companies.

IV.   The tradeoff between risk and expected return is central to most financial decisions.

   A.   The rate of return during a period of time is:

   $$\text{Holding period rate of return} = \frac{\text{Ending price - Beginning price + Distributions}}{\text{Beginning price}}$$

   where distributions would be interest on debt or dividends on stock.

   B.   When many rates of return are possible, risk is measured in terms of the variability of possible returns around the expected return.

   C.   In an efficient market, security prices will be bid to a level where the expected return equals the required return. When new information about the expected returns or riskiness of a security is made known to participants in financial markets, the price of the security will quickly adjust to reflect this new information.

   D.   Risk and return will be studied in future chapters. In general, investors expect a risk premium above and beyond the risk-free return in order to compensate themselves for making risky investments:

   Expected return = risk-free return + risk premium.

   E.   The risk-free rate of return is comprised of two elements:

   1.   The real rate of return is the return that investors would require

from a security having no risk of default during a period of no inflation.

    2.   An inflation premium is the compensation investors require for expected purchasing power losses due to inflation.

F.   The required return of a security also is influenced by its maturity. The term structure of interest rates is the pattern of interest rate yields for debt securities that are similar in all respects except for their length of time to maturity.

    1.   A graph or plot of interest rates against time to maturity is called a yield curve.

    2.   A positively-sloped yield curve is often an indicator that future interest rates are expected to rise; a downward-sloping yield curve indicates that future interest rates are expected to be lower.

G.   The risk structure of interest rates is the pattern of interest rates for debt securities that are similar in all respects except for risk of default. Risk of default and interest rates are directly related.

H.   Corporations issue many types of securities, with the most senior securities having the first claim on the company's assets in case of default. Examples of securities with differing seniority (from the least senior to the most senior) are: common stock, preferred stock, income bonds, subordinated debentures, debentures, second mortgage bonds, and first mortgage bonds.

I.   Business and financial risk premiums account for differences between the required rate of return between firms.

    1.   Business risk refers to the variability of the firm's operating earnings over time.

    2.   Financial risk refers to the variability of a company's earnings per share that results from the use of fixed cost sources of funds, such as debt or preferred stock.

J.   There is also marketability risk premium. Marketability risk refers to the ability of an investor to buy and sell a company's securities quickly without a significant loss of value.

K.   Different security types have significantly different returns over time, with a strong positive relationship between risk and return.

V.   Stock prices reflect a net present value estimate of the firm's expected cash flows, evaluated at an appropriate required rate of return.

A.   The required rate of return is determined by conditions in financial markets, including the supply of funds from savers, the investment demand for funds, and expectations regarding future interest rates.

B.   The required rate of return also is determined by firm specific characteristics such as the seniority and maturity of the security, the business and financial risk of the firm issuing the security, the risk of default, and the marketability of the security.

VI.   (Appendix to Chapter 2.) Federal income taxes are a major cash outflow for businesses, and it is necessary for you to have an understanding of the features of both corporate and individual income taxation. Please note that the tax system, overhauled recently in the Tax Reform Act of 1986, is much more complex than this overview and, furthermore, that the tax structure is frequently changed.

A.   The corporate tax rates on ordinary or operating income after July 1, 1987 are:

15% of the first $50,000 of taxable income,
25% of taxable income between $50,000 and $75,000, and
34% of taxable income over $75,000,
    plus an additional tax equal to
5% of taxable income between $100,000 and $335,000.

The effect of the 5% surcharge on income between $100,000 and $335,000 is that corporations with taxable incomes of $335,000 or greater pay a flat tax rate of 34% on all taxable income.

B.   Corporate capital gains income is taxed at the same marginal tax rate as ordinary income. Corporate capital losses are deductible only against capital gains. Prior to the TRA of 1986, corporate long-term capital gains were taxed at a lower rate than ordinary income.

C.   Intercorporate dividends (dividends received by a corporation from another corporation) are entitled to a 70% exclusion from federal income taxes. In other words, 30% of intercorporate dividends are taxable. If a corporation is in the 34% marginal bracket, the tax due would be 34% of 30% of dividends received, which is .30(.34) = 0.102 or 10.2% of dividends received. (Dividends paid are not a tax deductible expense.)

D.   The TRA of 1986 repealed the Investment Tax Credit. An Investment tax credit permits a credit against income taxes of an amount equal to some percentage of qualifying capital expenditures. The investment tax credit was a measure designed to encourage investment. A tax credit is a direct subtraction from a firm's tax bill. A tax deduction is a subtraction from taxable income, which then saves taxes equal to the firm's marginal tax rate times the amount of the tax deduction.

E. If a corporation sustains a net operating loss, the loss may be carried back three years to offset income in those years and to obtain a refund of taxes paid in prior years. The loss, if not fully utilized, may then be carried forward for fifteen future years to offset future income and taxes due until the loss carryover is exhausted.

F. When a corporation uses accelerated depreciation for tax purposes and straight-line depreciation for financial reporting purposes, the tax savings due to accelerated depreciation appear on income statements and balance sheets as deferred taxes.

G. The Internal Revenue Code allows certain small corporations called S corporations to allocate their business taxable income to their shareholders who must pay individual income taxes on the income. S corporations pay no income tax.

TRUE AND FALSE QUESTIONS

Agree with each of the statements or reject it and modify it so that it is acceptable.

1. The after-tax operating cash flow can be written as

$$CF = (R - O - Dep)(1-t) + Dep(t)$$

2. The net present value of an investment is equal to the present value of the investment's future returns minus the initial outlay.

3. Pension funds are an example of a thrift institution.

4. Financial intermediaries purchase primary securities from deficit spending units and sell secondary securities to surplus spending units.

5. A private placement is the sale of new securities directly to a few large investors instead of to the public.

6. Primary securities are not sold on secondary markets.

7. A yield curve shows the expected yield on debt securities as a function of risk of default.

8. Marketability risk concerns the ease with which an asset can be bought and sold without incurring substantial losses or transactions costs.

9. Senior securities have higher risk and lower required rates of return than less senior securities.

10. Business risk refers to the variability of a firm's operating earnings over time.

Answers to True and False Questions

1.   False. The after-tax operating cash flow is either.

   $$CF = (R - O)(1-t) + Dep(t)$$
   or
   $$CF = (R - O - Dep)(1-t) + Dep$$

2.   True.

3.   Savings and loan associations, mutual savings banks, and credit unions are classed as thrift institutions.

4.   True.

5.   True.

6.   Outstanding primary securities are sold on secondary markets.

7.   The yield curve shows the yields for debt securities with different maturities (that are otherwise identical) as a function of time to maturity.

8.   True.

9.   Senior securities have <u>lower</u> risk and lower returns.

10.   True.

CHAPTER 2 PROBLEMS

1.   One year ago, Sally Richardson bought shares of Cornhusker International for $37.00 per share. If Sally received dividends of $.75 per share and sold the stock today for $46.50, what is her percentage rate of return?

   Solution:

   $$\text{Holding period rate of return} = \frac{\text{Ending price - Beginning price + Distributions}}{\text{Beginning price}} \times 100\%$$

   $$= \frac{46.50 - 37.00 + .75}{37.00} \times 100\% = \frac{10.25}{37.00} \times 100\% = 27.70\%$$

2.   Phil Cooley bought a $1000, 10% bond one year ago for $960. If Phil receives two $50 coupon payments and sells the bond today for $900, what has been his percentage rate of return?

Solution:

$$\text{Holding period rate of return} = \frac{900 - 960 + 100}{960} \times 100\% = \frac{40}{960} \times 100\% = 4.17\%$$

3.   An outlay of $1,000 is expected to produce a cash flow of $1,150 in one year.

   a.   What is the present value of the expected future return if the required rate of return is 10%? What is the net present value?

   b.   What is the present value and net present value if the required return is 20%?

Solution:

multiply

   a. $\text{Present value} = \text{cash flow} \times \dfrac{1}{1 + i} = 1150 \times \dfrac{1}{1 + .10} = 1045$

      Net present value = present value - outlay

$$\text{NPV} = 1045 - 1000 = \$45$$

      This investment has a positive NPV.

   b. $\text{PV} = 1150 \dfrac{1}{1 + .20} = 1150 \dfrac{1}{1.20} = 958$

$$\text{NPV} = 958 - 1000 = -\$42$$

      At a higher required rate of return, the present value of the future cash flow decreases, and this project now has a negative NPV.

4.   Calculate the total tax due, average tax rate, and marginal tax rate for corporations with taxable incomes of $90,000, $200,000, and $400,000. Use the TRA of 1986 tax rates.

Solution:

over 335,000 drops to 34%

Taxable income	$90,000		$200,000		$400,000 34%	
	.15(50,000)	7,500	.15(50,000)	7,500	.15(50,000)	7,500
	.25(25,000)	6,250	.25(25,000)	6,250	.25(25,000)	6,250
	.34(15,000)	5,100	.34(125,000)	42,500	.34(325,000)	110,500
			.05(100,000)	5,000	.05(235,000)	11,750
Total tax due:	$18,850		$61,250		$136,000	

marginal tax rate

Average tax rates:

$$\frac{18,850}{90,000} = 20.9\% \qquad \frac{61,250}{200,000} = 30.6\% \qquad \frac{136,000}{400,000} = 34\%$$

Marginal tax rates: 34%   39%   34%

5. Winnetka Wine Corporation has wine sales of $3,000,000, cost of goods sold of $2,000,000, and selling and administrative costs of $500,000. In addition, WWC paid $50,000 of interest and $150,000 of dividends, received $100,000 of dividends from other corporations, and had a $100,000 long-term capital gain. Using the TRA of 1986 rates, what is Winnetka Wine's federal income tax liability?

Solution:

Sales		$3,000,000
Less expenses:		
Cost of goods sold	$2,000,000	
Selling and administrative	500,000	
Interest expense	50,000	2,550,000
Taxable ordinary income		$450,000
Plus 30% of intercorporate dividends		
.30(100,000)		30,000
Plus long-term capital gain		100,000
Total taxable income		$580,000

Since taxable income exceeds $335,000, use a 34% flat tax rate to calculate the tax liability.

Tax = .34(580,000) = $197,200

Dividends paid have no effect on Winnetka Wine's tax liability.

3

Evaluation of Financial Performance

Financial performance is frequently evaluated using financial statement analysis. The purposes of this chapter are to learn a critical mass of the more popular financial ratios, and to learn how to use financial ratio analysis.

I. Financial ratios are used in many ways by different people.

    A. Ratios are used internally by management for planning and for evaluating performance.

    B. Ratios are used by credit managers to estimate the riskiness of potential borrowers.

    C. Ratios are used by investors to evaluate the stocks and bonds of various corporations.

    D. Ratios are used by managers to identify and assess potential merger candidates.

II. Financial ratios are frequently grouped into four types of ratios.

    A. <u>Liquidity ratios</u> indicate the ability of the firm to meet short-term financial obligations.

    B. <u>Activity ratios</u> indicate how efficiently the firm is utilizing its resources.

C.   Leverage ratios indicate the firm's capacity to meet its debt obligations, both short-term and long-term.

D.   Profitability ratios measure the total effectiveness of management in generating profits on sales, assets, and owners' investment.

E.   In addition to these four types of ratios, there are market-based ratios which reflect the financial market's assessment of a company's stock.

F.   Common-size statements are also helpful in financial analysis.

1.   A common-size balance sheet shows the firm's assets and liabilities as a percentage of total assets (rather than as dollar amounts).

2.   A common-size income statement shows the firm's income and expense items as a percentage of net sales (rather than as dollar amounts).

III.   The data for constructing ratios generally comes from a firm's balance sheet, income statement, and sources and uses of funds statement.

A.   Liquidity Ratios:

1. $\text{Current Ratio} = \dfrac{\text{Current Assets}}{\text{Current Liabilities}}$

2. $\text{Quick (Acid Test) Ratio} = \dfrac{\text{Current Assets - Inventories}}{\text{Current Liabilities}}$

3.   An aging schedule shows the liquidity of accounts receivable. The aging schedule, for example, might show the amount and percentage of total accounts receivable in several age categories, such as less than 30 days old, 30 to 60 days old, 60 to 90 days old, and over 90 days old.

4.   The quick ratio can also be adjusted downward by removing accounts receivable over 90 days old from the numerator of the quick ratio.

B.   Activity Ratios:

1. $\text{Average Collection Period} = \dfrac{\text{Accounts Receivable}}{\text{Annual Credit Sales}/365}$

2. $\text{Inventory Turnover} = \dfrac{\text{Cost of Sales}}{\text{Average Inventory}}$

3. $\text{Fixed Asset Turnover} = \dfrac{\text{Sales}}{\text{Net Fixed Assets}}$

4.   Total Asset Turnover $= \dfrac{\text{Sales}}{\text{Total Assets}}$

C.   Leverage Ratios:

1.   Debt Ratio $= \dfrac{\text{Total Debt}}{\text{Total Assets}}$

2.   Debt to Equity Ratio $= \dfrac{\text{Total Debt}}{\text{Total Equity}}$

3.   Times Interest Earned $= \dfrac{\text{Earnings Before Interest and Taxes (EBIT)}}{\text{Interest Charges}}$

4.   Fixed Charge Coverage $=$

$$\dfrac{\text{EBIT + Lease Payments}}{\text{Int + Lease Pmts + Pref. Div. Before Tax + Before Tax Sinking Fund}}$$

D.   Profitability Ratios

1.   Gross Profit Margin $= \dfrac{\text{Sales - Cost of Sales}}{\text{Sales}}$

2.   Net Profit Margin $= \dfrac{\text{Earnings After Taxes (EAT)}}{\text{Sales}}$

3.   Return on Investment (ROI) $= \dfrac{\text{Earnings After Taxes (EAT)}}{\text{Total Assets}}$

4.   Return on Stockholders' Equity $= \dfrac{\text{Earnings After Taxes (EAT)}}{\text{Stockholders' Equity}}$

E.   Market-Based Ratios:

1.   Price to earnings ratio
     P/E = Market price per share/Current earnings per share.

2.   Market to Book Ratio (P/B)
     P/B = Market price per share/Book value per share.

IV.   The effective use of financial ratio analysis requires some experience and effort. There are some basic approaches to financial ratio analysis, some basic interrelationships among ratios, and sources of information which can enhance the analyst's effectiveness.

A.   Two common types of ratio analysis are time-series and cross-sectional analysis.

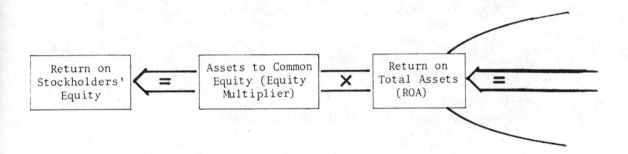

DUPONT CHART

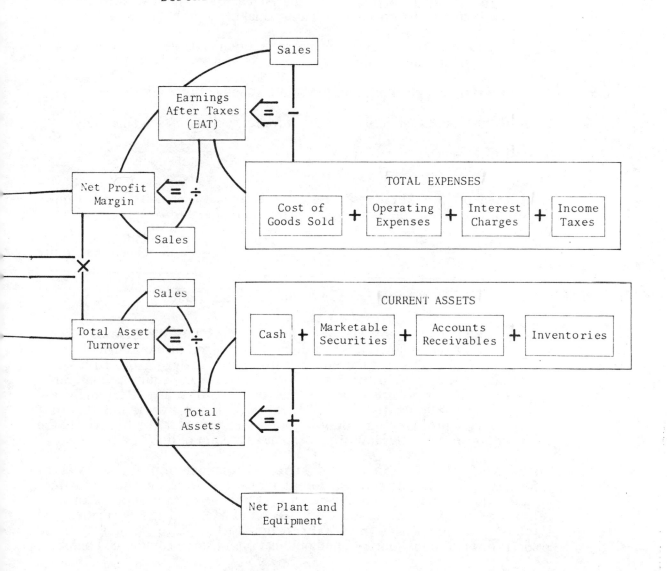

1. <u>Trend or time-series analysis</u>--This requires the analyst to examine the ratios of a firm for several periods. This shows whether the firm's financial condition is improving or deteriorating over time.

2. <u>Cross-sectional analysis</u>--The analyst compares the ratios of the firm to the industry norms or other individual firms in the industry.

3. Frequently time-series and cross-sectional analyses are pooled and performed simultaneously.

B.   There are simple logical relationships among many of the ratios.

1. Return on Investment = Net profit Margin x Total Asset Turnover.

$$\text{ROI} = \frac{\text{EAT}}{\text{Sales}} \quad x \quad \frac{\text{Sales}}{\text{Total Assets}} \quad = \quad \frac{\text{EAT}}{\text{Total Assets}}$$

2. Return on Stockholders' Equity = Return on Investment x Equity Multiplier. (The equity multiplier is the ratio of assets to equity).

$$\text{Return on Stockholders' Equity} = \frac{\text{EAT}}{\text{Total Assets}} \quad x \quad \frac{\text{Total Assets}}{\text{Stockholders' Equity}}$$

$$= \frac{\text{EAT}}{\text{Stockholders' Equity}}$$

3. <u>Dupont analysis</u>--A Dupont Chart, such as the one below presents some of the major ratios in a logical, organized fashion. This Dupont Chart provides a good starting point for analyzing the firm. For example, suppose a firm's return on stockholders' equity is considered low. Refer to the chart; is this because of a low ROI or a low equity multiplier (or both)? If the ROI is too low, is this due to a low net profit margin or low total asset turnover (or both)? If the net profit margin is low, which expenses are out of line?

C.   Sources of information on industries--The most popular sources of information about ratios for different industries are Dun and Bradstreet (D&B) and Robert Morris Associates. Other excellent sources include reports of the Federal Trade Commission (FTC) and the Securities and Exchange Commission (SEC), Prentice-Hall's <u>Ratio Almanac</u>, trade associations and trade journals, and publications of some commercial banks.

D.   There are several computerized data bases which can be used to assist in financial analysis. Standard and Poors provides the Compustat data base, which contains balance sheet, income statement, stock price and dividend information. The Value Line data base is available in both hard copy and microcomputer format (called Value Screen). There are also time sharing services such as Compuserve.

E.   The "quality" of a firm's earnings is positively related to the proportion of cash earnings to total earnings and to the proportion of recurring income to total income.

F.   The "quality" of a firm's balance sheet is positively related to the ratio of the market value of the firm's assets to the book value of assets and inversely related to the amount of its hidden liabilities.

V.   Discriminant analysis is a statistical technique which helps to classify observations (firms) into two or more predetermined groups based on certain characteristics of each of the firms.

A.   Edward Altman used discriminant analysis of financial ratios to predict bankruptcy of firms.

B.   The basic Altman model was based on five variables:

X_1 = Net working capital/Total assets (%)
X_2 = Retained earnings/Total assets (%)
X_3 = EBIT/Total assets (%)
X_4 = Market value of equity (common and preferred)/Book value of total debt (%)
X_5 = Sales/Total assets (number of times)

C.   The higher a firm's value for each of the five ratios (X_1 through X_5) the more likely the firm was to be solvent (and less likely to go bankrupt).

VI.   Ratios do not substitute for sound judgment and should be employed cautiously.

A.   Inflation can make it difficult to assess performance over time or across firms.

    1.   During inflation, the last-in, first-out (LIFO) inventory valuation method results in lower reported profits and lower taxes than the first-in, first-out (FIFO) method.

    2.   If inflation causes a rise in interest rates, the value of long-term debt will decline.

    3.   The Financial Accounting Standards Board requires that firms restate their income from operations as if depreciation were based on assets all purchased with the same purchasing power.

B.   Differing accounting practices can frustrate attempts to make meaningful comparisons between firms or between a firm and its industry.

C.   The dispersion (distribution) of ratios is not always known.

D.   A firm that is strong (or weak) within its own industry is not necessarily strong (or weak) compared to firms in other industries.

E.   Inflation can have an impact on a firm's reported earnings. For example, inventory valuation methods or cost accounting systems will influence earnings.

TRUE AND FALSE QUESTIONS

Agree with each of the statements or **reject** it and modify it so that it is acceptable.

1.   The current ratio will never exceed the quick ratio.

2.   Assuming a current ratio greater than one, the purchase of raw materials on credit decreases the current ratio.

3.   The gross profit margin is greater than the net profit margin.

4.   The average collection period is found by dividing a firm's year-end inventory by its average daily credit sales.

5.   Because total assets exceed net fixed assets, the total asset turnover must exceed the fixed asset turnover.

6.   A short average collection period is a sign of efficient accounts receivable management.

7.   The return on total assets equals the net profit margin times the total asset turnover.

8.   In the Altman model, a decrease in a firm's net working capital to total assets ratio would be interpreted as a decline in the firm's financial soundness.

9.   A change in inflation would have no effect on a firm's current ratio since the current ratio is based on short-term accounts.

10.   Firms with a current ratio below 2.0 are having liquidity problems.

Answers to True and False Questions

1.   The current ratio exceeds the quick ratio for all firms with an inventory.

2.   True.

3.   True.

4.   The average collection period is found by dividing the firm's year-end <u>accounts receivable</u> by its average daily credit sales.

5.   Because total assets exceed net fixed assets, the total asset turnover must <u>be less than</u> the fixed asset turnover.

6.   A short average collection period is not necessarily a sign of efficient accounts receivable management. It could also result from overly strict credit terms which can reduce the firm's sales and profitability.

7.   True.

8.   True.

9.   Inventory could be affected by the use of LIFO or FIFO.

10. The appropriate current ratio for a given firm can be substantially above <u>or</u> below 2.0 depending on the industry and circumstances relevant to the specific firm.

CHAPTER 3 PROBLEMS

1.   Please supply the missing figures:

	Net Profit Margin	Total Asset Turnover	Return on Investment	Equity Multiplier	Return on Stockholders' Equity
a.	20.0%	0.75	--	1.00	--
b.	--	2.00	8.0%	1.50	--
c.	2.5%	4.00	--	--	25.0%
d.	6.0%	--	9.0%	--	14.4%

Solution:

a.   ROI = NPM x TAT = 20.0%(.75) = 15.0%
     Return on Equity = ROI x Equity Multiplier
     = 15.0%(1.00) = 15.0%

b.   NPM = ROI/TAT = 8.0%/2.00 = 4%
     Return on Equity = ROI x Equity Multiplier
     = 8%(1.5) = 12.0%

c.   ROI = NPM x TAT = 2.5%(4.00) = 10%
     Equity Multiplier = Return on Equity/ROI = 25%/10%
     = 2.50

d. TAT = ROI/NPM = 9%/6% = 1.50
Equity Multiplier = Return on Equity/ROI = 14.4%/9%
    = 1.60

2. Find the sales of the Hudspeth Company using the following information:

Current ratio	2.0
Quick ratio	1.4
Current liabilities	$100,000
Inventory turnover	8.0
Gross profit margin	20%

Solution:

Current assets = 2.0(100,000) = $200,000
Current assets minus inventory = 1.4(100,000) = $140,000
Inventory = 200,000 - 140,000 = $60,000
Cost of sales = (100% - 20%) sales = (.8)sales
Sales = (cost of sales)/.8 = 480,000/.8 = $600,000

3. McKibben Oil & Grease has a net profit margin of 2%, a total asset turnover of 3.2, and an equity multiplier of 1.5. What is McKibben's return on investment and return on stockholders' equity?

Solution:

Return on investment = Net profit margin x Total asset turnover
Return on investment = 2% x 3.2 = 6.4%
Return on stockholders' equity = Return on investment x Equity multiplier
Return on stockholders' equity = 6.4% x 1.5 = 9.6%

4. Bill Lloyd forecasts sales of $4,000,000 for his firm next year. If the firm maintains its average collection period at 40 days and its inventory turnover at 8, what should be the firm's receivables and inventory levels? The gross profit margin is 22%.

Solution:

Accounts receivable = (40/365) 4,000,000 = $444,444
Cost of sales = (100%-gross profit margin) Sales
Cost of sales = 78% (4,000,000) = $3,120,000
Inventory = $3,120,000/8 = $390,000

5. Joyce Tilleman is planning for a small distributing firm she will operate after graduation. Her best guesses about several relevant financial variables are:

Sales	$100,000
Gross profit margin	40%
Average collection period (365 day year)	97 days
Inventory turnover	4.0

Minimum cash balance *CA* $5,000
Investment in fixtures and equipment ~ $10,000
Long-term bank loan ~ *CA* $15,000
 Current ratio   2.76
All other required assets are to be leased
All sales are credit sales

Complete the following pro forma balance sheet and indicate how much equity capital Joyce must invest in her firm.

BALANCE SHEET

Cash	$	Accounts payable	$
Accounts receivable	$	Bank loan	$____
Inventory	$____		
TOTAL CURRENT ASSETS	$	TOTAL LIABILITIES	$
		Stockholders' equity	$____
Long-term assets	$____	TOTAL LIABILITIES	
TOTAL ASSETS		& EQUITY	

AR is a current asset

Solution:

Cash = $5,000
Long-term assets = $10,000
Bank loan = $15,000
CA Accounts receivable = 100,000(97/365) = $26,575
Cost of sales = (100% - 40%)sales = (60%)100,000 = $60,000
Inventory = 60,000/4.0 = $15,000
Total current assets = 5,000 + 26,575 + 15,000 = $46,575
Total assets = 46,575 + 10,000 = $56,575
Current assets/current liabilities = 2.76
Accounts payable = current assets/2.76 = 46,575/2.76 = $16,875
Total liabilities = 16,875 + 15,000 = $31,875
Stockholders' equity = total assets - total liabilities
= 56,575 - 31,875 = $24,700

BALANCE SHEET

Cash	$ 5,000	Accounts payable	$ 16,875
Accounts receivable	26,575	Bank loan	15,000
Inventory	15,000		
TOTAL CURRENT ASSETS	$ 46,575	TOTAL LIABILITIES	$ 31,875
Long-term assets	10,000	Stockholders' equity	24,700
TOTAL ASSETS	$ 56,575	TOTAL LIABILITIES & EQUITY	$ 56,575

Joyce must invest $24,700 of equity capital in her business.

$$\frac{46,575}{16,875} = 2.76 \text{ current ratio} \qquad AP = \frac{46,575}{2.76}$$

6. From the financial statements of the Jackson Products Company, please provide a common-size balance sheet and common-size income statement.

JACKSON PRODUCTS COMPANY
Balance Sheet
December 31, 19X1

Cash and securities	$ 240,000	Accounts payable	$ 380,000
Accounts receivable	320,000	Notes payable	420,000
Inventory	1,040,000	Other current liabilities	50,000
Total current assets	$1,600,000	Total current liabilities	$ 850,000
Net plant & equipment	800,000	Long-term debt (10%)	$ 800,000
Total assets	$ 2,400,000	Common stock	400,000
		Retained earnings	350,000
		Total liabilities and stockholders' equity	$ 2,400,000

INCOME STATEMENT
for the Year Ended December 31, 19X1

Net sales (all on credit)		$ 3,000,000
Cost of sales		1,800,000
Gross profit		$ 1,200,000
Selling, general, and administrative expenses		860,000
Earnings before interest and taxes		$ 340,000
Interest:		
Notes	$ 37,800	
Long-term debt	80,000	
Total interest charges		117,800
Earnings before tax		$ 222,200
Federal income tax (40%)		88,880
Earnings after tax		$ 133,320

percentages

Solution:

JACKSON PRODUCTS COMPANY
Common-Size Balance Sheet
December 31, 19X1

Cash and Securities	10.00%	Accounts payable	15.83%
Accounts Receivable	13.33	Notes payable	17.50
Inventory	43.33	Other current liabilities	2.08
Total current assets	66.67	Total current liabilities	35.42%
Net plant and		Long-term debt	33.33
equipment	33.33	Common stock	16.67
Total assets	100.00%	Retained earnings	14.58
		Total liabilities and stockholders' equity	100.00%

JACKSON PRODUCTS COMPANY
Common-Size Income Statement

Net sales	100.00%
Cost of sales	60.00
Gross profit	40.00%
Selling, general, and administration expenses	28.67
Earnings before interest and taxes	11.33%
Total interest charges	3.93
Earnings before tax	7.40%
Federal income tax	2.96
Earnings after tax	4.44%

4

Cash Flow Analysis and Forecasting

Chapter 4 deals with cash flow analysis and cash flow forecasting. Several relevant forecasting tools are also covered.

I.   The firm's after-tax operating cash flow is equal to its earnings after tax plus noncash charges:

        CF   =   EAT +   Noncash charges.

Generally, the firm has two types of noncash expenses; depreciation and deferred taxes.

        A.   Depreciation is the systematic allocation of the cost of an asset over more than one year. Depreciation is an allocation of an asset's original cost and does not represent a cash outlay.

        B.   Deferred taxes occur when the company reports a different income tax expense than it actually paid in cash during the year.

                1.   Deferred taxes occur because of temporary differences in the stated amounts of assets and liabilities for financial reporting purposes and for tax purposes. Those differences most often occur in the accounting for depreciation, inventories, and pensions.

                2.   Many corporations use accelerated depreciation for tax purposes and straight-line depreciation for financial reporting purposes. This reduces the cash taxes due currently, and defers the payment of taxes into the future.

C.   The cash flow from operations is:

CF   =   Net earnings + Depreciation + Deferred taxes

D.   The statement of cash flows is a major portion of a company's financial statement. (The other major statements are the balance sheet and the income statement).

1.   The purpose of the statement of cash flows is to provide information about a company's cash receipts and cash disbursements during a particular accounting period.

2.   The statement of cash flows shows the effects of a company's operating, investing, and financing activities on its cash balance.

Net cash increase (decrease)   =   net cash provided (used) by operating activities

+   net cash provided (used) by investing activities

+   net cash provided (used) by financing activities

II.   Pro forma financial statements are used to show the results of an assumed or planned event instead of an actual event. Cash flow forecasting involves the projection of a firm's future cash needs.

A.   Percentage of sales forecasting relies on a forecast of sales and then obtains estimates of other variables which can be expressed as a proportion of sales.

1.   Total financing needed can be tied to a sales increase (ΔS):

Total Financing Needed = Forecasted Asset Increase -
    Forecasted Current Liability Increase

$$=   \frac{A}{S}(\Delta S) -   \frac{CL}{S}(\Delta S)$$

2.   A portion of total financing needed can be generated internally:

Internal Net Cash Provided = Forecasted Cash Flow (CF) - Dividends (D)

$$= CF - D$$

3.   The additional financing needed is the difference between the total financing needed and the internal financing provided.

Additional Financing Needed = Total Financing Needed - Internal Financing Provided

$$= \quad [\frac{A}{S}(\Delta S) - \quad \frac{CL}{S}(\Delta S)] - [NI - D]$$

B.   Cash budgeting plays a critical role in the firm's planning process.

    1.   A budget is simply a financial plan. Budgets are used to plan, coordinate, and control a firm's operations.

    2.   The cash budget projects the firm's cash receipts and disbursements over future periods of time.

        a.   Many cash receipts and disbursements are tied to projected sales. Receipts on credit sales will lag projected sales. Payments for purchases (of raw materials, merchandise, or supplies) to accommodate projected sales depend on how much the purchase precedes the sale and on credit terms received from suppliers.

        b.   Other expected receipts and disbursements of cash such as long-term loans, capital expenditures, dividend payments, wages and salaries, rent, etc., must be scheduled. Total disbursements are subtracted from total receipts and beginning cash to obtain an ending balance.

C.   A pro forma statement of cash flows can also be used to determine how much additional financing a company will need in a future period.

D.   Breakeven analysis is used to show the relationship between revenues, costs, and operating profits at various output levels.

    1.   The breakeven point is defined as the output level at which total revenues equal total operating costs. It is found by dividing fixed operating cost F, by the difference between the price, P, and variable cost per unit.

$$Q \quad = \quad \frac{F}{P-V}$$

    2.   For a cash breakeven point, noncash operating costs (depreciation) are subtracted from the fixed operating costs.

$$\text{Cash breakeven point} \quad = \quad \frac{F - Dep}{P - V}$$

The cash breakeven point in dollar sales is

$$\text{Cash breakeven sales} \quad = \quad \frac{F - Dep}{1 - (V/P)}$$

III.   Trend analysis, econometric models, and computerized financial planning models are also used as financial planning tools.

    A.   In trend analysis, the future value of some financial variable is predicted on the basis of past actual data. The trend can be linear or non-linear and the estimates can be extrapolated from a graph or obtained from statistical techniques such as regression analysis. Trend analysis assumes that future trends are a continuation of past trends.

    B.   Econometric techniques involve the development and empirical measurement of functional relationships between economic variables and one or more explanatory variables. An example might predict a company's sales as a function of gross national product.

    C.   A variety of specialized financial planning models are employed by businesses. These models are often computerized and sometimes use a number of quantitative techniques such as regression analysis and linear programming.

        1.   A deterministic model uses single-value forecasts of each financial variable. These values may not be optimal and nothing is specified about their probabilities. Management can perform sensitivity analyses, rerunning the model to see the sensitivity of the result to changes in forecasts or assumptions.

        2.   Probabilistic models utilize probability distributions for input data instead of single point estimates and provide probabilistic output.

        3.   Optimization models choose the optimal levels of some variables rather than having them specified beforehand.

IV.   (Appendix to Chapter 4) Breakeven analysis (also called cost-volume-profit analysis) describes the relationships among sales, profits, and costs.

    A.   If the firm sells its output at a constant price per unit (P), has a constant variable cost per unit (V), and has fixed costs (F), its profit is a function of the level of output (Q).

$$\text{Total operating cost} = TC = V(Q) + F$$
$$\text{Total revenue} = TR = P(Q)$$
$$\text{Profit} = EBIT = TR - TC$$
$$EBIT = P(Q) - V(Q) - F$$

    B.   When the firm is breaking even, profit equals zero and total revenue equals total costs. The breakeven level of output in units (Q_b) is $Q_b = F/(P - V)$.

The difference between the selling price per unit and the variable cost per unit is called the <u>contribution margin per unit</u>.

C.   <u>The break-even dollar sales volume (S_b) is easily found in one of two ways:</u>

1. $S_b = P(Q_b)$. $Sb = P\left(F/P-V\right)$

2. $S_b = \dfrac{F}{1 - (V/P)}$

V/P is the variable cost ratio, i.e., the variable costs per dollar of sales. $1 - (V/P)$ is the contribution margin per dollar of sales.

D.   The sales volume necessary to achieve some profit level other than zero (breakeven) is

$$\text{Target Volume (Units)} = \frac{\text{Fixed Costs + Target Profit}}{\text{Contribution Margin Per Unit}}$$

E.   Breakeven analysis is easy to see graphically.

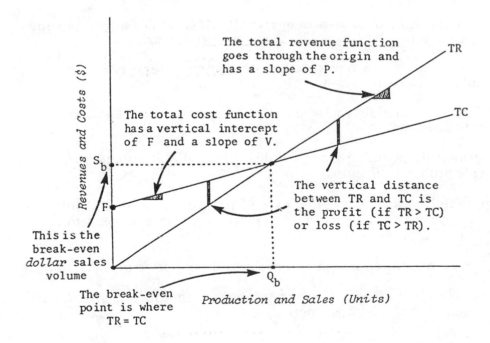

F.   <u>If the distribution of sales is known, the probability of an operating profit or loss can be determined.</u> If sales are normally distributed, let

$$Z = \frac{\text{breakeven point - expected (mean) sales}}{\text{standard deviation of sales}}$$

Z is the number of standard deviations the breakeven point differs from expected sales. This Z value can be looked up in a normal table to find the probability of an operating loss or profit.

TRUE AND FALSE QUESTIONS

Agree with each of the statements or reject it and modify it so that it is acceptable.

1. The principal disadvantage of financial forecasting with trend analysis is that the trend is assumed to be linear.

2. If the sales forecast is $10,000,000, the net profit margin is 12 percent and dividends are planned to be $500,000, the addition to retained earnings for the period should be $700,000.

3. The cash breakeven point is usually less than the breakeven point.

4. One advantage of a cash budget is that the cash budget can identify a cash shortage that may be covered by short-term borrowing.

5. Deferred taxes can occur when the company reports a different income tax expense than it paid in cash.

6. Optimization models find the optimal levels of variables rather than specifying them beforehand.

7. Deterministic planning models utilize probability distributions for input data and provide probabilistic output.

8. If planned uses of cash flow exceed planned sources and long-term external financing cannot make up the difference, the firm may need to reduce dividends or planned capital expenditures.

9. Budgets cannot be coordinated with the firm's projected financial statements.

10. Once a budget is agreed upon, managers should not attempt to change the document during the budget period.

Answers to True and False Questions

1. Non-linear trend analysis is used frequently.

2. True.

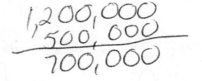

3.   True.

4.   True.

5.   True.

6.   True.

7.   This statement is true for probabilistic models. Deterministic models use single-value forecasts for input data.

8.   True.

9.   They can and should be coordinated.

10.   A budget is a financial plan, and plans should be flexible to accommodate changes through time.

CHAPTER 4 PROBLEMS

1.   Lori Franz needs a quick estimate of her financing needs. Briefly, the facts are these.

    Sales are forecasted to increase by $450,000
    Assets will increase by 80% of the sales increase
    Current liabilities will increase by 30% of the sales increase
    Projected operating cash flow is $125,000
    The dividends paid should be $65,000

How much additional financing is needed?

Solution:

Total financing needed = Forecasted asset increase - Forecasted current liability increase

$$\text{Total financing needed} = \frac{A(\Delta S)}{S} - \frac{CL(\Delta S)}{S}$$

$$= .80(450,000) - .30(450,000)$$
$$= 360,000 - 135,000 = \$225,000$$

Internal cash flow provided = Cash flow forecasted - Dividends

Internal cash flow provided = CF - D
$$= 125,000 - 65,000 = \$60,000$$

Additional financing needed
= Total financing needed - Internal cash flow provided
= 225,000 - 60,000 = $165,000

2. Paula Revere, financial analyst for the Austin Boston Corporation, needs a rough estimate of next year's external financing needs. She has the following information:

(1) Current sales of $10,000,000 are expected to increase 20 percent next year.
(2) The net profit margin is 9 percent.
(3) Dividends will be $500,000.
(4) Last year's balance sheet was:

BALANCE SHEET

Cash	$ 400,000	Payables	$1,500,000
Accounts receivable	2,000,000	Short-term bank loan	1,000,000
Inventory	3,000,000	Mortgage	2,500,000
Long-term assets	3,600,000	Net Worth	4,000,000
Total Assets	$9,000,000	Total Liabilities and Net Worth	$9,000,000

(5) The ratios of cash to sales, receivables to sales, inventory to sales, and payables to sales will remain constant.
(6) The sales increase can be handled by the existing amount of net long-term assets (and gross investment will equal depreciation).
(7) The principal amounts due on the short-term bank loan and mortgage will be unchanged.

Given these assumptions, Paula has only 15 minutes to predict external financing needs.

Solution:

Use ratio forecasting to construct a pro-forma balance sheet.

(a) Cash, receivables, inventories, and payables maintain the same ratio to sales. This ratio is multiplied by new sales to find the new level of each account.

$$\text{Cash} = \frac{400,000}{10,000,000}(12,000,000) = .04(12,000,000)$$

$$= \$480,000$$

$$\text{Accounts Receivable} = \frac{2,000,000}{10,000,000}(12,000,000) = .20(12,000,000)$$

$$= \quad \$2,400,000$$

Inventory $\quad = \quad \dfrac{3,000,000}{10,000,000}(12,000,000) = .30(12,000,000)$

$$= \quad \$3,600,000$$

Payables $\quad = \quad \dfrac{1,500,000}{10,000,000}(12,000,000) = .15(12,000,000)$

$$= \quad \$1,800,000$$

(b)   Next year's net income should be 9 percent of sales, or $.09(12,000,000) =$ $1,080,000$. The addition to retained earnings is net income less dividends, or $1,080,000 - 500,000 = \$580,000$. Net worth will be $4,000,000 + 580,000 = \$4,580,000$.

(c)   The pro-forma balance sheet should be

Cash	$ 480,000	Payables	$1,800,000
Accounts receivable	2,400,000	Short-term bank loan	1,000,000
Inventory	3,600,000	Mortgage	2,500,000
Long-term assets	3,600,000	Net Worth	4,580,000
Total Assets	$10,080,000	Subtotal	$9,880,000
		External Funds Needed	200,000
		Total Liabilities and Net Worth	$10,080,000

Total assets are forecasted to be $10,080,000 and total liabilities and net worth should be $9,880,000 prior to raising additional external financing. $200,000 of external funds are required to finance the firm next year.

3.   As a community service, Tau Alpha Sigma sorority runs Saturday afternoon movies for children, charging ten cents admission per child. The fixed costs are $40 per weekend for film rental and cleanup. Tau Alpha also sells candy, Coke,, and popcorn with a variable cost ratio (variable costs divided by selling price) of 0.40. The average child buys $.75 of junk food.

a.   What is the breakeven number of children?

b.   How many children are necessary to make a profit of $50?

$$\dfrac{F}{P-V}$$

Solution:

a.   Revenue per child = .10 + .75 = $.85
Variable cost per child = .4(.75) = $.30

$$Q_b = \dfrac{F}{P-V} = \dfrac{40.00}{.85 - .30} = \dfrac{40.00}{.55} = \text{72.7 children}$$

b.   Target volume (units) = $\dfrac{\text{Fixed Costs + Target Profit}}{\text{Contribution Margin Per Unit}}$

Target volume $= \dfrac{40 + 50}{.55} = \dfrac{90}{.55} = 163.6$ children

4.   The managers must prepare a cash budget for Brigham Jeans for the second quarter of 19X9. The sales forecast is:

	Total Sales	Credit Sales
March 19X9	$400,000	$300,000
April 19X9	500,000	375,000
May 19X9	700,000	525,000
June 19X9	600,000	450,000
July 19X9	500,000	375,000

Twenty percent of BJ's credit sales are collected in the month of the sale, and the remaining 80 percent is collected in the following month. The company's purchases are 70 percent of sales, and the purchases are made and paid for one month before the expected sales. Wages and salaries are estimated to be 9 percent of sales and are paid during the same month. Rent is $20,000 per month, and the company has forecasted additional cash operating expenses to be $50,000 in April, $60,000 in May, and $20,000 in June. A $40,000 tax payment and $40,000 dividend are expected in May. Brigham Jeans on April 1 expects a $125,000 cash balance and wishes to maintain a minimum balance of at least $100,000. BJ may borrow (or repay) needed funds from the bank in multiples of $5,000.

If no other receipts or expenditures are anticipated, prepare a monthly cash budget for April, May, and June.

Solution:

Brigham Jeans
Cash Budget, Second Quarter 19X9

	April	May	June
Sales	$500,000	$700,000	$600,000
Cash balance, beginning of month	$125,000	$100,000	$102,000
Receipts*			
Cash sales	125,000	175,000	150,000
Collection of current month credit sales	75,000	105,000	90,000
Collection of prior month credit sales	240,000	300,000	420,000
Total Cash Available	$565,000	$680,000	$762,000
Disbursements			
Payment for purchases**	$490,000	$420,000	$350,000
Wages and salaries	45,000	63,000	54,000
Rent	20,000	20,000	20,000
Other expenses	50,000	60,000	20,000
Dividends	--	40,000	--
Taxes	--	40,000	--
Total Disbursements	$605,000	$643,000	$444,000
Excess of available cash over disbursements	$(40,000)	$ 37,000	$318,000
Borrowing	140,000	65,000	--
Loan repayments	--	--	205,000
Cash balance, end of month	$100,000	$102,000	$113,000
Cumulative borrowing	$140,000	$205,000	-0-

*Cash sales are the current month's total sales less credit sales. Collections of credit sales are 20 percent of the amount in the current month and 80 percent one month after the credit sale.

**Purchases are 70 percent of the next month's total sales, and cash payment is made at the time of the purchase.

5.   Memphis Leisure Crafts makes rubber dinghies which they sell for $400 each. Their fixed costs are 75,000 and variable costs are $250 per dinghy. If the fixed costs include $18,000 of noncash depreciation charges, what is the cash breakeven point in units and in dollars?

Solution:

$$Q^c_b = \frac{F - N}{P - V} = \frac{75,000 - 18,000}{400 - 250} = \frac{57,000}{150} = 380 \text{ units}$$

$$S^c_b = 400(380) = \$152,000$$

6.   Rework the Brigham Jeans cash budgeting problem (#4 above) using the Lotus templates available with the textbook. As you will see in the template, very complicated cash budgeting problems can be done easily. The final output for the Brigham Jeans problem is on the following page.

CASH BUDGET			
SALES	$500,000	$700,000	$600,000
BEGINNING OF MONTH			
PROJECTED CASH BALANCE	$125,000	$100,000	$100,000
RECEIPTS			
CASH SALES	$125,000	$175,000	$150,000
RECEIVABLES COLLECTIONS	$315,000	$405,000	$510,000
NON-OPERATING CASH RECEIPTS	$0	$0	$0
CASH FROM SALE OF ASSETS	$0	$0	$0
CASH FROM FINANCING OPERATIONS	$0	$0	$0
TOTAL CASH AVAILABLE	$605,000	$680,000	$760,000
DISBURSEMENTS			
LABOR PAYMENTS	$45,000	$63,000	$54,000
LABOR (OTHER)	$0	$0	$0
MATERIALS PAYMENTS	$490,000	$420,000	$350,000
MATERIAL (OTHER)	$0	$0	$0
GENERAL AND ADMINISTRATIVE SALARIES	$0	$0	$0
RENT AND UTILITIES	$20,000	$20,000	$20,000
OTHER EXPENSES	$50,000	$60,000	$20,000
TAXES	$0	$40,000	$0
PURCHASE OF ASSETS	$0	$0	$0
INTEREST	$0	$0	$0
DIVIDENDS PAID	$0	$40,000	$0
REPAYMENT OF "OTHER" LOANS	$0	$0	$0
SINKING FUND PAYMENTS	$0	$0	$0
TOTAL DISBURSEMENTS	$605,000	$643,000	$444,000
EXCESS AVAIL CASH OVER DISBURSEMENTS	($40,000)	$37,000	$316,000
AVAILABLE CASH (NET OF LOAN)	($40,000)	($103,000)	$113,000
DESIRED CASH BALANCE	$100,000	$100,000	$100,000
LOAN REQUIRED TO MAINTAIN CASH BAL	$140,000	$203,000	$0
LOAN PAYMENT	$0	($63,000)	$203,000
END OF MONTH PROJECTED CASH BALANCE	$100,000	$100,000	$113,000

5

Financial Mathematics

Many managers make constant use of financial mathematics. Any decisions involving investing or financing where cash flows occur at different points in time require an understanding of the time value of money. This crucial topic is covered in Chapter 5.

I. In borrowing or lending money, the amount due can be calculated using simple interest or compound interest.

  A. The principal is the amount of money borrowed or invested, the term of a loan is the length of time or number of periods the loan is outstanding, and the rate of interest is the percent of the principal the borrower pays the lender per time period.

  B. Simple interest is the interest paid on the principal sum only

$$I = PV_0 \times i \times n$$

where I = simple interest in dollars, PV_0 = principal amount at time 0, i = interest rate per time period, and n = number of time periods.

  C. For simple interest, the present value of the loan is

$$PV_0 = \frac{I}{i \times n}$$

  D. The future value (amount due at time n) using simple interest is

$$FV_n = PV_0 + I$$
$$FV_n = PV_0 + (PV_0 \times i \times n) = PV_0 [1 + (i \times n)]$$

II.   Compound interest is due not only on the principal but on prior interest which has not been paid (or withdrawn). The amount of interest due each period is the interest rate times the principal amount at the beginning of the period.

   A.   For one period, the future (compound) value is

$$FV_1 = PV_0 (1 + i)$$

and for two periods, the future value is

$$
\begin{aligned}
FV_2 &= FV_1 (1 + i) \\
&= PV_0 (1 + i)(1 + i) = PV_0 (1 + i)^2
\end{aligned}
$$

   B.   In general, the future value at the end of year n for a sum compounded at interest rate i is

$$FV_n = PV_0 (1 + i)^n$$

   C.   In Table I in the text, compound value interest factors ($FVIF_{i,n}$) show the future value of \$1 invested for n years at interest rate i:

$$FVIF_{i,n} = (1 + i)^n$$

   D.   The future value of a sum can also be written as

$$FV_n = PV_0 (FVIF_{i,n})$$

III.   Present value calculations find the amount at time zero, or present value (PV_0), which is equivalent to some future amount FV_n.

   A.   The present value of a future amount received in n years discounted at interest rate i is:

$$PV_0 = FV_n \frac{1}{(1 + i)^n}$$

   B.   Table II includes present value interest factors ($PVIF_{i,n}$) which show the present value of \$1 discounted at interest rate i for n periods:

$$PVIF_{i,n} = \frac{1}{(1 + i)^n}$$

   C.   Using $PVIF_{i,n}$, the present value of amount FV_n is:

$$PV_0 = FV_n (PVIF_{i,n})$$

   D.   The present value interest factor is the reciprocal of the future value interest factor:

$$PVIF_{i,n} = 1/FVIF_{i,n}$$

IV.   An annuity is a series of periodic payments of equal size.

A.   An <u>ordinary annuity</u> is one where the payments or receipts occur at the end of each period, whereas an <u>annuity due</u> is one where the payments or receipts occur at the beginning of each period.

B.   The future value of an annuity can be found by investing each payment until the end of the annuity period and summing the future values of all the individual annuity payments.

C.   For an ordinary annuity, its future value at the end of year n is termed the compound sum of the annuity ($FVAN_n$), which can be found using Table III by multiplying the compound value of an annuity interest factor ($FVIFA_{i,n}$) times the annuity payment (R):

$$FVAN_n = R(FVIFA_{i,n})$$

D. $FVIFA_{i,n}$ is the value at time n of \$1 invested at the end of each of the next n periods earning interest rate i. For positive interest rates, the value of $FVIFA_{i,n}$ will exceed the value of n (i.e., $FVIFA_{i,n} > n$).

E.   A good financial calculator can be used for finding FVIFAs not shown in Table III. You can also use the formula:

$$FVIFA_{i,n} = \frac{(1 + i)^n - 1}{i}$$

F.   One common use of the FVIFA is to find the annuity amount that must be invested each year to produce a future value:

$$R = FVAN_n/(FVIFA_{i,n})$$

This is called the sinking fund problem.

V.   The present value of an annuity ($PVAN_0$) is the value at time 0 of a future stream of annuity payments.

A.   The present value of an annuity can be found by summing the present values of all of its individual future payments.

B.   For an ordinary annuity, the present value of the annuity ($PVAN_0$) can be found by multiplying the present value of an annuity interest factor ($PVIFA_{i,n}$) from Table IV times the annuity payment (R):

$$PVAN_0 = R(PVIFA_{i,n})$$

     C. $PVIFA_{i,n}$ is the value at time 0 of $1 received or paid at the end of each of the next n periods discounted at interest rate i. For positive interest rates, the value of $PVIFA_{i,n}$ will be less than the value of n (i.e., $PVIFA_{i,n} < n$).

     D.   A good financial calculator can be used for finding PVIFAs not given in Table IV. You can also use the formula:

$$PVIFA_{i,n} = \frac{1 - \dfrac{1}{(1 + i)^n}}{i}$$

     E.   Frequently, the PVIFA is used to find the annuity amount that is necessary to recover a capital investment:

$$R = PVAN_0/(PVIFA_{i,n})$$

This is called the capital recovery problem and an example of this problem would be to find the payments necessary to pay off a loan.

VI.   The formulas and table values in the chapter are for ordinary annuities, and they must be modified when dealing with an annuity due.

     A.   The future value of an annuity due is simply equal to the future value of an ordinary annuity times one plus the interest rate:

$$FVAND_n = R(FVIFA_{i,n})(1 + i)$$

     B.   The present value of an annuity due is equal to the present value of an ordinary annuity times one plus the interest rate:

$$PVAND_0 = R(PVIFA_{i,n})(1 + i)$$

VII.   A perpetuity is a financial instrument that promises to pay an equal amount of money per period into the indefinite future.

     A.   The present value of a perpetuity (which is an annuity with an infinite life) is

$$PVPER_0 = R/(1 + i)^1 + R/(1 + i)^2 + R/(1 + i)^3 + \ldots$$

$$PVPER_0 = \sum_{t=1}^{\infty} R/(1 + i)^t$$

where R is the equal periodic payment and $PVPER_0$ is the sum of the present values of these payments from time 1 to infinity.

B.   The present value of a perpetuity can be simplified to be

$$PVPER_0 = R/i$$

VIII.   Interest may be compounded more frequently than once per year.

A.   In semiannual compounding, the nominal interest rate i_{nom} is divided by two and credited twice per year; in other words, the interest rate $i_{nom}/2$ is earned in six months and six months later the interest rate $i_{nom}/2$ is earned on both the beginning of year principal and the interest earned at midyear.

B.   If m is the number of times interest is compounded per year (for semiannual compounding, m = 2), the future value is

$$FV_n = PV_0(1 + \frac{i_{nom}}{m})^{mn}$$

C.   For intrayear compounding, the present value of a future amount discounted at an annual nominal interest rate i_{nom} compounded m times per year is

$$PV_0 = FV_n \frac{1}{(1+i_{nom}/m)^{mn}}$$

D.   The more frequently an annual <u>nominal</u> rate of interest (i_{nom}) is compounded, the greater the <u>effective</u> rate of interest (i_{eff}) is. The rate of interest per period (where there is more than one compounding period per year), i_m, which results from an effective annual rate of interest, i, is

$$i_m = (1 + i_{eff})^{1/m} - 1$$

E.   Conversely, the effective annual rate of interest, i_{eff}, resulting from a rate of interest per period, i_m, compounded in times per year is

$$i_{eff} = (1 + \frac{i_{nom}}{m})^m - 1$$

IX.   (Chapter 5 Appendix) Continuous compounding is the case if interest is compounded a large number of times per year (i.e., if m approaches infinity).

A.   The future value (FV_n) of some initial amount (PV_0) compounded at a continuous interest rate i for n periods is

$$FV_n = PV_0 e^{in}$$

B.   The present value of a future lump sum discounted at continuous rate i is

$$PV_0 = FV_n/e^{in} = FV_n \, e^{-in}$$

C.   If the nominal interest (or growth) rate is i compounded continuously, the effective annual rate equivalent to this is

Effective (annual) rate $= i_{eff} = e^i - 1$

D.   If i is an annually compounded rate, the continuous rate equivalent to this is

Continuous effective rate $= \ln(1 + i_{eff})$

which is the natural logarithm of $1 + i_{eff}$

TRUE AND FALSE QUESTIONS

Agree with each of the statements or **reject** it and modify it so that it is acceptable.

1.   For a given i and n, the present value interest factor (PVIF) is the reciprocal of the future value interest factor (FVIF).

2.   The present value of an annuity interest factor (PVIFA) is the reciprocal of the future value of an annuity interest factor (FVIFA).

3.   If an annuity of $1.00 per year is extended by one year (i.e, from n to n + 1 years), the present value of the annuity increases by $1.00.

4.   If the discount rate increases, the present value of a given future payment decreases.

5.   If the interest rate increases, the compound sum of an annuity and the present value of an annuity both increase.

6.   If one bank pays eight percent compounded annually on its savings deposits and a second bank pays eight percent compounded semiannually, the second bank is paying approximately twice as much interest.

7.   The present value of an annuity interest factor ($PVIFA_{i,n}$) is equal to the present value of an annuity interest factor ($FVIFA_{i,n}$) times the present value interest factor ($PVIF_{i,n}$).

8.   A four-year ordinary annuity has equal payments occurring at times 1, 2, 3, and 4 (time 1 = one year from today, etc.) and a four-year annuity due has equal payments occurring at times 0, 1, 2, and 3.

9.   If n increases and i decreases, the present value of a single future cash flow decreases.

10.   The future value of an annuity due is greater than the future value of an ordinary annuity ($FVAND_n > FVAN_n$) and the present value of an annuity due is less than the present value of an ordinary annuity ($PVAND_0 < PVAN$).

Answers to True and False Questions

1.   True.

2.   False. It is true that the $PVIFA < n$ and the $FVIFA > n$ for $i > 0$.

3.   The present value of the annuity increases by the present value of $1, the extra dollar received, which is equal to

$$\frac{1}{(1 + i)^{n + 1}} < 1.00$$

4.   True.

5. $FVIFA_{i,n}$ increases and $PVIFA_{i,n}$ decreases.

6.   A bank paying eight percent compounded semiannually is actually paying four percent every six months, which is only slightly more than eight percent compounded annually. (Eight percent compounded semiannually is actually equivalent to 8.16% compounded annually).

7.   True.

8.   True.

9.   In this case, the present value might increase or decrease.

10. $FVAND_n = FVAN_n(1 + i)$, so it is true that $FVAND_n > FVAN_n$. However, $PVAND_0$

      $= PVAN(1 + i)$, so $PVAND_0 > PVAN$.

CHAPTER 5 PROBLEMS

1. If you deposit $500 in a savings account paying compound annual interest of 10%, what will the value of your account be in 1, 2, 3, 5, 10, and 20 years?

    Solution:

$$
\begin{aligned}
FV_n &= 500(1.10)^n &= 500(FVIF_{0.10,n}) \\
FV_1 &= 500(1.10)^1 &= 500(1.10) &= \$550 \\
FV_2 &= 500(1.10)^2 &= 500(1.21) &= \$605 \\
FV_3 &= 500(1.10)^3 &= 500(1.331) &= \$665.50 \\
FV_5 &= 500(1.10)^5 &= 500(1.611) &= \$805.50 \\
FV_{10} &= 500(1.10)^{10} &= 500(2.594) &= \$1,297 \\
FV_{20} &= 500(1.10)^{20} &= 500(6.728) &= \$3,364
\end{aligned}
$$

2. Fill in the missing information:

	PV	FV	i	n
a.	1000	--	10%	5
b.	--	50	1%	20
c.	144.25	250	4%	--
d.	600	3678	--	16

    Solution:

a. $FV = PV(1 + i)^n = PV(FVIF_{i,n})$
    $= 1000(1.611) = \$1,611$

b. $PV = FV \dfrac{1}{(1+i)^n} = FV(PVIF_{i,n})$

    $= 50(.820) = \$41$

c. $PV = FV \dfrac{1}{(1+i)^n} = FV(PVIF_{i,n})$

    $144.25 = 250(PVIF_{.04,n})$

    $PVIF_{.04,n} = 144.25/250 = .577$

    From Table II, n = 14

    OR

    $FV = PV(1 = i)^n = PV(FVIF_{i,n})$

    $250 = 144.25(FVIF_{.04,n})$

$FVIF_{.04,n} = 250/144.25 = 1.733$

From Table I, n = 14

d. $FV = PV(1 + i)^n = PV(FVIF_{i,n})$

$3678 = 600(FVIF_{i,16})$

$FVIF_{i,16} = 3678/600 = 6.130$

From Table I, i = 12%

OR

$PV = FV \dfrac{1}{(1+i)^n} = FV(PVIF_{i,n})$

$600 = 3678(PVIF_{i,16})$

$PVIF_{i,16} = 600/3678 = .163$

From Table II, i = 12%

3.   How long will it take to double your money if it grows at 10% annually?

Solution:

$FV_n = PV_0(FVIF_{i,n})$

$\$2 = \$1(FVIF_{.10,n})$

$FVIF_{.10,n} = 2.000$

From Table I, $FVIF_{.10,7} = 1.949$ and $FVIF_{.10,8} = 2.144$

So it will take between seven and eight years. (The actual answer is 7.18 years).

The "Rule of 72" gives a quick answer to the question. According to the rule, divide 72 by the interest rate percentage and this is the approximate number of years it takes the money to double (i.e., 72/10 = 7.2 years). Also, divide 72 by the number of periods to find the approximate interest rate per period required to double your money.

4.   Mark Cohen bought a stock 10 years ago for $20.00 a share. If it is now selling for $43.18 a share, what is the stock price's compound annual growth rate?

Solution:

$FV_n = PV_0(FVIF_{i,n})$

$$43.18 = 20.00(FVIF_{i,10})$$

$$FVIF_{i,10} = 43.18/20.00 = 2.159$$

From Table I, i = 8%

5. You may purchase a 5-year certificate at the local savings and loan association for $1,000. The note pays no interest but will be redeemed for $1539 at maturity. What is the interest rate on the note?

Solution:

$$1000\ (FVIF_{i,5}) = 1539$$

$$FVIF_{i,5} = 1.539$$

From Table I, i = 9%

6. Tom Berry sold a farm for $3,225 per acre. He says he owned the land for 20 years and that the value of the property appreciated at an 11% annual rate. What did Tom originally pay for the land?

Solution:

$$PV_0 = FV_n(PVIF_{i,n}) \quad OR \quad FV_n = PV_0(FVIF_{i,n})$$

$$PV_0 = 3225(.124) \qquad\qquad 3225 = PV_0(8.062)$$

$$PV_0 = \$399.90 \qquad\qquad PV_0 = 3225/8.062 = \$400$$

7. The Blue Fairy has offered to give you $1,000,000 in 20 years. Because of your incredulity, the BF has volunteered to deposit the present value of the $1,000,000 in a trust managed by a bank or insurance company of your choice. How much must the BF deposit if the investment earns 5%? 10%? 20%?

Solution:

$$PV_0 = 1,000,000\ \frac{1}{(1+i)^{20}} = 1,000,000(PVIF_{i,20})$$

$$\text{at } i=5\%,\ PV_0 = 1,000,000\ \frac{1}{(1.05)^{20}} = 1,000,000(.377) = \$377,000$$

$$\text{at } i=10\%,\ PV_0 = 1,000,000\ \frac{1}{(1.10)^{20}} = 1,000,000(.149) = \$149,000$$

$$\text{at } i=20\%,\ PV_0 = 1,000,000\ \frac{1}{(1.20)^{20}} = 1,000,000(.026) = \$26,000$$

8.   Suppose that the average house costs $70,000 in 1980. What annual inflation rate would cause the average house to cost $1,000,000 in the year 2000?

Solution:

$$FV_n = PV_0(FVIF_{i,n})$$

$$1,000,000 = 70,000(FVIF_{i,20})$$

$$FVIF_{i,20} = 1,000,000/70,000 = 14.286$$

From Table I, i would be between 14% and 15%. (It is actually 14.22%).

9.   Lawrence Laboratory's current $0.30 dividend is expected to grow at 25% annually for two years and then at 10% annually. What is the expected dividend in five years?

Solution: Skip

$$FV = .30(1.25)^2(1.10)^3 = .30(FVIF_{.25,2})(FVIF_{.10,3})$$

$$FV = .30(1.563)(1.331) = \$.624$$

10. Stan Hille is eligible for a student loan that will let him borrow $5000 at the bargain rate of 3%. The loan will be repaid in a single payment at the end of four years. Stan plans to invest the funds in a certificate of deposit which earns 8% compounded annually and matures in four years. What will be Stan's net profit on the date the certificate of deposit matures and he repays the loan?

Solution:

The future value of the loan is

$$FV = 5,000(FVIF_{.03,4}) = 5,000(1.126) = \$5,630$$

The future value of the certificate of deposit is

$$FV = 5,000(FVIF_{.08,4}) = 5,000(1.360) = \$6,800$$

Stan's profit in four years is the difference between these two values:

$$Profit = \$6,800 - \$5,630 = \$1,170$$

11. Brenda Jaeger is saving money for her daughter Sara's college education. Sara will begin college in eight years.

a.   If Brenda invests $500 at the end of each of the next eight years, how much will she have when Sara starts college? The interest rate is six percent.

b. What will she have if she makes the eight installments at the beginning of the year instead of the end?

Solution:

a. $FVAN_n = 500(FVIFA_{.06,8}) = 500(9.897) = \$4,948.50$

b. $FVAND_n = 500(FVIFA_{.06,8})(1.06)$

$FVAND_n = 500(9.897)(1.06) = \$5,245.41$

12. Find the present value of the following stream of cash flows discounted at 15%.

End of Year	Cash Flow
0	-$200
1	+$100
2	+$200
3	+$ 50

Solution:

$PV_0 = -200(PVIF_{.15,0}) + 100(PVIF_{.15,1}) + 200(PVIF_{.15,2})$

$+ 50(PVIF_{.15,3})$

$PV_0 = -200(1.000) + 100(.870) + 200(.756) + 50(.658)$

$PV_0 = -200 + 87.0 + 151.2 + 32.9 = \$71.10$

13. One of your weird relatives deposited $10,000 in each of three banks which pay 12% interest. Bank A compounds annually, Bank B compounds semiannually, and Bank C compounds quarterly. If no other deposits or withdrawals occur and the interest rates do not change, how much will your weird relative have on deposit at each bank after five years?

Solution:

$FV_n = PV_0(FVIF_{i,n})$

In Bank A, use i = 12%, n = 5

$FV = 10,000(FVIF_{.12,5})$

$= 10,000(1.762) = \$17,620$

In Bank B, use i = 6%, n = 10

$FV = 10,000(FVIF_{.06,10})$

$= 10,000(1.791) = \$17,910$

In Bank C, use $i = 3\%$, $n = 20$

$$FV = 10,000(FVIF_{.03,20})$$

$$= 10,000(1.806) = \$18,060$$

14. Dolt Briscoe hates Modine Gunch. However, he agreed to marry her for $1,000,000. Modine has invested $200,000 in a savings account earning 10% compounded annually which will eventually reach the required amount. Dolt figures he has a life expectancy of 40 more years and that he is safe. Is he? When should the marriage take place?

Solution:

$$FV_{40} = 200,000(1.10)^{40} = 200,000(FVIF_{0.10,40})$$

Note that $FVIF_{0.10,40} = (FVIF_{0.10,20})(FVIF_{0.10,20})$

$$FV_{40} = 200,000(6.728)(6.728) = 200,000(45.266) = \$9,053,200$$

Modine will have over nine times the million dollars before Dolt's death. Modine should have the $1,000,000 before 20 years. Let

$$FV_n = PV_0(1 + i)^n = PV_0(FVIF_{i,n})$$

$$1,000,000 = 200,000(FVIF_{.10,n})$$

$$FVIF_{.10,n} = 1,000,000/200,000 = 5.000$$

For $i = .10$, $FVIF_{.10,16} = 4.595$ and $FVIF_{.10,17} = 5.054$, so Dolt must marry Modine between 16 and 17 years from today.

15. Assume ordinary annuities with the following information given. Find the missing data.

a.	R = 100,	i = 10%,	n = 3,	FV =	____
b.	R = 100,	i = 10%,	n = 3,	PV =	____
c.	PV= 60,000,	i = 13%,	n = 25,	R =	____
d.	i = 8%,	n = 5,	FV= 20,000,	R =	____
e.	R = 198.71,	i = 10%,	PV= 1221,	n =	____
f.	R = 800,	n = 12,	PV= 4528,	I =	____

Solution:

a. $FVAN_n = R(FVIFA_{i,n}) = 100(3.310) = 331.00$

b. $PVAN = R(PVIFA_{i,n}) = 100(2.487) = 248.70$

c. $PVAN = R(PVIFA_{i,n})$

$$60,000 = R(7.330)$$

$$R = 60,000/7.330 = \$8,185.54$$

d. $FVAN_n = R(FVIFA_{i,n})$

$$20,000 = R(5.867)$$

$$R = 20,000/5.867 = \$3,408.90$$

e. $PVAN = R(PVIFA_{i,n})$

$$1221 = 198.71(PVIFA_{.10,n})$$

$$PVIFA_{.10,n} = 1221/198.71 = 6.145$$

From Table IV, n = 10

f. $PVAN = R(PVIFA_{i,n})$

$$4528 = 800(PVIFA_{i,12})$$

$$PVIFA_{i,12} = 4528/800 = 5.660$$

From Table IV, i = 14%

16.   You are comparing two alternative investments to augment your pension. Do this exercise for your own edification.

A.   Tax-sheltered medium: Take $2,000 of taxable income, invest the full amount at 5% interest at the end of each year for thirty years. At the end of thirty years, pay 40% taxes and see how much is left.

B.   Taxable medium: Pay 40% taxes on the $2,000 of taxable and invest the remaining $1,200 at the end of each year for 30 years. Because income is taxable, the investment will grow by 3% per year. At the end of the 30 years, however, no taxes are due.

Solution:

A.   Tax sheltered investment:

$$FVAN_n = 2,000(FVIFA_{.05,30}) = 2,000(66.439) = 132,878$$

Taxes = .40(132,878) = 53,151.20

Net proceeds = 132,878 - 53,151.20 = $79,726.80

B.   Taxable investment:

$$FVAN_n = 1,200(FVIFA_{.03,30}) = 1,200(47.575) = \$57,090$$

The tax sheltered investment results in a nest egg that is almost 40% larger than the taxable investment.

17.   Jim Rodriguez is borrowing \$50,000 to buy a home. If he pays equal annual installments for 30 years and 8% interest on the outstanding balance, what is the size of his annual payment? What would his payment be if the interest rate were 12%?

Solution:

$$PV = R(PVIFA_{i,n})$$

At 8%, $50,000 = R(PVIFA_{.08,30}) = R(11.258)$

$R = 50,000/11.258 = \$4,441.29$

At 12%, $50,000 = R(PVIFA_{.12,30}) = R(8.055)$

$R = 50,000/8.055 = \$6,207.32$

18.   What is the equal annual installment on a four-year note if the amount borrowed is \$10,000 and the interest rate is 20%? Prepare a table showing the interest paid and the remaining balance at the end of each year.

Solution:

$$PVAN = R(PVIFA_{i,n})$$

$$10,000 = R(PVIFA_{0.20,4}) = R(2.589)$$

$$R = 10,000/2.589 = \$3,862.50$$

Time	Payment	Interest	Principal Reduction	Remaining Principal
0	---	---	---	10,000.00
1	3862.50	2000.00	1862.50	8,137.50
2	3862.50	1627.50	2235.00	5,902.50
3	3862.50	1180.50	2682.00	3,220.50
4	3862.50	644.10	3218.40	2.10

The remaining balance should equal zero. If PVIFA is not rounded off to three places, the installment is \$3,862.89 and the remaining balance in the four years is almost exactly zero.

19.   Ann Hamilton is repaying a loan which currently has a remaining balance of \$20,000. Her next payment of \$4,000 is due in one year, and it will reduce the loan balance to \$18,200. What interest rate is Ann paying?

Solution:

payment = interest + principal reduction

4,000 = interest + (20,000 - 18,200)

interest = 4,000 - 1,800 = 2,200

interest rate = interest/previous balance

= 2,200/20,000 = .11 = 11%

20. Congratulations! You have just won $250,000 in a contest. You have your choice of (1) $25,000 every year for 10 years (at the end of the year), or (2) $125,000 in cash today. The appropriate discount rate is 8%.

Solution:

The present value of the annuity is

$$PVAN = R(PVIFA_{i,n})$$

$$= 25,000(6.710) = \$167,750$$

The annuity is worth more than $125,000.

21. The dean of the college considers Professor X to be totally incompetent and would like to fire him/her. Unfortunately (from the dean's perspective) under the terms of Professor X's contract, the professor cannot be fired for five years. If Professor X's salary will be $30,000 each year (paid at the end of each year), how much will it cost the dean to buy up the contract if the dean thinks Professor X will quit in exchange for 30% of the present value of his/her salary? The discount rate is 8%.

Solution:

$$PVAN = R(PVIFA_{i,n})$$

$$= 30,000(PVIFA_{.08,5}) = 30,000(3.993) = \$119,790$$

The offer should be 30% of $119,790, or .30(119,790) = $35,937.

22. James Smith is an indentured servant. Under his contract, he can buy his freedom for $1,000. If Smith can save $75 at the end of each year and he has nothing invested now, how long will it take for James Smith to become a free man? His investments earn 15%.

Solution:

$$FVAN_n = R(FVIFA_{i,n})$$

$$1000 = 75(FVIFA_{.15,n})$$

$$FVIFA_{.15,n} = 1000/75 = 13.333$$

From Table III, it will take about eight years.

23.   What is the present value of \$10,000 received in 4 years discounted at 20% compounded annually? compounded semiannually? compounded quarterly?

Solution:

For annual compounding, use $i = 20\%$ and $n = 4$

$$PV = \$10,000 \, (PVIF_{.20,4}) = \$10,000(.482)$$

$$PV = \$4,820$$

For semiannual compounding, use $i = 10\%$ and $n = 8$

$$PV = 10,000(PVIF_{.10,8}) = 10,000(.467)$$

$$PV = \$4,670$$
For quarterly compounding, use $i = 5\%$ and $n = 16$

$$PV = 10,000(PVIF_{.05,16}) = 10,000(.458)$$

$$PV = \$4,580$$

24.   You have \$2,000 of income to invest. You have two alternatives:

A.   Pay taxes at 30% on the income and invest the proceeds at 7% after taxes.

B.   Invest in an IRA, which earns 10% and is taxed at 30% on the amount withdrawn after retirement. If you withdraw prior to retirement, you are subject to a 10% penalty (or a 40% total tax).

If you reach retirement age in 25 years, how much do you net after taxes for each alternative if you withdraw your funds in one year? Five years? Twenty five years?

Solution:

A.   tax $= .30(2000) = 600$, leaving $2000 - 600 = 1400$
      one year: $FV = 1400(1.07)^1 = 1400 \, FVIF_{.07,1}$

$$FV = 1400(1.07) = \$1,498.00$$

five years: $FV = 1400(1.07)^5 = 1400 \, FVIF_{.07,5}$

$FV = 1400(1.403) = \$1,964.20$

25 years: $FV = 1400(1.07)^{25} = 1400 \, FVIF_{.07,25}$

$FV = 1400(5.427) = \$7,597.80$

B. Because of the penalty, if you withdraw prior to retirement, you net 60% of the withdrawal. After retirement, you net 70%.

one year: $FV = .60(2000)(1.10)^1 = 1200 \, FVIF_{.10,1}$

$FV = 1200(1.10) = \$1,320.00$

five years: $FV = .60(2000)(1.10)^5 = 1200 \, FVIF_{.10,5}$

$FV = 1200(1.611) = \$1,933.20$

25 years: $FV = .70(2000)(1.10)^{25} = 1400 \, FVIF_{.10,25}$

$FV = 1400(10.835) = \$15,169.00$

25. Willie Wilson plans to borrow \$1,500 at the beginning of each of his four years of college. He will repay the loan in ten equal annual installments at the end of each year starting one year after he graduates. If the interest rate is 8%, how large will the installments be?

Solution:

```
1500  1500  1500  1500  #  R  R  R           R  R
_____>
 0     1     2     3    4  5  6  7  .  .  .   13  14
```

This can be solved in different ways. One way is to find the future value of the four-year \$1,500 annuity due at t = 4 (his graduation date) and set this equal to the present value of a ten-year ordinary annuity of R dollars per year (at t = 4).

$\$1,500(FVIFA_{.08,4})(1.08) = R(PVIFA_{.08,10})$

$\$1,500(4.506)(1.08) = R(6.710)$

$6.710R = \$7299.72$

$R = \$1087.89$

26. Sarah N. Dippity believes the world will end in exactly five years. She has \$200,000 in a Savings and Loan Association earning 6% interest. Sarah wants to withdraw an equal amount at the beginning of each of the next five years and to

have exactly $50,000 left in five years to blow on one huge party just as the world is ending. What should be the size of her withdrawals?

Solution:

The $200,000 is the total present value of the five withdrawals (which are an annuity due) and the $50,000 future lump sum.

R	R	R	R	R	$50,000		withdrawals
0	1	2	3	4	5	-->	time

$200,000 = R(PVIFA_{.06,5})(1.06) + 50,000(PVIF_{.06,5})$

$200,000 = R(4.212)(1.06) + 50,000(.747)$

$200,000 = 4.465R + 37,350$

$4.465R = 200,000 - 37,350 = 162,650$

$R = 162,650/4.465 = \$36,427.77$

27. What is the present value of a perpetuity of $100 per year if the discount rate is 8%?

Solution:

$PVPER = R/i = 100/.08 = \$1,250$

28. What is the effective annual rate of a loan that charges 1.5% interest per month?

Solution:

Interest is compounded m = 12 times per year and the interest rate per month is 1.5%. The effective annual rate is

$i_{eff} = (1 + i_m)^m - 1 = (1 + .015)^{12} - 1 = (1.015)^{12} - 1$

$i_{eff} = 1.1956 - 1 = .1956$ or 19.56%

29. What is the future value in one year of $1,000,000 invested at:

  a. 12% compounded annually?
  b. 12% compounded semiannually?
  c. 12% compounded quarterly?
  d. 12% compounded monthly?
  e. 12% compounded continuously?

Solution:

a. $FV = 1,000(FVIF_{.12,1}) = 1,000,000(1.120) = \$1,120,000$

b. $FV = 1,000,000(FVIF_{.06,2}) = 1,000,000(1.124) = \$1,124,000$

c. $FV = 1,000,000(FVIF_{.03,4}) = 1,000,000(1.126) = \$1,126,000$

d. $FV = 1,000,000(FVIF_{.01,12}) = 1,000,000(1.127) = \$1,127,000$

e. $FV = 1,000,000e^{.12(1)} = 1,000,000(1.127) = \$1,127,000$

The future value increases the more frequently interest is compounded per year. Incidentally, the answers that would be obtained without rounding off the interest factors are:

a. $1,120,000
b. $1,123,600
c. $1,125,509
d. $1,126,825
e. $1,127,497

30.   What is the present value of $20,000 received in five years discounted at

a.   10% compounded annually?
b.   10% compounded semiannually?
c.   10% compounded continuously?

Solution:

a. $PV = 20,000(PVIF_{.10,5}) = 20,000(.621) = \$12,420$

b. $PV = 20,000(PVIF_{.05,10}) = 20,000(.614) = \$12,280$

c. $PV = 20,000\, e^{-.10(5)} = 20,000\, e^{-.5} = 20,000(.6065) = \$12,130$

31.   First National Bank pays 12% compounded continuously and First Bank and Trust pays 12.5% compounded annually. Which bank is paying the higher effective rate?

Solution:

In order to make a fair comparison, convert FNB's continuous rate to an effective annual rate.

$$\text{effective annual rate} = e^i - 1 = e^{.12} - 1$$

$$= 1.1275 - 1 = .1275 \text{ or } 12.75\%$$

The FNB effective annual rate of 12.75% is slightly higher than FB&T's 12.50%.

32.   Rework Problem 18 using the Lotus template accompanying the text. The result
       of your work should be as follows:

```
================================================================================
                            LOAN AMORTIZATION
================================================================================

                             DATE PAYMENTS START
PRINCIPAL       $10,000.00   MONTH (1-12)            12
YEARS                  4.0   YEAR                  1990
RATE                20.00%
PAYMENT          $3,862.89
                             TOTAL INTEREST:    $5,451.56
                             TOTAL PAYMENTS:   $15,451.56
                             AVERAGE PAYMENT:   $3,862.89
                             EFFECTIVE RATE:       20.00%
```

DATE	INTEREST RATE	PAYMENT	INTEREST	PRINCIPAL	BALANCE	CUMULATIVE INTEREST
12-1989					$10,000.00	
12-1990	20.00%	$3,862.89	$2,000.00	$1,862.89	$8,137.11	$2,000.00
12-1991	20.00%	$3,862.89	$1,627.42	$2,235.47	$5,901.64	$3,627.42
12-1992	20.00%	$3,862.89	$1,180.33	$2,682.56	$3,219.08	$4,807.75
12-1993	20.00%	$3,862.89	$643.82	$3,219.08	($0.00)	$5,451.56

33.   The Lotus templates allow you to work problems that would be very tedious if
       done by hand. For an example, do the following problem involving 36 loan
       payments instead of the 4 payments in the problem above.

       Calculate the loan payment and provide a loan amortization table for a $10,000, 36
       month car loan. The interest rate is 15%.

```
                          LOAN AMORTIZATION
```

```
                       DATE PAYMENTS START
PRINCIPAL       $10,000.00   MONTH (1-12)              1
MONTHS                36.0   YEAR                   1990
RATE               15.00%
PAYMENT            $346.65

                       TOTAL INTEREST:      $2,479.52
                       TOTAL PAYMENTS:     $12,479.52
                       AVERAGE PAYMENT:       $346.65
                       EFFECTIVE RATE:         15.00%
```

DATE	INTEREST RATE	PAYMENT	INTEREST	PRINCIPAL	BALANCE	CUMULATIVE INTEREST
12-1989					$10,000.00	
1-1990	15.00%	$346.65	$125.00	$221.65	$9,778.35	$125.00
2-1990	15.00%	$346.65	$122.23	$224.42	$9,553.92	$247.23
3-1990	15.00%	$346.65	$119.42	$227.23	$9,326.69	$366.65
4-1990	15.00%	$346.65	$116.58	$230.07	$9,096.62	$483.24
5-1990	15.00%	$346.65	$113.71	$232.95	$8,863.68	$596.94
6-1990	15.00%	$346.65	$110.80	$235.86	$8,627.82	$707.74
7-1990	15.00%	$346.65	$107.85	$238.81	$8,389.02	$815.59
8-1990	15.00%	$346.65	$104.86	$241.79	$8,147.22	$920.45
9-1990	15.00%	$346.65	$101.84	$244.81	$7,902.41	$1,022.29
10-1990	15.00%	$346.65	$98.78	$247.87	$7,654.54	$1,121.07
11-1990	15.00%	$346.65	$95.68	$250.97	$7,403.57	$1,216.75
12-1990	15.00%	$346.65	$92.54	$254.11	$7,149.46	$1,309.30
1-1991	15.00%	$346.65	$89.37	$257.29	$6,892.17	$1,398.67
2-1991	15.00%	$346.65	$86.15	$260.50	$6,631.67	$1,484.82
3-1991	15.00%	$346.65	$82.90	$263.76	$6,367.92	$1,567.71
4-1991	15.00%	$346.65	$79.60	$267.05	$6,100.86	$1,647.31
5-1991	15.00%	$346.65	$76.26	$270.39	$5,830.47	$1,723.57
6-1991	15.00%	$346.65	$72.88	$273.77	$5,556.70	$1,796.45
7-1991	15.00%	$346.65	$69.46	$277.19	$5,279.50	$1,865.91
8-1991	15.00%	$346.65	$65.99	$280.66	$4,998.84	$1,931.91
9-1991	15.00%	$346.65	$62.49	$284.17	$4,714.67	$1,994.39
10-1991	15.00%	$346.65	$58.93	$287.72	$4,426.95	$2,053.33
11-1991	15.00%	$346.65	$55.34	$291.32	$4,135.64	$2,108.66
12-1991	15.00%	$346.65	$51.70	$294.96	$3,840.68	$2,160.36
1-1992	15.00%	$346.65	$48.01	$298.64	$3,542.04	$2,208.37
2-1992	15.00%	$346.65	$44.28	$302.38	$3,239.66	$2,252.64
3-1992	15.00%	$346.65	$40.50	$306.16	$2,933.50	$2,293.14
4-1992	15.00%	$346.65	$36.67	$309.98	$2,623.52	$2,329.81
5-1992	15.00%	$346.65	$32.79	$313.86	$2,309.66	$2,362.60
6-1992	15.00%	$346.65	$28.87	$317.78	$1,991.87	$2,391.45
7-1992	15.00%	$346.65	$24.90	$321.75	$1,670.12	$2,416.37
8-1992	15.00%	$346.65	$20.88	$325.78	$1,344.34	$2,437.25
9-1992	15.00%	$346.65	$16.80	$329.85	$1,014.49	$2,454.05
10-1992	15.00%	$346.65	$12.68	$333.97	$680.52	$2,466.73
11-1992	15.00%	$346.65	$8.51	$338.15	$342.37	$2,475.24
12-1992	15.00%	$346.65	$4.28	$342.37	($0.00)	$2,479.52

6

Characteristics and Valuation of Long-Term Securities

Long-term debt, preferred stock, and common stock are the major sources of capital for a firm. Chapter 6 focuses on the characteristics and valuation of fixed income securities, namely long-term debt (bonds) and preferred stock.

I.   Long-term debt is a fixed-income security which usually has a specified maturity. Use of long-term debt exposes the firm to financial risk and provides the potential benefits of financial leverage.

    A.   Long-term debt can be classified in a number of ways according to the security, repayment provisions and other features.

        1.   Secured debt issues are called mortgage bonds; unsecured bonds are called debentures.

        2.   Senior debt issues have a higher priority claim to the earnings or assets of the firm than junior issues.

        3.   Debt may be subordinated or unsubordinated. In the event of liquidation or reorganization, claims of subordinated debenture holders are considered only after the claims of unsubordinated debt holders. The debt to which a debenture is subordinated varies from case to case.

    B.   Several special types of long-term debt can be identified.

71

1. <u>Equipment trust certificates</u> are used largely by railroads and trucking companies to purchase specific assets such as rolling stock. Technically, the certificate holders own the equipment and lease it to the firm. Oversight and payments are through a trustee.

2. <u>Collateral trust bonds</u> are backed by securities of other corporations. These are used primarily by holding companies which borrow against their interest in their subsidiaries and then re-lend the funds to the subsidiaries.

3. <u>Income bonds</u> promise to pay interest only if the firm has sufficient income. These are seldom used today.

4. <u>Pollution control bonds</u> and <u>industrial revenue bonds</u> are tax exempt securities issued by local governments for the benefit of a firm which guarantees the bonds.

C. Long-term debt contains a number of standard features and common optional features.

1. An indenture is a legal contract between the issuing firm and the lenders which specifies payment procedures and contains any restrictive covenants intended to enhance the security of the debt issue. Typical restrictions apply to minimum levels of working capital, limitations on dividends, and limitations on additional debt.

2. The Trust Indenture Act of 1939 requires that a trustee represent the debtholders in dealings with the firm. This role is usually performed by a commercial bank or trust company which is responsible for ensuring that all terms of the agreement are upheld.

3. A call feature is an option which allows the firm to redeem or call a debt issue prior to maturity. The call price is higher than the par value by an amount called the call premium. Bonds are most likely to be called when interest rates have declined since the time of issue.

4. A sinking fund provision requires the gradual retirement of a debt issue during its life either through repurchase in the open market, use of the call provision, or by contributions to a sinking fund account. The alternative chosen depends on the relative costs involved.

5. Debt is sometimes convertible at the option of the holder into common stock of the issuing company.

6. The coupon rates on new bonds are normally fixed and chosen so that the bond will sell at or near par value when issued. A few bonds have been issued with floating coupon rates that are pegged to another interest rate such as 91-day Treasury bills.

Original issue discount (OID) bonds are bonds issued with a coupon below prevailing rates and, therefore, are issued at a discount to par. Zero coupon bonds are OID bonds that pay no interest at all.

D.   Debt issues sold to the public usually range in size from $25 to $200 million although large companies occasionally issue larger amounts. Private placements are usually in the $5 to $10 million range.

E.   Long-term debt typically matures in 20 to 30 years although longer and shorter maturities do occur. Any debt with a maturity over 1 year is classified as long-term for accounting purposes.

F.   Most debt issues are traded over-the-counter although some widely traded issues are listed on the major exchanges. The financial press contains information on the secondary debt markets.

G.   Debt issues are rated according to risk. Moody's rates bonds from high to low as Aaa, Aa, A, Baa, Ba, B, Caa, Ca, C. Standard and Poor's uses the designations AAA, AA, A, BBB, BB, B, and so on.

        1.   Higher rated bonds generally carry lower market yields.

        2.   The interest rate spread between ratings is less during prosperity than during recessions.

        3.   Some companies in weak financial positions have issued high yield debt called junk bonds. These junk bonds are rated Ba or lower by Moody's (BB or lower by Standard and Poor's) and typically yield at least 3 percentage points more than high quality corporate bonds.

H.   The use of long-term debt has a number of advantages and disadvantages.

        1.   Tax deductibility of interest provides relatively low cost.

        2.   Financial leverage can increase potential EPS.

        3.   Ownership is not diluted through additional equity issues.

        4.   Financial risk is increased.

        5.   Bond indenture provisions may restrict the firm's flexibility.

II.   The value of an asset is based on the expected future benefits its owner will receive over the life of an asset.

        A.   The value of a financial asset is based on the expected cash returns it will generate.

B.   The capitalization-of-income method of valuation determines the value of an asset as the present value of the stream of future benefits discounted at an appropriate required rate of return.

1.   Algebraically, this approach is

$$V_0 = \frac{R_1}{(1 + k)^1} + \frac{R_2}{(1 + k)^2} + \ ... \ + \frac{R_n}{(1 + k)^n},$$

where R_t is the expected cash return at time t, k is the required rate of return or discount rate, n is the length of the holding period, and V_0 is the value of the asset.

2.   Using summation notation, the value is

$$V_0 = \sum_{t=1}^{n} \frac{R_t}{(1 + k)^t}$$

3.   The required rate of return k on an asset is a function of the asset's risk as well as the risk-free interest rate. If the asset's returns are known with certainty (there is no risk), the investor's required rate of return is the risk-free rate.

C.   The market value of an asset is determined by demand and supply.

1.   The transaction price at which an asset is sold is the market price.

2.   In market equilibrium there is no tendency for the price of an asset to change. However, when investors' required rates of return or expected returns from an asset change, the price should change.

3.   When large numbers of buyers and sellers operate in a market, the market price represents a consensus judgment about an asset or security's worth. If a security is not publicly traded, its value can be approximated by studying the prices of publicly traded firms of similar operating and financial characteristics.

D.   The book value of an asset is its accounting value-- historical acquisition cost minus accumulated depreciation. The book value of an asset does not have any necessary relationship to the market value of an asset.

III.   The value of a bond is the present value of its promised cash flows.

A.   Using the capitalization-of-income method, the value of a bond is

$$P_0 = \frac{I_1}{(1+k_d)^1} + \frac{I_2}{(1+k_d)^2} + \ldots + \frac{I_{n-1}}{(1+k_d)^{n-1}} + \frac{I_n + M}{(1+k_d)^n},$$

where P_0 is the present value of the bond, I_t is the interest payment, n the time to maturity, M the principal payment, and k_d the investor's required rate of return for the bond.

1. Since the interest payments are equal, the value can be expressed using summation notation as

$$P_0 = \sum_{t=1}^{n} \frac{I}{(1+k_d)^t} + \frac{M}{(1+k_d)^n}$$

2. Using present value factors, the value of the bond is

$$P_0 = I(PVIFA_{k_d,n}) + M(PVIF_{k_d,n})$$

3. There is an inverse relationship between a bond's value (P_0) and its required rate of return (k_d).

4. An equal change in the required rate of return changes the value of a long-term bond more than the value of a short-term bond.

B. A perpetual bond, or perpetuity, promises to pay interest indefinitely and has no maturity date.

1. The general valuation formula for a perpetual bond that pays interest (I) per period forever and has a required rate of return k_d is

$$P_0 = \sum_{t=1}^{\infty} \frac{I}{(1+k_d)^t}$$

2. This valuation formula may be simplified to $P_0 = I/k_d$.

C. The yield to maturity of a bond is the expected rate of return earned on a bond purchased at a given price and held to maturity.

1. The yield to maturity (r) is found by solving the following formula for r given values for P_0, I, M, and n.

$$P0 = \sum_{t=1}^{n} \frac{I}{(1+r)^t} + \frac{M}{(1+r)^n}$$

In practice, r may be found by using special bond tables, by using special financial calculators or computer routines, or by using trial and error.

2. An approximation of the yield to maturity can be found with this formula:

$$\text{approximate } r = \frac{I + (M - P_0)/n}{(P_0 + M)/2}$$

where $(M - P_0)$ is the discount (or premium if negative) on the bond, and $(M - P_0)/n$ is the annual amortization of the discount (or premium if negative) for the bond.

3. For zero coupon bonds that pay no interest over their lives, the only payment to holders is the principal payment at maturity. The yield to maturity on a zero coupon bond can be found directly from the relationship

$$P_0 = \frac{M}{(1 + k_d)^n}$$

$$P_0 = M\,(PVIF_{k_d,n})$$

4. The yield to maturity for a perpetual bond is $r = I/P_0$.

5. If sold prior to maturity, the realized rate of return for a bond will generally differ from its yield to maturity. Variation in the market value of a fixed income security (and in realized rates of return) due to fluctuations in interest rate levels is called interest rate risk.

IV. The characteristics of preferred stock place it in an intermediate position between common stock and long-term debt. It is a part of stockholders' equity like common stock; but it is considered a fixed income security like debt and increases the financial leverage of the firm.

A. Dividends on preferred stock are not tax deductible like interest on debt. This makes the effective cost considerably higher than debt and limits the popularity of preferred stock.

B. Preferred stock is so called because it usually has preference over common stock with regard to claims against the firm's earnings, assets, or both.

1. Dividends may not be paid on common stock unless the preferred dividend for the period has been paid.

2. Preferred stock usually has a higher claim (than common stock) against the assets of the company in the event of bankruptcy or liquidation.

C. Preferred stock is characterized by a number of features.

1.   The selling price is the price at which preferred shares are sold to the public.

2.   The par value is the value assigned to the stock by the firm for accounting purposes.

3.   Preferred stock is usually designated by the annual dollar dividend per share.

4.   Recently, some adjustable rate preferred stock has been issued. The dividends on adjustable rate preferred stock are reset periodically and are tied to some interest rates specified in their indentures.

5.   Most preferred stock is cumulative. No common dividend may then be paid unless all unpaid back preferred dividends have been paid.

6.   Most preferred stock is non-participating. Participating preferred shares in increased earnings of the firm.

7.   Although some preferred stock is perpetual with no maturity, many preferred issues have sinking fund provisions which guarantee retirement over a specified period.

8.   Preferred stock may have options of callability and convertibility like long-term debt.

9.   Preferred stock is usually nonvoting although special provisions may give preferred stockholders some voting rights if dividends are in arrears.

10.   Preferred shares are traded both on the major exchanges and over-the-counter.

11.   Utility companies are the most frequent users of preferred stock, although it is often used in mergers and by companies requiring capital which are restricted in their borrowing abilities or suffering from depressed prices of their common stock.

D.   Preferred stock has a number of advantages and disadvantages.

1.   Preferred stock increases financial leverage with less serious consequences in the event of missed dividends than defaulted interest payments.

2.   Preferred stock is expensive when compared to long-term debt because preferred dividends are not a tax deductible expense.

V.   Most preferred stock resembles a perpetuity, promising fixed dividends forever. The value of preferred stock, then, is

$$P_0 = \sum_{t=1}^{\infty} \frac{D_p}{(1+k_p)^t}$$

where D_p, is the fixed dividend per period and k_p is the required rate of return. This valuation formula reduces to $P_0 = D_p/k_p$.

TRUE AND FALSE QUESTIONS

Agree with each of the statements or reject it and modify it so that it is acceptable.

1. Secured debt issues are called mortgage bonds; unsecured bonds are called indentures. *debentures*

2. Income bonds are bonds which guarantee regular interest income to investors.

3. Sinking fund provisions may be met by purchasing bonds in the open market.

4. If a preferred stock is cumulative, no common dividend may be paid until all preferred dividends in arrears have been paid.

5. Preferred stock is frequently more expensive than debt.

6. The value of an asset is the present value of its expected future net income stream discounted at an appropriate discount rate.

7. While the market value of an asset may be above or below book value in the short run, on average book value equals market value.

8. There is an inverse relationship between the value of a bond and its required rate of return.

9. If two bonds with different maturities have the same price and yield to maturity, the short-term bond's price will change less in response to a change in interest rates than the long-term bond's price will change in response to an equal interest rate change.

10. For a perpetual bond, the yield to maturity and coupon yield will be equal.

Answers to True and False Questions

1. Unsecured bonds are called debentures. The legal agreement of a bond issue is called the indenture.

2. Income bonds pay interest only if earnings are sufficient to pay it. Otherwise no obligation exists.

3.   True.

4.   True.

5.   True.

6.   The value of an asset is the present value of its expected future cash flows.

7.   There is no necessary relationship between book and market values.

8.   True.

9.   True.

10.   True.

CHAPTER 6 PROBLEMS

1.   If a perpetual bond pays fixed interest of $80 at the end of each year, what is the value of the bond if the investor's required rate of return is 6%? 8%? 10%?

Solution:

$P_0 = I/k_d$

At 6%, P_0 = 80/.06 = $1,333.
At 8%, P_0 = 80/.08 = $1,000.
At 10%, P_0 = 80/.10 = $800.

2.   Suppose that General Motors (GM) has two issues of preferred stock outstanding, one paying a dividend of $3.75 per year and the other paying $5.00 annually. If the $3.75 GM preferred is selling for $35.50 and the $5.00 GM preferred is selling for $47.50, what are the required rates of return for each issue?

Solution:

$k_p = D_p/P_0$

For the $3.75 preferred, k_p = 3.75/35.50 = .1056 or 10.56%.
For the $5.00 preferred, k_p = 5.00/47.50 = .1053 or 10.53%.

3.   If Crown Zellerbach has a 9 1/4% bond which matures at the end of the year 2005, what will its value be at the end of 1985 if the yield to maturity at that time is 8%? 11%?

Solution:

$$P_0 = \sum_{t=1}^{n} \frac{I}{(1 + k_d)^t} + \frac{M}{(1 + k_d)^n}$$

$$P_0 = I(PVIFA_{k_d,n}) + M(PVIF_{k_d,n})$$

At 8%, $P_0 = 92.50(PVIFA_{.08,20}) + 1000(PVIF_{.08,20})$

$$= 92.50(9.818) + 1000(.215) = 908.16 + 215$$
$$= \$1,123.16.$$

At 11%, $P_0 = 92.50(PVIFA_{.11,20}) + 1000(PVIF_{.11,20})$

$$= 92.50(7.963) + 1000(.124) = 736.58 + 124$$
$$= \$860.58.$$

4.   Suppose Pacific Gas and Electric (PGE) has a 9 3/8% bond outstanding that matures in 30 years. If the bond has an annual coupon and is selling for 72 7/8 (72 7/8% of $1,000 or $728.75),

a.   what is the exact yield to maturity?

b.   what is the yield to maturity calculated using the approximation formula?

Solution:

a. $$P_0 = \sum_{t=1}^{n} \frac{I}{(1+i)^t} + \frac{M}{(1+i)^n}$$

$$P_0 = I(PVIFA_{i,n}) + M(PVIF_{i,n})$$

The yield to maturity may be found using trial and error. Since the bond is selling for a discount, its yield to maturity is above the coupon rate.

Trial 1: i = 14% P_0 = 93.75(7.003) + 1000(.020) = $676.53
Trial 2: i = 12% P_0 = 93.75(8.055) + 1000(.033) = $788.16
Trial 3: i = 13% P_0 = 93.75(7.496) + 1000(.026) = $728.75

The yield to maturity is 13%.

b. $$i = \frac{I + (M - P_0)/n}{(M + P_0)/2}$$

$$i = \frac{93.75 + (1000 - 728.75)/30}{(1000 + 728.75)/2} = \frac{93.75 + 9.04}{864.375} = \frac{102.79}{864.375}$$

$$= .1189 \text{ or } 11.89\%$$

5.   a.   What would Walt Eckardt have to pay for a 10-year, $1000 face value bond with a 6.5% annual coupon if its yield to maturity is 8.0%?

     b.   If the yield increases to 9.0% one year after Walt purchases the bond, what is the new bond value and Walt's realized rate of return if he sells it?

     c.   If the yield drops to 7.0% one year after Walt buys the bond, what is the bond value and realized rate of return?

Solution:

a.
$$P_0 = \sum_{t=1}^{n} \frac{I}{(1+k_d)^t} + \frac{M}{(1+k_d)^n}$$

$$P_0 = I(PVIFA_{k_d,n}) + M(PVIF_{k_d,n})$$

$$P_0 = \$65.00(PVIFA_{.08,10}) + \$1,000(PVIF_{.08,10})$$

$$P_0 = \$65.00(6.710) + \$1,000(.463)$$

$$P_0 = \$436.15 + \$463.00 = \$899.15$$

b.
$$P_1 = \$65.00(PVIF_{.09,9}) + \$1,000(PVIF_{.09,9})$$

$$P_1 = \$65.00(5.995) + \$1000(.460)$$

$$P_1 = \$389.68 + \$460.00 = \$849.68$$

$$\text{Realized return} = \frac{P_1 - P_0 + I}{P_0}$$

$$\text{Realized return} = \frac{\$849.68 - \$899.15 + \$65.00}{\$899.15}$$

$$\text{Realized return} = \frac{\$15.53}{\$899.15} = .0173 \text{ or } 1.73\%$$

c.
$$P_1 = \$65.00(PVIFA_{.07,9}) + \$1,000(PVIF_{.07,9})$$

$$P_1 = \$65.00(6.515) + \$1,000(.544)$$

$$P_1 = \$423.48 + \$544.00 = \$967.48$$

$$\text{Realized return} = \frac{P_1 - P_0 + I}{P_0}$$

$$\text{Realized return} = \frac{\$967.48 - \$899.15 + \$65.00}{\$899.15}$$

$$\text{Realized return} = \frac{\$133.33}{\$899.15} = .1483 \text{ or } 14.83\%$$

6.   What is the value of a share of Wisconsin Gas $2.55 preferred stock if the investor's required rate of return is

   a.   8%?
   b.   11%?
   c.   14%?

Solution:

$$P_0 = D_p/k_p$$

   a. $P_0 = 2.55/.08 = \$31.875$.
   b. $P_0 = 2.55/.11 = \$23.18$.
   c. $P_0 = 2.55/.14 = \$18.21$.

7.   A zero coupon bond with a current market price of $480.30 promises to pay $1000 at maturity in six years. What is the yield-to-maturity?

Solution:

$$P_0 \quad = \quad M(PVIF_{k_d,n})$$

$$480.30 = 1000 \, (PVIF_{k_d,n})$$

$$PVIF_{k_d,n} = .4803$$

$$\text{for } n = 6, \, k_d = 13\%$$

8.   International Velvet Company has $20 million of 12% debentures outstanding. After tax net income is $3 million. The bond indenture requires that the debt coverage ratio as measured by times-interest-earned be maintained at 2.5 or better. Their tax rate is 40%.

   a.   What is their times-interest-earned ratio?

   b.   How much additional debt at 10% could they have without violating the restrictive covenant?

Solution:

   a.   Net income = (Earnings before taxes)(1 - t)

   $3 million = (Earnings before taxes)(.6)

   Earnings before taxes = $5 million

   EBIT = EBT + Interest = $5 million + .12($20 million) = $7,400,000

TIE = EBIT/Interest = 7,400,000/2,400,000 = 3.08

b.   Maximum allowable interest occurs when 2.5 x interest = EBIT so maximum allowable interest = 7,400,000/2.5 = 2,960,000.

Maximum allowable interest - current interest = allowable increase

2,960,000 - 2,400,000 = 560,000

$5,600,000 of additional debt at 10% can be incurred without exceeding the restrictive covenant.

9.   Lesscan B. More, Inc. is considering whether to purchase bonds yielding 14% or preferred stock yielding 10%. Their tax rate is 40%.

a.   What after tax yield can they expect from the bonds?

b.   What after tax yield can they expect from the preferred?

Solution:

a.   After tax yield = (Before tax yield) (1-t) = 14% x .6 = 8.4%

b.   Dividends received by a corporation are 70% exempt from taxation.

After tax yield   = before tax yield - taxes

= before tax yield - before tax yield x .30 x tax rate

= 10% - (10% x .30 x .40) = 8.8%

7

Characteristics and Valuation of Common Stock

Chapter 7 describes the various characteristics of common stock and develops various models which can be used to value this security.

I. Common stock is the permanent long-term financing of the firm and represents the true residual ownership of the firm.

   A. Three balance sheet accounts are associated with the common stock of the company.

      1. The common stock account contains the par value of common stock issued.

      2. Contributed capital in excess of par, also known as additional paid in capital or sometimes capital surplus, represents the difference between the proceeds of issuing the common stock and the par value of the stock.

      3. Retained earnings represents the accumulation of net income which has been reinvested in the business.

      4. The book value per share is found by dividing total common stockholders' equity by the number of shares outstanding.

   B. Common stockholders have a number of general rights.

1. All common stockholders have a right to share equally on a per share basis in any dividends paid and in assets remaining after senior claims are satisfied in liquidation.

2. Unless the stock is specifically nonvoting, common stockholders have the right to vote on stockholder matters.

3. Some common stock carries a preemptive right which gives stockholders the right to share proportionately in any new stock sold.

C. Firms may create more than one class of common stock. Nonvoting stock may be issued to maintain control.

D. Several actions may be taken by management which affect common stockholders.

1. In order to attract more purchasers to a stock, the stock may be split to create a larger number of lower valued shares.

a. A stock split of itself has no value.

b. A stock split may increase the wealth of existing shareholders if the lower price increases market activity so that the overall market value of the common stock increases.

c. A stock split does not change any accounts. The par value and number of shares outstanding are the only changes.

2. A reverse stock split may be used to reduce the number of shares and increase the market price of the stock if it is felt that the stock is so low priced as to discourage investors because of commission costs or a low-price stigma.

3. A stock dividend is an increase in the number of shares outstanding.

a. Stock dividends are usually much smaller than stock splits in terms of the increase in shares.

b. Stock dividends involve a transfer from retained earnings to common stock and additional paid in capital.

c. Unless market activity is increased due to the reduced price, stock dividends have no real value.

4. Firms sometimes repurchase their own stock, which is known as treasury stock. Management may repurchase stock if they feel it is a good investment if the stock is undervalued. Repurchased stock may also be available for use in mergers or executive stock option plans. By issuing debt and repurchasing stock, the firm can increase its leverage and accomplish a financial restructuring. Share repurchases

can dispose of excess cash and can also be a tactic to help reduce takeover risk.

E. There are a number of advantages and disadvantages to common stock financing.

    1. Common stock financing is flexible since no fixed obligation exists.

    2. Common stock financing can reduce the financial leverage and lower the cost of capital if leverage is excessive.

    3. Issuing common stock dilutes earnings per share until the new investments pay off.

    4. Flotation costs make issuing common stock relatively expensive.

II. The valuation of common stock is based on the same principles underlying the valuation of bonds or preferred stock: the value of common stock is the capitalized (discounted) value of the stock's expected stream of returns.

A. The valuation of common stock is more difficult than other securities.

    1. The returns from owning common stock are a mixture of dividends and capital gains (or losses).

    2. Dividends are not constant and typically are expected to grow over time.

    3. The future returns from common stock are much more uncertain than the returns from bonds and preferred stock.

B. The present value of a share of common stock is based on the expected dividends received during the investor's holding period and the expected selling price at the end of the holding period.

    1. The one-period model is

$$P_0 = \frac{D_1}{(1 + k_e)^1} + \frac{P_1}{(1 + k_e)^1}$$

where k_e is the required rate of return, D_1 is the expected dividend at time 1, and P_1 is the expected selling price at time 1.

    2. The two-period dividend valuation model is

$$P_0 = \frac{D_1}{(1 + k_e)^1} + \frac{D_2}{(1 + k_e)^2} + \frac{P_2}{(1 + k_e)^2}$$

where the investor receives dividends for two periods and the stock is sold at the end of the second period.

3.   The n-period dividend valuation model is

$$P_0 = \frac{D_1}{(1 + k_e)^1} + \frac{D_2}{(1 + k_e)^2} + \ldots + \frac{D_n}{(1 + k_e)^n} + \frac{P_n}{(1 + k_e)^n}$$

or

$$P_0 = \sum_{t=1}^{n} \frac{D_t}{(1 + k_e)^t} + \frac{P_n}{(1 + k_e)^n}$$

where the investor receives dividends for n periods and P_n is the selling price after n periods.

C.   The value of the stock at the end of the holding period (P_n) depends on the value of future dividends after time n. The value of common stock at time zero (P_0) depends directly on dividends received during the holding period and indirectly on dividends after the holding period (through their effect on P_n). The general dividend model simply establishes the value of a firm's common stock to the investor to be equal to the present value of the expected future dividend stream.

$$P_0 = \sum_{t=1}^{\infty} \frac{D_t}{(1 + k_e)^t}.$$

III.   The general dividend valuation model can be simplified if the dividends follow a regular pattern. Three patterns considered here are constant growth, zero growth, and above-normal growth.

A.   The constant growth dividend valuation model assumes that dividends grow at a constant rate g per period forever.

1.   The future dividend at time t is $D_t = D_0(1 + g)^t$.

2.   The general dividend model becomes

$$P_0 = \sum_{t=1}^{\infty} \frac{D_0(1 + g)^t}{(1 + k_e)^t}$$

3.   Assuming $k_e > g$, this model reduces to

$$P_0 = \frac{D_1}{k_e - g}$$

where D_1 is the next period's dividend, $D_1 = D_0(1+g)$.

4. This constant growth dividend model is usually referred to as the Gordon model.

5. If P_0, g, and D_1 are given, the Gordon model can be used to find the investor's required rate of return on equity $k_e = (D_1/P_0) + g$. The investor's required rate of return is equal to the expected dividend yield (D_1/P_0) plus the capital gains yield (g).

B. The constant dividend model is the simplest dividend valuation model.

1. If the dividends are expected to be constant forever, the general valuation model is

$$P_0 = \sum_{t=1}^{\infty} \frac{D}{(1+k_e)^t}$$

2. The value is the present value of a perpetuity, $P_0 = D/k_e$. This can also be visualized as a special case of the Gordon model where g = 0.

C. The above-normal growth model allows rapid above-normal growth of dividends for a period of time after which the growth rate of dividends is lower.

1. Assume that dividends grow at a rate g_1 over the first m years and that dividends grow at a rate g_2 after that. The value of the stock can be expressed as

$$P_0 = \sum_{t=1}^{m} \frac{D_0(1 + g_1)^t}{(1 + k_e)^t} + \frac{P_m}{(1 + k_e)^m}$$

This gives the present value of the first m dividends plus the present value of the value of the stock at end of year m (P_m).

2. Because dividends will grow at a constant rate g_2 beginning in year m + 1, the Gordon model may be used to find the stock value in year m: $P_m = D_{m+1}/(k_e - g_2)$. By substituting this into the equation for P_m above, the above-normal growth dividend valuation model becomes

$$P_0 = \sum_{t=1}^{m} \frac{D_0(1+g_1)^t}{(1 + k_e)^t} + \frac{1}{(1 + k_e)^m} \left(\frac{D_{m+1}}{k_e - g_2}\right)$$

TRUE AND FALSE QUESTIONS

Agree with each of the statements or reject it and modify it so that it is acceptable.

1.   A 2 for 1 stock split doubles shareholders' wealth.

2.   The future returns from common stock are generally more uncertain than the future returns from bonds and preferred stock.

3.   In the Gordon model, the dividend growth rate is assumed to be zero.

4.   In the Gordon model, the value of the stock is inversely related to the dividend growth rate.

5.   In the general dividend valuation model, the value of a firm's common stock is equal to the present value of the expected dividend stream.

6.   In the basic Gordon model, the dividend is assumed to grow at a rate g, and because the stock value increases as dividends increase, the stock price should also grow at a rate g.

Answers to True and False Questions

1.   Unless market activity is increased resulting in a real increase in the total value of the stock, a split has no value.

2.   True.

3.   The growth rate is assumed to be constant.

4.   All other things held constant, the value of common stock and the dividend growth rate are positively related.

5.   True.

6.   True.

CHAPTER 7 PROBLEMS

1.   You bought a stock at $27 per share and sold it at $34. While you owned it you received a $2 per share dividend. What was your percentage return?

Solution:

$$\text{Percentage return} = \frac{\text{selling price - cost + dividend}}{\text{cost}}(100)$$

$$= \frac{34 - 27 + 2}{27}(100) \quad = \quad 33.3\%$$

2. Aardvark Exterminators Inc. has the following financial statements and other information.

Balance Sheet (millions)

Current assets	$ 80	Current liabilities	$30
Other assets	100	Long-term debt	40
		Preferred stock	20
		Common stock ($2 par)	10
		Additional paid in capital	35
		Retained earnings	45
Total assets	$180	Total liabilities and capital	$180

Income Statement (millions)		Miscellaneous	
Sales	$82	Preferred dividends	$2 million
Cost of goods sold	51	Common dividends	$5 million
EBIT	31	Market price common	$ 33/share
Interest expense	4		
EBT	27		
Taxes @ 37%	10		
Net Income	$17		

Find the following:

a. Earnings per share common
b. Price-earnings ratio on common
c. Book value of common
d. Interest coverage
e. Dividend yield on common
f. Dividend payout ratio

Solution:

a. $\text{EPS} = \dfrac{\text{Earnings available to common}}{\text{No. of shares}}$

$= \dfrac{\text{Net income-Preferred dividends}}{\text{Common stock account/par value}}$

$= \dfrac{17,000,000-2,000,000}{10,000,000/2} = \$3$

b.   Price/Earnings = 33/3 = 11x

c.
Common Stock	$10 million
+ Additional paid in capital	35 million
+ Retained Earnings	45 million
Total Common Equity	$90 million
(No. of shares	5 million
Book Value per share	$18

d.   Interest coverage = EBIT/Interest = 31/4 = 7.75x

e.   Dividend yield = dividend/price = 1/33 = 3.03%

f.   Payout ratio = dividends per share/earnings per share = 1/3 = 33.33%

3.   Suppose Aardvark (Problem 4) declares a 10% stock dividend. Show the changes in the stockholders' equity portion of their balance sheet.

Solution:

Preferred Stock	20	
Common Stock	11	= 10 + (.5 million new shares)($2 par)
Additional Paid in Capital	50.5	= 35 + (new shares)(market price-par)
Retained Earnings	28.5	= 45 - (new shares)(market price)
Total	110.0	

4.   Fred Easton can buy shares of Amalgamated Rockbuster for $25.00. Fred expects dividends to be $2.00 in one year and $4.00 in two years, and he expects to sell the stock for $28.00 in two years. Should Fred buy any Rockbuster? Fred feels that 20% is the appropriate discount rate.

Solution:

$$P_0 = \frac{D_1}{(1 + k_e)} + \frac{D_2}{(1 + k_e)^2} + \frac{P_2}{(1 + k_e)^2}$$

$$P_0 = 2.00(PVIF_{.20,1}) + 4.00(PVIF_{.20,2}) + 28.00(PVIF_{.20,2})$$

$$= 2.00(.833) + 4.00(.694) + 28.00(.694)$$

$$= 1.666 + 2.776 + 19.432 = \$23.87$$

Fred should not invest in Rockbuster because its estimated value of $23.87 per share is less than the $25.00 he would have to pay for it.

5.   Blather Broadcasting's current dividend per share of $3.20 is expected to grow at 5% per year indefinitely. What is the value of a Blather share if the required rate of return is

a.   10%?
b.   12%?
c.   14%?

Solution:

Next year's dividend should be 5% greater than the current dividend.

$D_1 = D_0(1 + g) = 3.20(1.05) = 3.36$

a. $P_0 = \dfrac{D_1}{ke-g} = \dfrac{3.36}{.10-.05} = \dfrac{3.36}{.05} = \$67.20$

b. $P_0 = \dfrac{3.36}{.12-.05} = \dfrac{3.36}{.07} = \$48.00$

c. $P_0 = \dfrac{3.36}{.14-.05} = \dfrac{3.36}{.09} = \$37.33$

6.   Union Aquatech Company has a current share price of $11.00 and an expected dividend of $0.66 in one year.

a.   If the dividend growth rate is 7%, what is the required rate of return for Union Aquatech shares?

b.   If the required rate of return is 11.5%, what dividend growth is expected if the Gordon model fits this stock?

Solution:

a. $k_e = (D_1/P_0) + g = (.66/11.00) + .07 = .06 + .07 = .13$ or 13%

b. $k_e = (D_1/P_0) + g$

$.115 = (.66/11.00) + g$

$g = .115 - .06 = .055$ or 5.5%

7.   Because of a lucky breakthrough, Philadelphia Pharmaceutical's current dividend per share of $2.00 is expected to grow at a very high 32% per year for the next three years and then to grow at a more normal 6% per year. What is the value of a Philadelphia share if the investors' required rate of return is 20%?

Solution:

The above-normal growth dividend valuation model may be used. The current value of the common stock would be the present value of the first three dividends plus the present value of the stock in three years (which is found with the Gordon model).

Present value of the first three years dividends:

Year	Dividend	$PVIF_{.20,n}$	Present value of D_t
1	$2.00(1 + .32)^1 = 2.64$	.833	2.20
2	$2.00(1 + .32)^2 = 3.48$	.694	2.42
3	$2.00(1 + .32)^3 = 4.60$	.579	2.66
			7.28

Value of stock at end of year three, $P_3 = D_4/(k_e - g_2)$
$D_4 = D_3(1 + g_2) = 4.60(1 + .06) = 4.88$

$P_3 = 4.88/(.20 - .06) = 4.88/.14 = 34.86$

Present value of $P_3 = P_3/(1 + k_e)^3$

$PV(P_3) = 34.86/(1 + .20)^3 = 34.86(PVIF_{.20,3}) = 34.86(.579) = 20.18$

Value of common stock $= P_0 = PV$(first three dividends) $+ PV(P_3)$

$P_0 = 7.28 + 20.18 = \$27.46$

8.   Rework Problem 7 using the Lotus template accompanying the text. The result is:

```
================================================================
        STOCK VALUATION    --    DISCOUNTED CASH FLOW METHOD
================================================================


REQUIRED RATE OF RETURN             20.00%
CURRENT DIVIDEND (D0)               $2.00
CONSTANT GROWTH RATE                 6.00%
STOCK VALUE
      UNDER ZERO GROWTH                            $10.00
      UNDER CONSTANT GROWTH                        $15.14
      UNDER SUPER-NORMAL GROWTH                    $27.44
```

8

Analysis of
Risk and Return

This chapter defines risk, looks at alternative measures of risk, and then considers the relationships between risk and security returns and values. The concepts in this chapter are very important ideas for financial theory and practice.

I.   Several important concepts are utilized when evaluating risky securities or investments.

   A.   Risk refers to the potential variability of returns from a project. A project is considered risk-free if the dollar returns from a project are known with certainty.

   B.   Probability distributions are the probabilities of every particular outcome. These probability distributions may be objectively or subjectively determined.

   C.   The expected value of a variable is a weighted average of individual possible outcomes:

$$\hat{R} = \sum_{j=1}^{n} R_j P_j$$

where

$\hat{R}$ = expected value
R_j = outcome for the jth case, where there are n possible outcomes
P_j = probability of occurrence of the jth outcome

95

D.   The standard deviation is an absolute measure of risk. It is defined as the square root of the weighted average of the squared deviations of individual observations from the expected value.

$$\sigma = \sqrt{\sum_{j=1}^{n} (R_j - \hat{R})^2 P_j}, \text{ where } \sigma = \text{standard deviation}$$

If the outcomes are normally distributed, the actual outcome should be between $\pm$ 1 standard deviation of the expected value 68.26 percent of the time, and between $\pm$ 2 standard deviations of the expected value 95.44 percent of the time.

E.   The coefficient of variation is a <u>relative</u> measure of risk. It is defined as the ratio of the standard deviation to the expected value

Coefficient of variation $= v = \sigma/\hat{R}$

F.   Risk often is an increasing function of time with early returns being less risky than distant returns.

II.   The evaluation of risk becomes more difficult when the firm diversifies and invests in more than a single investment.

A.   A <u>portfolio</u> is simply a collection of assets. When the firm is viewed as a portfolio of assets, it may not be appropriate to consider independently the risk of an individual project. When using a portfolio viewpoint, an individual project should be evaluated on the basis of its own returns and also in the light of the relationship between its returns and the returns of other existing or potential projects.

B.   The <u>portfolio effect</u> is the risk reduction accompanying diversification. The size of the portfolio effect is inversely related to the correlation between a project's cash flows and those of the rest of the firm: a project having cash flows or returns with a low (or perhaps even negative) correlation to the rest of the firm's returns or cash flows will reduce the overall risk of the firm more than a project with a higher correlation.

III.   The expected return and risk of a portfolio is a function of the characteristics of the securities (or assets) comprising the portfolio and how much of each security is in the portfolio.

A.   The expected return from a portfolio $(\hat{R}_p)$ is a weighted average of the expected returns from the individual securities.

$$\hat{R}_p = W_A \hat{R}_A + W_B \hat{R}_B$$

and $W_A + W_B = 1$

B.   The standard deviation of the portfolio return (r_p) is used as a measure of risk. For a two-security portfolio, the standard deviation is

$$p = \sqrt{W_A^2 \sigma_A^2 + W_B^2 \sigma_B^2 + 2W_A W_B \rho_{AB} \sigma_A \sigma_B}$$

where σ_A^2 and σ_B^2 are the variances of returns for securities A and B, σ_A and σ_B are their standard deviations, and ρ_{AB} is the correlation coefficient of return between securities A and B.

C.   The lower the correlation coefficient (ρ_{AB}), the greater will be the risk reduction accompanying diversification between A and B.

D.   An efficient portfolio has the highest possible return for a given standard deviation and has the lowest possible standard deviation for a given expected return.

    1.   The efficient frontier is the set of risk-return choices associated with efficient portfolios. On a graph of expected return on one axis and standard deviation of return on the other axis, the efficient frontier is a curved line.

    2.   The capital market line is a straight line starting at the risk-free rate and tangent to the efficient frontier. The capital market line shows the risk and return caused by lending at the risk-free rate and investing in the risky portfolio associated with the tangency on the efficiency frontier or borrowing at the risk-free rate and investing in that risky portfolio.

IV.   A well-known method for analyzing the relationship between risk and return for risky assets is the Capital Asset Pricing Model (CAPM).

A.   There are two types of risk inherent in all securities: systematic risk and unsystematic risk.

    1.   Systematic risk is the portion of the variability of a security's returns caused by factors affecting the market as a whole.

        a.   Some of these general factors include interest rate changes, changes in purchasing power, or changes in investor expectations about the economy.

        b.   Systematic risk is nondiversifiable; diversifying across more securities does not affect systematic risk.

    2.   Unsystematic risk is caused by factors unique to the firm.

        a.   Firm-specific factors such as management's decisions and capabilities, strikes, the availability of raw materials, some government actions and regulations, and foreign competition, can affect unsystematic risk.

b.   To the extent these factors are unique to the firm and do not affect the market as a whole, the unsystematic risk inherent in individual securities can be eliminated through diversification.

B.   In a well-diversified portfolio, the relevant risk to be considered for each individual security is its systematic risk (because the unsystematic risk has already been diversified away).

C.   The security market line (SML) shows the relationship between the required rate of return for a security and its systematic risk.

The SML may be expressed as

$$k_j = r_f + \theta_j$$

where k_j is security j's required rate of return, r_f is the risk-free rate, and θ_j is the risk premium required by investors.

D.   The risk-free rate (r_f) is composed of two parts, a real return and a premium for expected inflation. Changes in inflationary expectations would change the risk-free rate in the SML for all securities and change their required rates of return.

E.   The most commonly used measure of the systematic risk of a security is its beta.

1.   The beta is determined by the standard deviation of the security's returns (σ_j), the standard deviation of the returns from the market portfolio (σ_m), and the correlation between the security and market returns (ρ_{jm}).

2.   Security j's beta is equal to the covariance of the returns on security j and the market portfolio divided by the variance of the returns on the market portfolio.

$$b_j = \text{Covariance}_{j,m} / \text{Variance}_m$$

which is also equal to

$$b_j = \rho_{jm}\sigma_j \sigma_m / \sigma_m^2$$

3.   In practice, beta may be computed as the slope of a regression line where the return on security j is the dependent variable and the return on the market portfolio is the independent variable.

$$R_j = a_j + b_j R_m + e_j$$

where R_j is the return for security j, R_m is the return of the market index, a_j is the constant term in the regression, b_j is the regression coefficient (slope term) which is the beta for security j, and e_j is a random error term. This equation is estimated from a number of observations over a historical period. A regression equation of the form above is called security j's characteristic line.

4.   The beta of a portfolio of n securities is a weighted average of the individual security betas

$$b_p = \sum_{j=1}^{n} W_j b_j$$

5.   Using beta as a systematic risk measure, the risk premium for a security is proportional to its beta:

$$\theta_j = b_j(k_m - r_f)$$

The security market line gives the required rate of return for security j (k_j) and is written as

$$k_j = r_f + b_j(k_m - r_f)$$

where k_m is the required rate of return for the market, r_f is the risk-free rate and, of course, b_j is the beta for security j.

F.   The capital asset pricing model may be used to estimate the cost of equity capital for the firm. Given estimates of r_f, k_m, and b_j, the security market line (SML) equation immediately above is used to find k_j.

G.   The capital asset pricing model (CAPM) is based on a number of crucial assumptions.

1.   These assumptions are:

a.   Investors hold well-diversified portfolios and are influenced by the systematic risk (rather than total risk) of each security.

b.   Securities are actively traded in a competitive market, where information is freely available.

c.   Investors can borrow and lend at the risk-free rate which is constant over time.

d.   There are no brokerage charges for buying and selling securities.

e.   There are no taxes.

        f.   Investors are risk averse.

        g.   All investors have homogeneous expectations regarding the expected returns, variances, and correlations of returns among all assets.

    2.   While these assumptions are restrictive, the CAPM has been used somewhat successfully in the face of violations of assumptions.

    3.   In practical applications of the CAPM, some of the major problems encountered are:

        a.   Estimating expected future market returns.

        b.   Determining an appropriate risk-free rate.

        c.   Determining the best estimate of an asset's future beta.

        d.   Assuming that systematic risk is the relevant risk measure in some instances where unsystematic risk should not be ignored.

        e.   Betas are frequently unstable over time.

        f.   There is some evidence that required returns are determined by factors in addition to the risk-free rate of interest and the systematic risk of a security.

V.   A model known as the Arbitrage Pricing Theory (APT) uses multiple risk factors to explain security returns.

    A.   The APT postulates that the rate of return on a security is a linear function of a set of economic factors common to all securities.

$$k_j = \hat{k}_j + b_{1j} \ (\text{factor 1}) \ + b_{2j} \ (\text{factor 2}) \ + \ldots$$
$$+ \ b_{mj} \ (\text{factor m}) + e_j$$

where

    k_j = actual (realized) return on security j

    $\hat{k}_j$ = expected return on security j

    (factor i)   = deviation of the ith factor return from its expected value.

    b_j = sensitivity of security j returns to factor i

e_j = random error term for security j
(with an expected value equal to 0)

B.   Unlike the CAPM which assigns a risk premium based on a single factor (a security's beta), the APT assigns several risk premia equal to the product of the expected return on the factor times the sensitivity of the security's returns to the corresponding factor.

C.   The APT does not specify what risk factors should be used in determining security returns. Empirical studies have used the unanticipated charges in

1.   industrial production

2.   inflation

3.   bond default risk premiums, and

4.   the slope of the yield curve

VI.   Risk of failure is not necessarily captured by risk measures that focus on return variability (total variability measured by a standard deviation or coefficient of variation or systematic variability measured by a beta).

A.   For undiversified investors, risk of failure is especially relevant.

B.   If a failing firm goes into bankruptcy, it suffers costs including:

1.   The loss of funds that occurs when assets are sold at distressed prices during liquidation,

2.   The legal fees and selling costs incurred when a firm enters bankruptcy proceedings, and

3.   The opportunity costs of funds unavailable to investors during extended bankruptcy proceedings.

VII.   In addition to diversification, there are many other methods that financial managers use to reduce the risk of their resource allocation decisions.

A.   Acquisition of additional information can reduce the risk arising from the lack of information.

1.   There are many examples of this in marketing, production, and finance. Firms will "test market" a new product before making a larger commitment. Oil companies have well designed strategies for exploring and developing oil fields. Companies often pay a bond rating agency to rate a prospective new bond issue so they will have

a better idea about the interest rate before they finally issue the bond.

> 2. Additional information is costly. A firm should be willing to invest in additional information as long as the marginal value of that information exceeds its marginal cost.

B. Hedging can limit the risk associated with fluctuations in the value of an investment position. A hedge is accomplished by taking a position by buying or selling a futures (or forward) contract to offset an investment position.

> 1. A futures contract is a standardized contract, traded on an organized exchange, to buy or sell a fixed quantity of a defined commodity at a set price in the future.

> 2. A forward contract is a contractual agreement between two parties to exchange a commodity at a set price in the future. Unlike a futures contract, forward contracts are not traded on an organized exchange and there is the risk that one party to the contract will not perform as promised.

> 3. Option contracts give the buyer the right (but not the obligation) to buy or sell a commodity at a specific price.

> 4. Futures markets exist for many commodities, including minerals (copper, gold, silver and crude oil), agricultural commodities (corn, wheat, live hogs, cotton, and cattle), and financial instruments (Treasury Bills, Treasury Bonds, foreign currencies, commercial paper, and stock indexes such as Standard and Poor's 500 Stock Index).

C. Insurance, gaining control over the operating environment, and limiting use of firm

> 1. For a certain periodic cost (the insurance premium) insurance companies will assume the consequences of many specific risks.

> 2. Controlling the operating environment (such as buying a source of raw materials, getting exclusive dealerships, or harassing competitors with lawsuits) can be attempted to reduce risk.

> 3. Highly specialized, firm-specific assets might be avoided because they reduce the firm's flexibility.

TRUE AND FALSE QUESTIONS

Agree with each of the statements or reject it and modify it so that it is acceptable.

1.   A riskless security should have an expected rate of return of zero.

2.   The standard deviation is defined as $\quad \sigma = \sum_{j=1}^{n} (R_j - \hat{R})^2 P_j$

3.   The expected portfolio return and standard deviation of the portfolio return are weighted averages of the individual security expected returns and standard deviations.

4.   The portfolio standard deviation is directly related to the correlation coefficients between securities.

5.   Systematic risk cannot be eliminated through diversification.

6.   Changes in the level of interest rates are one source of unsystematic risk.

7.   The characteristic line shows the relationship between the required rate of return for a security and its systematic risk.

8.   Beta, a commonly used systematic risk measure, is the covariance between a security's return and the market return divided by the variance of the market return.

9.   A portfolio beta is a weighted average of its individual security betas.

10.   According to the security market line, the required rate of return for a security is equal to the risk-free rate plus a risk premium that is proportional to the security's beta.

Answers to True and False Questions

1.   The risk premium for a riskless security should be zero and its expected return should be equal to the risk-free rate of return.

2. $\sigma = \sqrt{\sum_{j=1}^{n} (R_j - \hat{R})^2 P_j}$

3.   The expected portfolio return is a weighted average of the individual security expected returns. However, the portfolio standard deviation is a weighted average of the individual security standard deviations only if the securities are perfectly correlated ($\rho = +1.0$). When the correlations are less than 1.0, the portfolio standard deviation is less than the weighted average of individual security standard deviations.

4.   True.

5.   True.

6.   Changing interest rates would affect all securities and therefore would be part of nondiversifiable or systematic risk.

7.   The security market line shows the relationship between the required rate of return and systematic risk. The characteristic line is a regression with the security returns as the dependent variable and the market returns as the independent variable.

8.   True.

9.   True.

10.   True.

CHAPTER 8 PROBLEMS

1.   Joe Carreras owns a piece of property which has the following distribution of returns:

Probability	Return
.1	5.00%
.2	7.50%
.4	10.00%
.3	12.50%

a.   What is the expected return on Joe's property?

b.   Compute the standard deviation.

c.   Compute the coefficient of variation.

Solution:

R_j	P_j	R_jP_j	$(R_j\text{-}\hat{R})$	$(R_j\text{-}\hat{R})^2$	$(R_j\text{-}\hat{R})^2P_j$
5.00	.1	0.50	-4.75	22.5625	2.25625
7.50	.2	1.50	-2.25	5.0625	1.01250
10.00	.4	4.00	0.25	.0625	.02500
12.50	.3	3.75	2.75	7.5625	2.26875
	1.0	9.75			5.56250

$$\hat{R} = \sum_{j=1}^{4} R_jP_j = 9.75\%$$

b. $\sigma = \sqrt{\sum_{j=1}^{4} (R_j - \hat{R})^2 P_j} = \sqrt{5.5625} = 2.3585\%$

c.   Coefficient of variation = $v = \sigma/\hat{R} = 2.3585 / 9.75 = .242$

2.   An investment has an expected return of 30% and a standard deviation of 20%. If the returns are normally distributed,

   a.   what is the probability of a negative return?

   b.   what is the probability of a return below 30%?

   c.   what is the probability of a return above 50%?

Solution:

   a.   Probability of a return less than zero = $P(R < 0)$

   The critical $Z = \dfrac{R - \hat{R}}{\sigma} = \dfrac{0 - 30}{20} = -1.5$

   $P(R < 0) = R(Z < -1.50) = .067$

   b. $Z = \dfrac{R - \hat{R}}{\sigma} = \dfrac{30 - 30}{20} = 0$

   $P(R < 30) = P(Z < 0) = .50$

   c. $Z = \dfrac{R - \hat{R}}{\sigma} = \dfrac{50 - 30}{20} = 1.0$

   $P(R > 50) = P(Z > 1.0) = .159$

3.   Terry Robinson is investing in four securities with the following expected returns:

Security	Expected Return (%)
W	16
X	15
Y	26
Z	12

   a.   If Terry invests 40% of her money in Security W, 30% in X, 20% in Y, and 10% in Z, what is the expected portfolio return?

b.   If Terry invests 10% in W, 20% in X, 30% in Y, and 40% in Z, what is the portfolio return?

c.   How could Terry earn the highest possible and lowest possible returns?

Solution:

a. $\hat{R} = \displaystyle\sum_{i=1}^{4} W_i \hat{R}_i = .40(16)+.30(15)+.20(26)+.10(12) = 17.3\%$

b. $\hat{R} = \displaystyle\sum_{i=1}^{4} W_i \hat{R}_i = .10(16)+.20(15)+.30(26)+.40(12) = 17.2\%$

c. If Terry invested 100% of her funds in Y, the expected return would be 26%. 100% invested in Z results in a 12% expected return.

4.   Two securities have the following expected returns and standard deviations:

	Security 1	Security 2
Expected return	.12	.20
Standard deviation	.08	.30

If you invest 40% of your money in Security 1 and 60% of your money in Security 2:

a.   What is your expected portfolio return?

b.   What is your portfolio standard deviation if the correlation coefficient is +1.0, +.05, 0.0, -0.5, and -1.0?

Solution:

a. $\hat{R}_p = W_1 \hat{R}_1 + W_2 \hat{R}_2 = .4(.12) \quad + .6(.20) \quad = .168$

b. $\sigma_p = \sqrt{W_1^2 \sigma_1^2 + W_2^2 \sigma_2^2 + 2 W_1 W_2 \rho_{12} \sigma_1 \sigma_2}$

For $\rho_{12} = 1.0$: $\sigma = \sqrt{(.4)^2(.08)^2+(.6)^2(.30)^2+2(.4)(.6)(1.0)(.08)(.30)}$

$= \sqrt{.001024 + .0324 +.01152} = \sqrt{0.044944} = .2120$

For $\rho_{12} = 0.5$: $\sigma = \sqrt{(.4)^2(.08)^2+(.6)^2(.30)^2+2(.4)(.6)(.5)(.08)(.30)}$

$= \sqrt{.039184} = .1979$

For ρ_{12} = 0: $\sigma = \sqrt{(.4)^2(.08)^2 + (.6)^2(.30)^2 + 2(.4)(.6)(0)(.08)(.30)}$

$= \sqrt{.033424} = .1828$

For ρ_{12} = -0.5: $\sigma = \sqrt{(.4)^2(.08)^2 + (.6)^2(.30)^2 + 2(.4)(.6)(-.5)(.08)(.30)}$

$= \sqrt{.027664} = .1663$

For ρ_{12} = -1.0: $\sigma = \sqrt{(.4)^2(.08)^2 + (.6)^2(.30)^2 + 2(.4)(.6)(-1.0)(.08)(.30)}$

$= \sqrt{.021904} = .1480$

5. New Mexico Mining Company has a standard deviation on its common stock of 60% and a correlation with market returns of 0.65. The market's standard deviation and expected return are 15% and 14%, respectively, and the risk-free rate of return is 8%.

   a.   What is New Mexico Mining's beta?

   b.   Calculate New Mexico Mining's expected rate of return.

Solution:

   a. $b_j = \rho_{jm}\sigma_j\sigma_m / \sigma_m^2$

        $b_j = .65(60\%)(15\%) / (15\%)^2 = 2.60$

   b. $k_j = r_f + b_j (k_m - r_f)$

        $k_j = 8\% + 2.60(14\% - 8\%)$

        $k_j = 8\% + 15.6\% = 23.6\%$

6. Sharon Conn has invested 50% of her portfolio in Atlantic Richfield, 20% in Coca Cola, and 30% in Union Pacific. Assume that the betas for Atlantic Richfield, Coca Cola, and Union Pacific are 1.20, 0.85, and 1.30, respectively. What is her portfolio beta?

Solution:

$$b_p = \sum_{j=1}^{n} W_j b_j$$

$b_p = (.50)(1.20) + (.20)(0.85) + (.30)(1.30) = 1.16$

7. Abqaiq Baking expects to pay \$2.40 dividend next year (D_1 = 2.40) and the dividend is expected to grow at 4% annually. Abqaiq has an estimated standard deviation of .24, the market portfolio has a standard deviation of .12, the market expected return is .13 and the risk-free rate is .05. The correlation between Abqaiq and market returns is 0.8.

    a.   What is Abqaiq's beta?

    b.   What is the required rate of return?

    c.   What is the value of a share of stock?

    Solution:

    a. $b = \rho_{jm}\sigma_j\sigma_m/\sigma_m^2$ = .8(.24)(.12)/(.12)^2 = 1.6

    b. $k_j = r_f + b_j(k_m-r_f)$ = .05 + 1.6(.13-.05) = .05 + .128 = .178

    c. $P = \dfrac{D_1}{k\text{-}g} = \dfrac{2.40}{.178-.04} = \dfrac{2.40}{.138} = \$17.39$ per share.

8. Consider the following information about two securities.

Security	Expected Return	Std. Deviation	Beta	% Invested (W)
OHV	10%	20%	.85	.30
Turbo	12%	28%	1.15	.70

    a.   Compute the expected portfolio return.

    b.   If the returns of the two securities have a correlation of 0.50, compute its portfolio standard deviation.

    c.   Compute the beta of the portfolio.

    Solution:

    a. $\hat{R}_p = W_1\hat{R}_1 + W_2\hat{R}_2 = .30(.10) + .70(.12) = .114$

    b. $\sigma_p = \sqrt{W_1^2\sigma_1^2 + W_2^2\sigma_2^2 + 2W_1W_2\rho_{12}\sigma_1\sigma_2}$

    $\sigma_p = \sqrt{(.3)^2(.20)^2 + (.7)^2(.28)^2 + 2(.3)(.7)(.5)(.20)(.28)}$

    $\sigma_p = \sqrt{.0036 + .038416 + .01176} = \sqrt{.053776} = .232$

    c. $b_p = W_1b_1 + W_2b_2$

    $b_p = .3(.85) + .7(1.15) = 1.06$

9.   David Brown has $12,000 invested in American Cyanamid, $15,000 in Gannett Company, and $3,000 in Texas International. If American Cyanamid has a beta of 1.05, Gannett a beta of .85, and Texas International a beta of 1.30, what is David's portfolio beta?

Solution:

The total portfolio is $12,000 + $15,000 + $3,000 = $30,000. The portfolio weights are:

American Cyanamid: W_1= 12,000/30,000 = 0.40
Gannett Company: W_2= 15,000/30,000 = 0.50
Texas International: W_3= 3,000/30,000   = 0.10

The portfolio beta is

$$b_p = W_1 b_1 + W_2 b_2 + W_3 b_3$$

$$b_p = .40(1.05) \quad + .50(.85) \quad + .10(1.30) \quad = 0.975$$

9

Capital Budgeting and Cash Flow Analysis

Chapter 9 provides an overview of the capital budgeting process and shows how to estimate the relevant cash flows associated with an investment project.

I.   Capital expenditure decisions can be the most complex decisions facing the firm's management.

    A.   Capital budgeting is the process of planning for purchases of assets whose returns are expected to continue beyond one year.

    B.   A capital expenditure is a cash outlay which is expected to generate a flow of future cash benefits. Normally, a capital project is one with a life of more than one year.

    C.   Capital budgeting models are used to evaluate a wide variety of capital expenditure decisions, including:

        1.   investments in assets to expand an existing product line or to enter a new line of business.

        2.   replacement of an existing capital asset.

        3.   expenditures for an advertising campaign.

        4.   expenditures for research and development.

        5.   investments in permanent increases in inventory or receivables levels.

      6.   investments in education and training.

      7.   refunding an old bond issue with new bonds paying a lower interest rate.

      8.   leasing decisions.

      9.   merger and acquisition decisions.

   D.   The firm's <u>cost of capital</u> is the overall cost of funds which are supplied to the firm. The cost of capital is also called the investors' required rate of return, because it is the minimum rate of return which must be earned on the capital invested in the firm. The required rate of return helps provide a basis for evaluating capital investment projects.

   E.   Projects under consideration may be independent of each other or have some types of interdependencies.

      1.   An independent project is one whose acceptance or rejection has no effect on other projects under consideration.

      2.   Two projects are mutually exclusive if one or the other can be accepted, but not both.

      3.   A contingent project is one whose acceptance is contingent upon the adoption of one or more other projects.

      4.   One additional complication is capital rationing, which occurs when the firm has a limited total amount of dollars available for investment and the outlay for profitable investments exceeds this limit. On the other hand, when the firm has sufficient funds available to invest in all profitable projects, we say the firm is operating without a funds constraint.

II.   The basic framework for capital budgeting is widely employed.

   A.   Economic theory demonstrates that the firm should expand its output until marginal revenue equals marginal cost.

   B.   In capital budgeting, the firm should invest in its most profitable projects first and should continue accepting projects as long as the last project's rate of return exceeds the marginal cost of funds to the firm.

   C.   Some practical problems are encountered when using this capital budgeting model.

      1.   All capital projects may not be known to the firm at one time. Changing markets, technology, and corporate strategies can make some current proposals obsolete and make new ones profitable.

2.   The behavior of the marginal cost of capital may be difficult to determine. This topic is discussed extensively later in the text.

3.   Estimates of future costs and revenues can be made subject to varying degrees of uncertainty.

D.   The capital budgeting process can be broken into four steps. (The first two are discussed in this chapter and the last two are in the following chapter).

1.   Generating capital investment project proposals.

2.   Estimating cash flows.

3.   Evaluating alternatives and selecting projects to be implemented.

4.   Reviewing or post-auditing prior investment decisions.

III.   The initial step in the capital budgeting process is generating capital investment project proposals.

A.   The process of soliciting and evaluating investment proposals varies greatly among firms.

B.   Investment projects can be classified as:

1.   projects generated by growth opportunities in existing product lines or new lines.

2.   projects generated by cost reduction opportunities.

3.   projects required to meet legal requirements and health and safety standards.

C.   The size of an investment proposal frequently determines who has authority to approve the project. A very large outlay might require approval of the corporation president or board of directors and successively smaller outlays can be authorized by lower and lower levels of management.

D.   If an investment decision is critical and must be made fast, a lower level manager can approve it or it can by- pass the normal time-consuming review process to reach the appropriate responsible manager as fast as possible.

IV.   Estimating the cash flows associated with investment projects is crucial to the capital budgeting process. The cash flows associated with a project are the basis for evaluation rather than the project's accounting profits.

A.   Cash flows should be measured on an incremental basis. The cash flow stream for a project is the difference between the cash flows to the firm with the project compared to the cash flows to the firm without adopting the project.

B.   Cash flows should be measured on an after-tax basis.

C.   All the indirect effects of a project should be included in the cash flow estimates. For example, increases in cash balances, receivables, and inventory necessitated by a capital project should be included in the project's net investment.

D.   Sunk costs should not be considered since sunk costs result from previous decisions, they are not truly incremental costs.

E.   Resources should be measured in terms of their opportunity costs. The opportunity costs of resources are the cash flows they would generate if not used in the project under consideration.

V.   The net investment (NINV) is the cash outlay for a project (usually at time zero).

A.   A four-step procedure for estimating the net investment is

Step 1   Asset cost
            + Shipping costs
            + Installation costs   = $ xxx
      plus:

Step 2   Increase in net working capital
            Cash, receivables, inventories)   = $ xxx
      minus:

Step 3   Proceeds on sale of old asset   = $ xxx
      plus or
      minus:

Step 4   Taxes due on old asset if sold for profit
or   - Tax savings if old asset sold for loss   = $ xxx

Net Investment   = $ xxx
                                                                     ====

B.   Some projects involve outlays over more than one year. The NINV for a multiple-period investment is the present value of the series of outlays discounted at the firm's cost of capital.

VI. The future net cash flows (NCF) are easily computed:

A.   1. $NCF = \Delta EAT + \Delta Dep$ where

NCF = net cash flow

ΔEAT = change in earnings after tax, and
ΔDep = change in depreciation

B.   The change in net income after tax is

$\Delta EAT = \Delta EBT(1 - t)$

where

ΔEBT = change in earnings before tax, and
t = tax rate

C.   The change in earnings before tax is $\Delta EBT = \Delta R - \Delta 0 - \Delta D$ where

$\Delta R = R_2 - R_1$ = change in revenues

R_2 – revenues with project

R_1 = revenues without project

$\Delta 0 = 0_2 - 0_1$ = change in cash operating costs

0_2 = cash operating costs with project

0_1 = cash operating costs without project

$\Delta Dep = Dep_2 - Dep_1$ = change in depreciation

Dep_2 = depreciation with project

Dep_1 = depreciation without project

D.   Based on these definitions, two useful expanded versions of the basic NCF equation are

$$NCF = (\Delta R - \Delta 0 - \Delta Dep)(1 - t) + \Delta Dep$$

$$NCF = [(R_2-R_1)-(0_2-0_1)-(Dep_2-Dep_1)](1-t) + (Dep_2-Dep_1)$$

VII.   There are two potential cash flows at the end of a project's life.

A.   Cash inflow due to the incremental salvage must be included at the end of the project. The incremental salvage is the difference between the salvage with the project and without the project. There will be taxes due or saved when an asset is sold for more or less than book value.

B.   Recovery of net working capital can be a cash inflow. There are no tax
       consequences of liquidating working capital.

VIII. It is important to note that interest charges were not considered in estimating a
       project's net cash flows. This was done so that measures of the value of a
       project (in the next chapter) can be constructed independent of how a project is
       financed. Furthermore, if interest charges are deducted from cash flows and then
       the remaining cash flows are discounted to adjust for the time value of money,
       this would constitute a double counting of the time value of money when
       evaluating the value of an asset.

IX.   Federal income taxes figure prominently in the cash flows from capital budgeting
       projects.

       A.   The Investment Tax Credit (ITC) was abolished by the Tax Reform Act of
              1986. An investment tax credit reduces the net outlay for a capital project
              and, when used, is a stimulus to investment.

       B.   Depreciation is the allocation of the cost of an asset over more than one
              year.

              1.   For tax purposes, depreciation charges affect the cash flows of the
                     firm.

                     Cash flow = Net income after taxes + Depreciation

              With a 34% tax rate, an additional $1.00 depreciation charge will reduce
              earnings before taxes by $1.00, reduce taxes by $.34, reduce net income
              after taxes by $.66, and increase the period's cash flow by $.34.

              2.   For tax purposes, depreciation charges are calculated using the
                     Modified Accelerated Cost Recovery System, which is usually called
                     the Modified ACRS. This system assigns depreciable assets into one
                     of several property classes.

Recovery Period and Asset Class	Property Included in Class
3-year	A small class of short-lived assets including some special tools, some tractors, and race- horses (over 2 years old)
5-year	Automobiles, light trucks, heavy general purpose trucks, buses, oil drilling equipment, information systems, certain semiconductor, textile, chemical, electronic, and manufacturing equipment, dairy and breeder cattle

7-year*   Most manufacturing equipment, railroad track, office furniture and equipment, railroad cars and locomotives, airplanes, amusement parks, and mining equipment

10-year   Vessels, barges, petroleum refining equipment, railroad tank cars, some manufacturing equipment

15-year   Electric generation and distribution systems, cement manufacturing equipment, nuclear power plants, natural gas pipelines, billboards, sewage treatment plants, telephone distribution plants

20-year   Most public utility property, sewer pipes, railroad structures

27.5-year, Straight-line class   Residential rental property

31.5-year, Straight-line class   Non-residential real property such as offices

*Most equipment is contained in the 7-year class.

  3.   Under the Modified ACRS, the depreciable basis of an asset is usually equal to the purchase price plus installation and shipping charges.

  4.   If you are not familiar with the Modified ACRS depreciation method, you should review the Appendix to this chapter in the Study Guide summarizing straight- line, sum-of-the-years' digits, double declining balance, and 150% declining balance depreciation.
        The Modified ACRS is an adaptation of the 200% and 150% declining balance methods. For all of the asset classes using 200% or 150% declining balance depreciation above, a half-year convention is used. This means that the Internal Revenue Service assumes that an asset is placed in service in the middle of the year and that only one half of the first year's depreciation is allowed in year 1. For example, for 5-year property, only one half of a year's depreciation will be allowed in year 1 and one-half year's depreciation will be in year 6. A switchover from declining balance depreciation to straight-line depreciation is made late in the depreciable life of the asset whenever the straight-line charge exceeds the declining balance charge. Salvage value is ignored in calculating ACRS depreciation.
        Because the calculations for the Modified ACRS depreciation can be tedious, the following table shows the percentage depreciation allowed each year during an asset's life (rounded to the nearest .01%).

Depreciation Percentages for ACRS Property Classes

Year	3-year 200% DB	5-year 200% DB	7-year 200% DB	10-year 200% DB	15-year 150% DB	20-year 150% DB	Year
1	33.33%	20.00%	14.29%	10.00%	5.00%	3.750%	1
2	44.45	32.00	24.49	18.00	9.50	7.219	2
3	14.81	19.20	17.49	14.40	8.55	6.677	3
4	7.41*	11.52*	12.49	11.52	7.70	6.177	4
5		11.52	8.93*	9.22	6.93	5.713	5
6		5.76	8.92	7.37	6.23	5.285	6
7			8.93	6.55*	5.90*	4.898	7
8			4.46	6.55	5.90	4.522	8
9				6.56	5.91	4.462*	9
10				6.55	5.90	4.461	10
11				3.28	5.91	4.462	11
12					5.90	4.461	12
13					5.91	4.462	13
14					5.90	4.461	14
15					5.91	4.462	15
16					2.95	4.461	16
17						4.462	17
18						4.461	18
19						4.462	19
20						4.461	20
21						2.231	21

*switchover to straight-line

5. For residential real property (in the 27.5-year, straight-line class) and for nonresidential real property (in the 31.5-year, straight-line class), the depreciation charges depend on the month of the first year in which the property is place in service.

6. The Modified ACRS recovery periods are generally shorter than the expected economic life for an asset. After the ACRS recovery period, no depreciation charge is available.

X. (Appendix to Chapter 9) The most common depreciation methods besides ACRS are the straight-line method and declining balance methods. These methods, as well as the sum-of-the-years'- digits methods are easily summarized.

A. In the straight-line depreciation method, the annual depreciation charge is

$$\text{Annual depreciation amount} = \frac{\text{Cost - Estimated salvage value}}{\text{Estimated economic life (years)}}$$

B. The declining balance amount allows the firm to take a percentage depreciation amount for the first year depreciation amount that is greater than straight-line. Then this percentage is applied to the remaining undepreciated amount in subsequent years.

1.   Three common versions of declining balance depreciation are the 200 percent declining balance (double declining balance), 150 percent declining balance, and 125 percent declining balance.

2.   Tax laws have permitted a switch from declining balance to straight-line when the latter results in larger depreciation charges. This can happen near the end of the asset's life.

3.   With declining balance, the salvage value is not deducted from the cost of the asset when calculating depreciation charges. However, the asset cannot be depreciated below its reasonable salvage value.

C.   In the sum-of-the-years'-digits method, annual depreciation charges are computed by multiplying a declining fraction times the asset's original cost (minus salvage value). The denomination of the fraction is the sum from 1 to n where n is the life of the asset. The numerator of the fraction is n the first year, n-1 the second year, on down to 1 the last or nth year. For example, if the asset's life is 4 years, the denominator is $1+2+3+4 = 10$. The depreciation fraction is 4/10 the first year, 3/10 the second year, 2/10 the third year, and finally, 1/10 the last year.

TRUE AND FALSE QUESTIONS

Agree with each of the statements or reject it and modify it so that it is acceptable.

1.   If Investment B can be made only after Investment A is made, then the two investments are mutually exclusive.

2.   A decision to keep the old machine or replace it with a new one can be a mutually exclusive decision.

3.   The president of the firm ordinarily accepts or rejects investment proposals regardless of their size.

4.   MACRS stands for Modified Accelerated Cost Recovery System.

5.   If an old asset has been fully depreciated to zero and is sold for less than original cost, there is no tax liability because the asset has been written off.

6.   For capital budgeting purposes, interest paid is not deducted when finding a project's future net cash flows.

7.   Because a business has no choice about paying taxes, taxes are generally ignored in evaluating capital projects.

8.   Given the same revenues and costs, a larger depreciation charge would result in a smaller net income and a larger net cash flow.

9. Such costs are an important component of the net investment outlay in many capital budgeting decisions.

10. If the tax rate is 40 percent, an additional one dollar depreciation charge results in a sixty cent net cash flow.

Answers to True and False Questions

1. Investment B is contingent upon Investment A.

2. True.

3. Presidential (or board) approval might be required for very large investments, but authority to accept or reject smaller projects is normally delegated to lower management levels.

4. True.

5. Taxes are due on the gain over current book value (zero) at the ordinary tax rate.

6. True.

7. Taxes must be deducted to find the net cash flow.

8. True.

9. Sunk costs should not be considered since they result from previous decisions and are not truly incremental costs.

10. The net cash flow will be the tax rate times the additional depreciation charge, or only forty cents. In the basic equation NCF $= (\Delta R - \Delta 0 - \Delta Dep)(1 - t) + \Delta Dep$, let ΔR and $\Delta 0$ be zero:

$$NCF = -\Delta Dep(1 - t) + \Delta Dep = t\Delta Dep = .40(\$1)$$
$$= \$.40$$

CHAPTER 9 PROBLEMS

1. McCoin Company is considering a new machine which would increase annual revenues by $100,000, increase annual cash operating expenses by $40,000, and increase depreciation charges by $20,000 per year. If McCoin is in the 40 percent tax bracket, what annual net cash flows result from this investment?

Solution:

NCF $= \Delta EAT + \Delta Dep = (\Delta R - \Delta 0 - \Delta Dep)(1 - t) + \Delta Dep$

$= (100{,}000 - 40{,}000 - 20{,}000)(1 - .4) + 20{,}000$

$= 40{,}000(.6) + 20{,}000$

$= 24{,}000 + 20{,}000 = \$44{,}000$

2.   Consolidated Construction bought a small crane ten years ago for $140,000. The crane is being depreciated over a 15 year life to a salvage value of $20,000. Consolidated pays taxes equal to 48% of ordinary income and 30% of capital gains. What is the tax liability (or saving) if the crane is sold not for

    a. $60,000

    b. $44,000

    c. $92,000

    d. $160,000

Solution:

This asset was installed before 1981 and is being depreciated using a pre-ACRS straight-line method.

Annual depreciation $= (\$140{,}000 - \$20{,}000)/15 = \$8{,}000$
Current book value $= \$140{,}000 - \$8{,}000(10) = \$60{,}000$

    a.   The selling price equals the current book value so there is no tax consequence.

    b.   Tax saving equals the ordinary rate times the loss.
        Tax saving $= .48(60{,}000 - 44{,}000) = .48(16{,}000) = \$7{,}680$.

    c.   Tax liability equals the ordinary rate times the gain.
        Tax $= .48(92{,}000 - 60{,}000) = .48(32{,}000) = \$15{,}360$.

    d.   Tax liability equals the ordinary rate times (140,000 - 60,000) plus the capital gains rate times (160,000 - 140,000).
        Tax $= .48(140{,}000 - 60{,}000) + .30(160{,}000 - 140{,}000)$
             $= .48(80{,}000) + .30(20{,}000) = 38{,}400 + 6{,}000 = \$44{,}400$.

3.   What is the after-tax cash proceeds for Consolidated Construction for each selling price above in Problem 2?

Solution:

a. $60,000

b. $44,000 + $7,680 = $51,680

c. $92,000 - $15,360 = $76,640

d. $160,000 - $44,400 = $115,600

4.   Barry's Texas Bar BQ bought a light duty truck in 1988 for $60,000. What will be Barry's future depreciation charges. Modified ACRS rules apply.

Solution:

Barry's truck is classed as 5-year property and there is no investment tax credit. The depreciation charges will be:

Year	ACRS rate	Rate x $60,000
1	20.00%	$12,000
2	32.00	19,200
3	19.20	11,520
4	11.52	6,912
5	11.52	6,912
6	5.76	3,456
7 and after	0.00	0

5.   Charlie's Cleaners is considering replacing its old equipment with more efficient equipment. The old equipment was purchased five years ago for $90,000. New equipment would cost $135,000 plus $5,000 for shipping and $10,000 for installation. Under Modified ACRS rules, the new equipment is classed as 7-year property. The new equipment has a 10-year economic life and a $10,000 estimated salvage. The new equipment would have no effect on sales, but it would reduce annual cash operating expenses by $10,000 (from $60,000 per year with the old equipment to $50,000 with the new). No change in receivables or inventories will be associated with the new equipment. Charlie's Cleaners is in the 34 percent tax bracket.

a.   If Charlie buys the new equipment, what is his net investment at time zero?

b.   If Charlie buys the new equipment, what is his net cash flow for each of the next ten years?

Solution:

a.   The net investment can be found in four steps.

Step 1	Asset cost	$135,000		
	Shipping cost	5,000		
	Installation cost	10,000		$150,000
Step 2	Increase in working capital	0	+	0
Step 3	Proceeds on sale of old assets (before tax)	30,000	-	30,000
Step 4	Tax saving on old asset sold at loss*	10,200	-	10,200
	Net Investment			$109,800

*The book value on the old equipment = 90,000 - 5(6,000) = $60,000.
The loss was 60,000 - 30,000 = $30,000.
The tax saving was .34(30,000) = $10,200.

b.   The annual depreciation on the old equipment for each year is 90,000/15 = $6,000.

The depreciable basis of the new equipment is $150,000. The depreciation charges for the new equipment will be:

Year	ACRS Rate	Depreciation ACRS Rate x $150,000
1	14.29%	$21,435
2	24.49	36,735
3	17.49	26,235
4	12.49	18,735
5	8.93	13,395
6	8.92	13,380
7	8.93	13,395
8	4.46	6,690
9	0.00	0
10	0.00	0

The annual operating net cash flows are computed with the formula

$$NCF = (\Delta R - \Delta O - \Delta Dep)(1 - t) + \Delta Dep$$

$$NCF = [(R_2 - R_1) - (O_2 - O_1) - (D_2 - D_1)](1 - t) + (D_2 - D_1)$$

For all 10 years, $\Delta R = 0$

For all 10 years, $\Delta O = 50,000 - 60,000 = -\$10,000$

The depreciation charge is

Year	new depr	old depr	ΔDep
1	$21,435	$6,000	$15,435
2	36,735	6,000	30,735
3	26,235	6,000	20,235
4	18,735	6,000	12,735
5	13,395	6,000	7,395
6	13,380	6,000	7,380
7	13,395	6,000	7,395
8	6,690	6,000	690
9	0	6,000	-6,000
10	0	6,000	-6,000

Year $(\Delta R - \Delta O - \Delta Dep)(1 - t) + \Delta Dep = \Delta EAT + \Delta Dep = NCF$

Year							
1	(0 + 10,000 - 15,435)(1-.34)	+ 15,435	= -3,587	+ 15,435	= 11,848
2	(0 + 10,000 - 30,735)(1-.34)	+ 30,735	= -13,685	+ 39,735	= 17,050
3	(0 + 10,000 - 20,235)(1-.34)	+ 20,235	= -6,755	+ 20,235	= 13,480
4	(0 + 10,000 - 12,735)(1-.34)	+ 12,735	= -1,805	+ 12,735	= 10,930
5	(0 + 10,000 - 7,395)(1-.34)	+ 7,395	= 1,719	+ 7,395	= 9,114
6	(0 + 10,000 - 7,380)(1-.34)	+ 7,380	= 1,729	+ 7,380	= 9,109
7	(0 + 10,000 - 7,395)(1-.34)	+ 7,395	= 1,719	+ 7,395	= 9,114
8	(0 + 10,000 - 690)(1-.34)	+ 690	= 6,145	+ 690	= 6,835
9	(0 + 10,000 + 6,000)(1-.34)	- 6,000	= 10,560	- 6,000	= 4,560
10	(0 + 10,000 + 6,000)(1-.34)	- 6,000	= 10,560	- 6,000	= 4,560

In addition, in year 10, Charlie's Cleaners will sell the new equipment for salvage for $10,000, which will be taxed at 34%. So the year 10 net cash flow will be

$$NCF_{10} = 4,560 + 10,000 - .34(10,000) = \$11,160.$$

6.   Using each of the following depreciation methods, compute the annual depreciation charge, and year-end book value, for an asset with a $100,000 original cost, a zero salvage value, and an expected useful life of five years.

a. Straight-line

b. Sum-of-the-years'-digits

c. Double declining balance

d. 150 percent declining balance

Solution:

Let D_i = depreciation in year i, and

BV_i = book value at end of year i

a. Straight-line

$$1 + 2 + 3 + 4 + 5 = 15$$

$$D = \frac{100{,}000 - 0}{5} = 20{,}000$$

$D_1 = 20{,}000$ $BV_1 = 100{,}000 - 20{,}000 = 80{,}000$
$D_2 = 20{,}000$ $BV_2 = 80{,}000 - 20{,}000 = 60{,}000$
$D_3 = 20{,}000$ $BV_3 = 60{,}000 - 20{,}000 = 40{,}000$
$D_4 = 20{,}000$ $BV_4 = 40{,}000 - 20{,}000 = 20{,}000$
$D_5 = 20{,}000$ $BV_5 = 20{,}000 - 20{,}000 = 0$

b. Sum-of-the-years'-digits

$D_1 = (5/15)(100{,}000) = 33{,}333$ $BV_1 = 100{,}000 - 33{,}333 = 66{,}667$
$D_2 = (4/15)(100{,}000) = 26{,}667$ $BV_2 = 66{,}667 - 26{,}667 = 40{,}000$
$D_3 = (3/15)(100{,}000) = 20{,}000$ $BV_3 = 40{,}000 - 20{,}000 = 20{,}000$
$D_4 = (2/15)(100{,}000) = 13{,}333$ $BV_4 = 20{,}000 - 13{,}333 = 6{,}667$
$D_5 = (1/15)(100{,}000) = 6{,}667$ $BV_5 = 6{,}667 - 6{,}667 = 0$

c. Double declining balance (fraction = 200% (1/5) = .40)

$D_1 = .40(100{,}000) = 40{,}000$ $BV_1 = 100{,}000 - 40{,}000 = 60{,}000$
$D_2 = .40(60{,}000) = 24{,}000$ $BV_2 = 60{,}000 - 24{,}000 = 36{,}000$
$D_3 = .40(36{,}000) = 14{,}400$ $BV_3 = 36{,}000 - 14{,}400 = 21{,}600$
$D_4 = .40(21{,}600) = 8{,}640$ $BV_4 = 21{,}600 - 10{,}800 = 10{,}800$
   vs. 10800*
$D_5 = 10{,}800$ $BV_5 = 10{,}800 - 10{,}800 = 0$

*Switch to straight-line here and spread out 21,600 evenly over remaining two years.

d. 150 percent declining balance (fraction = 150%(1/5) = .30)

$D_1 = .30(100{,}000) = 30{,}000$ $BV_1 = 100{,}000 - 30{,}000 = 70{,}000$
$D_2 = .30(70{,}000) = 21{,}000$ $BV_2 = 70{,}000 - 21{,}000 = 49{,}000$
$D_3 = .30(49{,}000) = 14{,}700$ $BV_3 = 49{,}000 - 16{,}333 = 32{,}667$
   vs. 16,333*
$D_4 = 16{,}333$ $BV_4 = 32{,}667 - 16{,}333 = 16{,}334$
$D_5 = 16{,}333$ $BV_5 = 1$(rounding error)

*Switch to straight-line here and depreciate 49,000 evenly over remaining three years.

═══════════ C H A P T E R ═══════════

10
Capital Budgeting
Decision Criteria

This chapter explains four commonly used capital budgeting criteria, discusses project review and post audit procedures, and discusses how capital rationing and inflation are included in capital budgeting analysis.

I.   Four capital budgeting techniques are widely known and used.

    A.   The net present value (NPV) of an investment project is defined as the present value of the stream of future net cash flows from a project minus the project's net investment.

        1.   The net present value is:

$$NPV = \sum_{t=1}^{n} \frac{NCF_t}{(1 + k)^t} - NINV$$

        where:
            NPV = net present value
            NCF_t = expected net cash flow in period t
            n = expected project life
            k = cost of capital
            $NINV$ = net investment

        2.   The NPV decision rule is to accept a project when the NPV is greater than zero (because the present value of the project's net cash flows exceeds the project's net investment outlay) and to reject

127

a project when its NPV is less than zero (the present value of the net cash flows is less than the outlay).

3.   The NPV criterion is superior to the PB criterion because it accurately accounts for the time value of a project's cash flows over its entire life. It is easy to use because positive NPV's increase the wealth of the firm's owners while negative NPV's have the opposite effect: accept/reject decisions are clearer with the NPV criterion (compared to PB).

4.   A disadvantage is that the NPV is not as easily understood by untrained persons as the payback or internal rate of return.

B.   The internal rate of return (IRR) is defined as the rate of discount that equates the present value of net cash flows of a project with the present value of the net investment. In other words, the IRR is the discount rate which makes a project's NPV equal zero.

1. $$\sum_{t=1}^{n} \frac{NCF_t}{(1 + r)^t} = NINV \text{ where } r = IRR = \text{internal rate of return.}$$

2.   The IRR decision rule is to accept a project when its IRR exceeds the cost of capital (k) and to reject a project when its IRR is less than k.

3.   Like the NPV, the IRR takes account of the magnitude and timing of a project's net cash flows over its entire life.

4.   One occasional difficulty with the IRR is that an unusual cash flow pattern (cash flows switching signs from positive to negative and vice versa) can result in multiple rates of return.

5.   When two or more mutually exclusive projects are acceptable using the IRR and NPV criteria, and if the two criteria disagree on which is best, the NPV criterion is generally preferred.

6.   Both the NPV and IRR criteria will always agree on accept/reject decisions (i.e., if NPV > 0, then IRR > k, and if NPV < 0, then IRR < k), even if they do not rank projects the same.

7.   Different rankings result from the implicit reinvestment rate assumptions of the two techniques: the NPV assumes that cash flows over the project's life may be reinvested at the cost of capital k while the IRR assumes that cash flows may be reinvested at the IRR.

C.   The profitability index (PI) or benefit-cost ratio is the ratio of the present value of future net cash flows over the life of the project to the net investment.

1.   Algebraically, the profitability index is

$$PI = \frac{\sum\limits_{t=1}^{n} \dfrac{NCF_t}{(1+k)^t}}{NINV}$$

2.   The PI decision rule is to accept a project whose PI is greater than or equal to one and to reject a project whose PI is less than one.

3.   The PI has the same advantages and disadvantages as the NPV criterion.

4.   The NPV is an <u>absolute</u> measure of the amount of wealth increase from a project, whereas the PI is a <u>relative</u> measure showing the wealth increase per dollar of investment.

D.   The <u>payback (PB) period</u> of an investment is the number of years required for the cumulative net cash inflows from a project to equal the initial cash outlay.

1.   If the future net cash inflows are equal in each year, the payback period is simply the ratio of the net investment to the annual cash inflows.

$$PB = \frac{net\ investment}{annual\ net\ cash\ flow}$$

When the future net cash flows are unequal, interpolation is frequently used in the final period to get an accurate payback period.

2.   The advantages of the payback method are that it is simple, it provides a measure of project liquidity, and, in a sense, it may also be a measure of risk.

3.   On the other hand, the payback period is not a true measure of profitability and, therefore, is not a good criterion for decision making. The payback period ignores cash flows after the payback is reached and it ignores the time value of money of the cash flows occurring within the payback period.

II.   Capital budgeting analysis is complicated by capital rationing, that is, when the total outlay for projects exceeds available funds. One method for maximizing the wealth of the firm given a funds constraint is the profitability index approach. It involves the following steps:

A.   Calculate the profitability index (PI) for each of a series of investment projects.

B.   Array the projects from the highest to the lowest PI.

C.   Starting with the project with the highest ratio, proceed through the list and accept until the entire capital budget is utilized.

D.   If some capital investment funds cannot be fully utilized because the next acceptable project is too large, there are three alternatives:

1.   Search for another combination of projects, perhaps including some smaller, less profitable projects, which will allow for a more complete utilization of available funds and increase the NPV of the combination of projects.

2.   Attempt to relax the funds constraint so that sufficient resources are available to accept the last project.

3.   Accept as many projects as possible and invest any excess funds in short-term securities until the next period, or pay out the excess funds to reduce outstanding debt or as common stock dividends.

III.   Reviewing or post-auditing is a final step to review the performance of investment projects after they have been implemented.

A.   While projected cash flows are uncertain and one should not expect actual values to agree with predicted values, the analysis should attempt to find systematic biases or errors by individuals, departments, plants, or divisions and attempt to identify reasons for these errors.

B.   Another reason to audit project performance is to decide whether to abandon or continue projects that have done poorly.

IV.   Inflation is easily incorporated into the basic capital budgeting criteria.

A.   Make sure the cost of capital takes account of inflationary expectations.

B.   Make sure that future cash flow estimates also include expected price and cost increases.

C.   If these are done, the capital budgeting techniques outlined in these chapters serve the financial decision maker reasonably well.

V.   (Appendix) When two or more mutually exclusive projects have unequal lives, the net present value and internal rate of return criteria can be unreliable unless the projects are being evaluated for an equal period of time. The two basic approaches to evaluate unequal lives, mutually exclusive projects are the replacement chain approach and the equivalent annual annuity approach.

A.   In the replacement chain approach, follow these logical steps:

1.   Find the least common multiple of the projects' lives (i.e., find the smallest number that is an integer multiple of each project's life).

2.   For each project, lay out the replacement chain cash flows over the least common multiple of lives (you may have to reinvest in each project one or more times over a long time period).

3.   Find the net present value of the replacement chain cash flows for each project. Choose the alternative with the best NPV.

B.   In the equivalent annual annuity approach, follow these steps:

1.   Compute the net present value of each project over its expected economic life.

2.   Obtain an equivalent annual annuity for each project by dividing its net present value by the present value of an annuity factor (PVIFA) over its original life. Choose the project with the better equivalent annual annuity.

3.   If a net present value is desired, the net present value for each project may be found by assuming the equivalent annual annuity is a perpetuity. The net present value of a perpetuity is found by dividing the equivalent annual amount by the cost of capital. Choose the project with the greater NPV. (This will always agree with your decision in step 2.)

TRUE AND FALSE QUESTIONS

Agree with each of the statements or reject it and modify it so that it is acceptable.

1.   A project with a rapid payback will have a positive net present value (NPV).

2.   Assume a project has a positive NPV. If the net investment, expected future cash flows, and cost of capital all double, then the NPV doubles.

3.   If an investment's cash flows are discounted at its internal rate of return (IRR), the resulting NPV is zero.

4.   The NPV and IRR criteria agree on accept/reject decisions for individual projects, but they may rank a set of projects differently.

5.   The profitability index (PI) decision rule is to accept a project whose PI exceeds zero and to reject a project with a negative PI.

6. When the cost of capital increases, the NPV and IRR decrease and the payback increases.

7. If Project A's NPV is $2,000 and its IRR is 15%, and Project B's NPV is $3,000, then Project B's IRR is greater than 15%.

8. The NPV criterion is not a true measure of profitability and an objective criterion for decision making because it ignores the cash flows after the payback is reached.

9. One reason to review or post-audit the performance of investment projects after they have been implemented is to decide to abandon or continue projects that have done poorly.

10. One way that inflation may be incorporated into capital budgeting criteria is by making sure that inflationary expectations are reflected in both the cost of capital and future cash flow estimates.

Answers to True and False Questions

1. A project with a rapid payback can have a negative payback. For example, if you lend me $1,000 for one year and I pay you back, you have an investment with a one-year payback and a negative NPV.

2. If the net investment and expected future cash flows double while the cost of capital stays the same, then the NPV would double.

3. True.

4. True.

5. Accept if PI $\geq$ 1.0 and reject if PI < 1.0.

6. The higher discount rate decreases the NPV but does not change the calculated IRR and payback.

7. The NPV and IRR may rank projects differently.

8. The NPV criterion evaluates all cash flows. The comment in the statement applies to the payback criterion, not to the NPV criterion.

9. True.

10. True.

CHAPTER 10 PROBLEMS

1.   An outlay of $50,000 is expected to yield the following cash flows:

Year	Net Cash Flow
1	5,000
2	10,000
3	20,000
4	15,000
5	5,000
6	5,000

The depreciation tax benefits and salvage value are already included in the cash flows and the cost of capital is 14 percent.

a.   What is the payback period?
b.   What is the project's NPV?
c.   Should the project be adopted?

Solution:

a.   Payback = 4.0 years (cumulative cash inflow = $50,000 after 4 years).

b.

Year	NCF $_t$	PVIF @ 14%	PV Cash Flows
1	5,000	.877	4,385
2	10,000	.769	7,690
3	20,000	.675	13,500
4	15,000	.592	8,880
5	5,000	.519	2,595
6	5,000	.456	2,280
			39,330
	Less: Net Investment		(50,000)
		NPV=	$-10,670

c.   The project should be rejected because of its negative NPV.

2.   What is the internal rate of return for the cash flows in Problem 1?

Solution:

We can find the IRR with trial and error and interpolation.

Year	NCF$_t$	PVIF @ 5%	PV of Cash Flows	PVIF @ 6%	PV of Cash Flows
1	5,000	.952	4,760	.943	4,715
2	10,000	.907	9,070	.890	8,900
3	20,000	.864	17,280	.840	16,800
4	15,000	.823	12,345	.792	11,880
5	5,000	.784	3,920	.747	3,735
6	5,000	.746	3,730	.705	3,525
			51,105		49,555
Less:		NINV	(50,000)		(50,000)
		NPV =	$ 1,105	NPV =	$ -445

Interpolation of IRR:

$$r = 5\% + \frac{1,105}{1,105 + 445}(6\%\text{-}5\%) = 5\% + .71(1\%) = 5.71\%$$

The IRR criterion rates the project as unacceptable because the IRR (5.71%) is less than the cost of capital (14%).

3.   Two mutually exclusive projects have the following cash flows:

Year	NCF for A	NCF for B
0	-10,000	-10,000
1	4,000	0
2	4,000	0
3	4,000	0
4	4,000—	19,000—

a.   Find the net present value of each project discounted at 0%, 5%, 10%, 15%, and 24%. Plot the NPVs as a function of the discount rate.

b.   What is the IRR of each project?

c.   Assuming a cost of capital of 10%, which project should be chosen?

Solution:

a.

Discount Rate	NPV for A	NPV for B
0%	-10,000+4,000(4.0) =6,000	-10,000+19,000(1.0) = 9,000
5%	-10,000+4,000(3.546)=4,184	-10,000+19,000(.823)= 5,637
10%	-10,000+4,000(3.170)=2,680	-10,000+19,000(.683)= 2,977
15%	-10,000+4,000(2.855)=1,420	-10,000+19,000(.572)= 868
20%	-10,000+4,000(2.589)= 356	-10,000+19,000(.482)= -842
24%	-10,000+4,000(2.404)=- 384	-10,000+19,000(.423)=-1,963

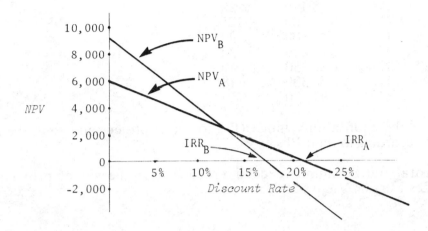

b.   Discounted at 21%, NPV_A = -10,000 + 4,000(2.540) = 160

Discounted at 22%, NPV_A = -10,000 + 4,000(2.494) = -24

Interpolating for IRR:

$$r = 21\% + \frac{160}{160+24}(22\% - 21\%) = 21\% + .87(1\%)$$

$$= 21.87\%$$

Discounted at 17%, NPV_B = -10,000 + 19,000(.534) = 146

Discounted at 18%, NPV_B = -10,000 + 19,000(.516) = -196

Interpolating for IRR:

$$r = 17\% + \frac{146}{146+196}(18\% - 17\%) = 17\% + .43(1\%)$$

$$= 17.43\%$$

c.   If the cost of capital is 10%, NPV_A = 2,680 and NPV_B = 2,977, which means that Project B is superior. However, IRR_A = 21.87% and IRR_B = 17.43%, implying that Project A is superior. The choice of projects would depend on which reinvestment assumption was appropriate. For example, if the NPV reinvestment assumption of 10% (the cost of capital) is correct, then Project B would be chosen.

4.   The Mission Viejo Company is evaluating the following seven independent projects

Project	Outlay	NPV
A	$ 100	$ 20
B	500	125
C	400	90
D	200	20
E	250	40
F	300	18
G	50	9

a. Calculate the profitability index (PI) for each project and rank the seven projects according to their PI's.

b. If the total outlay cannot exceed $750, choose the set of projects that maximizes Mission Viejo's NPV.

Solution:

a.

Project	Outlay	NPV	PV*	PI**	Rank
A	100	20	120	1.200	3
B	500	125	625	1.250	2
C	400	90	490	1.225	1
D	200	20	220	1.100	6
E	250	40	290	1.160	5
F	300	18	318	1.060	7
G	50	9	59	1.180	4

*PV = present value of future NCF's = Outlay + NPV

**PI = PV/Outlay

b. This can be solved by trial and error. Generally, projects with high PI's are chosen, but in this case, the best two projects (C and B) cannot both be bought because they exceed the $750 budget.

Projects	Total Outlay	Total NPV
B, E	$750	$165
A, C, E	750	150
B, A, G	650	154
B, D, G	750	154

Projects B and E are the set of projects that maximizes your NPV subject to the $750 capital outlay constraint.

5. Calculate the NPV of the equipment replacement decision being considered by Charlie's Cleaners. The cost of capital is 8%. (Refer back to Problem 5 in Chapter 9.)

Solution:

Time	Cash flow	PVIF @ 8%	PV @ 8%
0	-$109,800	1.000	-$109,800.00
1	11,848	.926	10,971.25
2	17,050	.857	14,611.85
3	13,480	.794	10,703.12
4	10,930	.735	8,033.55
5	9,114	.681	6,206.63
6	9,114	.630	5,741.82
7	9,114	.583	5,313.46
8	6,830	.540	3,688.20
9	4,560	.500	2,280.00
10	4,560	.463	5,167.08
		Total	-$37,083.04

This is an unprofitable investment with a negative NPV of -$36,083.

6.   Tom Sale is evaluating a capital budgeting project for his employer.   Tom has determined the relevant facts to be as follows:

installed cost = $100,000
project life = 10 years
incremental revenue = $45,000 annually
incremental cash operating expenses = $20,000
cost of capital = 10%
tax rate = 40%
depreciation: straight-line over ten years to a salvage value of $10,000.
liquidation value in 10 years = $10,000
investment in working capital = zero

Please use this information to find (a) the project's payback period, (b) net present value, (c) profitability index, and (d) internal rate of return.

Solution:

Annual depreciation = (100,000 - 10,000)/10 = $9,000
NCF = $(\Delta R - \Delta O - \Delta D)(1 - t) + \Delta D$
NCF = (45,000 - 20,000 - 9,000)(1 - .4) + 9000
NCF = 9,600 + 9,000 = 18,600

a.   Since the future cash flows are equal,
     PB = net investment/annual net cash flow
     PB = 100,000/18,600 = 5.38 years

b.

Year	NCF	Interest Factors @ 10%	PV of Cash Flows
1-10	18,600	6.145	114,297
10	10,000	.386	3,860
			118,157
	Less:	NINV	(100,000)
		NPV =	$ 18,157

c.   PI = PV of Cash Flows/NINV
     PI = 118,157/100,000 = 1.18

d.   We will use trial and error and interpolation to get the IRR.

Year	NCF	PVIF @ 13%	PV of Cash Flows	PVIF @ 14%	PV of Cash Flows
1-10	18,600	5.426	100,923.60	5.216	97,017.60
10	10,000	.295	2,950.00	.270	2,700.00
			103,873.60		99,717.60
	Less:	NINV	(100,000.00)		(100,000.00)
		NPV =	$ 3,873.60	NPV =	$ -282.40

Interpolating:

$$r = 13\% + \frac{3,873.60}{3,873.60 + 282.40} \quad (14\% - 13\%) = 13\% + .93(1\%)$$

$$= 13.93\%$$

This is a profitable project. It has a positive net present value, a profitability index greater than 1.0, and an internal rate of return greater than the cost of capital.

7.   Reevaluate Problem 6 in the Study Guide applying the TRA of 1986 corporate tax rules. The relevant data are now:

installed cost = $100,000
no investment tax credit
project life = 10 years
incremental revenue = $45,000 per year
incremental cash operating expenses = $20,000 per year
cost of capital = 10%
tax rate = 34%
depreciation: Modified ACRS, 7-year class, 200% declining balance
liquidation value in 10 years = $10,000
investment in working capital = zero

Please use this information to find (a) the project's payback period, (b) net present value, (c) profitability index, and (d) internal rate of return.

Solution:

Year	ACRS rate	Depreciation (rate x $100,000)
1	14.29%	$14,290
2	24.49%	24,490
3	17.49%	17,490
4	12.49%	12,490
5	8.93%	8,930
6	8.92%	8,920
7	8.93%	8,930
8	4.46%	4,460
9	0.00%	0
10	0.00%	0

Year $(\Delta R - \Delta O - \Delta D)(1 - t) + \Delta D = NCF$

1	(45,000 - 20,000 - 14,290)(1 - .34)	+	14,290	=	21,358.60
2	(45,000 - 20,000 - 24,490)(1 - .34)	+	24,490	=	24,826.60
3	(45,000 - 20,000 - 17,490)(1 - .34)	+	17,490	=	22,446.60
4	(45,000 - 20,000 - 12,490)(1 - .34)	+	12,490	=	20,746.60
5	(45,000 - 20,000 - 8,930)(1 - .34)	+	8,930	=	19,536.20
6	(45,000 - 20,000 - 8,920)(1 .34)	+	8,920	=	19,532.80
7	(45,000 - 20,000 - 8,930)(1 - .34)	+	8,930	=	19,536.20
8	(45,000 - 20,000 - 4,460)(1 - .34)	+	4,460	=	18,016.40
9	(45,000 - 20,000 - 0)(1 - .34)	+	0	=	16,500.00
10	(45,000 - 20,000 - 0)(1 - .34)	+	0	=	16,500.00

In year 10, the cash flow also increases by the salvage value and declines by the tax on the gain on salvage.

$$NCF_{10} = 16,500 + 10,000 - .34(10,000) = 23,100$$

a. To find the PB, we see how long it takes for the cumulative cash flow to equal the outlay.

Year	Cash Flow	Cumulative Cash Flow
1	21,358.60	21,358.60
2	24,826.60	46,185.20
3	22,446.60	68,631.80
4	20,746.60	89,378.40
5	19,536.20	108,914.60
6	19,532.80	128,447.40
7	19,536.20	147,983.60
8	18,016.40	166,000.00
9	16,500.00	182,500.00
10	23,100.00	205,600.00

It takes between 4 and 5 years to recover the $100,000 net investment. Interpolating for the payback gives:

$$PB = 4 \text{ years} + \frac{100,000.00 - 89,378.40}{108,914.60 - 89,378.40} (1 \text{ year}) = 4.54 \text{ years}$$

b.

Year	NCF	PVIF @ 10%	PV of NCF
1	21,358.60	.909	19,414.97
2	24,826.60	.826	20,506.77
3	22,446.60	.751	16,857.40
4	20,746.60	.683	14,169.93
5	19,536.20	.621	12,131.98
6	19,532.80	.564	11,016.50
7	19,536.20	.513	10,022.07
8	18,016.40	.467	8,413.66
9	16,500.00	.424	6,996.00
10	23,100.00	.386	8,916.60
			128,445.88
	Less: NINV		100,000.00
	NPV		28,445.88

c.   PI = PV of cash flows / NINV

PI = 128,446.21/100,000.00 = 1.284

d.   Using trial and error, the IRR is between 16% and 17%.

Year	NCF	PVIF @ 16%	PV of NCF
1	21,358.60	.862	18,411.11
2	24,826.60	.743	18,446.16
3	22,446.60	.641	14,388.27
4	20,746.60	.552	11,452.12
5	19,536.20	.476	9,299.23
6	19,532.80	.410	8,008.49
7	19,536.20	.354	6,915.81
8	18,016.40	.305	5,495.00
9	16,500.00	.263	4,339.50
10	23,100.00	.227	5,243.70
			101,999.39
	Less: NINV		100,000.00
	NPV		1,999.39

skip

Year	NCF	PVIF @ 17%	PV of NCF
1	21,358.60	.855	18,261.60
2	24,826.60	.731	18,148.24
3	22,446.60	.624	14,006.68
4	20,746.60	.534	11,078.68
5	19,536.20	.456	8,908.51
6	19,532.80	.390	7,617.79
7	19,536.20	.333	6,505.55
8	18,016.40	.285	5,134.67
9	16,500.00	.243	4,009.50
10	23,100.00	.208	4,804.80
			98,476.02
	Less: NINV		100,000.00
	NPV		-1,523.98

Interpolating for the IRR:

$$r = 16\% + \frac{1,999.71}{1,999.71 + 1,523.61}(1\%) = 16\% + .57(1\%) = 16.57\%$$

8.   Gus Kalogeras must choose between two mutually exclusive projects with differing lives. Project F requires a $20,000 outlay and produces an after-tax net cash flow of $12,000 each year over its three-year life. Project G involves a $30,000 outlay and generates $13,000 each year for four years. Both projects have no salvage value. Project G, then, involves a larger outlay than Project F, but it provides a slightly larger cash inflow over the first 3 years and then provides $13,000 in year 4 when Project F has expired. The services of either project are required more or less indefinitely, it is simply a question of which is more profitable. Assume a 10% cost of capital.

   a.   Calculate the net present value of a replacement chain for each project over the least common multiple of the project's lives.

   b.   Calculate the equivalent annual annuity for each project.

Solution:

a.   The least common multiple of 3 and 4 (the lives of F and G) is 12.

The cash flows for 12 years would be:

Time	Outlay(F)	Net Cash Flow(F)	Outlay(G)	Net Cash Flow(G)
0	20,000	--	30,000	--
1		12,000		13,000
2		12,000		13,000
3	20,000	12,000		13,000
4		12,000	30,000	13,000
5		12,000		13,000
6	20,000	12,000		13,000
7		12,000		13,000
8		12,000	30,000	13,000
9	20,000	12,000		13,000
10		12,000		13,000
11		12,000		13,000
12		12,000		13,000

The net present value of each project over the 12 year period is:

$$NPV_F = 12,000(PVIFA_{.10,12}) - 20,000(PVIF_{.10,0}) - 20,000(PVIF_{.10,3})$$
$$- 20,000(PVIF_{.10,6}) - 20,000(PVIF_{.10,9})$$

$$NPV_F = 12,000(6.814) - 20,000(1) - 20,000(.751) - 20,000(.564)$$
$$- 20,000(.424)$$

$$NPV_F = 81,768 - 20,000 - 15,020 - 11,280 - 8,480$$

$$NPV_F = \$26,988$$

$$NPV_G = 13,000(PVIFA_{.10,12}) - 30,000(PVIF_{.10,0}) - 30,000(PVIF_{.10,4})$$
$$- 30,000(PVIF_{.10,8})$$

$$NPV_G = 13,000(6.814) - 30,000(1) - 30,000(.683) - 30,000(.467)$$

$$NPV_G = 88,582 - 30,000 - 20,490 - 14,010$$

$$NPV_G = \$24,082$$

Apparently, Project F has the superior net present value ($26,988 compared to $24,082).

b.   Find the NPV of each project over its original life:

$\text{NPV}_F = -20,000 + 12,000(\text{PVIFA}_{.10,3})$

$\text{NPV}_F = -20,000 + 12,000(2.487) = \$9,844$

$\text{NPV}_G = -30,000 + 13,000 \, (\text{PVIFA}_{.10,4})$

$\text{NPV}_G = -30,000 + 13,000(3.170) = \$11,210$

Find the equivalent annual annuity EAA for each project by dividing its NPV by the present value of an annuity factor for its original life:

$\text{EAA}_F = \text{NPV}_F/(\text{PVIFA}_{.10,3})$

$\text{EAA}_F = \$9,844/2.487 = \$3,958$

$\text{EAA}_G = \text{NPV}_G/(\text{PVIFA}_{.10,4})$

$\text{EAA}_G = \$11,210/3.170 = \$3,536$

Choose Project F because it provides an annuity of $3,958 per year while G provides a lesser $3,536. If a net present value of a perpetuity is desired, divide the equivalent annual annuity for each project by the cost of capital:

$\text{NPV}_F = \$3,958/.10 = \$39,580$

$\text{NPV}_G = \$3,536/.10 = \$35,360$

Project F has the greater NPV for such a long-lived chain.

9.   Rework Problem 7 using the Lotus templates accompanying the text. The results of doing this are on the following pages. If you do this, you should notice how much faster you can do this problem, and also that you can readily attack much more complicated problems with the help of a spreadsheet program.

```
==================================================================
               CAPITAL BUDGETING INVESTMENT ANALYSIS
==================================================================


INFORMATION ON OLD ASSET
------------------------
ORIGINAL INSTALLED COST OF ASSET                                  $0
NET WORKING CAPITAL REQUIRED FOR ASSET                            $0
INVESTMENT TAX CREDIT AT                    0.00%                 $0
ORIGINAL ESTIMATE OF SALVAGE VALUE                                $0
ECONOMIC LIFE OF ASSET                                             0
DEPRECIABLE CLASS OF ASSET (# OF YEARS UNDER ACRS)                 0
DEPRECIATION METHOD
   (1)-PRE-ACRS STRAIGHT-LINE  (2)-ACRS
   (3)-MODIFIED ACRS                                               0
YEARS DEPRECIATED                                                  0
ACCUMULATED DEPRECIATION                                          $0
BOOK VALUE (ADJUSTED FOR ITC RECAPTURE)                           $0


INFORMATION ON NEW ASSET
------------------------
DEPRECIABLE CLASS OF NEW ASSET (# OF YEARS UNDER ACRS)             7
ECONOMIC LIFE OF NEW ASSET                                        10
SALVAGE VALUE OF NEW ASSET                                   $10,000
DEPRECIATION METHOD
   (1)-PRE-ACRS STRAIGHT-LINE  (2) MODIFIED ACRS                   2

COST OF NEW ASSET                                          $100,000
DELIVERY AND INSTALLATION                                         $0
NET WORKING CAPITAL REQUIRED FOR ASSET                            $0
PROCEEDS FROM SALE OF OLD ASSET                                   $0
TAX EFFECTS
   CAPITAL GAINS TAX RATE                   34.00%
   MARGINAL TAX RATE                        34.00%
TAX ON SALE OF OLD ASSET                                          $0
RECAPTURE OF ITC                                                  $0


INFORMATION ON REAL PROPERTY
----------------------------
ORIGINAL COST OF LAND                                             $0
ESTIMATED VALUE AT END OF PROJECT                                 $0


ORIGINAL COST OF BUILDING                                         $0
MONTH BUILDING IS PLACED IN SERVICE (1-12)                         0
DEPRECIABLE LIFE OF BUILDING (27.5 OR 31.5)                      0.0
ESTIMATED VALUE AT END OF PROJECT                                 $0

   NET INVESTMENT                                         $100,000
```

NET CASH FLOW CALCULATION		0	1	2
CASH INFLOWS				
	GROWTH RATE			
REVENUES WITH PROJECT (STREAM #1)	0.00%		$45,000	$45,000
REVENUES WITH PROJECT (STREAM #2)	0.00%		$0	$0
REVENUES WITHOUT PROJECT (STREAM #1)	0.00%		$0	$0
REVENUES WITHOUT PROJECT (STREAM #2)	0.00%		$0	$0
INCREMENTAL REVENUE			$45,000	$45,000
CASH OUTFLOWS				
	GROWTH RATE			
COSTS WITH PROJECT (STREAM #1)	0.00%		$20,000	$20,000
COSTS WITH PROJECT (STREAM #2)	0.00%		$0	$0
COSTS WITHOUT PROJECT (STREAM #1)	0.00%		$0	$0
COSTS WITHOUT PROJECT (STREAM #2)	0.00%		$0	$0
INCREMENTAL COST			$20,000	$20,000
DEPRECIATION				
DEPRECIATION ON BUILDING			$0	$0
DEPRECIATION WITH PROJECT			$14,286	$24,490
DEPRECIATION WITHOUT PROJECT			$0	$0
INCREMENTAL DEPRECIATION			$14,286	$24,490
INCREMENTAL EARNINGS BEFORE TAXES			$10,714	$510
TAXES			$3,643	$173
RECAPTURE OF ASSET SALVAGE VALUE				
RECAPTURE OF WORKING CAPITAL				
RECAPTURE OF LAND SALVAGE VALUE				
RECAPTURE OF BUILDING SALVAGE VALUE				
ADDITIONAL WORKING CAPITAL (AFTER INITIAL INVESTMENT)			$0	$0
NET CASH FLOW		($100,000)	$21,357	$24,827

NET CASH FLOW CALCULATION	3	4	5	6
CASH INFLOWS				
REVENUES W PROJECT (STREAM #1)	$45,000	$45,000	$45,000	$45,000
REVENUES W PROJECT (STREAM #2)	$0	$0	$0	$0
REVENUES WO PROJECT (STREAM #1)	$0	$0	$0	$0
REVENUES WO PROJECT (STREAM #2)	$0	$0	$0	$0
INCREMENTAL REVENUE	$45,000	$45,000	$45,000	$45,000
CASH OUTFLOWS				
COSTS WITH PROJECT (STREAM #1)	$20,000	$20,000	$20,000	$20,000
COSTS WITH PROJECT (STREAM #2)	$0	$0	$0	$0
COSTS WITHOUT PROJECT (STREAM #1)	$0	$0	$0	$0
COSTS WITHOUT PROJECT (STREAM #2)	$0	$0	$0	$0
INCREMENTAL COST	$20,000	$20,000	$20,000	$20,000
DEPRECIATION				
DEPRECIATION ON BUILDING	$0	$0	$0	$0
DEPRECIATION WITH PROJECT	$17,493	$12,495	$8,925	$8,925
DEPRECIATION WITHOUT PROJECT	$0	$0	$0	$0
INCREMENTAL DEPRECIATION	$17,493	$12,495	$8,925	$8,925
INCREMENTAL EARNINGS BEFORE TAXES	$7,507	$12,505	$16,075	$16,075
TAXES	$2,552	$4,252	$5,466	$5,466
RECAP OF ASSET SALVAGE VALUE				
RECAP OF WORKING CAPITAL				
RECAP OF LAND SALVAGE VALUE				
RECAP OF BLDG SALVAGE VALUE				
ADDITIONAL WORKING CAPITAL	$0	$0	$0	$0
NET CASH FLOW	$22,448	$20,748	$19,534	$19,534

NET CASH FLOW CALCULATION	7	8	9	10
CASH INFLOWS				
REVENUES W PROJECT (STREAM #1)	$45,000	$45,000	$45,000	$45,000
REVENUES W PROJECT (STREAM #2)	$0	$0	$0	$0
REVENUES WO PROJECT (STREAM #1)	$0	$0	$0	$0
REVENUES WO PROJECT (STREAM #2)	$0	$0	$0	$0
INCREMENTAL REVENUE	$45,000	$45,000	$45,000	$45,000
CASH OUTFLOWS				
COSTS WITH PROJECT (STREAM #1)	$20,000	$20,000	$20,000	$20,000
COSTS WITH PROJECT (STREAM #2)	$0	$0	$0	$0
COSTS WITHOUT PROJECT (STREAM #1)	$0	$0	$0	$0
COSTS WITHOUT PROJECT (STREAM #2)	$0	$0	$0	$0
INCREMENTAL COST	$20,000	$20,000	$20,000	$20,000
DEPRECIATION				
DEPRECIATION ON BUILDING	$0	$0	$0	$0
DEPRECIATION WITH PROJECT	$8,925	$4,462	$0	$0
DEPRECIATION WITHOUT PROJECT	$0	$0	$0	$0
INCREMENTAL DEPRECIATION	$8,925	$4,462	$0	$0
INCREMENTAL EARNINGS BEFORE TAXES	$16,075	$20,538	$25,000	$25,000
TAXES	$5,466	$6,983	$8,500	$8,500
RECAP OF ASSET SALVAGE VALUE				$6,600
RECAP OF WORKING CAPITAL				$0
RECAP OF LAND SALVAGE VALUE				$0
RECAP OF BLDG SALVAGE VALUE				$0
ADDITIONAL WORKING CAPITAL	$0	$0	$0	$0
NET CASH FLOW	$19,534	$18,017	$16,500	$23,100

```
SUMMARY INFORMATION
=========================

DISCOUNT RATE                                    10.00%
INITIAL GUESS FOR IRR                            10.00%
NET PRESENT VALUE                              $28,459
IRR                                              16.56%
PROFITABILITY INDEX                               1.28
PAYBACK (YEARS)                                      5

REINVESTMENT RATE                                10.00%
GROSS TERMINAL VALUE OF CASH FLOWS            $333,190
ADJUSTED NET PRESENT VALUE                     $28,459
ADJUSTED INTERNAL RATE OF RETURN                 12.79%

EQUIVALENT ANNUAL ANNUITY                       $4,632
NET PRESENT VALUE (INFINITE CHAIN)             $46,316
```

CHAPTER

11
Capital Budgeting and Risk

In Chapters 9 and 10, investments were evaluated using the firm's weighted cost of capital (required rate of return). This requires that the projects being considered are exactly as risky as the firm as a whole. When a project being evaluated is more or less risky than the firm's average risk level, other techniques and principles (such as those in Chapter 5) are required.

I.   It can be important to distinguish between the <u>total project risk</u> and the <u>portfolio</u> or <u>beta</u> risk of an investment.

    A.   Total project risk is the risk that a project performs below expectations. This is the risk of a project considered in isolation and some of total project risk can be diversified away.

    B.   Portfolio or beta risk depends on the risk of the project relative to the market--portfolio or beta risk cannot be diversified away.

II.   To adjust for portfolio or beta risk, the capital asset pricing model can be used to estimate risk-adjusted discount rates for capital budgeting.

    A.   After estimating the project's beta, the project's risk- adjusted discount rate is found with the SML equation.

$$k^* = r_f + (r_m - r_f)b$$

B.   The firm is a portfolio of assets and the firm's beta is a weighted average of the asset betas. The firm's weighted cost of capital is based on the firm's beta. Individual projects will have a greater (or smaller) required rate of return than the weighted cost of capital if the project's beta is great (or less than) the firm's beta.

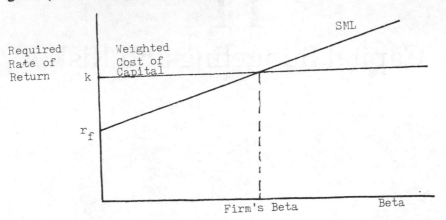

The weighted cost of capital is correct only when the project beta equals the firm's beta. When the project beta is less than (or greater than) the firm's beta, the weighted cost of capital is greater than (less than) the project's risk-adjusted rate of return from the SML.

C.   The beta of another firm in the line of business of a proposed investment can be used to proxy for the beta of a proposed investment. The proxy firm's beta, however, reflects both the operating and financing risks of that firm, so an adjusted beta is found in two steps.

1.   Calculate an unleveraged beta

$$b_u = \frac{b_1}{1 + (1-t)\,(B/E)}$$

where

b_u is the unleveraged beta

b_l is the leveraged beta of the proxy firm

t is the firm's tax rate

B/E is the proxy firm's debt to equity ratio (market value of debt/market value of equity)

2.   Then calculate a new leveraged beta for your investment where

$$b_l = b_u[1 + (1-t)(B/E)]$$

t is the firm's tax rate

B/E is the debt/equity ratio employed by your firm

3.   This adjustment is only an approximation of the effect of leverage on beta. More sophisticated treatments of this problem exist, but are not shown here.

D.   The projects net present value is

$$NPV = \sum_{t=1}^{n} \frac{NCF_t}{(1+k^*)^t} - NINV$$

where

k^* is the risk-adjusted discount rate estimated with the capital asset pricing model.

E.   The capital asset pricing model can also be used to compute divisional costs of capital. Projects in each division are discounted by that division's cost of capital.

1.   The firm's weighted average beta is a weighted average of the divisional betas.

2.   The firm's weighted average cost of capital is a weighted average of the divisional costs of capital.

III.   A variety of techniques are used to adjust for the total project risk for an individual investment (neglecting portfolio effects).

A.   NPV-Payback Approach--to be accepted, a project must have a positive NPV and a payback of less than a critical number of years (such as 4 years).

B.   Risk-adjusted discount rate approach--when finding the NPV, an individual project is discounted at a discount rate adjusted to the riskiness of the project instead of discounting all projects at one rate (the firm's cost of capital). The firm carries a risk premium which depends on its riskiness.

$$\theta = k - r_f$$

where
θ = average risk premium for the firm
r_f = risk-free rate

k = cost of capital (required rate of return) for projects of same risk as firm

The risk premiums applied to individual projects usually are chosen in a subjective manner. Many firms establish risk classes (such as low, medium, high), assign individual projects to these classes, and discount all the projects in each class by a discount rate arbitrarily chosen for that class.

Given a risk premium θ_A for project A, the risk adjusted discount rate for Project A, k^*_A, would then be

$$k^*_A = r_f + \theta_A$$

and the net present value for Project A is

$$NPV_A = \sum_{t=1}^{n} \frac{NCF_t}{(1 + k^*_A)^t} - NINV.$$

C.   Hurdle rate approach--the project's risk-adjusted discount rate, k^*_A, is computed (as above) and compared to the project's IRR. If IRR $> k^*_A$, the project is accepted.

D.   The certainty equivalent approach involves converting expected risky cash flows to their certainty equivalents and then computing the net present value of the project.

1.   The risk-free rate, r_f, not the firm's risky cost of capital, k, is used as the discount rate.

2.   The certainty equivalent cash flow is a certain cash flow that the decision-maker feels is equivalent to the risky cash flow. (At time t, the decision-maker would be indifferent between the risky cash flow and the certainty equivalent). The certainty equivalent factor ($_t$) is the ratio of the certainty equivalent cash flow to the risky cash flow.

$$\alpha_t = \frac{\text{certainty equivalent at time t}}{\text{expected risky cash flow at time t}}$$

3.   The certainty-equivalent net present value is:

$$NPV = -NINV(\alpha_0) + \sum_{t=1}^{n} \frac{NCF_t \alpha_t}{(1 + r_f)^t}$$

where

α_0 = certainty equivalent factor associated with the net investment (NINV) at time 0

α_t = certainty equivalent factor associated with expected risk cash flows (NCF_t) at time t

r_f = risk-free rate

n = economic life of the project

E.   Simulation approach--the probability distribution of each element which influences the cash flows of a project is estimated. These elements include the number of units sold, market price, unit production costs, unit selling costs, net investment, project life, and the cost of capital. A numerical value for each of these items is randomly chosen and a net present value calculated. This process is repeated many times until a probability distribution of the project's NPV can be estimated.

F.   Sensitivity analysis--sensitivity analysis involves systematically changing relevant variables to find to which variables the NPV (or IRR) seems most "sensitive."

   1.   It can be useful to make sensitivity curves to show the impact of changes in a variable (such as the price of the output, the cost of capital, the tax rate, etc.) on the project's NPV.

   2.   Electronic spreadsheets and other financial modeling software available on microcomputers and large-scale computers make sensitivity analysis easy to perform.

TRUE AND FALSE QUESTIONS

Agree with each of the statements or reject it and modify it so that it is acceptable.

1.   If a project's return has a zero standard deviation, then it is considered to be risk-free.

2.   A project's portfolio risk can be diversified away.

3.   In the risk-adjusted discount rate approach, a project's NPV is found by discounting with the weighted cost of capital.

4.   The certainty equivalent factor is the ratio of the present value of a risky cash flow to the expected cash flow.

5.   The internal rate of return is not used for capital budgeting under risk.

6.   Discounting all projects at the cost of capital instead of the risk-adjusted discount rate might cause the firm to reject some high risk projects that should be accepted and to accept some low risk projects that should be rejected.

7.   Computer simulation can be used for evaluating risky projects.

8.   A project with a beta less than the overall beta of the firm should have a required rate of return less than the firm's weighted cost of capital.

9.   Diversified investors should use a systematic risk measure such as beta and nondiversified investors should use a total risk concept.

10.   When portfolio effects are present, the capital asset pricing model approach is recommended to find the appropriate risk- adjusted discount rate.

Answers to True and False Questions

1.   True.

2.   Portfolio risk <u>cannot</u> be diversified away.

3.   The risk-adjusted discount rate, not the weighted cost of capital, is used as the discount rate.

4.   The certainty equivalent factor ($_t$) is the ratio of the certainty equivalent cash flow at time t to the expected risky cash flow at time t.

5.   The IRR is compared to the risk-adjusted discount rate (k^*) instead of the cost of capital (k).

6.   The errors are the opposite of the ones named. Using the cost of capital instead of risk-adjusted discount rates might cause the firm to accept some bad high-risk projects and to reject some good low-risk projects.

7.   True.

8.   True.

9.   True.

10.   True.

CHAPTER 11 PROBLEMS

1.   Louisiana Land and Minerals uses a combined NPV-Payback approach to capital budgeting: a project must have a payback of three years or less and a positive NPV. Which of the following projects are acceptable, if the cost of capital is 12%

		Project A	Project B
Outlay:		100,000	40,000
Cash flow:	1 year	50,000	12,000
	2 years	40,000	12,000
	3 years	20,000	12,000
	4 years	20,000	12,000
	5 years	20,000	12,000
	6 years	0	12,000

Solution:

Payback $_A$ = 2.5 years

Year	NCF	12% Present Value Interest Factor	PV of NCF
1	50,000	.893	44,650
2	40,000	.797	31,880
3	20,000	.712	14,240
4	20,000	.636	12,720
5	20,000	.567	11,340
			114,830
	Less: Net Investment		100,000
	NPV$_A$ =		$ 14,830

Payback $_B$ = $\dfrac{40,000}{12,000}$ = 3.33 years

Year	NCF	12% Present Value Interest Factor	PV of NCF
1-6	12,000	4.111	49,332
	Less: Net Investment		40,000
	NPV$_B$ =		$9,332

Project A meets both the NPV and payback criterion while Project B's payback does not meet Louisiana Land's payback cutoff.

2. Abdul Al Hashim estimates the outlay for a risky project to be $900,000. He also expects after-tax net cash flows of $300,000 for each of the first three years and $240,000 for years 4 and 5. His certainty equivalent factors are estimated to be:

α_0 = 1.00
α_1 = .90
α_2 = .87
α_3 = .83
α_4 = .80
α_5 = .80

156   Contemporary Financial Management

the cost of capital is 20% and the risk-free rate is 8%. Use the
certainty-equivalent method to obtain a net present value.

Solution:

Year	NCF$_t$	α_t	NCFα_t	PVIF@8%	PV
0	-$900,000	1.00	-$900,000	1.000	-$900,000
1	300,000	.90	270,000	.926	250,020
2	300,000	.87	261,000	.857	223,677
3	300,000	.83	249,000	.794	197,706
4	240,000	.80	192,000	.735	141,120
5	240,000	.80	192,000	.681	130,752
				NPV =	$ 43,275

3.   Howie Rutledge is an accountant for a small oil company. He has been asked by
the company's chief executive officer to estimate the required rate of return for
an investment in oil storage facilities. Rutledge, after two weeks of study, has
found these to be very risky investments. He estimates the standard deviation of
the return on oil storage facilities to be 30% per year and that the correlation
between the returns on oil storage facilities and returns on investments in general
to be 0.75. Current market conditions would argue for a 9% riskless rate of
return, a 15% rate of return in the market for risky assets, and a 10% standard
deviation for the market return.

a.   What is the beta for oil storage facilities?
b.   What is the required rate of return on this investment?

Solution:

a.   beta = $\dfrac{\rho_{jm}\sigma_j\sigma_m}{\sigma^2_m}$ = $\dfrac{.75(.30)(.10)}{(.10)^2}$ = 2.25

b. $k_j = r_f + b_j(r_m - r_f)$ = .09 + 2.25(.15 - .09) = .09 + .135

= .225 or 22.5%

4.   The risk-free rate is 5%, the firm's beta is 0.8, and the required rate of return
for the market is 10%. The firm is evaluating the following investment projects:

Project	Internal Rate of Return	Beta
A	7.0%	1.00
B	11.0%	1.40
C	14.0%	1.10
D	10.0%	0.70
E	7.5%	0.60
F	13.0%	1.00
G	11.0%	1.25
H	12.0%	1.70
I	8.5%	0.60
J	8.5%	0.75

a. What is the weighted cost of capital or required rate of return for the firm? If this is used as the hurdle rate for all projects, which projects will be selected?

b. If a separate required rate of return is estimated for each project, which projects will be selected?

Solution:

a. $WCC = r_f + b_j(r_m - r_f) = 5\% + .8(10\% - 5\%) = 5\% + 4\% = 9\%$

Accept all projects with IRR above 9%.

Accept: B C D F G H   Reject: A E I J

b. $k_j = r_f + b_j(r_m - r_f)$

Required Rate of Return	Internal Rate of Return	Decision
$k_A = 5 + 1.0(5) = 10\%$	7.0%	Reject
$k_B = 5 + 1.4(5) = 12\%$	11.0%	Reject
$k_C = 1.1(5) = 10.5\%$	14.0%	Accept
$k_D = 5 + .7(5) = 8.5\%$	10.0%	Accept
$k_E = 5 + .6(5) = 8.0\%$	7.5%	Reject
$k_F = 5 + 1.0(5) = 10.0\%$	13.0%	Accept
$k_G = 5 + 1.25(5) = 11.25\%$	11.0%	Reject
$k_H = 5 + 1.7(5) = 13.5\%$	12.0%	Reject
$k_I = 5 + .6(5) = 8.0\%$	8.5%	Accept
$k_J = 5 + .75(5) = 8.75\%$	8.5%	Reject

Accept any projects with IRR above its RRR.

Accept: C D F I   Reject: A B E G H J

Note that the two approaches select different projects. The WCC approach accepted projects B, G and H that should have been rejected and rejected project I that was a good project.

5.   Blansett Airways is considering an investment in a small commuter route. A proxy firm in that line of business has a beta of 1.5, and a debt/equity ratio of 3.0 (i.e., 75% debt, 25% equity), and a tax rate of 40%.

   a.   If Judy Blansett has a 40% tax rate and plans to finance her investment with 50% equity, what should she use as the project's beta.

   b.   If the current risk-free rate is 7% and the market return is 16%, what should Judy use as the project's cost of capital?

Solution:

a. $b_u = \dfrac{b_1}{1 + (1\text{-}t)(B/E)}$ for proxy firm

   $b_u = \dfrac{1.50}{1 + (1\text{-}.4)(3)} = .536$

   $b_l = b_u [1 + (1\text{-}t)(B/E)]$ for Blansett

   $b_l = .536 \ [1 + (1\text{-}.4)(1)] = .8576$

b. $k = r_f + (r_m - r_f)b$

   $k = .07 + (.16 - .07).8576$

   $k = .07 + .077 = .147 = 14.7\%$

Judy should use 14.7% as her cost of capital for the commuter route investment.

12

The Cost of Capital

One of the key variables in capital budgeting decisions is the cost of capital. The cost of capital can be thought of as what the firm must pay for capital or the return required by investors in the firm's securities. It can also be thought of as the minimum rate of return required on new investments undertaken by the firm. The cost of capital is determined in the capital markets and depends on the risk associated with the firm's activities.

I. The required return, k, on any security may be thought of as consisting of a risk-free rate of return plus a premium for the risk inherent in the security, or:

$$k = r_f + \text{risk premium}$$

A. The risk-free rate of return is usually measured by the rate of return on risk-free securities such as short term Treasury securities.

1. The risk-free rate increases with expectations of future inflation.

2. The risk-free rate depends on the overall supply and demand for funds in the economy.

B. There are four major risk components which determine the risk premium on a security.

1. Business risk arises from the variability of the firm's operating income and is determined by the variability of sales revenues and expenses and by the amount of operating leverage the firm uses.

2. <u>Financial risk</u> arises from the additional variability of the firm's net earnings associated with the use of financial leverage together with the increased risk of bankruptcy associated with the use of debt.

3. <u>Marketability risk</u> refers to the ability to quickly buy and sell the securities. Securities which are widely traded have less marketability risk than those which are less actively traded.

4. <u>Interest rate risk</u> refers to the variability in returns on securities arising from changes in interest rates. Increases in interest rates reduce the market price of the security. Decreases in interest rates reduce the rate at which intermediate interest payments can be reinvested.

C. The cost of funds may increase with the amount of financing required.

D. The cost of funds obtained from a particular type of security increases the lower the security ranks in its claims on the firm. The cost of common equity is higher than that for preferred stock. The return required on preferred stock is higher than that for unsecured debt which is higher than that for secured debt.

E. The cost of capital to the firm is equal to the equilibrium rate of return demanded by investors in the capital markets for securities of that degree of risk.

II. Regardless of the specific source of financing used at a particular time, a weighted composite cost of capital dependent on component costs and the proportions of the components in the target capital structure is used for capital budgeting decisions.

A. Before tax considerations, the cost of debt is the rate of return, k_d, that equates the present value of the future cash flows from interest and principal to P_0, the offering price of the security.

1. The before-tax cost of debt can be found by using the methods for calculating yield-to-maturity illustrated in the chapter on bond valuation.

2. Because most new debt is sold at or close to par value, the before tax cost of debt can usually be approximated by the coupon interest rate:

$$k_d = \text{coupon interest rate.}$$

3. Interest payments on debt are deductible in arriving at taxable income. The after-tax cost of debt, k_i, is given by:

$$k_i = k_d (1 - \text{tax rate})$$

B. The cost of preferred stock is the rate of return required by investors in the preferred stock of the firm adjusted for flotation costs.

    1. The preferred stock valuation model tells us:

$$P_0 = D_p/k_p$$

    where P_0 is the price, D_p is the dividend, and k_p is the investor's required rate of return.

    2. The cost of preferred stock is given by:

$$k_p = D_p/P_{net}$$

    where P_{net} is the net proceeds to the firm after subtracting flotation costs.

    3. Dividends on preferred stock are not deductible in arriving at taxable income, so no tax adjustment is made. Because of this the cost to the firm of preferred stock is usually higher than that of debt, and firms prefer to obtain leverage from debt rather than from preferred stock.

C. The basic cost of equity capital is the equilibrium rate of return required by investors in the firm's common stock. Equity capital can be raised internally through retained earnings or externally through the sale of new common stock. Use of externally generated equity capital entails flotation costs in addition to the required return.

D. The cost of internally generated equity can be developed in several different ways.

    1. If dividends are expected to grow at a constant rate g, the price of common stock can be obtained as:

$$P_0 = D_1/(k_e - g)$$

    where k_e is the required rate of return and D_1 is the next anticipated dividend which is equal to the current dividend D_0 times $(1 + g)$. By simple algebra:

$$k_e = D_1/P_0 + g$$

    2. If dividends are expected to grow at a rate g_1 for m years followed by perpetual growth at a rate g_2 in later years, the valuation model can be generalized to:

$$P_0 = \sum_{t=1}^{m} \frac{D_0(1 + g_1)^t}{(1 + k_e)^t} + \frac{1}{(1 + k_e)^m} \times \frac{D_{m+1}}{k_e - g_2}$$

k_e must be solved for by trial and error.

3.   Dividend valuation models (frequently called DCF or discounted cash flow and models) are frequently used to calculate a firm's cost of equity. Analysts' forecasts of future earnings rates are a superior source of information for DCF models. Institutional Brokers Estimate Service (IBES) summarizes analysts' forecasts for the stocks of more than 3400 firms.

4.   The cost of equity capital can also be estimated using the capital asset pricing model (CAPM). In the CAPM, the required return on a stock depends on the risk-free rate, r_f, and a risk premium. The risk premium is determined by the difference between the expected return on the market as a whole and the risk-free rate, $(r_m - r_f)$ and by beta, b, which is a measure of the volatility of the stock relative to the volatility of the market index. Using the CAPM, the required return on equity is given by:

$$k_e = r_f + b(r_m - r_f)$$

5.   Another method of estimating the cost of equity is to add 6.8 percentage points to the cost of debt (for an average risk company). This is called the risk premium on debt approach. For a firm with a beta of 0.7, 3 to 4 points are added to the cost of debt.

E.   The cost of external equity capital is greater than the cost of retained earnings and must be measured slightly differently.

1.   The cost of new issues of common stock must include flotation costs.

2.   Because a new issue increases the supply of stock, the equilibrium price of the stock can be expected to drop so that the offering price of a new issue must be lower than the market price of the stock before announcement of the new issue.

3.   The cost of external equity, k'_e, can be determined as:

$$k'_e = \frac{D_1}{P_{net}} + g$$

where P_{net} is the actual proceeds to the firm.

F.   The weighted, or overall, cost of capital is obtained from the weighted costs of the individual components. The weights are equal to the proportion of each of the components in the target capital structure.

1.   The general expression for calculating the weighted cost of capital, k_a, is:

$$k_a = \text{(equity fraction)(cost of equity)} + \text{(debt fraction)(cost of debt)}$$

$$k_a = \frac{E}{D+E}(k_e) \;+\; \frac{D}{D+E}(k_d)(1-t)$$

where D = amount of debt and E = amount of equity.

2.   The appropriate component costs to use in determining k_a are the marginal costs or the costs associated with the next dollar of capital to be raised. These may differ from the historical costs of capital raised in the past.

G.   The weighted (marginal) cost of capital can be positively related to the amount of funds raised if internally generated funds (which would be used first) are cheaper than externally generated funds (because of flotation costs). The procedure for finding the weighted (marginal) cost of funds schedule can be understood by studying part a of problem 4 below.

H.   If the capital structure includes debt, preferred stock and common stock, the weighted cost of capital is:

$$k_a = \frac{E}{D+P_f+E}(k_e) \;+\; \frac{P_f}{D+P_f+E}(k_p) \;+\; \frac{D}{D+P_f+E}(k_i)$$

III.   Determination of the optimal capital budget and the weighted cost of capital must be an integrated procedure.

A.   As larger amounts of capital are raised, the marginal cost of capital increases because of the need to raise external equity and the increased cost associated with additional increments of debt. This requires that a marginal cost of capital schedule be developed which shows the costs associated with each increment or "package" of capital throughout the range of the potential capital budget. At each point where the cost of a component changes, a new package occurs. The resulting schedule of marginal costs can be plotted on a graph as a marginal cost of capital curve.

B.   An investment opportunities curve is developed by plotting expected returns against the total capital to be expanded.

C.   The information contained in the investment opportunities curve and the marginal cost of capital curve is combined so that the optimal capital budget contains all projects for which the expected return lies above the marginal cost of capital curve. This procedure is illustrated in the solved problem number 4 below.

IV.   For some firms depreciation is a major source of funds for investment.

A.   The cost of funds generated by depreciation is taken as equal to the firm's weighted cost of capital based on retained earnings and the lowest cost debt.

B.   The availability of funds from depreciation shifts the marginal cost of capital curve to the right.

TRUE AND FALSE QUESTIONS

Agree with each of the statements or reject it and modify it so that it is acceptable.

1.   Business risk does not depend on the capital structure of the firm so it does not affect the firm's cost of capital.

2.   Marketability risk refers to the risk that the products of the firm will not have an adequate market.

3.   Unsecured debt has a higher cost than secured debt.

4.   The component cost of debt sold at its par value is equal to the coupon rate of interest on the debt.

5.   The component cost of preferred stock must be adjusted for taxes which the stockholders must pay on the dividends.

6.   Using the dividend model, the cost of equity capital is given by

$$k_e = (D_0/P_0) + g$$

7.   The cost of external equity is higher than the cost of retained earnings.

8.   If a firm uses preferred stock, the expression for the weighted cost of capital is

$$\frac{E}{D + E + P}(k_e) \quad + \quad \frac{D}{D + E + P}(k_d)(1 - t) \quad + \quad \frac{P}{D + E + P}(k_p)$$

where P is the amount of preferred stock.

9.   All potential capital investment projects are evaluating using a single cost of capital.

10.   Marginal cost of capital refers to the cost of the next dollar of capital to be raised.

11.   Funds derived from depreciation are free.

Answers to True and False Questions

1. Business risk is a component of the risk of the firm and the cost of capital depends on this risk.

2. Marketability risk refers to the ability to buy and sell the firm's securities quickly and easily.

3. True.

4. True.

5. Preferred dividends are not deductible in arriving at the taxable income of the firm so no adjustment is needed. Stockholders' taxes do not directly affect the cost of preferred stock to the firm.

6. Using the dividend model, the cost of equity capital is given by

$$k_e = (D_1/P_0) + g$$

7. The cost of external equity is higher than the cost of retained earnings because of flotation costs.

8. True.

9. The optimal capital budget and determination of the cost of capital must be integrated. The marginal cost of capital increases as the package of sources of capital changes with the amount of capital to be raised. High risk projects should be evaluated at a cost of capital that is consistent with project risk.

10. True.

11. Since the funds could be returned to the stockholders or used to retire debt, the appropriate opportunity cost is the firm's weighted cost of capital.

CHAPTER 12 PROBLEMS

1. The ICU Keyhole Company is planning to issue $15 million of 6- 2/3% preferred stock at a price of $150 per share. Flotation costs will be $7 per share. ICU's tax rate is 40%. Calculate the after tax cost of the preferred stock assuming:

    a. The stock is perpetuity

    b. The stock is callable in 7 years at $169 per share and is expected to be called at that time.

Solution:

a. The cost of perpetual preferred stock is given by $K_p = D/P_{net}$. No adjustment for taxes is required.

$$D = 6\text{-}2/3\% \text{ of } \$150 = \$10$$

$$P_{net} = \$150 - \$7 = \$143$$

$$k_p = 10/143 = .07 \text{ or } 7\%$$

b. The general principle is that the cost of a component of capital is equal to the discount rate that equates the present value of expected cash flows to the proceeds from the issue. Here we want

$$P_{net} = \sum_{t=1}^{7} \frac{D}{(1+k_p)^t} + \frac{\text{Call Price}}{(1+k_p)^7}$$

$$143 = \sum_{t=1}^{7} \frac{10}{(1+k_p)^t} + \frac{169}{(1+k_p)^7}$$

$$k_p = 9\%$$

2.   The following information is available concerning the Pan-T- Hose Company.

Per share current market price	$15.00
Per share current dividend	0.60
Per share current earnings	2.00
Expected growth rate in EPS	10%
Beta	1.2
Risk-free rate	6.0%
Expected market return	13.5%

The dividend payout ratio is expected to remain constant. Earnings are expected to grow at a constant rate for the foreseeable future. Calculate the cost of retained earnings using:

a. The dividend capitalization approach

b. The CAPM approach

Solution:

a. The dividend capitalization approach uses the formula

$$k_e = (D_1/P_0) + g$$

The constant payout ratio implies that dividends will grow at the same rate as EPS so $g = .10$.

We are given that $D_0 = .60$, $D_1 = D_0(1 + g)$ so we have $D_1 = .60(1 + .1) = .66$.

We are given that $P_0 = \$15$ so we have

$$k_e = (.66/15) + .10 = .144$$

b. The CAPM approach uses

$$k_e = r_f + b(r_m - r_f) \text{ so we have}$$

$$k_e = .06 + 1.2(.135 - .06) = .15.$$

3. The Lever Crowbar Company has a target capital structure of 70% long-term debt and 30% equity. Long-term debt will cost 8% and the cost of retained earnings is 15%. The firm's tax rate is 40%. Calculate the weighted cost of capital.

Solution:

The weighted cost of capital is given by

$$k_a = (\text{Fraction of Equity})(k_e) + (\text{Fraction of Debt})(k_d)(1-t)$$

$$= (.30)(.15) + (.70)(.08)(.60) = .0786$$

4. The Parr Golf Company is working on their capital budget. Four projects have been identified with the following characteristics:

Project	Investment	IRR
A	$2 million	11%
B	$5 million	10%
C	$4 million	12%
D	$3 million	13%

The company can issue up to $5 million of debt at a cost of 9% and any reasonable additional amount at 12%. The target capital structure calls for equal amounts of debt and equity. Anticipated net income from which earnings will be retained for reinvestment in the business is $7,025,000. The current stock price is $55 and there are 1.1 million shares outstanding. The most recent dividend was $2.50 per share. Dividends are expected to grow at 10% per year. Additional shares can be issued at $53 before a $3 per share flotation cost. The firm's marginal tax rate is 40%.

Determine the following:

a. The marginal cost of capital schedule
b. The investment opportunities schedule
c. The size of the optimal capital budget and the projects it contains.

Solution:

a. The first step in finding the MCC schedule is to find the costs of the individual components. The before tax costs for debt are given, but the costs of retained earnings and new equity must be found.

Based on the nature of the information provided, the cost of retained earnings must be found using the dividend capitalization approach. This is

$$k_e = (D_1/P_0) + g$$

We are given that P_0 = $55, D_0 = $2.50 and g = .10. From this we have D_1 = 2.50(1.1) = 2.75.

$$k_e = (2.75/55) + .10 = .15$$

The cost of new equity capital is calculated similarly except that we use P_{net} rather than P_0.

$$P_{net} = \text{Issue cost - flotation costs} = 53 - 3 = \$50$$

$$k'_e = (D_1/P_{net}) + g = (2.75/50) + .10 = .155$$

To complete the gathering of information regarding the individual components, we must determine the amount of retained earnings to be available. Net income is expected to be $7,025,000 out of which we expect to pay dividends of $2.75 per share on 1.1 million shares. This represents total dividends of $3,025,000 leaving retained earnings of $4 million.

We can now summarize the component costs and the amounts available at those amounts as follows.

Debt	Equity
1st $5 million: 9%	1st $4 million: 15.0%
any additional: 12%	any additional: 15.5%

We now examine the composition of the marginal packages of capital. To do this we first find the break points in the MCC schedule.

Break points occur as successively higher cost debt or equity are used.

We will have "used up" the 9% debt when the $5 million available represents 50% of the capital raised. This occurs when

$5 million = .5 x capital raised
capital raised = $5 million/.5 = $10 million

We will have "used up" the 15% equity when the $4 million available represents 50% of the capital raised. This occurs when

$4 million   = .5 x capital raised
capital raised = $8 million

Ordering these break points, they occur at $8 million and $10 million. From these calculations we now that the following packages are to be considered.

Total Capital $(w_e)(k_e) + (w_d)(k_d)(1 - t) = k_a$

less than 8 million $(.5)(.150) + (.5)(.09)(.6) = .1020$
8 million-10 million $(.5)(.155) + (.5)(.09)(.6) = .1045$
more than 10 million $(.5)(.155) + (.5)(.12)(.6) = .1135$

This is a schedule of the MCC from which a graph can be drawn.

b. Determination of the investment opportunities schedule consists of organizing the information about the potential investments. This is done by ordering the rates of return in descending order and determining the total amount of the capital budget for projects at each rate of return or higher.

Total Capital Budget	IRR
$ 3 million	13%
$ 7 million	12%
$ 9 million	11%
$ 14 million	10%

c. To determine the optimal capital budget, we can either graph the marginal cost of capital and investment opportunities schedules and determine where they cross or we can accomplish the same thing in a table as follows:

Total Capital Budget	IRR	MCC
$ 3 million	13%	10.20%
$ 7 million	12%	10.20%
$ 9 million	11%	10.45%
$ 14 million	10%	11.35%

The optimal capital budget will be for $9 million since that is the last point where the IRR exceeds the MCC. This capital budget will include those projects with IRR's of 11% and above. They are A, C, and D. Graphically, this solution is found as follows:

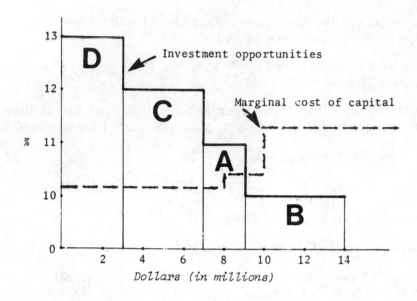

5. The Kinky Rope Company is determining their MCC schedule. They expect to generate $3 million from depreciation. Their target capital structure consists of 40% debt and 60% equity. Debt and equity capital can be raised according to the following schedule:

Debt		Equity	
1st $2 million	8%	1st $1.5 million	18%
next $4 million	10%	next $4.5 million	20%
any additional	13%	any additional	23%

Find the breakpoints in their MCC.

Solution:

To find the breakpoints, we look at the cumulative amounts of debt and equity available in successively higher cost increments and determine the total capital that can be raised with these amounts of debt and equity under the target capital structure. The breakpoints thus found are then adjusted for the funds available from depreciation.

Cumulative debt levels
$2 million

Total capital raised
$2 million/.4 = $5 million + $3 million = $8 million

$2 million + 4 million

$6 million/.4 = $15 million + $3 million = $18 million

Cumulative equity levels   Total capital raised
$1.5 million $1.5 million/.6 = $2.5 million + $3 million
                                 = $5.5 million

$6.0 million $6 million/.6 = $10 million + $3 million
                                 = $13 million

Sorting these into order we find breakpoints at $5.5 million, $8 million, $13 million, and $18 million. Each of these breakpoints has been increased by the $3 million available from depreciation resulting in the following packages:

Amount raised ($)	Component Costs	
0 - 5.5 million	8% debt	18% equity
5.5 - 8.0 million	8% debt	20% equity
8.0 -13.0 million	10% debt	20% equity
13.0 -18.0 million	10% debt	23% equity
over 18.0 million	13% debt	23% equity

13

The Capital Structure Decision

Capital structure is the relative amount of permanent short-term debt, long-term debt, preferred stock, and common stock used to finance the firm. This chapter summarizes some very important thinking on the capital structure decision. First, the value of the firm is shown to be independent of capital structure if capital markets are perfect and there are no corporate income taxes. Then the optimal capital structure is shown to be 100% debt if a corporate income tax exists and there are no bankruptcy or agency costs. Finally, if a corporate income tax, bankruptcy costs, and agency costs exist, an optimal capital structure is shown to consist of both debt and equity. The chapter also presents EBIT-EPS analysis, which gives a picture of what happens to EPS (earnings per share) as EBIT (earnings before interest and taxes) fluctuate if the firm uses different capital structures.

I.   Capital structure is one of the fundamental issues in financial management. Some important terms are:

  A.   Capital structure--the relative amounts of permanent short- term debt, long-term debt, preferred stock, and common stock used to finance a firm.

  B.   Financial structure--the relative amounts of total current liabilities, long-term debt, preferred stock, and common stock used to finance a firm.

  C.   Optimal capital structure--the capital structure that minimizes a firm's weighted cost of capital and, therefore, maximizes the value of the firm.

  D.   Target capital structure--the capital structure at which the firm plans to operate.

       E.   Debt capacity -- the amount of debt in the firm's optimal capital structure.

       F.   The optimal capital structure (and debt capacity) are determined by factors including: the business risk of the firm, the tax structure, bankruptcy potential, agency costs, and signalling affects.

II.   The discussion on capital structure is based on important assumptions.

       A.   Assume that the firm's investment policy is held constant. The capital structure changes the distribution of the firm's operating income (EBIT) among the firm's claimants, including debtholders, preferred stockholders, and common stockholders.

       B.   With a constant investment policy, investments are assumed to leave the debt capacity of the firm unchanged.

III.   Business risk is the variability or uncertainty of a firm's operating income (EBIT). There are many factors influencing a firm's business risk, including:

       A.   The variability of sales volume

       B.   The variability of selling prices

       C.   The variability of costs

       D.   The amount of market power the absence of present or future competition reduces the firm's risk.

       E.   The degree of operating leverage (DOL) Operating leverage involves the use of assets having fixed costs. The DOL is defined as the percentage change in EBIT resulting from a given percentage change in sales.

IV.   Financial risk refers to the additional variability of earnings per share and the increased probability of bankruptcy that result when the firm uses fixed cost sources of funds.

       A.   Financial leverage can increase the returns to common shareholders, but the increased returns are achieved at the expense of increased risk.

       B.   Financial ratios that can indicate financial risk are the debt-to-assets ratio, the debt-to equity ratio, the times interest earned ratio, and the fixed charge coverage ratio. Another financial risk measure is the degree of financial leverage, (DFL):

$$DFL = \frac{\% \text{ change in EPS}}{\% \text{ change in EBIT}}$$

C.   The probability distribution of profits also indicates the nature of financial risk.

V.   Capital structure theory studies the relationship between capital structure (the ratio of debt to assets) and the cost of capital (and the value of the firm). Capital structure models help to show the role of personal and corporate taxes, bankruptcy costs, and agency costs on the determination of an optimal capital structure.

A.   Franco Modigliani and Merton Miller (MM) showed that under certain assumptions, the firm's overall cost of capital (and the firm's value) were independent of capital structure. This classic article was published in 1958.

1.   MM made the following assumptions:

a.   No transaction costs for buying and selling securities

b.   Large numbers of buyers and sellers in the market

c.   Relevant information costless and readily available to all investors.

d.   All investors can borrow or lend at the same rate.

e.   Investors are rational and have homogeneous expectations of a firm's earnings.

f.   Firms can be put into homogeneous risk classes.

2.   In their model the cost of debt, (k_d), and the cost of capital, (k_a), are constant as capital structure changes. If leverage increases, the cost of equity, (k_e), increases to exactly offset the benefit of more debt financing, leaving the cost of capital constant.

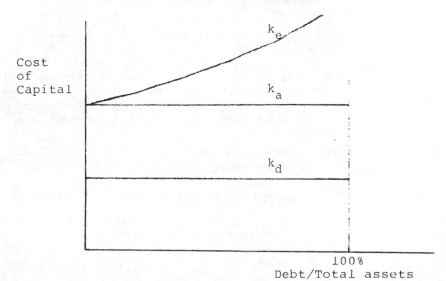

If the overall cost of capital is independent of capital structure, it follows that the firm's value is independent of capital structure.

3.   MM showed their theory to be correct using an arbitrage argument.

   a.   Suppose that there are two unlevered firms of identical business risk. If one of the firms issues some debt, then some people argue that its value would increase (and MM would argue the firm is overvalued relative to the unlevered firm).

   b.   Investors would sell the stock of the overvalued (levered) firm and take on personal debt of an amount similar to the debt behind the levered shares.

   c.   With the proceeds of the stock sale and personal borrowing, investors will buy enough of the unlevered firm's shares to service the debt and replace the income lost from the sale of the levered firm's shares. Because the unlevered firm is undervalued, some of the proceeds will be left over and the investor will have an arbitrage profit.

   d.   The selling of the overpriced (levered) stock drives its price down and the buying of the underpriced (unlevered) stock drives its price up until their values are in line and arbitrage profits are no longer possible. Assuming no taxes, the values of the two firms are easily given. The value of the unlevered firm is

$$\text{Value of U} = \frac{\text{DIV}}{k_e}$$

where DIV is dividends paid.

The value of the levered firm is

$$\text{Value of L} = \frac{\text{DIV}}{k_e} + \frac{I}{k_d}$$

The dividends paid to L's stockholders are reduced by the amount of interest paid on the debt and k_e is higher for L because of the additional leverage-induced risk. The values of U and L are identical due to arbitrage.

B.   With corporation income taxes, the value of the levered firm will be more than the value of the levered firm. MM established this in 1963.

   1.   The values of U and L are still given by the same two equations

$$\text{Value of U} = \frac{\text{DIV}}{k_e}$$

$$\text{Value of L} = \frac{DIV}{k_e} + \frac{I}{k_d}$$

2. The dividends distributed to U's stockholders are reduced by the taxes paid on operating income, so the value of U drops. However, for L, dividends paid are operating income minus interest and taxes. Since interest is tax deductible, so the levered firm realizes a tax saving relative to U.

$$\text{Tax shield} = i\,B\,t$$

where i = interest rate, B = value of debt, and t = tax rate

3. The value of the tax shield to L is capitalized at the interest rate on the debt, so the present value of the tax shield equals the tax rate times the amount of debt.

$$\text{Present value of tax shield} = \frac{iBt}{i} = Bt$$

4. The value of the levered firm equals the value of the unlevered firm thus the value of the tax shield.

Value of levered firm = Value of unlevered firm + Value of tax shield

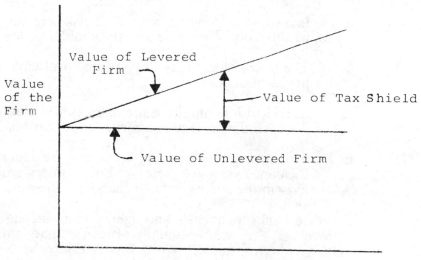

5. According to this result, the firm maximizes its value by choosing a capital structure that is all debt.

C. This section extends the analysis of capital structure by including bankruptcy costs and agency costs

1.   Increasing its leverage can increase the potential costs of financial distress, or bankruptcy. "Bankruptcy costs" come from several sources.

    a.   As the firm increases its debt level, lenders may demand higher interest rates.

    b.   Lenders may decline to lend at all, which imposes an opportunity cost on the firm from lost investment opportunities.

    c.   Customers may doubt the firm's ability to continue in existence and shift their business to other firms they feel are more likely to remain.

    d.   A company facing financial distress incurs extra accounting and legal costs.

    e.   Finally if a firm is forced to liquidate, its assets may have to be sold for less than their market values.

2.   Agency costs can arise in any agency relationship. In the stockholder-bondholder relationship, the bondholders are the principals and the stockholders are the agents. There are conflicts of interests between these two parties.

    a.   Investing in projects with high risk and low returns can shift wealth from bondholders to stockholders.

    b.   The stockholders may forego some profitable investments in the presence of debt.

    c.   Stockholders might issue high quantities of new debt and diminish the protection afforded to earlier bondholders.

    d.   Monitoring and bonding costs may be incurred to reduce the incidence of agency costs. Bondholders will shift these costs back to the agents through charging higher interest rates.

3.   Because bankruptcy costs and agency costs increase with the amount of leverage, they can eventually offset the marginal benefits from the value of the tax shield. With corporate income taxes and no agency or bankruptcy costs, the optimal capital structure is a corner solution with 100% debt financing. With the inclusion of agency and bankruptcy costs, the optimal capital structure will be an interior solution with a mixture debt and equity in the capital structure. The figure below illustrates this important result.

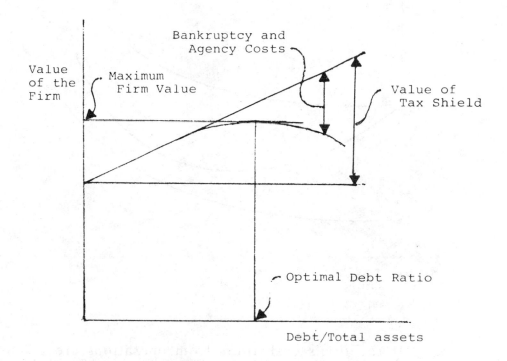

D.   The capital structure affects the riskiness of the debt and common stock of the firm and hence the cost of capital.

1.   The greater the proportion of debt used, the greater the risk of bankruptcy and the higher interest costs on the debt will be.

2.   The greater the proportion of debt used, the greater the variability of earnings per share and the higher the risk premium required by common stockholders.

3.   The after tax cost of debt is less than the cost of equity.

4.   The above relationships are shown in the graph below. For any level of $B/(B + E)$ (except 0), the weighted cost of capital is between k_e and $k_d(1 - t) = k_i$:

$$k_a \quad = \quad \frac{E}{B + E}(k_e) \quad + \quad \frac{B}{B + E}(k_i)$$

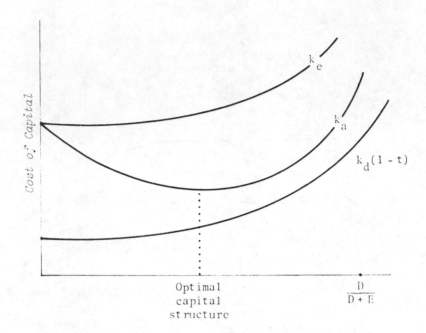

5.   If the firm's cash flows from operations are taken as given, discounting them at the lowest possible cost of capital maximizes the value of the firm. Hence the least cost capital structure is optimal.

E.   Personal tax effects, industry effects, signalling effects, and managerial preferences also impact the optimal capital structure.

1.   Miller (half of MM) in 1977 showed that if personal taxes rates are higher for interest income from debt than for equity income, this would reverse some or all of the tax benefit corporations receive from issuing debt instead of equity.

2.   Industry profitability and bankruptcy patterns tend to be reflected in different amounts of leverage across industries.

3.   When firms issue new securities, negative stock price responses frequently occur. Stock repurchases have had positive responses, and leverage increasing decisions have been received positively while leverage decreasing decisions have been received negatively.

4.   Managers seem to have a preference for internal financing. When external financing is used, debt financing seems to be preferred over equity. These preferences may reflect a desire by management to avoid the discipline and monitoring that occurs when new securities are sold publicly. This behavior is called the pecking order theory.

F.   Capital structure theory and related empirical research provide important insights for managers.

    1.   Capital structure is a centrally important management decision.

    2.   The benefits of the tax shield from debt provide an incentive to use debt financing to the point that increasing agency and bankruptcy costs offset the debt advantage.

    3.   The optimal capital structure is heavily influenced by business risk.

    4.   Changes in capital structure signal important information to investors.

VI.   Two practical techniques used by managers in their capital structure decisions are EBIT-EPS analysis and cash insolvency analysis.

A.   A useful technique for comparing alternative capital structures is EBIT-EPS analysis. EBIT-EPS analysis can be performed graphically or algebraically. In either case the intent is to determine the level of EBIT where EPS would be identical under either debt or equity financing.

    1.   EBIT-EPS analysis can be performed algebraically by use of the relationship

$$\frac{(EBIT - I_1)(1 - t)}{S_1} = \frac{(EBIT - I_2)(1 - t)}{S_2}$$

where I_1 and I_2 represent the amount of interest to be paid under plans 1 and 2. S_1 and S_2 represent the number of shares of common stock under each plan.

    2.   For graphical analysis of EBIT-EPS indifference points, we calculate earnings per share at each of two levels of EBIT for each of the financing plans. Drawing straight lines through the pairs of points for each financing plan provides a graphical representation of the effects of the different levels of debt on EPS. The point where lines cross indicates the indifference point.

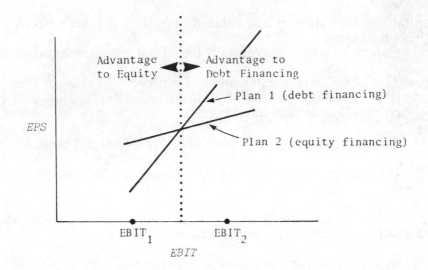

3.   If it is reasonable to expect that EBIT will be to the right of the indifference level, increased leverage is favorable in the sense that higher EPS results.

B.   In the case of a recession, liquidity is important.

1.   Liquidity ratios like the current and quick ratio show the ability of the firm to pay its maturing short term debt.

2.   The projected cash balance in a recession is also critical.

$$CB_R = CB_0 + NCF_R$$

where

CB_R =   cash balance in a recession

CB_0 =   cash balance at the beginning of a recession

NCF_R=   net cash flow during the recession

The firm needs cash (or access to cash) to survive a recession.

C.   Managers also adjust their capital structure to industry standards; to advice they receive from lenders, investment bankers, and bond rating agencies; to their own aversion to fixed debt obligations; and to their wish to maintain control (which could happen if they issue equity).

VII.   Multinational firms have a more complex capital structure decision than purely domestic firms.

A.   Exchange rate risk should lead firms to finance investments in a country with funds from that country's capital markets.

B.   Some countries use more financial leverage than others.

C.   Some governments restrict foreign investments in their countries.

D.   There is risk of expropriation in some countries.

E.   Some host countries provide low-cost financing to stimulate investment.

VIII. (Appendix to Chapter 13)   Operating and financial leverage are covered in this appendix.

A.   Operating leverage and business risk are related concepts.

1.   The firm's <u>degree of operating leverage</u> (DOL) is defined as the percentage change in earnings before interest and taxes (EBIT) resulting from a given percentage change in sales (or output).

a.   The formula for the DOL is

$$DOL = \frac{\text{Percentage Change in EBIT}}{\text{Percentage Change in Sales}}$$

$$DOL = \frac{\Delta EBIT/EBIT}{\Delta Sales/Sales}$$

$$DOL = \frac{(EBIT_1 - EBIT_0)/EBIT_0}{(Sales_1 - Sales_0)/Sales_0}$$

where $EBIT_0$ and $Sales_0$ are the original values of EBIT and sales and $EBIT_1$ and $Sales_1$ are the new values.

b.   Economists term the percentage change in one variable with respect to another variable its <u>elasticity</u>. For example, the DOL is the elasticity of EBIT with respect to sales.

If the breakeven model assumptions apply, the degree of operating leverage can also be found as

$$DOL = \frac{\text{Sales - Variable Costs}}{\text{EBIT}}$$

$$DOL = \frac{(P - V)Q}{(P - V)Q - F}$$

2.   Business risk is the inherent variability or uncertainty of a firm's EBIT.

    a.   One important factor affecting business risk is the degree of operating leverage. The greater a firm's DOL, all other factors held constant, the greater will be its business risk.

    b.   Another factor affecting business risk is the variability or uncertainty of sales.

    c.   Another factor is the variability or uncertainty of the selling price (P) or variable cost per unit (V).

    d.   These factors are interrelated. For example, an airline has a high DOL and relatively unstable sales and high business risk.

B.   Financial leverage occurs when the firm employs funds with fixed costs, such as debt with fixed interest payments and preferred stock with fixed preferred stock dividends.

1.   The use of debt or preferred stock financing changes the returns to common shareholders (earnings per share) and also affects the amount of change in earnings per share in response to a given change in EBIT.

2.   The degree of financial leverage (DFL) is defined as the percentage change in earnings per share (EPS) resulting from a given percentage change in earnings before interest and taxes (EBIT).

    a.   The formula for DFL is

$$DFL = \frac{\text{Percentage Change in EPS}}{\text{Percentage Change in EBIT}}$$

$$DFL = \frac{\Delta EPS/EPS}{\Delta EBIT/EBIT}$$

$$DFL = \frac{(EPS_1 - EPS_0)/EPS_0}{(EBIT_1 - EBIT_0)/EBIT_0}$$

where EPS_0 and $EBIT_0$ are the original values and EPS_1 and $EBIT_1$ are the new values.

    b.   An alternative formula for the DFL which is more easily calculated is:

$$DFL = \frac{EBIT}{EBIT - I - D_p/(1 - t)}$$

where

I = interest payments,
D_p = preferred dividend payments, and
t = the marginal tax rate.

Preferred dividends are divided by (1 - t) to find their fixed cost on a before-tax basis. Interest is tax-deductible, so no such adjustment is made to I.

c. A firm with a high fixed capital cost relative to EBIT will have a high DFL, i.e., financial risk. The amount of fixed capital costs depends on the mix of debt and equity in that firm's capital structure. The firm's capital structure is the makeup of its permanent long-term debt, preferred stock, and common stock equity.

3. The probability of negative (or positive) earnings per share can be found if the distribution of EBIT is known. If EBIT is normally distributed, let

$$Z = \frac{\text{loss level EBIT - expected EBIT}}{\text{standard deviation of EBIT}}$$

The loss level EBIT is the amount of EBIT needed to cover interest charges and preferred dividends (on a before-tax basis). This Z value can be looked up in a normal table to find the probability of a negative EPS.

C. Combined leverage is the effect of both operating leverage (fixed operating costs) and financial leverage (fixed capital costs) on the returns to a firm's common stockholders.

1. The degree of combined leverage (DCL) is the percentage change in earnings per share (EPS) resulting from a given percentage change in sales.

a. The basic formula for the DCL is

$$DCL = \frac{\text{Percentage Change in EPS}}{\text{Percentage Change in Sales}}$$

$$DCL = \frac{\Delta EPS/EPS}{\Delta Sales/Sales}$$

$$DCL = \frac{(EPS_1 - EPS_0)/EPS_0}{(Sales_1 - Sales_0)/Sales_0}$$

where EPS_0 and $Sales_0$ are the original values and EPS_1 and $Sales_1$ are the new values.

        b.   The degree of combined leverage is the product of the degree of operating leverage and the degree of financial leverage,

$$DCL = (DOL)(DFL)$$

        c.   The DCL also equals

$$DCL = \frac{Sales - Variable\ Costs}{EBIT - I - D_p/(1 - t)}$$

    2.   A firm can trade off operating and financial leverage to control its degree of combined leverage. For example, a firm with a high DOL may choose a capital structure with a low DFL to avoid a high DCL. Business risk and financial risk account for the total variability of the firm's earnings per share.

TRUE AND FALSE QUESTIONS

Agree with each of the statements or reject it and modify it so that it is acceptable.

1.   Capital structure refers to the composition of the right hand side of the balance sheet.

2.   Financial structure refers to the amount of long-term debt, preferred stock, and common equity of the firm.

3.   As leverage increases, the net income theory of capital structure assumes that cost of equity and cost of debt are constant and the overall cost of capital declines.

4.   The optimal capital structure minimizes the cost of equity.

5.   In their 1958 article, Modigliani and Miller showed that (in the absence of taxes, market imperfections) two firms of the same operating risk class and different capital structures would have the same overall cost of capital.

6.   The introduction of corporate income taxes had no impact on the optimal capital structure of a firm.

7.   An example of a bankruptcy cost imposed on highly levered firms is the reluctance of customers to do business with the firm if the customers doubt the continued existence of the firm.

8.   Firms should try to minimize their cost of capital.

9.   EBIT-EPS analysis can be used to determine when debt financing is advantageous.

10.   EBIT-EPS analysis implies that debt financing should be used when the expected level of EBIT is less than the indifference level of EBIT.

11.   Other things equal, investors in debt consider the debt less risky if the firm is less leveraged rather than more leveraged.

12.   The cost of equity capital decreases as the financial leverage increases because of the potential for higher EPS.

13.   The lower the cost of capital, the higher the value of the firm.

14.   An example of an agency cost in the shareholder-bondholder relationship would be a decision to invest in very risky projects that cause the value of the bonds to drop and the value of common stock to rise.

15.   The existence of bankruptcy and agency costs cause the firm to choose more leverage.

Answers to True and False Questions

1.   Capital structure refers to the composition of the long-term portion of the right hand side of the balance sheet.

2.   Financial structure refers to the composition of the right hand side of the balance sheet including the proportion of current liabilities.

3.   True.

4.   The optimal capital structure minimizes the weighted cost of capital.

5.   True.

6.   Assuming no agency or bankruptcy costs, the introduction of corporate income taxes creates a tax shield to debt such that the optimal capital structure is a corner solution with all debt financing.

7.   True.

8.   True.

9.   EBIT-EPS analysis alone is not sufficient basis. The effect of a change in leverage on the P/E multiple must also be considered in order to determine the effect on the stock price.

10.   EBIT-EPS analysis implies that debt financing should be used when the expected level of EBIT is more than the indifference level of EBIT.

11.   True.

12.   The cost of equity capital increases as financial leverage increases because of the increased volatility of EPS.

13.   True.

14.   True.

15.   Since bankruptcy and agency costs increase with leverage, they cause the firm to use less debt financing.

CHAPTER 13 PROBLEMS

1.   The U Company and the L Company are identical in every respect except that the U Company is unlevered while the L Company has $1,000 in 6 percent perpetual bonds outstanding (on which $60 of interest is paid each year). Both firms have expected net operating income of $300 (forever). Both firms distribute as dividends all income available to stockholders. There are no taxes. Assume no agency costs or bankruptcy costs. The cost of equity is 10 percent for the U Company and 12 percent for the L Company.

   a.   Calculate the market value of each firm.

   b.   Calculate the cost of capital for each firm.

   c.   What is the total income available annually to the firm's securityholders?

Solution:

   a.   Value of firm = Value of equity + Value of debt
        Value of firm = $Div/k_e + I/k_d$
        Value of U = 300/.10 + 0
                   = 3000 + 0 = $3,000

        Dividends for L = 300 - 60 = $240

        Value of L   =   240/.12 + 60/.06
                     =   2000 + 1000 = $3,000

   b. $k_a = \dfrac{E}{B+E} k_e + \dfrac{B}{B+E} k_d$

        For U

        $k_a = \dfrac{3000}{3000}(.10) + 0 = 10\%$

        For L

        $k_a = \dfrac{2000}{3000}(.12) + \dfrac{1000}{3000}(.06) = 10\%$

c.   For U, income distributed to security holders is $300 of dividends and $0 of interest.
     For L, the income distribution is $300, composed of $240 of dividends and $60 of interest.

Summary of results for Problem 1:

	U Company	L Company
Value of equity	$3000	$2000
Value of debt	0	1000
Value of firm	$3000	$3000
Cost of equity	.10	.12
Cost of debt	--	.06
Cost of capital	.10	.10
Net operating income	$ 300	$ 300
Less: Interest	0	60
Income available to stockholders	$ 300	$ 240
Total income available to securityholders	$ 300	$ 300

2.   Assume a 40 percent corporate income tax (with interest paid as a tax deductible expense). Reevaluate your answers to Problem 1.

Solution:

a.   Dividends for U are $300(1 - .40) = 180$ since taxes paid were $300(.40) = 120$

Value of U $= 180/.10 + 0 = \$1,800$

Dividends for L are $(300-60)(1 - .40) = \$144$ and taxes paid were $(300 - 60)(.40) = \$96$

$$\text{Value of L} = 144/.12 + 60/.06$$
$$= 1,200 + 1,000 = \$2,200$$

The value of L can also be equal to the value of the unlevered firm plus the present value of the tax shield.

$$\text{Value of L} = \text{Value of U} + Dt$$
$$= 1,800 + 1,000(.40)$$
$$= 1,800 + 400 = \$2,200$$

b.   The cost of capital is

$$k_a = \frac{E}{D+E} k_e + \frac{D}{D+E} k_d(1-t)$$

For U

$$k_a = \frac{1800}{1800}(.10) + 0 = 10\%$$

For L

$$k_a = \frac{1200}{2200}(.12) + \frac{1000}{2200}(.06)(1-.4) = 8.18\%$$

c.   For U, income distributed to securityholders is $180 of dividends to stockholders.

For L, income distributed to securityholders of $144 of dividends plus $60 of interest, which is a total of $204. Notice that the extra income distributed to L's securityholders, 204 - 180 = $24, is equal to the tax saving on interest charges, 60(.40) = $24.

Summary of Results for Problem 2:

	U Company	L Company
Value of equity	$1800	$1200
Value of debt	0	1000
Value of firm	$1800	$2200
Cost of equity	.10	.12
Cost of debt (after-tax)	--	.06(1-.4)=.036
Cost of capital	.10	.0818
Net operating income	$ 300	$ 300
Less: Interest	0	60
Taxable Income	$ 300	$ 240
Less: Taxes (40%)	120	96
Income available to stockholders	$ 180	$ 144
Total income available to securityholders	$ 180	$ 204

3.   The Even Break Glass Company is planning to raise $100 million of new capital. They currently have $20 million of 5% debt outstanding together with 5 million shares of common stock. They can raise the additional funds by using either 10% debt or issuing an additional 5 million shares at $20 per share. Their marginal tax rate is 40%.

a.   Algebraically determine the indifference level of EBIT.

b.   Graphically determine the indifference level of EBIT. (HINT: To get EPS results that graph easily, use EBIT levels of $16 million and $26 million).

Solution:

a. The indifference point occurs when EPS is the same under either plan. This occurs when we have

$$\frac{\text{EBIT - Interest Using Debt}}{\text{Shares Using Debt}} = \frac{\text{EBIT - Interest Using Equity}}{\text{Shares Using Equity}}$$

If we issue new equity, interest is $1 million on the existing debt and the number of shares increases to 10 million. If new debt is issued, interest increases by 10% of $100 million to $11 million and the number of shares remains at 5 million.

Thus we have

$$\frac{\text{EBIT - 11,000,000}}{5,000,000} = \frac{\text{EBIT - 1,000,000}}{10,000,000}$$

Solving gives EBIT = $21 million.

b. To determine the breakeven level of EBIT graphically, we first determine EPS at each of two levels of EBIT for each of the plans.

	Equity Alternative		Debt Alternative	
EBIT	16,000,000	26,000,000	16,000,000	26,000,000
- Interest	-1,000,000	-1,000,000	-11,000,000	-11,000,000
Taxable Income	15,000,000	25,000,000	5,000,000	15,000,000
Tax @ 40%	6,000,000	10,000,000	2,000,000	6,000,000
Net Income	9,000,000	15,000,000	3,000,000	9,000,000
Shares	10,000,000	10,000,000	5,000,000	5,000,000
EPS	.90	1.50	.60	1.80

The EBIT-EPS pairs are now graphed and used to establish straight lines for each of the plans.

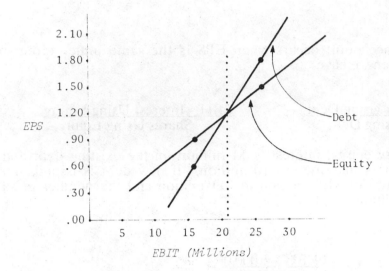

The breakeven point is seen to be at $21 million EBIT.

4.   For the Even Break Glass Company in Problem 3, which plan is riskier?

Solution:

Riskiness is measured by the variability of returns. Returns are more variable if the debt financing is used.

5.   The Mourning Glory Casket Company has determined the following costs of debt and equity capital for various capital structures.

Debt Fraction	k_e	$k_d(1-t)$
0.00	13.0	---
.10	13.1	6.0
.20	13.2	6.2
.30	13.4	6.4
.40	13.6	6.6
.50	14.0	7.0
.60	16.0	9.0

Determine the company's optimum capital structure and the associated cost of capital.

Solution:

To determine the optimum capital structure, we find the weighted cost of capital at each capital structure and choose the capital structure with the minimum weighted cost.

(Debt Fraction)	x $k_d(1-t)$) +	(Equity Fraction)	x (k_e)	= k_a
0.00	-	1.00	13.0	13.00
.10	6.0	.90	13.1	12.39
.20	6.2	.80	13.2	11.80
.30	6.4	.70	13.4	11.30
.40	6.6	.60	13.6	10.80
.50	7.0	.50	14.0	10.50
.60	9.0	.40	16.0	11.80

The minimum cost of 10.5% occurs with a capital structure consisting of 50% debt and 50% equity.

6.   The Wacky Tabakky Company needs $40 million for expansion. They currently have 10 million shares outstanding and $20 million of 5% long-term debt. They can raise the new capital by issuing an additional 4 million shares at $10 per share or by issuing $40 million of long-term debt at an interest cost of 10%.

   a.   Determine the indifference level for EBIT.

   b.   If the expected level of EBIT is $18 million and the standard deviation for EBIT is $5 million, what is the probability that equity financing will be preferred to the debt financing?

Solution:

   a.   The indifference level for EBIT can be found by using the general solution

$$\frac{(EBIT - I_1)(1-t)}{S_1} = \frac{(EBIT - I_2)(1-t)}{S_2}$$

S_1 and I_1 are the number of shares outstanding and the total interest cost under one of the plans and S_2 and I_2 are the corresponding amounts under the alternative plan. Taking debt financing as Plan 1 and equity financing as Plan 2, we solve the equation above:

$$EBIT = \frac{(14,000,000)(5,000,000) - (10,000,000)(1,000,000)}{14,000,000 - 10,000,000}$$

$$EBIT = \$15,000,000$$

   b.   Equity financing is preferred if EBIT is less than $15 million. Using the normal distribution, we are looking for the shaded area shown below.

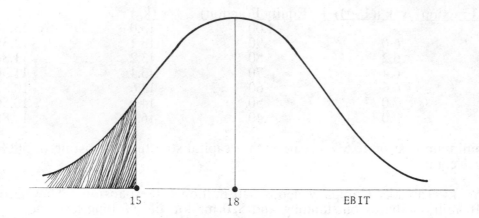

Transforming to the standard normal distribution we get:

$$Z = \frac{\$15,000,000 - \$18,000,000}{\$5,000,000} = -0.6$$

Using a Normal Table, we find the probability of being more than 0.6 standard deviations below the mean is 0.2743.

7.   Memphis Leisure Crafts makes rubber dinghies which they sell for $400 each. Their fixed costs are $75,000 and variable costs are $250 per dinghy.

a.   What is the breakeven point in units and in dollars?

b.   If their sales level is 800 units, what is the percentage increase in EBIT and the degree of operating leverage if sales increase 20 percent?

c.   What is the degree of operating leverage at a sales level of 1000 dinghies?

Solution:

a. $Q_b = \dfrac{F}{P-V} = \dfrac{75,000}{400-250} = \dfrac{75,000}{150} = 500$ dinghies

$S_b = 400(500) = \$200,000$.

b.   At 800 units, EBIT $=$ $PQ - VQ - F$
$=$ $400(800) - 250(800) - 75,000$
$=$ $320,000 - 200,000 - 75,000 = \$45,000$.

At 960 units, EBIT $=$ $400(960) - 250(960) - 75,000$
$=$ $384,000 - 240,000 - 75,000 = \$69,000$.

Increase in EBIT $= 69,000 - 45,000 = \$24,000$.

Percentage increase in EBIT = $\frac{24,000}{45,000}(100\%) = 53.33\%$.

$$DOL = \frac{\text{Percentage Increase in EBIT}}{\text{Percentage Increase in Sales}} = \frac{53.33\%}{20.00\%} = 2.67$$

c. $DOL = \frac{(P - V)Q}{(P - V)Q - F} = \frac{(400 - 250)(1000)}{(400 - 250)(1000) - 75,000}$

$$= \frac{150,000}{150,000 - 75,000} = 2.00$$

8.   The Brass Monkey has operating profits of $200,000 and a degree of operating leverage of 1.5. Forecast the Brass Monkey's operating profits if sales increase by 10%.

Solution:

$$DOL = \frac{\text{Percentage Increase in EBIT}}{\text{Percentage Increase in Sales}}$$

Percentage increase in EBIT = 1.5(10%) = 15%

Increase in EBIT = 15%($200,000) = $30,000

New EBIT level = $200,000 + $30,000 = $230,000

9.   Charles Mims has two financing plans for his new business:

Plan I   All equity (ten thousand shares sold for $10 per share).

Plan II   50% equity, 50% debt (five thousand shares sold for $10 per share plus $50,000 of debt paying 12% interest).

The business is in the 40% tax bracket.

a.   If EBIT is $20,000, what is the earnings per share for each financing plan?

b.   If EBIT is 20% greater, what is the EPS for each plan? What is the degree of financial leverage?

c.   Construct an EPS-EBIT graph for each plan (plot both of the EPS-EBIT functions on the same graph). What is the level of EBIT when the two functions intersect?

Solution:

a.	Plan I	Plan II
EBIT	$20,000	$20,000
Interest	0	6,000
EBT	$20,000	$14,000
Taxes (@ 40%)	8,000	5,600
EAT	$12,000	$ 8,400
Number of Shares	10,000	5,000
EPS	$ 1.20	$ 1.68

b.   If EBIT increases by 20%, EBIT = $24,000.

	Plan I	Plan II
EBIT	$24,000	$24,000
Interest	0	6,000
EBT	$24,000	$18,000
Taxes (@ 40%)	9,600	7,200
EAT	$14,400	$10,800
Number of Shares	10,000	5,000
EPS	$ 1.44	$ 2.16

With Plan I, the percentage increase in EPS is

$$\frac{1.44 - 1.20}{1.20}(100\%) = \frac{.24}{1.20}(100\%) = 20\%$$

With Plan II, the percentage increase in EPS is

$$\frac{2.16 - 1.68}{1.68}(100\%) = \frac{.48}{1.68}(100\%) = 28.57\%$$

$$DFL = \frac{\%\text{ Change in EPS}}{\%\text{ Change in EBIT}}$$

For Plan I, $DFL_I = 20\%/20\% = 1.00$. For Plan II, $DFL_{II} = 28.57\%/20\% = 1.43$. The degree of financial leverage can also be calculated as

$$DFL = \frac{EBIT}{EBIT - I - D/(1 - t)}$$

$$DFL_I = \frac{20,000}{20,000 - 0} = \frac{20,000}{20,000} = 1.00$$

$$DFL_{II} = \frac{20,000}{20,000-6,000} = \frac{20,000}{14,000} = 1.43$$

c.

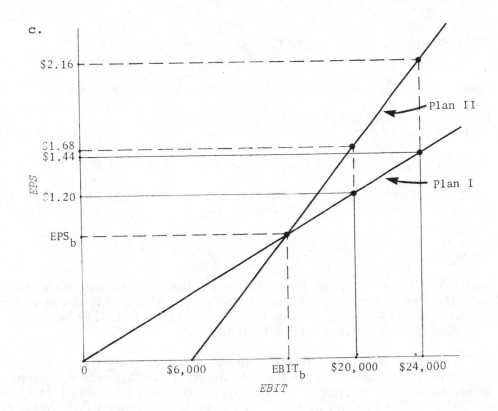

For Plan I, EPS will be zero if EBIT = 0, so the graph goes through the origin. If EBIT increases $1,000, net income increases $600 (taxes are $400), so earnings per share increase $.06 per $1,000 increase in EBIT. ($.06 = $600/10,000 shares).

For Plan II, EPS will be zero if EBIT equals the interest charge, or $6,000. If EBIT increases $1,000, net income increases $600 (taxes are $400 again, interest charges are unchanged), so earnings per share increase $.12 per $1,000 increase in EBIT. ($.12 = $600/5,000 shares). Because there are fewer shares with Plan II, a given EBIT change has a larger impact on EPS than with Plan I.
Notice that EPS will be greater with Plan II as long as EBIT is above the level where the two EPS-EBIT functions intersect. When they intersect, the EPS is the same for both plans. We can find this EBIT level easily.

$$\text{EPS} = \frac{(\text{EBIT} - I)(1 - t)}{\text{Number of shares}}$$

$$\text{EPSI} = \frac{(\text{EBIT} - 0)(1 - .4)}{10,000}$$

$$\text{EPSII} = \frac{(\text{EBIT} - 6,000)(1 - .4)}{5,000}$$

We set $\text{EPS}_I = \text{EPS}_{II}$ and solve for EBIT.

$$\frac{(EBIT - 0)(.6)}{10,000} = \frac{(EBIT - 6,000)(.6)}{5,000}$$

If we multiply both sides by 10,000 and divide both sides by .6, we have

$$EBIT = 2.0(EBIT - \$6,000) = 2EBIT - \$12,000$$
$$EBIT = \$12,000$$

When EBIT is \$12,000, $EPS_I = EPS_{II}$ (When EBIT = \$12,000, EPS = \$.72)

An important relationship is to compare the ratio EBIT/Assets to the interest rate. The assets in this business are \$100,000, so

$$\frac{EBIT}{Assets} = \frac{\$12,000}{\$100,000} = 12\%$$

when both plans have the same EPS. Of course, the interest rate on the debt is equal to 12%. Leverage will increase earnings per share only if the operating rate of return, EBIT/Assets, exceeds the interest rate. If EBIT/Assets are less than 12%, Plan II would have a lower EPS than Plan I.

10. Rework Problem 9 using the Lotus templates accompanying the text. Use the indifferent point template. In addition to answers for Problem 9, assume that EBIT is normally distributed with a mean of \$20,000 and a standard deviation of \$10,000. What is the probability that Plan II results in higher EPS? What is the probability of a loss under Plan I and Plan II? This is the output from the template.

```
==============================================================================
                        INDIFFERENCE POINT ANALYSIS
==============================================================================

BEFORE FINANCING:
-----------------
CURRENT INTEREST PAYMENTS              $0
PREFERRED DIVIDENDS                    $0
NUMBER OF COMMON SHARES                 0

FINANCING PROPOSALS:
--------------------                        OPTION 1        OPTION 2
                                          ------------    ------------
AMOUNT OF DEBT FINANCING (1ST SOURCE)         $0           $50,000
COST OF DEBT FINANCING (1ST SOURCE)         0.00%           12.00%
AMOUNT OF DEBT FINANCING (2ND SOURCE)         $0               $0
COST OF DEBT FINANCING (2ND SOURCE)         0.00%            0.00%
AMOUNT OF PREFERRED STOCK FINANCING           $0               $0
NUMBER OF PREFERRED SHARES                     0                0
PREFERRED DIVIDEND PER SHARE               $0.00            $0.00
AMOUNT OF EQUITY FINANCING               $100,000          $50,000
NET COMMON PROCEEDS (PER SHARE)            $10.00           $10.00
   TOTAL -- PROPOSED FINANCING          $100,000         $100,000

MARGINAL TAX RATE                    40.00%

IMPACT OF FINANCING PROPOSALS
-----------------------------               OPTION 1        OPTION 2
                                          ------------    ------------
INTEREST PAYMENTS                             $0            $6,000
PREFERRED DIVIDENDS                           $0               $0
NUMBER OF COMMON SHARES                     10,000           5,000


INDIFFERENCE POINT (EBIT*)      $12,000
EARNINGS PER SHARE AT EBIT*                  $0.72           $0.72
                                          ============    ============

EXPECTED EBIT                   $20,000
STANDARD DEVIATION              $10,000
EARNINGS PER SHARE                           $1.20           $1.68
                                          ============    ============

PROBABILITY OF OPERATING INCOME LESS THAN EBIT*                21.19%
PROBABILITY OF OPERATING INCOME GREATER THAN EBIT*             78.81%

PROBABILITY OF OPERATING INCOME LESS THAN THE INTEREST PAYMENT:

                                UNDER OPTION 1                 2.28%
                                UNDER OPTION 2                 8.07%
```

11.   Use the leverage and breakeven analysis template for this problem. Sales are $400,000, fixed costs are $100,000, and variable costs arc 50% of sales. The firm has $150,000 of debt on which it pays 12% interest. The tax rate is 34%.

    a.   What is the firm's EPS?
    b.   What is the DOL, DFL AND DCL?
    c.   What happens to EPS if sales increase 10%?

```
=====================================================================
                  LEVERAGE AND BREAK EVEN ANALYSIS
=====================================================================


   SUMMARY OF INPUT
   - - - - - - - - - - - - - - - -
   TOTAL SALES                                          $400,000
   FIXED OPERATING COSTS                                $100,000
   VARIABLE COST RATIO                                    50.00%
   NUMBER OF COMMON SHARES                                 5,000
   MARGINAL TAX RATE                                      34.00%
   ANALYSIS OF % CHANGE IN SALES                          10.00%

   SUMMARY OF FINANCIAL OBLIGATIONS:


              PRINCIPAL      INTEREST RATE           INTEREST
              $150,000           12.00%              $18,000
                   $0            0.00%                   $0
                   $0            0.00%                   $0
                   $0            0.00%                   $0
                   $0            0.00%                   $0
                                                  - - - - - - - - - - - - - - - -
   TOTAL INTEREST OBLIGATION                            $18,000

   PREFERRED DIVIDENDS:                                      $0
```

```
=============================================================
                    REVISED INCOME STATEMENT
=============================================================


TOTAL SALES                                                 $400,000
FIXED COSTS                                                 $100,000
VARIABLE COSTS AT           50.00%                          $200,000
                                                    ------------------
OPERATING INCOME (EBIT)                                     $100,000
INTEREST PAYMENTS                                            $18,000
                                                    ------------------
INCOME BEFORE TAXES                                          $82,000
TAXES AT                    34.00%                           $27,880
                                                    ------------------
NET INCOME                                                   $54,120
PREFERRED DIVIDENDS                                               $0
                                                    ------------------
EARNINGS AVAILABLE TO COMMON                                 $54,120
                                                    ==================
NUMBER OF COMMON SHARES                      5,000
EARNINGS PER SHARE                                            $10.82
                                                    ==================
```

```
=============================================================
         BREAK EVEN SALES LEVEL AND SUMMARY OF LEVERAGE MEASURES
=============================================================


BREAK EVEN DOLLAR SALES                                    $200,000

DEGREE OF
    OPERATING LEVERAGE                                         2.00
    FINANCIAL LEVERAGE                                         1.22
    COMBINED LEVERAGE                                          2.44

FORECASTED EARNINGS PER SHARE
IF SALES CHANGE BY              10.00%                       $13.46
                                                    ==================
```

14

Dividend Policy

The value of a firm is influenced by its capital budgeting decisions, its capital structure decisions, and its dividend decisions. These types of decisions all interact since the size of the capital budget is affected by the amount and cost of capital available; the capital structure and cost of capital are affected by the amount of earnings retained in the business; and retained earnings and dividends are alternative uses of available net income. These decisions must be made jointly to choose a set of decisions which will maximize shareholder wealth.

I. Dividend decisions are affected by consideration of a number of issues concerning legality, taxes, bond indenture provisions, liquidity, earnings prospects, the economic environment, and shareholder preferences.

   A. Most states impose three types of regulations on the payment of dividends by firms which are chartered in that state.

      1. Dividends cannot be paid out of capital. Depending on the state, capital is defined as either the commonstock account or that account together with other contributed capital in excess of the par value of the common stock.

      2. Dividends must be paid only out of present and past net earnings.

      3. Dividends cannot be paid when a firm is insolvent which means that its liabilities exceed its assets. This is to protect the creditors of the firm.

B.   The IRS code prohibits excessive accumulation of profits for the purpose of protecting stockholders from paying taxes on the dividends they would otherwise receive. A tax is imposed on excessive accumulations.

C.   Since the Tax Reform Act of 1986, the personal marginal tax rates on dividend income and long-term capital gains are the same. Prior to the TRA of 1986, capital gains were taxed at lower rates, which favored the retention of earnings (and, hopefully, future capital gains) over distributing cash dividends.

D.   Restrictive covenants in bond indentures, loan agreements, lease contracts, and preferred stock agreements may prohibit or limit dividend payments.

E.   Payment of dividends requires liquidity--ultimately cash. Earnings do not necessarily result in cash available for dividend payments.

F.   Available investment opportunities together with the availability of capital may dictate that earnings be retained in the business rather than paid out as dividends.

G.   Firms are often reluctant to lower their dividend payments once they are established. Firms with stable earnings are able to pay higher dividends without risk of cutting them than are firms with unstable earnings.

H.   Firms in rapid growth industries with a substantial need for capital must frequently retain earnings for investment or face the higher cost of external equity capital.

I.   Inflation may decrease a firm's ability to pay high dividends because funds generated by depreciation will not be adequate for the firm to maintain itself in the face of rising equipment costs.

J.   Inflation may decrease a firm's liquidity because of the rising dollar investment in inventories and accounts receivable for the same volume level of business.

K.   In closely-held corporations, dividend policy may be subject to the desires of stockholders with regard to dividends versus reinvestment.

L.   In broadly-held firms, it is suggested that dividend policy, once established, provides a basis by which shareholders sort themselves out according to their preferences. The "clientele" theory of dividends suggests that maintaining a steady policy will account for the preferences of a firm's stockholders.

M.   If payment of large dividends results in the need to raise external equity capital and existing shareholders cannot maintain their proportionate share of ownership, their control in the company may be diluted.

II.   There are two schools of thought regarding the effect of dividend policy on a firm's value. One school, led by Miller and Modigliani, argues that dividend policy is irrelevant, that dividend policy does not affect firm value. The other school obviously disagrees.

  A.   The Miller and Modigliani (MM) group contends that the value of a firm is based on its investment decisions. The payment of a particular dividend is only a mere financing detail since a dividend policy can be offset by other forms of financing, such as selling new shares of common stock.

   1.   The MM irrelevance of dividends argument is based on several assumptions:

       No taxes
       No transactions costs
       No flotation costs (on the issuance of new securities)
       A fixed investment policy

   2.   If a dividend is financed by issuing new shares of stock, the value of the old shares will be diluted and will fall by the amount of the dividend received. Conversely, if stockholders forego a dividend, their stock should appreciate by this amount. The wealth of a shareholder (cash received from dividends plus the value of shares owned) is not affected by dividend policy.

   3.   Dividends can have informational content. If dividends are raised, is this a mere financing detail, or is it a signal that the earning capacity of the firm has increased?

   4.   Changes in dividend payments represent a <u>signal</u> to investors concerning the future earnings and cash flows of the company.

   5.   MM claim that the existence of clienteles of investors favoring a particular firm's dividend policy should have no effect on share value. Some investors may sell a company's stock after a dividend policy change, but others will buy, and no net change in the stock's value should result.

  B.   A second school believes that the MM argument is reasonable, but that MM's restrictive assumptions would cause dividend policy to be important if the assumptions were relaxed.

   1.   Risk averse investors might prefer cash dividends now over the promise of more income later.

   2.   Brokerage costs make it expensive for stockholders to sell part of their holdings to substitute for cash dividends.

   3.   Capital gains tax treatment once was favorable to the taxation of dividends.

4.   High flotation costs make it expensive for a firm to sell external equity (sell new shares of stock) to finance a cash dividend payment.

5.   The payment of dividends can reduce agency costs between shareholders and management. Paying cash dividends causes a firm to raise more capital in external markets, which subject the firm to scrutiny by regulators and potential investors. This serves as a monitoring function of managerial performance.

III.   A number of alternative dividend strategies are frequently used as the basis for a dividend policy. The actual choice of a policy is influenced by the practical considerations above.

A.   The passive residual policy integrates the dividend decision with the optimal capital budget--marginal cost of capital decision of Chapter 12.

1.   If the optimal capital budget can be financed with a package that does not fully utilize available earnings, the earnings not required for retention are paid out in dividends.

2.   If the optimal capital budget fully uses the available earnings, no dividend is paid.

3.   Under this policy, dividends can fluctuate significantly from year to year depending on the firm's investment opportunities.

4.   In practice the dividends can be smoothed by recognizing that it is acceptable for the actual capital structure to vary around the target by borrowing more in years with a high demand for funds and using more equity in years with less demand for funds.

5.   The residual theory suggests that "growth" firms will normally have lower dividend payout ratios than non- growth firms.

B.   Much evidence indicates that most firms and stockholders prefer reasonably stable dividend policies.

1.   Stable dividends are characterized by a reluctance to reduce the dollar level of dividends from one period to the next.

2.   Under a policy of stable dividends, increases in dividends tend to lag behind increases in earnings to insure against a need to decrease them in the future.

3.   Stable dividends are desirable for a number of reasons.

a.   Dividends are often interpreted as an indication of the firm's longer run profit potential.

b.   Many shareholders depend on dividends for their cash income requirements.

c.   Stability of dividends may be taken as an indication of the riskiness of the firm and affect the capitalization rate and cost of capital.

d.   Many financial institutions such as banks, pension funds, and insurance companies are restricted in the types of common stock they can own to that of firms which have a record of continuous and stable dividends.

C.   Some firms attempt to maintain a fairly constant payout ratio. If a firm's earnings fluctuate substantially, a constant payout ratio causes dividends to fluctuate also.

D.   Some firms follow a policy of paying a small regular dividend plus year-end extras.

1.   Stockholders can depend on the regular payout.

2.   The policy can accommodate changing earnings and investment requirements.

IV.   Corporations generally pay dividends quarterly.

A.   The board of directors declares dividends that follow the following pattern:

1.   Declaration date--the board of directors announces a dividend to be payable to shareholders of record on the record date. (example: January 15)

2.   Record date--the firm takes its list of shareholders from its stock transfer books. (example: February 15) These shareholders of record will receive dividend checks mailed on the payment date.

3.   Ex-dividend date--the major stock exchanges require four business days prior to the record date. (example: February 11) Persons buying the stock on February 11 or later are buying the stock ex-dividend, meaning without the dividend.

4.   Payment date--the date the dividend checks are actually mailed. (example: March 1)

B.   Many firms have dividend reinvestment plans.

1.   Under these plans, shareholders can elect to have their cash dividends reinvested automatically in additional shares.

2.   Some plans purchase existing shares on the open market (through a trustee) and other plans purchase newly issued shares. The latter plan raises new equity capital for the firm.

3.   Brokerage commissions are not charged for these plans.

4.   Investors are still liable for income taxes on dividends reinvested even though they received no cash.

V.   Dividends are usually taken to mean cash dividends. Sometimes firms declare stock dividends which result in the payment of additional shares of stock to the common stockholders.

A.   Stock dividends are usually stated as a percent of shares outstanding.

B.   Stock dividends increase the number of shares outstanding.

C.   An accounting transaction transfers the pre-dividend market value of the dividend from retained earnings to the capital accounts.

1.   The par value of the new shares is credited to common stock.

2.   Any additional value is credited to contributed capital in excess of par.

D.   Because each shareholder's proportionate claim on the firm's net worth and earnings is unchanged, the market price of each share of stock should decline in proportion to the number of new shares issued.

$$\text{Post stock dividend price} = \frac{\text{original price}}{1 + \text{Percent stock dividend rate}}$$

A 10% stock dividend would reduce the stock price 9.09%.

E.   Although the theoretical value of a stock dividend is zero, firms declare them for several reasons.

1.   A stock dividend may broaden the ownership of the firm's shares since many stockholders sell the stock from the dividend.

2.   If the firm pays a cash dividend, a stock dividend results in an effective increase in cash dividends provided that the level of the cash dividend is not reduced.

3.   The reduction in share price may broaden the appeal of the stock to investors resulting in a real increase in market value.

VI.   Stock splits are similar to stock dividends. They increase the number of shares and reduce the price of each share.

VII.   Some firms distribute funds to investors through repurchasing shares of the stock rather than paying dividends.

A.   Stock may be repurchased by a tender offer, in the open market, or by negotiation with larger holders.

B.   Repurchased stock is known as treasury stock.

C.   Stock repurchases reduce the number of shares outstanding and hence increase the EPS.

D.   Plans for a repurchase are usually announced so that investors know the reason for the additional trading in the stock and can wait for the anticipated price increase before selling their shares.

E.   In theory, repurchases are a desirable way of distributing earnings.

1.   Repurchases allow the stockholder to exercise his/her preference for current income or longer term capital gains.

2.   The IRS will not permit a firm to regularly repurchase a stock as an alternative to paying cash dividends because repurchases convert ordinary income to capital gains which receive preferential tax treatment. Regular stock repurchases are viewed as equivalent to cash dividends and taxed accordingly.

TRUE AND FALSE QUESTIONS

Agree with each of the statements or reject it and modify it so that it is acceptable.

1.   Dividends may be paid only out of current earnings.

2.   Inflation causes dividends to increase because of the increased revenues from higher prices.

3.   The clientele theory of dividends suggests that dividend policy should seldom be changed.

4.   The residual theory of dividends integrates the dividend decision with the capital budgeting and cost of capital decisions.

5.   Growth firms usually pay large dividends in order to make new issues of common stock more attractive.

6. A policy of stable dividends means the firm always pays a stable percentage of earnings.

7. Individuals who buy a stock anytime before the record date receive the dividend.

8. Stock dividends are more valuable to shareholders than cash dividends because the value of the stock received is usually much more than the amount of a typical cash dividend.

9. Regular repurchases are a good way to help stockholders avoid income taxes.

10. Stock repurchases reduce the number of shares outstanding and hence increase EPS.

Answers to True and False Questions

1. Dividends may be paid only out of current or past earnings.

2. Inflation may limit the ability to pay dividends because of the need to invest funds in higher priced inventory, larger accounts receivable, and the replacement of equipment not adequately covered by depreciation.

3. True.

4. True.

5. Growth firms often must retain a larger portion of their earnings in order to meet their investment needs.

6. A policy of stable dividends means that a firm attempts to pay a dividend which will not need to be reduced.

7. Individuals who buy the stock before the ex-dividend date will receive the dividend.

8. Unless a stock dividend results in an effective increase in cash dividends or in a higher market price for the firm because of the increased attractiveness of the lower share price, it is worthless.

9. The IRS views regular repurchases as equivalent to cash dividends and taxes them accordingly.

10. True.

CHAPTER 14 PROBLEMS

1. The ICU Keyhole Company has the following equity accounts on its balance sheet:

Common stock ($5 par, 1 million shares)	$ 5,000,000
Contributed capital in excess of par	7,000,000
Retained earnings	15,000,000
Total Common Equity	$27,000,000

a. If the capital impairment laws of the state define capital as the par value of the common stock, what is the maximum dividend that can be paid?

b. If capital is defined as common stock and contributed capital in excess of par, what is the maximum dividend that can be paid?

Solution:

a. If capital is defined as the par value of the common stock, then dividends can be paid out of retained earnings and contributed capital in excess of par for a total of $22,000,000.

b. If capital is defined as the par value of the common stock and contributed capital in excess of par, then up to $15,000,000 of dividends may be paid out of retained earnings.

2. The Moyer Foyer Tile Company has EBIT of $150,000. Annual depreciation is $60,000 and interest expense is $50,000. They must make a payment of $30,000 annually into a sinking fund for retirement of the debt. What is the maximum per share dividends they can pay on their 300,000 shares of common stock if the bond indenture requires that cash flow must be at least equal to dividends, interest, and sinking fund requirements? Their tax rate is 40%.

Solution:

The first step is to determine available cash flow.

EBIT	$150,000
- Interest Expense	50,000
Taxable Income	$100,000
x (1 - t)	.60
Net Income	$ 60,000
+ Depreciation	60,000
Cash Flow	$120,000

The maximum total dividend is equal to the available cash flow less the interest and sinking fund requirements:

Cash Flow	$120,000
- Interest Expense	50,000
- Sinking Fund Requirements	30,000
Available for Dividends	$ 40,000
÷ 300,000 Shares	
Maximum per share dividend	$ 0.13

3.   The Left-Over Recycling Company believes in the residual theory of dividends. Their target capital structure calls for equal amounts of debt and equity. Anticipated earnings amount to $3 million. The after tax cost of debt is 6%, the cost of retained earnings is 20%, and the cost of new equity is 24%.

   a.   If their investment opportunities include $5 million worth of projects with a return greater than 13%, what amount of dividends should they pay?

   b.   If their investment opportunities include $7 million worth of projects with a return greater than 15%, what amount of dividends should they pay?

Solution:

   a.   The first step is to determine the marginal cost of capital schedule. The target package of capital consists of equal mounts of retained earnings and debt. Potential retained earnings of $3 million permit financing up to $6 million of projects with this package. The weighted cost is given by

$$.5(.06) + .5(.20) = .13$$

   The next increment of capital must contain equal amounts of new equity with a cost of 24% and debt with an after tax cost of 6%. The weighted cost of this package is

$$.5(.06) + .5(.24) = .15$$

   The optimal capital budget will use a total of $5 million of capital at a cost of 13%. This $5 million consists of $2.5 million of debt and $2.5 million of retained earnings leaving $3.0 - 2.5 = $.5 million of earnings available for dividends.

   b.   All $7 million of investment opportunities will be taken and the entire first package of capital will be used along with $1 million of the second package. All earnings are retained and no dividends are paid.

4.   The C-Thru Glass Company has the following equity accounts on its balance sheet:

Common Stock ($2 par, 100,000 shares)	$200,000
Contributed capital in excess of par	$100,000
Retained Earnings	$700,000

The current price of stock is $10 per share. If C-Thru declares a 5% stock dividend, what is the effect on the firm's capital accounts?

Solution:

A 5% stock dividend involves creation of an additional 5,000 shares. The market value of these shares is transferred from retained earnings to the common stock account and the contributed capital in excess of par account. Market value of the dividend is 5,000 shares x $10 = $50,000. $2 per share, the par value, is transferred to the common stock account and the remaining $40,000 to the contributed capital in excess of par amount. The resulting capital accounts appear as follows:

Common Stock ($2 par, 105,000 shares)	$210,000
Contributed capital in excess of par	$140,000
Retained Earnings	$650,000

15

Managing Intermediate-Term Funding Sources

Intermediate term financing is defined as obligations maturing in more than one year and less than ten years. Two major sources of intermediate term financing are term loans and leases.

I. A term loan is defined as any debt obligation having an initial maturity between one and ten years.

    A. Term loans are available from a wide variety of sources including banks, insurance companies, pension funds, small business investment companies, government agencies and equipment suppliers.

    B. Particularly in smaller amounts, term loans are usually less expensive than issuing bonds or common stock.

    C. Term loans are often better suited for financing than short-term loans because of a reduction of the problems of future interest rate variability and ability to renew the loan. This is particularly true for financing small additions to plant and equipment where the cash flows from the investment often cover the servicing requirements of the debt.

    D. Term loans can also be used to finance moderate increases in working capital if the length of the loan approximately matches the time the working capital will be needed or until the debt can be amortized out of earnings.

E.   Term loans usually require that the principal be amortized over the life of the loan. Amortization requires that the borrower make regular periodic payments of principal and interest.

   1.   A common arrangement is for the borrower to make regular equal payments so that the present value of the annuity of payments is equal to the amount of the loan.

   2.   Another arrangement calls for equal reductions in principal during the life of the loan together with payment of interest on the outstanding balance.

   3.   Partial amortization may be used which results in a lump payment called a "balloon payment" at the maturity of the loan.

   4.   Term loans may call for periodic payment of interest with a final balloon payment equal to the amount of the loan (bullet loan).

F.   Interest costs on term loans depend on a number of factors--particularly the general level of interest rates. Variable rates dependent on the prime rate or another indicator are sometimes used.

G.   Term loan agreements often call for the borrower to keep a percentage of the loan balance on deposit as a compensating balance. This can increase the effective interest rate on the loan.

H.   In the case of higher risk loans to companies with promising growth potential, a term loan agreement may call for issuance to the lender of a warrant giving the lender an option to purchase equity in the company at a future date.

I.   Security provisions in term loans are dependent on the credit standing of the borrower. Security provisions can take many forms:

   1.   Assignment of payments due under a particular contract.

   2.   Assignment or pledging of inventories, receivables or securities.

   3.   A mortgage on property, plant or equipment.

   4.   An assignment of the cash surrender value of a life insurance policy.

J.   Affirmative covenants outline actions which a firm agrees to take during the term of the loan. These include such things as providing financial statements and cash budgets, carrying insurance on assets and against insurable business risks, maintaining minimum levels of net working capital, and maintaining personnel acceptable to the lender.

K.   Negative covenants outline actions which a firm agrees not to take during the term of the loan. These may include agreements not to merge with other firms, not to pledge assets as security to other lenders, or not to make loans to other firms.

L. Restrictive covenants limit the firm's potential actions but do not prohibit them. Restrictions might limit dividends, limit employee compensation, limit additional borrowing and limit investment activities.

M. Term loan agreements contain default provisions which permit the lender to insist on immediate repayment under certain conditions.

II. Term loans are available from a number of sources.

A. Although banks prefer loans having relatively short maturities, they are a major source of term loans.

B. Insurance companies and pension funds are a source of term loans.

1. Insurance companies and pension funds prefer longer term loans.

2. Prepayment of loans from these sources may involve penalties.

3. Loans from insurance companies and pension funds are usually secured.

4. Due to the longer maturity and lack of compensating balance arrangements, loans from these institutions tend to have slightly higher stated interest rates than those from banks.

C. The Small Business Administration (SBA), an agency of the Federal government, was established to make credit available to small businesses.

1. SBA loans are usually secured.

2. Most SBA loans are participation loans obtained from a bank with the SBA guaranteeing up to 90% of the amount.

3. Direct loans are available from the SBA on a limited basis.

4. Economic opportunity loans up to $25,000 and 15 years maturity are available from SBA to assist economically and socially disadvantaged individuals who own their own firms.

D. Small business investment companies (SBIC's) are licensed by the government to make debt or equity investments in small firms.

1. SBIC's obtain capital by borrowing from the SBA and other sources.

2. SBIC's specialize in firms with growth potential.

3.   Because the borrowers tend to have above average risk, these loans tend to be more expensive than banks loans.

E.   Industrial Development Authorities (IDA's), organized by state and local governments, issue bonds and use the proceeds to build facilities which are then leased to a firm. Because the bonds are tax exempt, the financing costs are often lower than on directly issued corporate bonds.

F.   Municipalities issue pollution control revenue bonds. The proceeds are used to assist industry in acquiring pollution control equipment. Because the bonds are tax exempt, the financing costs are lower than if industry raised the funds directly.

G.   Equipment financing loans are loans to purchase equipment which then serves as collateral on the loan.

1.   The equipment is usually of a type which is readily marketable such as motor vehicles.

2.   These loans are usually amortized over the expected life of the equipment.

3.   Equipment financing loans are available from the usual financial intermediaries as well as from equipment sellers themselves.

4.   Two legal forms are common for equipment financing loans.

a.   Conditional sales contracts are common when financing is from the equipment seller. In a conditional sales contract, the purchaser usually makes a down payment and a series of periodic payments. Title does not pass to the purchaser until the contract is fulfilled.

b.   Chattel mortgages are often used by financial intermediaries. A chattel mortgage is a mortgage on property other than real estate.

III.   Traditionally leasing is a means of obtaining plant and equipment for a specific period of time without actually owning it. Such "true leases" are an alternative to term financing for many purposes. Special lease arrangements to transfer tax benefits also exist.

A.   There are two major classes of true leases

1.   An operating lease, sometimes called a service or maintenance lease, is an agreement for period to period use of an asset. Maintenance and insurance are usually included in the lease.

2.   A <u>financial</u> or <u>capital lease</u> is noncancellable. The lessee is usually responsible for maintenance and possibly for insurance and property taxes.

   a.   A financial lease may originate as a direct lease in which the lessee acquires use of an asset it has not owned.

   b.   A financial lease may originate as a sale and leaseback in which the lessor purchases the asset from the lessee and then leases it back to him.

3.   A leveraged lease is a three-party financial lease consisting of the lessee who acquires use of the asset, the lessor who holds an equity interest in the asset, and a lender who finances the purchase of the asset by the lessor.

B.   Analysis of leasing opportunities from the lessor's perspective consists of present value analysis similar to capital budgeting decisions.

1.   The lessor's required payment is an annuity payment than can be found with this three-step process:

   Step 1:   Compute the lessor's amount to be amortized

       Initial Outlay
       Less: Present value of after-tax salvage
       Less: Present value of depreciation tax shelter
       Equals: Amount to be amortized

   Step 2:   Compute after-tax lease income requirement

       Amount to be amortized =   Present value of after tax lease payment

   Step 3:   Compute before-tax lease payment

       Lease payment = $\dfrac{\text{after-tax lease income requirements}}{1 - \text{lessor's marginal tax rate}}$

2.   An example of finding the required lease payment from the lessor's perspective is given in Problem 3. There are a couple of things to keep in mind.

   a.   The discount rate is the lessor's after-tax required rate of return.

   b.   Lease payments are usually due at the beginning of the period, in which case the computation of the present value of the lease payments must be for an annuity due rather than an ordinary annuity.

C. Often one of the advantages of true leases is derived from tax considerations.

1. Care must be taken that the arrangement is recognized as a lease rather than an installment purchase plan by the IRS.

a. The remaining useful life of the equipment at the end of the lease must be the greater of 1 year or 20% of the cost of the property.

b. Leases may not exceed 30 years for tax purposes.

c. The lessor must receive a reasonable return of investment.

d. Renewal options must be closely related to the economic value of the asset. ˙

e. If the agreement contains a purchase option at the end of the lease, the purchase price must be based on the asset's market value at the time.

f. For leveraged leases, the lessor must provide at least 20% equity.

g. Property valuable only to the lessee may not be leased.

2. Because annual lease payments are deductible, leasing of land can provide tax benefits similar to those which would be obtained if land could be depreciated.

3. If a lease contract is disallowed for tax purposes, taxes are applied as though the asset had been sold to the lessee and pledged to the lessor as security on a loan.

D. The Financial Accounting Standards Board requires that financial leases be capitalized.

1. A liability equal to the present value of the lease payments discounted at the firm's borrowing rate for a secured loan of similar maturity is shown.
2. The asset value of the lease is also reported.

3. Further details must be provided in the footnotes to the financial statements.

E. There are a number of potential advantages and disadvantages to leasing.

1. Lease agreements tend to be more flexible than loan agreements particularly with regard to restrictive covenants.

2.   Leasing is often more convenient than negotiating term loans or selling securities.

3.   Payments may be lower because of the tax benefits to the lessor.

4.   The lessee may avoid some of the risk of obsolescence.

5.   Earnings are smoother and EPS in the early years is higher under leasing because the accelerated depreciation does not show on the lessee's income statement.

6.   Leasing provides essentially 100% financing.

7.   Leasing can reduce pressures on the lessee's liquidity.

8.   Leasing is often more expensive than ownership.

9.   The lessee loses the benefit of the salvage value. This is particularly significant in real estate.

10.   Approval for modifications of the asset may be difficult to obtain.

11.   Financial leases may not be cancelled without a substantial penalty.

F.   Lease-Buy analysis from the lessee's perspective compares leasing to the alternative to borrowing to buy.

1.   The basic approach of the lease-buy analysis model is to compute the net advantage to leasing (NAL):

	Installed cost of the asset
Less:	Present value of the after-tax lease payment
Less:	Present value of the depreciation tax shield
Plus:	Present value of after-tax operating costs incurred if owned but not if leased
Less:	Present value of the after-tax salvage value
Equals:	Net Advantage to Leasing (NAL)

2.   If the NAL is positive, it is cheaper for the lessee to lease the asset than to borrow and buy it. If the NAL is negative, leasing is unattractive. It is easy to see how each of the items above affects the attractiveness of leasing. For example, a larger lease payment reduces the NAL.

3.   Problem 4 illustrates the calculation of the lessee's net advantage of leasing. There are several things to keep in mind.

a.   The installed cost is the purchase price plus installation and shipping charges.

b.   The present value of the after-tax lease payment is found by discounting at the lessee's after- tax marginal cost of borrowing. The lease payment is usually an annuity due.

c.   The annual depreciation tax shield is the depreciation times the lessee's marginal tax rate. The present value of the depreciation tax shield is found using the lessee's after-tax marginal cost of borrowing.

d.   If leased, some operating costs (such as property tax payments, insurance, and some maintenance costs) may be paid by the lessor. If so, these savings are discounted at a rate reflecting their relative certainty, frequently the lessee's after-tax marginal cost of borrowing.

e.   Because the salvage value belongs to the lessor, this amount lost to the lessee is discounted at a rate reflecting its uncertainty, frequently the lessee's weighted cost of capital (which is higher than the after-tax cost of borrowing).

TRUE AND FALSE QUESTIONS

Agree with each of the statements or **reject** it and modify it so that it is acceptable.

1.   A term loan is a long-term debt obtained from sources other than bonds.

2.   Term loans avoid the renewal risk present in short-term loans.

3.   Term loans are usually amortized.

4.   Longer maturity term loans are usually obtained from banks while shorter maturity ones are usually obtained from insurance companies and pension funds.

5.   Most SBA loans are made directly from the SBA to the borrower and provide financing for new businesses with no assets available for security.

6.   Industrial Development Authorities provide a means to channel the proceeds of tax exempt bonds to private industry.

7.   Operating leases are noncancellable.

8.   In order to qualify as a lease under IRS regulations, a lease agreement must contain a renewal option at the same payment rate as the original lease.

9.   Financial leases provide a means of obtaining assets in exchange for an agreement to make periodic payments without increasing the debt on the balance sheet.

10.   In finding the lessee's net advantage of leasing, the various cash flows are discounted at the firm's cost of capital.

Answers to True and False Questions

1.   A term loan is intermediate term debt with a maturity of 1-10 years.

2.   True.

3.   True.

4.   Banks prefer to make shorter term loans while insurance companies and pension funds prefer longer term loans.

5.   Most SBA loans are participation loans and require security.

6.   True.

7.   Financial leases are noncancellable; operating leases may be cancelled.

8.   Renewal options should reflect the economic value of the asset at the time of renewal.

9.   Generally financial leases must be capitalized so that the present value of the debt is reflected in both the assets and liabilities.

10.   When calculating the lessee's net advantage of leasing, the after-tax lease payment and the depreciation tax shelter are discounted at the lessee's after tax marginal cost of borrowing.

PROBLEM 15 PROBLEMS

1.   The Old Parr Bank will lend you $1 million at a nominal interest rate of 8% to be repaid over 5 years. Compute the amortization schedule for each of the following repayment schemes. Be sure to distinguish between principal and interest for each payment.

   a.   Five equal annual installments
   b.   A "bullet" loan
   c.   Five equal annual installments plus a $500,000 balloon
   d.   Five equal principal payments plus interest on the unpaid balance

   Solution:

   a.   Determine the amount of the equal payments.

$1,000,000 = \text{Payment} \times \text{PVIFA}_{0.08,5} = \text{Payment} \times 3.993$

Payment = $250,438

For an amortization schedule we set up a table showing the balance at the beginning of each year, the payment, the amount of the payment representing interest, and the amount paid toward the principal. For each year, the interest is 8% of the beginning balance; the principal payment is the difference between the payment and the interest. New balance is old balance less principal.

Year	Payment	Interest	Principal Repayment	Remaining Balance
0	---	---	---	1,000,000
1	250,438	80,000	170,438	829,562
2	250,438	66,365	184,073	645,489
3	250,438	51,639	198,799	446,690
4	250,438	35,735	214,703	231,987
5	250,438	18,559	231,879	108 [*]

*The remaining balance does not equal zero because of rounding. A payment of $250,456.45 would be more precise.

b.   In a bullet loan, only the accrued interest is paid during years 1-4. The final payment includes the final interest payment and the entire principal amount.

Year	Payment	Interest	Principal Repayment	Remaining Balance
1	80,000	80,000	0	1,000,000
2	80,000	80,000	0	1,000,000
3	80,000	80,000	0	1,000,000
4	80,000	80,000	0	1,000,000
5	1,080,000	80,000	1,000,000	0

c.   This balloon loan payment scheme can be viewed as a $500,000 loan amortized with equal annual payments together with a $500,000 bullet loan. For years 1-4, the total payment is the amortization payment on $500,000 plus the interest on the remaining $500,000. The Final payment consists of the amortization payment, the interest on the bullet, and the principal payment on the bullet. Once the payments are determined, operations in the table are identical to those for an amortized loan. Interest is 8% of the balance. Principal is payment less interest, the next year's balance is the old balance less the principal payment. The payment for years 1 to 4 on the amortized portion is determined by

$500,000 = \text{Payment} \times \text{PVIFA}_{.08,5} = \text{Payment} \times 3.993$

Payment = $125,219

The payment of the bullet portion is simply

Payment = .08 x 500,000 = $40,000

The total payment is the sum of the two parts or $165,219.

This final payment is equal to the regular payments plus the $500,000 balloon or $665,219.

A second way to visualize this is:

$$1,000,000 = \text{payment} \times \text{PVIFA}_{.08,5} + \text{PVIF}_{.08,5}$$

$$1,000,000 = \text{payment} \times 3.993 + 500,000 \times .681$$

$$1,000,000 = \text{payment} \times 3.993 + 340,500$$

$$\text{payment} \times 3.993 = 659,500$$

$$\text{payment} = \$165,164$$

This payment differs from the others due to rounding error in the present value factors. The first four payments are $165,164 and the fifth is $165,164 + $500,000 = $665,164. Using $165,219 as the payment, the amortization table is:

Year	Payment	Interest	Principal Repayment	Remaining Balance
0	---	---	---	1,000,000
1	165,219	80,000	85,219	914,781
2	165,219	73,182	92,037	822,744
3	165,219	65,820	99,399	723,345
4	165,219	57,868	107,351	615,994
5	665,219	49,280	615,939	55[*]

[*]A payment of 165,228.23 would reduce this to zero.

d.   In this case, the total payment varies. The payment on the principal amount is always equal to $1,000,000/5 = $200,000. The interest payment is equal to 8% of the beginning balance for the year. The total payment is the sum of the two.

Year	Payment	Interest	Principal Repayment	Remaining Balance
0	---	---	---	1,000,000
1	280,000	80,000	200,000	800,000
2	264,000	64,000	200,000	600,000
3	248,000	48,000	200,000	400,000
4	232,000	32,000	200,000	200,000
5	216,000	16,000	200,000	0

2. The 29th National Bank of Lubbock will lend you $10,000 for 3 years with a stated interest rate of 8.29% to be paid in advance for the entire three years. What is the effective annual percentage cost?

Solution:

The total interest is given by

Interest = Principal x Rate x Years = 10,000 x .0829 x 3 = 2,487

The net cash flow from the loan at the time it is made is equal to 10,000 - 2,487 = 7,513. To find the effective rate we use

$PV = FV \times PVIF_{i,n}$

$7,513 = 10,000 \times PVIF_{i,3}$

$i = 10\%$

3. United Leasing Corporation wishes to lease some new forging and grinding equipment to the Utah Manufacturing Company. What lease payment should United charge? The relevant information is:

  installed cost = $20,000,000.

  20 year lease with lease payments at the beginning of each year.

  straight-line depreciation (of the full $20,000,000) over 20 years to a zero salvage value.
  expected salvage value is $5,000,000 (which will be a taxable gain).

  United's marginal tax rate is 34 percent.

  United wishes a 10% after tax rate of return.

Solution:

Let us follow the three-step procedure outlined in the text.

Step 1: Compute the lessor's amount to be amortized

  PV of after-tax salvage

   $= 5,000,000(1-.34)PVIF_{.10,20}$

   $= 3,300,000(.149) = \$491,700$

  PV of depreciation tax shelter

   $= 1,000,000(.34)PVIFA_{.10,2}$

$$= 340,000(8.514) = \$2,894,760$$

20,000,000	Initial outlay
- 491,700	PV of after-tax salvage
- 2,894,760	PV of depreciation tax shelter
$16,613,540	Amount to be amortized

Step 2:   Compute after tax lease income required (Recall that this is an annuity due.)

$$16,613,540 = (\text{After-tax income})(PVIFA_{.10,20})(1.10)$$

$$16,613,540 = (\text{After-tax income})(8.514)(1.10)$$

After-tax income required = $1,773,927

Step 3:   Compute the before-tax lease payment

$$\text{Lease payment} = \frac{\text{after-tax lease income requirement}}{1 - \text{lessor's marginal tax rate}}$$

$$\text{Lease payment} = \frac{1,773,927}{1 - .34} = \frac{1,773,927}{.66} = \$2,687,769$$

4.   J. O. Osborne, Inc., has asked you to recommend how it should finance the acquisition of a needed piece of equipment. The asset has an installed cost of $600,000 and would be depreciated as 5-year, 200% class property over its six year economic life. The estimated salvage value in six years is predicted to be $50,000, which would be taxable at ordinary rates. The equipment is not eligible for an investment tax credit. If purchased, the needed funds can be borrowed at a 10.6% pre-tax rate. If leased, the lessor will charge Osborne a lease payment of $120,000 at the beginning of each of the next six years. If leased, Osborne will save $5,000 of operating costs that it would have incurred if it owned the asset. Osborne's weighted average cost of capital is 12% and Osborne is in the 34% marginal tax bracket.

a.   Compute Osborne's net advantage to leasing?

b.   Should Osborne lease the equipment or borrow the funds to purchase it?

Solution:

a. The installed cost of the asset is $600,000.

The after-tax lease payment is (120,000)(1-.34) = $79,200. The lease payment is an annuity due.

The after-tax operating costs if owned = 5,000(1-.34) = $3,300.

The after-tax salvage is 50,000(1-.34) = $33,000.

The depreciation tax shield each year is:

Year	ACRS Rate	Depreciation Rate x $600,000	Tax Shield .34 x Depreciation
1	20.00%	$120,000	$40,800.0
2	32.00	192,000	65,280.0
3	19.20	115,200	39,168.0
4	11.52	69,120	23,500.8
5	11.52	69,120	23,500.8
6	5.76	34,560	11,750.4

End of Year (1)	Installed Cost (2)	Lease Payment After-Tax (3)	Depreciation Tax Shield (4)	Additional Oper. Cost If Owned (5)	Cash Flow Except Salvage (6) (2)-(3) -(4)+(5)
0	600,000	79,200	-	-	520,800
1	-	79,200	40,800	3,300	-116,700
2	-	79,200	65,280	3,300	-141,180
3	-	79,200	39,168	3,300	-115,068
4	-	79,200	23,500.8	3,300	-99,400.8
5	-	79,200	23,500.8	3,300	-99,400.8
6	-	-	11,750.4	3,300	-8,450.4

PVIF @ 7% (7)	Present Value (8) (6)x(7)	After-Tax Salvage (9)	PVIF @ 12% (10)	PV of Salvage (11) (9)x(10)	Net Adv. of Leasing (12) (8)-(11)
1.000	520,800.00	-	-	-	520,800.00
.935	-109,114.50	-	-	-	-109,114.50
.873	-123,250.14	-	-	-	-123,250.14
.816	-93,895.49	-	-	-	-93,895.49
.763	-75,842.81	-	-	-	-75,842.81
.713	-70,872.77	-	-	-	-70,872.77
.666	-5,627	33,000	.507	16,731	-23,358.97

Net Advantage to Leasing = 25,465.32

b.   Since the net advantage to leasing is positive, Osborne is better off leasing the equipment.

16

Managing Long-Term Funding Sources

In addition to issuing simple long-term debt, preferred stock, and common stock, a firm has two other alternatives available. These include convertible issues of debt and preferred stock and warrants. Convertible securities and warrants are forms of options, which are securities giving the right to buy or sell another asset under specified conditions.

I. An option is a security that gives its holder the right, but not the obligation, to buy or sell an asset at a set price during a specified time period.

   A. A call option is an option to buy a particular asset whereas a put option is an option to sell it. The set price at which the option holder can buy (or sell) an asset is called the exercise price or strike price.

   B. A warrant is a call option issued by a company on its own securities, usually on its own stock.

   C. A convertible security is a fixed income security with a call option on common stock. A convertible bond can be exchanged for a set number of shares of common stock.

II. There are several variables that affect the value of an option.

   A. There are boundaries or limits to the value of a call option.

      1. At maturity (when the option expires), if the stock price is above the exercise price.

229

Value of a call option at maturity = Stock price - Exercise price

2.   Prior to maturity, a call option sells for more than this amount

Value of a call option prior to maturity > Stock price - Exercise price

3.   Under no conditions will an investor pay more for an option than the stock price

Maximum value of call option = Stock price

4.   An option cannot have negative value (such as if exercising an option when the exercise price is above the stock price) because a rational investor will simply not exercise the right to buy the stock.

Minimum value of a call option   = 0

B.   Several variables affect the value of a call option.

1.   An increase in the stock price (with the exercise price and everything else constant) will increase the value of a call option.

2.   A higher exercise price (everything else the same) reduces the value of a call option.

3.   The longer the time remaining until expiration the higher the option value (all other things being equal).

4.   The higher the level of interest rates, the higher is the call option's value (all other things being equal).

5.   The greater the volatility of the stock price, the higher is the call option value (all other things being equal).

C.   Investors take a variety of positions in the options market.

1.   Investors who feel a stock is going to rise will buy a call option and investors who feel a stock is going to drop will buy a put option.

2.   Selling an option is frequently called "writing" an option.

3.   If a person sells a call option on shares he or she owns, this is called covered option writing. Writing a call option without owning the underlying stock is called uncovered or naked option writing.

D.   Any firm with debt and equity outstanding can be analyzed in an options framework.

1. The stockholders can be viewed as having sold the firm to the debtholders. The stockholders have an option to buy back the firm from the debtholders (by paying the promised debt payments).

2. At the time the debt is due, if the value of the firm exceeds the debt claim, the stockholders will exercise their option by paying off the debt. On the other hand, if the value of the firm is less than the debt claim, the stockholders will let their option expire by not repaying the debt (i.e., defaulting on the debt).

3. One implication of this analysis is that risk-increasing investments that may benefit stockholders at the expense of debtholders. High payoffs benefit stockholders and low payoffs increase the probability of defaults on debt.

III. Both debentures and preferred stock can be convertible into shares of the firm's common stock. Issuance of these securities usually represents a future issuance of common stock since ultimate conversion is anticipated.

A. The terms of conversion are represented in the conversion price.

1. At conversion, the convertible security is surrendered for a quantity of common stock which, when priced at the conversion price, has a total value equal to the par value of the convertible.

2. The number of shares which can be obtained in conversion is called the conversion ratio. The conversion ratio is given by:

Conversion ratio = Par value of security/Conversion price

3. The conversion price is higher than the stock price at the time the securities are issued. The difference is called the conversion premium.

B. There are several reasons for issuing convertibles:

1. To make the fixed income security more attractive so that lower interest or dividends may be paid.

2. To "sell" common stock in the future when the price will be higher.

3. To allow time for investments financed with the funds from issuance of the security to begin to pay benefits before the additional common stock is used in the calculation of EPS.

4. Relatively small, risky companies whose common stock is publicly traded are the principal issuers of convertibles. Convertibles can lessen the agency conflict between stockholders and debtholders. Since convertible owners have an equity stake in the company, they

will be entitled to some of the benefits that stockholders can receive if they invest in high risk projects.

C. Because convertible securities are a cross between fixed income securities and common stock, their valuation is more complex than that of simple securities.

    1. The conversion value is the value of the common stock that could be obtained in conversion. This is given by:

        Conversion value = Conversion ratio x Stock price

    2. The straight-bond value or investment value of a convertible is the value it would have if it did not have the conversion feature. This is equal to the present value of its future cash flows discounted at a rate k_d which is the current yield to maturity for similar nonconvertible securities.

    3. The market value is the price the security trades for in the market.

        a. The market value is usually slightly above the higher of the conversion value or the investment value.
        b. The difference between the market value and the higher of the conversion value or the investment value is the premium.

D. Convertible securities can be converted voluntarily by investors or conversion can be forced by the issuing company.

    1. Voluntary conversion can occur at any time prior to expiration of the conversion feature.

    2. Conversion can be forced by utilizing the call privilege of the security. If the conversion value is higher than the call price, investors will convert to common stock rather than have the security called.

IV. A warrant is an option, issued by the firm, to purchase a specific number of shares at a specified price during the life of the warrant.

A. Warrants are usually issued in conjunction with an issue of other securities in order to make them more attractive.

B. Warrants are characterized by the exercise price and the expiration date.

    1. The exercise price is the price at which shares of common stock may be purchased. The exercise price is usually 10% to 30% above the market price of the common stock at the time the warrant is issued.

2.   The expiration date is the date when the option to purchase the common stock ends. Most warrants have an expiration date 5 to 10 years after the date of issue.

C.   Warrants can usually be traded separately from the security with which they are originally issued.

D.   The exercise or expiration of warrants does not affect the security with which they were issued on the books of the firm.

E.   The primary reason for issuing warrants is to "sweeten" the security with which they are issued by allowing purchasers to participate in increases in the common stock price and to sell common stock in the future.

F.   The valuation of warrants is more complex than that of simple securities.

1.   The basic value of a warrant is the greater of $0 or the profit which could be made by exercising the warrant and immediately selling the stock. This is given by:

$$\text{Formula value of a warrant} = \max\left[0;\ \left(\begin{array}{c}\text{common stock}\\ \text{market price}\\ \text{per share}\end{array} - \begin{array}{c}\text{exercise}\\ \text{price}\\ \text{per share}\end{array}\right) \times \begin{array}{c}\text{No. of shares}\\ \text{obtainable with}\\ \text{each warrant}\end{array}\right]$$

2.   The market value of a warrant usually exceeds the formula value. The difference is called the premium.

3.   Warrants carry a premium because of the potential for price appreciation of the common stock during the life of the warrant.

G.   Warrants provide leverage to investors because the warrant holder can obtain the benefits of increasing stock prices for an investment in the warrant which is less than would be required for the stock.

V.   Companies that have convertible securities and warrants outstanding must calculate EPS in two ways.

A.   Primary earnings per share $= \dfrac{\text{Earnings available to common}}{\text{Common shares outstanding}}$

B.   Fully diluted EPS $= \dfrac{\text{Earnings available to common}}{\text{Common shares if warrants \& convertibles are exercised}}$

Under certain circumstances, calculation of the denominator may be more complex.

VI.   Capital markets are classified as primary or secondary markets.

    A.   New securities are traded in the primary markets.

    B.   Securities which are already outstanding are traded in the secondary markets.

       1.   Although no new capital is raised in the secondary markets, their existence and operation provides liquidity for investors in the primary market. This encourages investment and may reduce the cost of new capital.

       2.   Secondary markets can be further classified as listed security exchanges and over-the-counter markets.

          a.   Listed security exchanges include the New York Stock Exchange, the American Stock Exchange, and several regional exchanges.

          b.   Securities which are not traded on the listed exchanges are traded over-the-counter. The OTC system consists of securities firms which deal in OTC securities and often carry inventories in them. Trading in the securities is linked by the automated quotation system operated by the National Association of Security Dealers (NASDAQ).

    C.   The _Wall Street Journal_ and the business section of larger daily newspapers contain economic and security market news.

       1.   Stock quotations for listed stocks usually give the high and low over the last 52 weeks; an abbreviated name of the company; the current annual dividend; dividend yield; the price-earnings ratio; the sales volume in hundreds of shares; the high, low, and closing price for the day; and the change between the day's closing price and that for the previous day.

       2.   Over-the-counter stocks are usually quoted in terms of their bid and asked price.

       3.   Bond quotations are usually given as a percentage of par value.

       4.   Stock market indexes such as the Dow Jones Industrial Average and Standard and Poor's 500 Stock Index give a broad indication of how the market or a segment of it performed during the day.

       5.   Securities can be purchased in part with funds borrowed from brokers. The fraction of money put up by the investor is called _margin_. The minimum margin percentage is regulated by the Federal Reserve.

6.   Investors can sell securities that they do not own by borrowing them in the hope of replacing the borrowed securities at a lower cost. This is called <u>short selling</u>.

D.   Both the individual states and the federal government regulate the securities business. Major federal regulation arose after the stock market crash of 1929. These laws make no judgments regarding the quality of securities.

     1.   The Securities Act of 1933 requires complete disclosure of all pertinent facts when new securities are issued.

     2.   The Securities Exchange Act of 1934 extended coverage to include trading in existing securities and created the Securities and Exchange Commission (SEC).

VII.   Investment bankers are experts in capital market issues including long-range financial planning, issuance of securities, the arrangement of long-term loans and leases, and the negotiation of mergers.

A.   Securities are sold in the primary market to the pubic in public cash offers, to a few large investors in private or direct placements, or to existing stockholders of the firm through a rights offering.

     1.   Public cash offerings are usually purchased by an investment banker or an investment banking syndicate and then resold to the general public. This process is called <u>underwriting</u>. The underwriting agreement is determined by negotiation or competitive bid. The underwriters are compensated by the difference between their purchase price and the price to the public. This difference is called the <u>underwriting discount</u> or <u>underwriting spread</u>. In some cases, the investment bankers only market the securities on a "best effort" basis without actually underwriting them.

     2.   Direct or private placement of securities with one or more institutional investors is often arranged by an investment banker in exchange for a "finder's fee." Direct placement avoids underwriting costs and registration requirements and offers greater flexibility in terms although interest rates are often slightly higher.

     3.   Common stock may be sold through the issuance of "rights" to existing stockholders which entitle them to purchase the new stock at a subscription price below the current market price. For these issues, investment bankers encourage rights holders to purchase the issue. In a standby underwriting, they also agree to purchase any unsold shares at the subscription price.

     4.   Flotation costs consist of the underwriting spread and all other issue

expenses of the company. Flotation costs are usually directly related to the riskiness of the security.

VIII. Several new and innovative securities are being used in their financing. The "financial engineering" creations can be grouped as debt or equity innovations.

    A.   The following are examples of debt innovations.

        1.   Adjustable Rate Notes. The interest rate varies and is based on an index, such as the 3-month Treasury bill rate.

        2.   Bonds Linked to a Commodity Price. The interest and/or principal is adjusted to changes in the price of a commodity, such as silver.

        3.   Extendible Notes. The interest rate is reset every 2-3 years, at which time the holders can accept the new rate (extending the loan for a longer time) or they can put the notes back to the issuer at par.

        4.   Interest Rate Reset Notes. The interest rate is reset, for example, three years after issuance to give the notes a predetermined market value such as 101 percent of par value. However, the interest rate cannot be lowered.

        5.   Interest Rate Swap. This is an argument between two companies in which one company's floating rate debt repayment obligation is traded for another company's fixed rate obligation. These swaps are a means of shifting interest rate risk from one company to another.

        6.   Puttable Bonds. The investor has a put option to sell the puttable bond back to the issuing company at par. This protects the investor against increases in interest rates or a deterioration of the company's credit quality.

    B.   The following are examples of equity innovations.

        1.   Adjustable Rate Preferred Stock. The quarterly dividend is reset each quarterly dividend is reset each quarter and is usually tied to Treasury notes.

        2.   Additional Class(es) of Common Stock. Companies can create an additional class of common stock whose dividends are based on the earnings of a subsidiary. A separate market value for the subsidiary is established, although the parent company retains 100 percent voting control.

        3.   Master Limited Partnership. This is a business set up as a partnership but that is publicly owned and traded as if it were a corporation. The purpose of the master limited partnership is to

lower taxes, only the partners are taxed, not the corporation. This tax benefit is being phased out.

TRUE AND FALSE QUESTIONS

Agree with each of the statements or reject it and modify it so that it is acceptable.

1. A put option is a security that gives its holder the right to buy an asset at a set price during a specified time period.

2. At expiration, a call option will sell for (1) the excess of the stock price over the exercise price or (2) zero, whichever is greater.

3. Options frequently have negative value.

4. An increase in the stock price increases the value of a call option (all else the same).

5. An increase in the stock price volatility reduces the value of a call option on the stock (all else the same).

6. Both debentures and preferred stock can be convertible into shares of the firm's common stock.

7. The number of debentures required to obtain one share of stock is called the conversion ratio.

8. At the time of issue, the conversion value is usually less than the market price of the stock to ensure that conversion will occur.

9. The conversion value represents a floor for the price of the convertible security.

10. A firm often calls a convertible security in order to prevent it from being converted.

11. The market price of a convertible is usually slightly less than the lesser of the conversion value or the investment value.

12. When a warrant is exercised, the security with which it was issued is cancelled and removed from the books of the company.

13. Warrants are attractive to investors because they provide leverage.

14. Primary earnings per share is the earnings available if the dividend on a convertible preferred is ignored.

15. Warrants are traded on the Chicago Board Options Exchange.

16. Primary markets consist of the major exchanges while the smaller regional exchanges are called secondary markets.

17. NASDAQ is the National Association of Security Dealers Automated Quotation system.

18. In an OTC stock quotation, the bid price is always greater than the asked price.

19. Margin refers to money borrowed from a broker to purchase securities.

20. Short selling consists of selling borrowed securities.

21. The Securities and Exchange Commission insures that all securities sell for a price within a reasonable range of the actual value.

22. An underwriting investment banker in a public cash offering assists the issuing firm on a best efforts basis.

23. Flotation costs are usually higher for high quality securities.

24. An underwriting discount is a special price break for firms which often issue new securities.

25. Privately placed debt usually carries a higher interest cost than debt issued through underwriters.

Answers to True and False Questions

1. A call option is a security that gives its holder the right to buy an asset at a set price during a specified time period.

2. True.

3. Options can be worthless, but they cannot have negative value because the holder will not exercise options if it is not in the investor's best interests to do so.

4. True.

5. An increase in the stock price volatility increases the value of a call option on the stock (all else the same).

6. True.

7. The number of shares of stock obtainable from one debenture is called the conversion ratio.

8. At the time of issue, the conversion value is usually less than the investment

(bond) value of the security. This ensures that the funds are available for use for a while before the number of common shares will increase.

9. The investment (bond) value represents a floor for the price of the convertible security.

10. A firm often calls a convertible security in order to force holders to convert it.

11. The market price of a convertible is usually greater than the higher of the conversion value or the investment value.

12. Exercise of a warrant has no effect on the security with which it was issued.

13. True.

14. Primary earnings per share is the earnings available to common stock after preferred dividends are considered. This ignores the potential increase in the number of shares from exercise of warrants and convertibles.

15. Warrants are traded on the stock exchanges. Warrants, issued by the firm, are not the same as options traded on the CBOE which are not issued by the firm and cannot result in an increase in the number of common shares outstanding.

16. Primary markets consist of markets where new securities are issued.

17. True.

18. In an OTC stock quotation, the bid price is lower than the ask price. The bid is the price at which dealers are willing to buy the stock. The asked price is the price at which they are willing to sell.

19. Margin refers to the fraction of the purchase cost put up by the investor.

20. True.

21. The SEC regulates trading but makes no judgment as to the value of a security.

22. An underwriting investment banker purchases the issue from the firm and then resells it. Assistance provided on a best effort basis is not underwriting.

23. Flotation costs are usually higher for more risky securities.

24. An underwriting discount is the difference between the price the underwriter pays the firm for the security and sells the security to the public.

25. True.

CHAPTER 16 PROBLEMS

1.   The Hide-Away Bed Company has an issue of convertible debentures outstanding. Par value is $1,000 and the conversion price is $40. The coupon interest rate is 5% paid annually. The bonds mature in 10 years and are callable at 105. The company has a tax rate of 40%.

    a.   If the company's stock is selling at $30, calculate the conversion value.
    b.   Assume that similar straight debt yields 8%. Calculate the investment value of the convertible.
    c.   What should the approximate market value of the convertible be?
    d.   What is the minimum stock price at which the company should call the debentures and force conversion?

Solution:

    a.   Conversion value = stock price x   (par value/conversion price)

$$= \quad 30 \quad x \quad (1000/40) \quad = \quad \$750$$

    b.   Investment value =   price as straight bond

$$= \quad 50 \times PVIFA_{0.08,10} + 1000 \times PVIF_{0.08,10}$$

$$= \quad 50 \times 6.710 + 1000 \times .463 = \$798.50$$

    c.   The convertible should be selling for slightly more than the higher of the conversion value or the investment value. It should be selling for somewhat more than $750.

    d.   In order to force conversion, the stock price must be high enough that the conversion value exceeds the call value. Investors are indifferent if conversion value equals call value.

$$(\text{stock price})(\text{conversion ratio}) = \text{call value}$$

$$(\text{stock price})(\text{par value/conversion price}) = \text{call value}$$

$$(\text{stock price})(1000/40) = \$1050$$

$$(\text{stock price})(25) = \$1050$$

$$\text{stock price} = \$42$$

If the debenture is called when the stock price is greater than $42 per share, conversion should occur.

2.   The ICU Keyhole Company has an issue of warrants outstanding. Each warrant entitles the holder to purchase two shares of the company's common stock at an

exercise price of $15 per share. The current market price of the warrant is $13 and the price of the common is $20. What is the premium on the warrant?

Solution:

The formula value of the warrant is the greater of $0 or

(stock price - exercise price)(shares per warrant) = (20-15)(2) = 10

The premium is the difference between the market price of the warrant and its formula value.

Warrant premium = $13 - $10 = $3

3. Your firm is considering issuing $20 million of convertible debentures. The conversion price is $50 per share. The present capital structure appears as follows.

Long-term debt	$100 million
Common stock ($5 par)	50 million
Additional paid-in capital	100 million
Retained earnings	200 million

a. Show the capital structure if the convertibles are issued.

b. Show the capital structure after conversion takes place.

Solution:

a.

Long-term debt	$120 million
Common stock ($5 par) (10 million shares)	50 million
Additional paid-in capital	100 million
Retained Earnings	200 million

b.

Long-term debt	$100 million
Common stock ($5 par) (10.4 million shares)	52 million
Additional paid-in capital	118 million
Retained earnings	200 million

The convertible debentures have been converted to common stock. The par value is added to the common stock account and the remainder to the additional paid-in capital. The debt is cancelled.

4. When a company's stock was trading at $12, outstanding warrants on the stock were trading at $3. When the stock was trading at $15, the warrants were trading at $6. Calculate the percentage returns to an investor who bought the stock at $12 and sold at $15 and the returns to another investor who traded in the warrants at the same time.

Solution:

The percentage return on the stock is $100(15 - 12)/12 = 25\%$.

The percentage return on the warrants is $100(6 - 3)/3 = 100\%$.

5.   An issue of 8% convertible debentures is issued at par and will mature in 30 years. The conversion ratio is 10. Conversion is expected to occur in 10 years when the stock price is $130. The company has a 40% tax rate. Find the component cost of capital. (Hint: Try 7%.)

Solution:

The after-tax cost of capital associated with a convertible is found by using the relation:

Issue price = (coupon interest)$(1 - t)(PVIFA_{r,n}) + (CV_n)(PVIF_{r,n})$

where r is the after-tax cost of capital, n is the expected number of years until conversion, and CV_n is the expected conversion value in n years. r is found by trial and error. In the present problem we have:

$$1000 = (80)(.6)(PVIFA_{r,10}) + (10)(130)(PVIF_{r,10})$$

Trying 7% we get

$$\$998 = (80)9.6)(7.024) + (10)(130)(.508)$$

Appendix 16

I.   Bond refunding occurs when a company redeems a callable issue and replaces it with a lower cost issue.

A.   Bond refunding decisions are based on the present value of the cash flows associated with maintaining the old issue versus those of refunding.

B.   Because the cash flows associated with refunding decisions are known with certainty, the after-tax cost of the new debt is used for discounting rather than the firm's cost of capital.

C.   Factors included in the refunding decision are the savings in periodic interest payments, the call premium on the old bonds, the flotation cost on the new bonds, the unamortized flotation costs on the old bonds, and the double interest payments between the time the new debt is issued and the old recalled.

1.   The value of the interest savings is computed as

Annual interest, old issue = (issue size)(coupon)(1-tax rate)
Annual interest, new issue = (issue size)(coupon)(1-tax rate)
Annual after-tax interest savings

The present value of the annual after-tax savings is computed using the after-tax interest rate on the new debt.

PV interest saving = (annual after-tax savings)$(PVIFA_{r,n})$

2.   The call premium is tax deductible. The call premium after taxes is computed as (call premium) (1 - t)

3.   Flotation costs on the new bonds are an immediate cash outflow. These costs are amortized over the life of the issue. Each year, the amortization is deducted from taxable income. The present value effect is given by

Present Value of
flotation costs =   costs - (costs/years)(tax rate)$(PVIFA_{r,n})$
of new issue

4.   The unamortized portion of the flotation costs for the old issue will be taken as an expense immediately rather than being amortized over the remaining life of the issue. The present value effect of this is given by

Present Value of
flotation costs = unamortized costs(t) - $\dfrac{\text{unamortized cost}(t)(PVIFA_{r,n})}{\text{years left}}$
of old issue

5.   In order to prevent a gap in financing, the new bonds are usually issued before the old bonds are retired. The interest expense on the new issue during this overlap is called the overlapping interest.

Overlapping Interest = (size of issue)(coupon rate)(1-t)(overlap as fraction of year)

6.   The present value of the net investment in refunding is

Call Premium
+   PV of flotation costs on new issue
-   PV of flotation costs on old issue
+   Overlapping interest
Net Investment (cash outflow)

7.   The interest savings and the net investment are combined to obtain the net present value of refunding.

NPV of refunding = PV of interest savings - PV Net Investment

8.   Refunding is undertaken if the NPV is greater than zero. Consideration should also be given to the possibility that more advantageous refunding opportunities may occur in the relatively near future.

II.   One of the rights of stockholders is the right to elect the board of directors. Two rules for electing the Board of Directors are commonly used.

A.   Majority voting requires that a group have more than 50% of the votes to elect a director.

B.   Cumulative voting makes it easier for minorities to elect a favorable board member.

C.   Under cumulative voting, the number of shares required to obtain representation on the Board is given by

$$\text{No. of shares} = \frac{\text{No. of directors desired} \times \text{No. of shares outstanding}}{\text{No. of directors being elected} + 1} + 1$$

III.   If a company's charter contains a provision for preemptive rights then any new common stock must be sold through a rights offering. Other companies may choose to issue new equity through a rights offering rather than the underwriting procedure of a public offering.

A.   A single right attaches to each outstanding share.

B.   The ratio of outstanding shares to shares to be issued determines the number of rights required to purchase one new share.

C. Possession of the required number of rights allows the holder to purchase one share of stock at the subscription price.

D. To provide an incentive for stockholders to exercise their rights, the subscription price is less than the current market price.

E. Stockholders who do not wish to exercise their rights can sell them in the open market.

F. Like dividends, rights are subject to a shareholder of record date. As in the case of dividends, a purchaser becomes a holder of record five trading days after purchase. A stock trades "rights-on" until it goes "ex- rights." The stock goes ex-rights four days before the holder of record date.

G. Rights have economic value.

1. The theoretical value of a right while the stock is selling "rights-on" is given by

$$R = (M_0 - S)/(N + 1)$$

where M_0 is the rights-on price of the stock, S is the subscription price, and N is the number of rights required to purchase one share.

2. The theoretical value of a right after it is detached from the stock is given by

$$R = (M_e - S)/N$$

where M_e is the ex-rights price of the stock.

H. Rights usually trade in the market for a price greater than the theoretical value because of the potential for the price of the stock to increase before they are exercised.

TRUE AND FALSE QUESTIONS

Agree with each of the statements or reject it and modify it so that it is acceptable.

1. Bond refunding frequently occurs in order to replace a high interest debt issue with an issue of lower cost.

2. If interest rates decline, a bond issue should be refunded.

3. Overlapping interest must be paid because the new issue is usually sold before the old issue is retired.

4.   Cumulative voting provisions make it easier for groups of stockholders with minority views to obtain representation.

5.   Other things equal, the value of a right attached to the stock is identical to the value of a right which is detached from the stock.

Answers to True and False Questions

1.   True.

2.   This is over simplified. The present value of interest savings must be compared to the present value of the net investment in the refunding process including call premium, changes in flotation cost amortization, and overlapping interest.

3.   True.

4.   True.

5.   True. (The formulas differ because of the fact that the stock price right-on includes the value of the right. Dividing by N+1 prevents double counting of the value of the right.)

APPENDIX 16 PROBLEMS

1.   The Sure-Bond Glue Company has outstanding $100 million of 12% bonds with 20 years to maturity. These bonds are callable at 105. $600,000 of flotation costs have not yet been amortized. Sure-Bond is considering replacing the outstanding bonds with an issue of the same maturity bearing interest at 10%. Flotation costs will amount to 1% of the amount issued. If the refunding is undertaken, there will be a 4 week overlap between the time the new bonds are issued and the old retired. The company's tax rate is 40%. Find the net present value of refunding. For simplicity, assume that the tax benefits of writing off the flotation costs of the old issue are available immediately. Assume interest is paid annually.

Solution:

We begin by finding the present value of the interest savings.

$$
\begin{aligned}
\text{After tax interest on old issue} &= 100 \text{ million} \times 12\% \times .6 = \$7,200,000 \\
-\ \underline{\text{After tax interest on new issue}} &= \underline{100 \text{ million} \times 10\% \times .6 = \$6,000,000} \\
\text{After tax interest savings} &\qquad\qquad\qquad\qquad \$1,200,000 \\
\times\ \underline{\text{PVIFA}_{0.06,20} \text{ (use after tax rate on new bonds)}} &\qquad\qquad\qquad\qquad\ \underline{11.470} \\
\text{Present value of after tax interest savings} &\qquad\qquad\qquad \$13,764,000
\end{aligned}
$$

The next step is to determine the present value of the net investment in refunding. The components of this include the call premium, the unamortized flotation costs on the old issue, the flotation costs on the new issue, and the overlapping interest.

The after tax cash flow associated with the call premium on the old issue is:

(size of issue)(call premium)(1 - t)

($100,000,000)(.05)(.6) = $3,000,000

If the old issue is refunded, the unamortized flotation costs will be written off immediately rather than amortized over the remaining 20 years. This results in a current tax deduction of the unamortized costs but a reduction in future tax benefits. The result is given by:

Present value of flotation costs of old issue

$$= \frac{\text{Unamortized costs}}{\text{Years left}} (t)(PVIFA_{0.06,20})-(\text{Unamortized costs})(t)$$

$$= \frac{600,000}{20}(.4)(11.470)-(600,000)(.4)=-102,360$$

The negative sign indicates that this is a net cash inflow since the immediate writeoff is more valuable than the amortized writeoff.

The flotation costs on the new issue represent an immediate cash outflow which will be partially offset by the tax benefits arising from the annual amortization. Thus we have

Present value of flotation costs of new issue

$$= \quad \text{costs} \quad - \quad (\text{costs/years})(t)(PVIFA_{.06,20})$$

$$= \quad 1,000,000 \quad - \quad (1,000,000/20)(.4)(11.470) = 770,600$$

Overlapping interest is given by

Overlapping interest

$$= (\text{size of issue})(\text{rate on new issue})(\text{fraction of year})(1-t)$$

$$= (100,000,000)(.10)(4/52)(.6) = 461,538$$

The net investment in refunding is summarized as:

Call premium	3,000,000
Flotation costs on old issue	-102,360
Flotation costs on new issue	770,600
Overlapping interest	461,538
Net investment in refunding	4,129,778

The net present value of refunding is:

Present value of interest savings - present value of net investment

$$= 13,764,000 - 4,129,778 = \$9,634,222$$

2.   The Dawson Trail Gold Company is issuing new common stock through a rights offering. The stock is selling for $45 per share. The subscription price is $42. Five rights are needed to purchase one share.

   a.   Calculate the theoretical value of the right while the stock is selling rights-on.

   b.   Other things equal, what should the price of the stock be immediately after going ex-rights?

   c.   Calculate the value of the right after the stock goes ex- rights.

   d.   If the stock goes back to $45, find the ex-rights value.

   Solution:

   a.   Value rights-on $= \dfrac{\text{Stock price-Subscription price}}{1 + \text{no. of rights for 1 share}}$

   $= \dfrac{45 - 42}{5 + 1} = \$.50$

   b.   Other things equal, the price of the stock should decline by the value of the right. The new price should be $44.50.

   c.   Value ex-rights $= \dfrac{\text{Stock price-Subscription price}}{\text{No. of rights for 1 share}}$

   $= \dfrac{44.50 - 42}{5} = \$.50$

   d.   The formula is the same as in part c, but the numbers are:

   $\dfrac{45 - 42}{5} = \$.60$

3.   The K.E.N. Arrow Company has 12 members on their board of directors. Three positions are up for election at the annual meeting. The company has 20 million shares of common stock outstanding. You are a member of a group which wishes to be assured of electing at least one of your group members to the board of directors. How many shares of stock must your group control?

   a.   If a simple majority voting rule is followed?
   b.   If the company uses cumulative voting?

Solution:

a.   Under simple majority voting, you must have 50% of the stock outstanding plus one share or 10,000,001 shares.

b.   Under cumulative voting, the number of shares required is given by

No. of shares

$$= \frac{\text{No. of directors desired} \times \text{No. of shares outstanding}}{\text{No. of directors being elected} + 1} + 1$$

$$= \frac{1 \times 20,000,000}{3 + 1} + 1$$

$$= \quad 5,000,001 \text{ shares}$$

17

Working Capital Policy

The management of working capital is concerned with decisions involving the firm's current assets and current liabilities. These decisions include the composition of current assets and liabilities, their use, and their relationship to the risk of the firm.

I. Working capital management is concerned with current assets and current liabilities and their relationship to the rest of the firm.

    A. Working capital refers to the total investment in current assets while net working capital refers to the difference between current assets and current liabilities.

    B. Working capital management involves a number of types of decisions:

        1. The level of investment in current assets.

        2. The proportion of short-term versus long-term debt the firm uses to finance its assets.

        3. The investment in each type of current asset.

        4. The specific sources and mix of current liabilities.

    C. Working capital represents assets that flow through the business at a relatively rapid rate. Working capital is needed because of the asynchronous nature of cash receipts and disbursements.

251

D.   The operating cycle of a manufacturing firm can be characterized by the time intervals between the following dates:

Date 1	(Sept 1)	Purchase of resources
Date 2	(Oct 1)	Pay for resource purchases
Date 3	(Oct 15)	Sell product on credit
Date 4	(Dec 1)	Collect receivables

1.   The time interval from the purchase of resources until the collection of receivables is the operating cycle. This interval from date 1 to date 4 in the example above is 90 days long.

2.   The inventory conversion period is the period between the purchase of resources and sale of the product (from date 1 to date 3 - 45 days). The receivables conversion period is the period between the sale of the product on credit and the receivable collection (between date 3 and date 4 - 45 days).

3.   The payables deferral period is the period between the purchase of resources and the payment for these resources (from date 1 to date 2 - 30 days). The cash conversion cycle is the period between when the firm pays for its resources and when the firm collects on its own sales (from date 2 to date 4 - 60 days).

4.   These time periods also can be seen as:

memorize

Operating cycle = Inventory conversion period + Receivables conversion period

$$\text{Inventory conversion period} = \frac{\text{Average inventory}}{\text{Cost of sales}/365}$$

$$\text{Receivables conversion period} = \frac{\text{Accounts receivable}}{\text{Annual credit sales}/365}$$

$$\text{Payables deferral period} = \frac{\text{Accounts payable + salaries, benefits \& payroll taxes payable}}{(\text{Cost of sales + Selling, general and admin. expense})/365}$$

Cash conversion cycle = Operating cycle - payables deferral period

E.   The net working capital position of a firm is a measure of the firm's riskiness in terms of its ability to pay its bills on time.

F.   The size and nature of a firm's investment in current assets depend on a number of factors:

1.   The type of products manufactured

2.   The length of the operating cycle

3.   Requirements for inventory to support sales

4.   Inventory policies regarding safety stock and probabilities of running out of goods

5.   Credit policies affecting levels of accounts receivable

6.   Efficiency of current asset management.

G.   Determination of the appropriate level of working capital involves a tradeoff between risk and profitability.

1.   More conservative policies involve holding a greater amount of current assets relative to sales. More aggressive policies hold less.

2.   More conservative working capital policies have lower expected profitability since more assets are used to produce a given level of income.

3.   More conservative working capital policies have a lower risk of insufficient cash to pay bills and insufficient inventory to meet demand. More conservative policies often result in lost sales due to restrictive credit policies.

4.   The optimal level of working capital investment is the level which is expected to maximize shareholder wealth.

II.   In addition to the level of current assets, the firm must consider the proportions of short-term and long-term financing used to support them. This decision involves tradeoffs between profitability and risk.

A.   The relationship between debt maturity and interest rates is known as the term structure of interest rates. The term structure may be displayed as a graph called a yield curve.

1.   The yield curve is generally upward sloping.

2.   Sometimes the yield curve is downward sloping or approximately flat.

3.   Even if the yield curve is downward sloping, the cost of financing working capital with long-term debt may be higher than that of short-term debt because long- term debt is less flexible and may require payment of interest on funds which are needed only part of the time.

B.   The risk associated with financing working capital with short-term debt is greater than that for long-term debt.

1.   There is a risk the firm will not be able to refund the short-term debt.

2. Short-term interest rates tend to fluctuate more than long-term rates so that the cost is less certain.

C. Current assets can be divided into permanent current assets and fluctuating current assets.

1. Fluctuating current assets are those which are affected by seasonal or cyclical demand.

2. Permanent current assets are those which are *not* affected by seasonal or cyclical demand.

3. One approach to financing working capital is to attempt to match the maturity of the debt to the maturity of the assets. Under this approach, permanent working capital is financed from long-term sources while fluctuating working capital is financed with short-term debt.

a. A more conservative approach uses a higher proportion of long-term financing. This usually involves higher cost and lower profitability, with reduced risk of unavailable funding and interest rate changes.

b. A more aggressive approach uses a higher proportion of short-term debt.

D. The optimal combination of long- and short-term financing for working capital is the combination which maximizes shareholder wealth. This varies from firm to firm depending on other factors affecting risk and profitability.

TRUE AND FALSE QUESTIONS

Agree with each of the statements or reject it and modify it so that it is acceptable.

1. F Net working capital = working capital - current liabilities. *current assets - current liabilities*

2. If a firm finances its working capital entirely with short-term debt, it will have no net working capital.

3. The amount of working capital needed is determined by the amount of the firm's current liabilities.

4. The amount of working capital required increases faster than sales.

5. Working capital policies which hold a smaller amount of working capital for a given level of sales are more aggressive.

6.   The optimal level of working capital is that which gives a current ratio equal to the industry average.

7.   Fixed assets are a part of permanent working capital.

8.   A given working capital policy can be made more conservative by either increasing the proportion of long-term debt relative to short-term debt or by increasing the level of working capital relative to sales.

Answers to True and False Questions

1.   True.

2.   True.

3.   The amount of working capital is determined by the nature of the firm's business, length of the operating cycle, level of sales, and attitudes toward risk.

4.   The amount of working capital required usually increases slower than sales.

5.   True.

6.   The optimal level of working capital is that which maximizes stockholder wealth.

7.   Only current assets are included in working capital. Permanent working capital consists of the minimum long-term level of current assets.

8.   True.

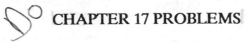 **CHAPTER 17 PROBLEMS**

1.   Gentry Manufacturing has the following balance sheet and income statement for 1992:

BALANCE SHEET

Cash	$ 500,000	Accounts payable	$ 750,000
Accounts receivable	1,500,000	Salaries payable	250,000
Inventories	2,000,000	Other current liabilities	1,500,000
Fixed assets, net	2,000,000	Long-term debt	1,000,000
	$ 6,000,000	Stockholders' equity	2,500,000
			$6,000,000

INCOME STATEMENT

Net sales	$ 7,500,000
Cost of sales	4,500,000
Selling, general and administrative expenses	1,000,000
Other expenses	1,000,000
Earnings after tax	$ 500,000

Calculate the following:

a.   the inventory conversion period.
b.   the receivables conversion period.
c.   the length of the operating cycle.
d.   the payables deferral period.
e.   the length of the cash conversion cycle.

Solution:

a.
$$\text{Inventory conversion period} = \frac{\text{Average inventory}}{\text{Cost of sales}/365}$$

$$= \frac{2,000,000}{4,500,000/365} = 162.22 \text{ days}$$

b.
$$\text{Receivables conversion period} = \frac{\text{Accounts receivable}}{\text{Annual credit sales}/365}$$

$$= \frac{1,500,000}{7,500,000/365} = 73.00 \text{ days}$$

c.   Operating cycle = Inventory conversion period + Receivables conversion period

$$= 162.22 \text{ days} + 73.00 \text{ days} = 235.22 \text{ days}$$

d.
$$\text{Payables deferral period} = \frac{\text{Accounts payable + salaries, benefits \& payroll taxes payable}}{(\text{Cost of sales + Selling, general and admin. expense})/365}$$

$$= \frac{750,000 + 250,000}{(4,500,000 + 1,000,000)/365} = 66.36 \text{ days}$$

e.   Cash conversion cycle = Operating cycle - payables deferral period

$$= 235.22 \text{ days} - 66.36 \text{ days} = 168.86 \text{ days}$$

2.   The Anadarko Company is considering three levels of working capital. Because of expected lost sales from low levels of working capital, expected sales and EBIT depend on the level of working capital. The company currently has $30 million of fixed assets. The alternative policies and the associated expected operating results are as follows:

Policy	Working Capital	Sales	EBIT
A	$30 million	$48 million	$18 million
B	35 million	50 million	20 million
C	40 million	52 million	22 million

a.   Which alternative is the most aggressive and which is the most conservative?

b.   For each alternative, find EBIT/Total assets.

Solution:

a.   A has the least investment in working capital and is the most aggressive. C is the most conservative.

		A	B	C
b.	Current Assets	$30 million	$35 million	$40 million
	Fixed Assets	30 million	30 million	30 million
	Total Assets	60 million	65 million	70 million
	EBIT	18 million	20 million	22 million
	EBIT/Total Assets	18/60 = .300	20/65 = .308	22/70 = .314

For this case, an examination of the risk and return indicates that because of the relationship between EBIT, sales, and working capital, the most conservative is also the most profitable. Generally, however, higher risk working capital policies tend to be associated with higher returns.

3.   Anadarko Company in Problem 2 currently has $30 million of working capital. Because of the analysis in Problem 1, they wish to increase this to $40 million. Currently their liabilities and capital consist of:

Current liabilities (short-term debt)	$20 million
Long-term debt	$10 million
Common equity	$30 million

They are considering financing the additional working capital in three different ways; interest costs depend on the method of financing chosen. Relevant facts are summarized as:

Policy	Increase STD	Increase LTD	Cost STD	Cost LTD
A	$2 million	$8 million	10.5%	12.5%
B	5 million	5 million	10.0%	12.0%
C	8 million	2 million	9.5%	11.5%

a.   Which policy is the most conservative?

b.   For each policy determine the return on equity and the current ratio. Assume a tax rate of 40%.

Solution:

a.   Policy A is the most conservative.

b.

	A	B	C
Current Assets	$40 million	$40 million	$40 million
Fixed Assets	30 million	30 million	30 million
Total Assets	70 million	70 million	70 million
Current Liabilities	22 million	25 million	28 million
Long-term Debt	18 million	15 million	12 million
Common Equity	30 million	30 million	30 million
EBIT	22 million	22 million	22 million
Interest on STD	2,310,000	2,500,000	2,660,000
Interest on LTD	2,250,000	1,800,000	1,380,000
Taxable Income	17,440,000	17,700,000	17,960,000
Net Income	10,464,000	10,620,000	10,776,000
Return on Equity	34.9%	35.4%	35.9%
Current Ratio	1.82	1.60	1.43

18

Management of Cash and Marketable Securities

Cash and marketable securities are the most liquid of a firm's assets. Cash consists of currency and deposits in checking accounts. Marketable securities consist of short-term investments made with idle cash in order to receive interest. Cash management includes the issues of the optimal size of the firm's balances of liquid assets, control of the collection and disbursement of cash, and the types and amounts of short-term investments the firm makes.

I.   Firms hold liquid asset balances for several main reasons including day-to-day transactions needs, precautions against unexpected cash requirements, balances to meet future requirements, balances held for speculative reasons, and compensating balances required by banks.

   A.   Cash inflows and outflows are seldom synchronized.

      1.   The first step in cash management is development of a cash budget showing the forecasted receipts and disbursement as well as a forecast of any cumulative shortages or surpluses expected during the budget period.

      2.   Many firms prepare a series of cash budgets with the nearest period being budgeted on a daily basis and longer-term budgets being prepared on a weekly or monthly basis.

   B.   Requirements for compensating balances are a common means for banks to receive a portion of their payment for their services.

1. Significant services include the maintenance of disbursement and payroll checking accounts, collection of deposits, lines of credit, term loans, handling of dividend payments, and the registration and transfer of the firm's stock.

2. Less tangible services may include supplying credit information and consulting advice.

3. Compensating balance requirements may be stated in terms of absolute minimum balances or minimum average balances.

4. Firms should occasionally shop around and determine whether the fee schedule and compensating balance requirements offered by their bank are competitive with those offered by other banks.

II. A major concern in cash management is the determination of the optimal size of liquid asset balances. This involves weighing the costs and benefits of liquid assets.

A. Compensating balance requirements establish a lower limit on the liquid assets which must be held.

B. Holding of excess liquid assets results in an opportunity cost resulting from the income that the firm could earn if these funds were invested in other productive assets.

C. Inadequate liquid balances result in "shortage" costs such as missing cash discounts, deterioration of the firm's credit rating, higher interest costs on borrowed funds, and the risk of insolvency.

III. The processes of cash collection and disbursement provide the firm with opportunities to increase the available cash balance without additional total investment.

A. Float is the difference between the checking account balances shown in the firm's books and those of the bank.

1. Positive or disbursement float occurs when the balance on the bank's books exceeds that on the firm's books. This occurs because of the delays caused by mailing disbursement checks and the clearing process.

2. Negative or collection float occurs when the firm shows a higher balance than the bank. This depends on the time it takes for deposited checks to clear.

3.   Management of collections and disbursements consists of attempts to maximize the net balance of positive and negative float through speeding collections and slowing disbursements.

B.   The components of the cash collection process include mail time, processing time, and check clearing time. A number of systems may be used to reduce the time involved in one or more of the components.

1.   A decentralized collection system consists of several strategically located collection centers which receive payments, deposit checks, and report information to the firm's headquarters.

a.   Decentralized collection systems reduce mailing time and check clearing time by being closer to customers.

b.   The decentralized banks regularly forward funds to a small number of larger accounts at concentration banks.

c.   Use of a larger number of collection centers may decrease collection time but involve larger fees and compensating balances because of the larger number of banks involved.

2.   A lock-box system consists of post office boxes maintained by local banks to receive deposits for the firm.

a.   In a lock-box system, the local bank empties the box and deposits payments in the firm's accounts and sends the firm a report of payments received.

b.   Funds in excess of required compensating balances are sent to a concentration bank from which the firm makes disbursements.

c.   Lock-box systems involve significant fees and are usually more beneficial for relatively small numbers of larger deposits than for large numbers of small deposits.

d.   Evaluation of a lock-box collection system involves comparison of the costs of the system versus the benefits of faster collection.

3.   Wire transfers are funds sent electronically from one bank to another through the Federal Reserve System.

a.   Wire transfers are the fastest way of moving funds between banks since no mail or clearing time is involved.

b.   Wire transfers are used extensively in moving funds from local collection centers and lock-box banks to concentration banks.

4. A mail depository transfer check (DTC) is an unsigned, nonnegotiabie check drawn on the local collection bank and payable to the concentration bank. Each day, a DTC in the amount of the deposits at the local collection bank will be mailed to the concentration bank. A DTC is cheaper than a wire transfer. An electronic depository transfer check (EDTC) can also be used to forward funds electronically through the Automated Clearing House (ACH) System.

5. Very large remittances may justify the use of a courier service to pick up checks and present them for collection at the bank on which they are drawn.

6. A preauthorized check (PAC) resembles an ordinary check except that it does not require the signature of the person (or firm) on whose account it is being drawn. PAC's are used by many insurance companies, utilities, savings and loans and others to collect amounts due from their customers.

C. Several means are available by which a firm can slow disbursements. These do not include late payment which can impair the firm's credit rating and cost the firm in lost cash discounts.

1. A zero-balance system involves the use of a master or concentration account together with a number of disbursement accounts.

   a. Transfers are made from the concentration account to the disbursement accounts as checks clear through the disbursement accounts.

   b. The disbursements accounts are called zero- balance accounts because transfers to them are in the exact amount required for the cleared checks so that the balance at the end of the day is always zero.

   c. Use of zero-balance accounts minimizes the balances kept in disbursement accounts.

2. The use of drafts rather than checks permits a firm to keep smaller balances in its disbursement accounts.

   a. A draft is similar to a check but is not payable on demand.

   b. When drafts are used, funds do not have to be deposited until the draft is presented for payment.

   c. Drafts are usually more expensive than checks because of the lower account balances and increased processing costs on the part of the bank.

3.   With accurate estimates of disbursement float, a firm can synchronize deposits in disbursement accounts with expected check clearings.

D.   Electronic funds transfer (EFT) can replace the paper (check) systems.

    1.   Electronic funds transfer eliminate disbursement float and collection float.

    2.   Large payments are commonly made by means of wire transfers or through an automated clearinghouse (ACH).

E.   There are some ethical (and sometimes legal) issues associated with systems that delay payments and accelerate collections. A large (or sophisticated) firm might be able to exploit smaller (or less sophisticated) firms in its cash management policies.

IV.   Investments in marketable securities provide a means for a firm to earn interest on cash in excess of daily requirements as well as liquid assets kept for precautionary reasons or being accumulated for later investment.

A.   In choosing marketable securities, a firm should consider the default risk, marketability, maturity, and rate of return.

    1.   Default risk is lowest on U.S. Treasury securities followed by other Federal agency securities and finally by corporate and municipal securities. Default risk and expected return are usually inversely related.

    2.   Marketability requires that a security be able to be sold quickly and at a price fairly close to the amount paid for it.

    3.   Investment in marketable securities is usually limited to those with fairly short maturities which have less risk of price fluctuation due to changing interest rates.

B.   Purchases of marketable securities are usually confined to money market instruments which are high-grade, short-term debt instruments having original maturities less than 1 year. A number of money market instruments are available.

    1.   U.S. Treasury Bills (T-Bills) are the most popular marketable securities.

        a.   T-Bills are sold at weekly auctions through Federal Reserve banks. T-Bills are issued at a discount and then redeemed for the full face amount at maturity.

        b.   T-Bills have standard maturities of 91 days, 182 days, and 1 year.

     c.   An active secondary market insures the marketability of T-Bills.

     d.   Because of their safety and marketability, Treasury bills usually offer the lowest yield of the available instruments.

2.   Other Treasury issues can be used.

     a.   Notes and bonds become short-term instruments as their maturity approaches.

     b.   Tax Anticipation Bills mature approximately one week after quarterly corporate tax payments are due and can be used to pay income taxes.

3.   Other Federal agency issues which are not a legal obligation of the U.S. Government provide a slightly higher yield and very low risk.

4.   Short-term municipal securities are a suitable investment. Municipal yields are lower than other issues because municipal interest is free of Federal income tax. The yields on municipals will vary with the credit-worthiness of the particular state or local government issuer.

5.   Negotiable certificates of deposit (CDs) are issued by commercial banks.

     a.   Negotiable CDs differ from the smaller non-negotiable CDs usually purchased by individuals.

     b.   CDs offer a higher return than Federal agency issues.

     c.   Negotiable CDs have initial maturities ranging from 30 days to 18 months and are highly marketable.

6.   Commercial paper consists of short-term promissory notes issued by large corporations and finance companies.

     a.   Maturities range from 2 or 3 days to 270 days.

     b.   Commercial paper is not highly marketable.

     c.   Low marketability and high default risk result in higher yields than most other money market instruments.

7.   Repurchase agreements are arrangements in which investors acquire short-term securities subject to a commitment from the selling bank or security dealer to repurchase them on a specified date.

8.   A banker's acceptance is a short-term debt instrument issued by a firm and guaranteed by a commercial bank. They often originate in international trade.

9.   Eurodollar deposits are dollar denominated deposits in banks or bank branches located outside the United States.

10. Money market preferred stock has a dividend that is adjusted regularly so that the price of this security stays close to par. The advantage of money market preferred stock is that its dividends are eligible for the 70 percent intercorporate dividend exemption.

11. Smaller firms which do not have the funds to invest in the relatively large denomination securities may invest in a money market mutual fund that pools the funds of smaller investors to obtain larger denomination investments.

12. Commercial banks also have money market accounts that pay competitive interest rates.

V.   There are some unique elements of cash management for a multinational corporation (MNC).

A.   Three differences in cash management for MNCs are:

1.   It is sometimes difficult and costly to convert cash from one currency to another.

2.   Some less developed countries lack integrated international cash transfer facilities.

3.   There are a greater variety of investment opportunities for excess cash balances.

B.   MNCs usually have a centralized cash management function that tracks the firm's cash balances around the world and identifies the best sources for short-term borrowing and lending.

C.   MNCs use a process called multilateral netting. Cross-border transactions are netted off to minimize costly transactions. Funds that cross a border unnecessarily are called misdirected funds.

TRUE AND FALSE QUESTIONS

Agree with each of the statements or reject it and modify it so that it is acceptable.

1.   Firms hold liquid assets for transaction purposes, precautionary motives, and compensating balances.

2.   Cash budgets are seldom used in managing liquid assets.

Contemporary Financial Management

3. A firm should never hold more cash than that required for compensating balances.

4. Positive float is usually associated with the collection process.

5. A lock-box should be maintained by a bank expecting night deposits.

6. A zero-balance account is likely to result in a notice of insufficient funds from the bank.

7. Long-term government bonds are usually an acceptable investment for idle cash.

8. A strong secondary market exists for commercial paper.

9. Treasury bills are the most popular marketable security.

10. Smaller firms can invest idle cash in money market mutual funds.

Answers to True and False Questions

1. True.

2. Cash budgets are fundamental to the management of cash.

3. Compensating balance requirements establish the minimum cash that a firm can hold.

4. Positive float is associated with the disbursement process and arises from the mailing time, processing time by the recipient, and the check clearing time.

5. A lock-box is a means of speeding up collections.

6. A zero-balance account is used in conjunction with a concentration account to minimize idle balances by depositing funds as checks clear.

7. Long-term bonds involve significant risk of price fluctuations due to interest rate changes. They become acceptable only when close enough to maturity to be effectively short-term instruments.

8. The secondary market for commercial paper is relatively weak.

9. True.

10. True.

CHAPTER 18 PROBLEMS

1. The Immobile Oil Company has found that 9 days pass between the time payment is received from a customer and the funds become collected and available for use by the firm. The firm's annual sales are $547.5 million.

    a. If Immobile could reduce the 9-day interval to 7 days, what would be the increase in the firm's average cash balance?

    b. Suppose that the additional cash were used to reduce outstanding debt which has a cost of 7%. Determine the annual pre-tax savings in interest.

    Solution:

    a. Assuming that receipts are spread evenly over a 365-day year, receipts amount to $1.5 million per day. A reduction of 2 days in the amount outstanding would increase the cash balance by 2 x $1.5 million = $3 million.

    b. If the $3 million is used to reduce outstanding debt costing 7%, pre-tax earnings would increase by 7% x $3 million = $210,000.

2. The Boomer Construction Company in Soonerville, Oklahoma receives large progress payments on contracts. These checks are deposited in the local bank and the funds become available 5 days later. Boomer is considering the value of receiving the use of the funds sooner by sending a messenger to the Dallas bank on which they are usually drawn. A trip to Dallas by courier costs $120. If Boomer can earn 9% on the funds in the money market, what size check will justify the use of a courier?

    Solution:

    If Boomer uses a courier, they will earn 5 days of interest at an annual rate of 9%. They wish to find the size of the payment for which $(5/365)(.09)(\text{payment}) = 120$. Solving we find the minimum payment size is $97,333.

3. Passport Card, a major bank credit card, processes all its payments through its main office in San Francisco. They are considering establishing a lock-box collection system through a bank in Keokuk, Iowa. Under this arrangement, average mailing time for customers east of the Mississippi will be reduced from 17 days to 15 days. Check processing and clearing time would be reduced by 2 days. Annual collections from the East average $325 million from a total of 5 million payments. The Keokuk bank will process the payments for an annual fee of $95,000 plus $.06 per payment. The San Francisco processing center will save $60,000 per year. If Passport can invest the funds for 12%, should they undertake the lock-box arrangement?

Solution:

Using a 365-day year, average daily collections amount to 325,000,000/365 = $890,411 per day. A saving of 4 days in the collection process would make available 4 x 890,411 = $3,561,644. Invested at 12%, these funds would earn .12 x 3,561,644 = $427,397 per year. The net value would be:

Annual earnings earned on released funds	$427,397
Annual savings at San Francisco office	60,000
- Cost of lock box arrangement	
(95,000 + .06 x 5,000,000)	-395,000
Net increase in pre-tax earnings	$ 92,397

The lock-box arrangement would result in an increase of $92,397 in pre-tax earnings and should be undertaken.

4.   The True-Balance Scale Company is considering establishing a zero-balance system for its payroll account. Total payroll amounts to $1.44 million per month paid on the last Friday of the month. The firm currently deposits the entire amount on Friday, but most checks do not clear until the following week. True-Balance can earn 8% on funds which are released from the payroll account. The typical distribution of check clearings is as follows:

Day	Amount Clearing
Friday	$ 300,000
Monday	444,000
Tuesday	350,000
Wednesday	200,000
Thursday	146,000
Total	$1,440,000

Determine the monthly pre-tax returns the firm would realize from use of the zero-balance system.

Solution:

To determine the annual pre-tax returns, we examine the daily balance under the present system and the lost interest on that balance. Saturday and Sunday must be included. Interest at 8% amounts to .08/365 = .000219 per day.

To be explicit, we assume that the funds needed for Monday clearings would earn interest for Friday through Sunday; Tuesday's deposit will earn interest for Friday through Monday; and so on.

Day	Clearings	No. of Days	Interest Earned
Friday	$300,000	0	0
Monday	444,000	3	291.71
Tuesday	350,000	4	306.60
Wednesday	200,000	5	219.00
Thursday	146,000	6	191.84

Total pre-tax earnings: $ 1,009.15

19

Management of Accounts Receivable and Inventories

Accounts receivable consist of the credit a firm grants its customers in the course of making sales. Accounts receivable can take the form of either trade credit granted to other firms or consumer credit granted to final consumers. Inventories serve to uncouple the various segments of the procurement, production, and sales cycle of the firm by acting as buffers between the elements. The inventory operation is similar for manufacturing firms and for those engaged in wholesale and retail trade, although the relationships are more complex for a manufacturing firm.

I.   Extension of credit is essentially an investment decision. An optimal credit extension policy requires that the firm extend credit whenever the marginal returns from extending credit exceed the marginal costs.

    A.   A more liberal credit policy, other things equal, should provide returns in the form of increased sales leading ultimately to increased gross profits.

    B.   Costs associated with granting credit include the cost of the funds employed, costs of credit checking, and possibly an increase in bad debt expense.

II.   A credit policy includes as major variables: credit standards, credit terms, and the collection effort.

    A.   Credit standards are the criteria the firm uses to screen credit applications to determine whether and in what amount credit should be extended. This allows the firm to control the quality of accounts which are accepted. Quality has two important facets.

1.   One facet is the time a customer takes to repay given that the credit is repaid.

2.   The probability that the customer will fail to repay which is known as the default risk.

3.   Overall measures of the quality of accounts accepted are the average collection period and the bad-debt ratio.

B.   Credit terms specify the conditions under which credit extended must be repaid.

1.   The credit period is the time allowed for payment.

2.   Cash discounts are discounts allowed if payment is made within a specified period of time. Cash discounts are usually specified as a percentage of the invoiced amount and are granted to speed up collection of accounts receivable.

3.   Seasonal datings are special terms sometimes offered to retailers on seasonal merchandise. The retailer is encouraged to order and accept delivery of merchandise well ahead of the peak season and to pay shortly after the peak sales. This assists retailers in financing inventory and allows producers to smooth their production and distribution over a longer period of time.

C.   The collection effort consists of the methods employed to attempt to collect payment on past due accounts.

1.   The collection effort must be a balance between excessive leniency and the risk of alienating customers.

2.   An important part of managing accounts receivable is monitoring their status.

a.   Aging of accounts is a useful means of monitoring them.

b.   An aging analysis consists of classifying accounts into categories according to the number of days they are past due.

c.   Changes in the age composition of accounts may reveal changes in the quality of the firm's accounts receivable.

D.   Analysis of a change in credit policy is based on the potential changes in profit resulting from a change in policy.

1.   An increase in the credit period may increase the quantity of goods sold. This would have the following effects on pre-tax profits:

a.   An increase in pre-tax profits equal to the profit contribution per dollar of sales times the anticipated increase in sales.

b.   A cost increase resulting from additional investment in receivables (and inventories in some cases).

c.   A cost increase resulting from additional bad debts.

2.   Liberalization of cash discount policies may result in the following effects:

a.   An increase in sales.

b.   A reduction in the receivables balance resulting in either additional income from alternative investments or a decrease in the cost of funds invested in receivables.

c.   A reduction in cash revenues resulting from the discount itself.

3.   Increases in collection effort and methods might result in:

a.   Reduced sales.

b.   Increased collection expenses.

c.   Reduced bad-debt losses.

III.   The evaluation of credit applicants is based on the firm's credit and collection policies. Several main steps are common to most credit evaluation processes:

A.   Information on the credit worthiness of an applicant is gathered from sources such as financial statements submitted by the applicant, credit reporting organizations, banks, and the firm's prior experience with the customer.

B.   In analyzing the credit worthiness of customers, the cost of analysis should be considered.

C.   The "five C's" of credit provide a useful framework for organizing information about an applicant.

1.   Character concerns the applicant's willingness to meet credit obligations.

2.   Capacity refers to the applicant's ability to meet obligations based on his liquidity and projected cash flows.

3.   Capital refers to the applicant's overall financial strength based on net worth.

4. <u>Collateral</u> refers to assets that may be pledged as security. In trade credit decisions, collateral is seldom a major consideration since foreclosing on the pledged assets is often an expensive and time-consuming process which does not adequately substitute for prompt receipt of cash.

5. <u>Conditions</u> refer to the general economic climate and outlook which may affect the customer's willingness and ability to pay.

D. Numerical scoring systems are sometimes useful, particularly in consumer credit.

IV. Manufacturing firms usually hold three types of inventories consisting of raw materials, work-in-process and finished goods.

A. The raw materials inventory consists of stores of items used in production.

1. Raw materials inventories allow firms to take quantity discounts.

2. Raw materials inventories assure supply in times of scarcity.

B. Work-in-process inventories consist of items currently at some intermediate state of completion.

1. Work-in-process occurs naturally as materials are put into production.

2. Work-in-process allows for asynchronous schedules among departments.

3. The size of the work-in-process inventory usually increases with the length and complexity of the firm's production cycle.

C. Finished goods inventories consist of items ready and available for sale.

1. The finished goods inventory permits prompt filling of orders.

2. The finished goods inventory allows production runs which are large enough to attain economies of scale by minimizing fixed set-up costs.

V. Three distinct types of costs are usually associated with an inventory policy.

A. Ordering costs represent the costs of placing and receiving an order of goods.

1. For external purchases, ordering costs include the cost of preparing the purchase order, expediting, receiving the goods, and handling payment.

2.   For internally produced goods, the order costs consist mainly of the production set-up costs.

3.   While some order costs may vary with the size of the order, most simple inventory control models assume them to be fixed.

B.   Carrying costs consist of the costs of holding items in inventory for a given period of time.

1.   Carrying costs include storage and handling costs, obsolescence and deterioration costs, insurance, taxes, and the cost of funds invested in inventory.

2.   Carrying costs are usually expressed in terms of a cost per unit per period or as a percentage of the inventory value per period.

C.   Stockout costs are incurred when a firm is unable to fill an order because the item is not available in inventory. Stockout costs may involve lost sales, costs of rescheduling production, and the costs of placing and expediting special orders.

VI.   Inventory models are available which can assist in determining the optimal inventory level of each item. These models can vary considerably in their complexity.

A.   The ABC inventory classification system is helpful in guiding the extent of control that should be applied to different inventory items.

1.   Group A items include the items which have the largest dollar value. The C items are the items with the smallest dollar value. The B items are in between.

2.   The A items might include 10% - 20% of the total number of items and account for 80% - 90% of the total dollar value of inventory. The C items may contain 50% of the number of items and account for less than 10% of the dollar value of inventory. Group B includes the remaining items.

3.   Group A items would be subjected to very careful monitoring and management while the C items will be managed much less intensely.

B.   A major determinant of the complexity of an inventory model is the nature of the assumption regarding demand for the item.

1.   Deterministic models assume that demand is constant over time.

2.   Probabilistic models assume that demand fluctuates randomly.

C.   The simplest model is the deterministic economic order quantity model.

1. In its simplest form, the EOQ model assumes known demand which occurs uniformly over the year and no lags from order to receipt of the goods.

2. In the simplest EOQ model, the annual inventory cost is given by the formula

$$TC = \frac{D}{Q}(S) + \frac{Q}{2}(C)$$

where
Q = quantity ordered;
S = fixed order cost;
D = annual demand for the item; and
C = the cost of carrying 1 unit for 1 year.

The economic order quantity Q^* is

$$Q^* = \sqrt{\frac{2SD}{C}}$$

where Q^* = order quantity that minimizes total inventory cost.

3. The time between orders T is given by

$$T = \frac{Q}{D/365} = \frac{365 \times Q}{D}$$

D. The EOQ can be made more complex by relaxing some of the simplifying assumptions.

1. If the lead time between ordering and receiving items is constant but not zero, the order quantity is not affected but the order is placed before the inventory reaches zero. The order should be placed when the remaining inventory is just enough to last through the lead time.

$$Q_r = n(D/365)$$

where:
Q_r = reorder point;
n = lead time (in days), and
D/365 = daily demand.

2. The existence of quantity discounts affects the EOQ model. If a quantity discount is available, the total cost for the quantity indicated by the EOQ is compared with the total inventory cost for the discount quantity less the discount savings. Total inventory cost is given by

$$TC = \frac{D}{Q}(S) + \frac{Q}{2}(C)$$

If TC^* is the total inventory cost using the EOQ and TC' is the cost using the order quantity required for receiving a discount, the increase in inventory costs

$$\Delta TC = TC' - TC^*$$

is compared to the savings from discounts received.

Discount savings are given by

(Discount per unit)(Annual demand in units)

If the discount savings are greater than the increase in inventory costs (DTC), then it is profitable to take the discount.

3.   When demand is not constant due to uncertain total demand, a safety stock may be maintained. There is a tradeoff between carrying costs and stockout costs. For example, a business can reduce its stockout costs by maintaining a larger safety stock, but a larger safety stock increases its carrying costs.

4.   Just-in-time inventory models have been popularized by the Japanese. This system tries to eliminate the safety stocks many American firms use. The idea is that the required inventory items are supplied to production at exactly the right time and in exactly the right quantities. Just-in-time requires very close cooperation between the company buying the inventory and the supplier selling it. This system is best applied to well-planned manufacturing operations.

TRUE AND FALSE QUESTIONS

Agree with each of the statements or reject it and modify it so that it is acceptable.

1.   Methods used for analyzing the credit-granting decision are highly unique.

2.   A firm should attempt through its credit policy to minimize its bad debt expense.

3.   Default risk refers to the probability that a customer will fail to pay.

4.   Credit terms of 2/10, net 30 means that the customer must pay 2% of the invoice within 10 days and the balance in 30 days.

5.   The average collection period and bad-debt loss ratios are overall measures of the quality of accounts accepted.

6.   The average collection period can be found as (365)(AR)/Credit Sales.

7. Credit should never be granted until all available sources of information regarding the applicant have been utilized.

8. Collateral is seldom of major importance in trade credit.

9. Liberalization of credit terms may result in an increase in the investment in inventory.

10. Conditions as used in the five C's of credit refers to the terms of credit.

11. Inventories act as buffers between the segments of the firm's procurement, production, and sales cycles.

12. The size of the work-in-process inventory can be totally controlled by management.

13. Carrying costs represent transportation-in on goods purchased.

14. All firms should determine optimal order quantities according to the formula:

$$Q = \sqrt{\frac{2SD}{C}}$$

15. When lead time is not zero, the optimal order size must be modified.

16. Uncertainty regarding demand or lead time can be accounted for by use of a safety stock.

17. Probabilistic inventory control models allow demand to be a random variable.

18. The cost of financing inventory is a component of ordering costs.

19. The EOQ model can be used only for externally purchased goods which have an order cost.

20. The objective of the EOQ model is to minimize the total of order and carrying costs.

21. In the EOQ model, an increase in the carrying cost per unit of inventory would decrease the EOQ.

22. An increase in the lead time would raise the reorder point.

23. In the ABC classification system, the A items account for the preponderance of the dollar value of inventory.

24. Just-in-time inventory systems rely on large safety stocks.

25. The offering of quantity discounts can make it attractive to increase the order

size if the discounts received exceed the increase in the total of carrying and ordering costs.

Answers to True and False Questions

1.   Credit granting decisions are essentially investment decisions.

2.   Minimizing bad debts may result in credit policies which are overly stringent and result in lost sales. Credit policies should be based on profitability.

3.   True.

4.   Credit terms of 2/10, net 30 mean that the customer may take a discount of 2% of the invoice amount if he pays within 10 days. The net amount of the invoice is due in 30 days.

5.   True.

6.   True.

7.   Credit policies must consider the cost of collecting and evaluating information. Decisions should be based on the least cost analysis which will produce a satisfactory decision.

8.   True.

9.   True.

10. Conditions refers to the general economic climate and outlook which may affect the customer's willingness and ability to pay.

11. True.

12. The size of the work-in-process inventory depends in part on the length and complexity of the production cycle.

13. Carrying costs represent the costs of holding inventory for a period of time.

14. Use of this formula is appropriate only if the assumptions of known uniform demand, fixed order costs, and constant per unit carrying costs are approximately met. Otherwise, the model must be appropriately modified.

15. The economic order quantity is not affected by non-zero lead time. The timing of placing the order is changed.

16. True. (More sophisticated methods may be required for determining the appropriate safety stock, however.)

17. True.

18. The cost of financing inventory is a component of carrying costs.

19. The EOQ model can be used also for internally produced goods. The order cost consists of production set-up costs.

20. True.

21. True.

22. True.

23. True.

24. Just-in-time systems attempt to achieve very small or even zero safety stocks.

25. True.

CHAPTER 19 PROBLEMS

1. National Iron Monger, Inc. wholesales hardware. Annual credit sales are $25 million spread evenly throughout the year. Their accounts receivable balance is $2.5 million. Terms of credit are net 30. Determine:

   a. Average daily credit sales

   b. Average collection period

   Solution:

   a. Assuming 365 days per year, average daily credit sales are:

   $$25,000,000/365 = \$68,493.15$$

   b. Average collection period = accounts receivable/daily credit sales

   $$= 2,500,000/68,493.15 = 36.5 \text{ days}$$

2. Connie Sewer Wines wishes to speed up collection of its receivables. Connie Sewer currently offers credit terms of 1/15, net 30. It is considering changing to terms of 2/10, net 30. The collection period is expected to be reduced from 40 to 25 days. The percentage of customers paying within the discount period is expected to increase from 60% to 80%. Bad debt losses average 5% of sales and are not expected to change under the proposed policy. Annual billings are $5 million. The variable cost ratio is 60%. The pre-tax return on funds made available by this change in policy is 20%. Assuming that the change in terms is made, determine the following:

a.   The amount of funds released by the decrease in receivables

b.   The earnings on the funds released

c.   The cost of the additional cash discounts taken

d.   The net effect on Connie Sewer's pre-tax profits.

Solution:

(handwritten annotations: "collection period", "annual billings", "copy", "pretax return")

a.   AR (Current) = 40 days x $5,000,000/365 = $547,945

AR (Proposed) = 25 days x $5,000,000/365 = $342,466

Funds released = Current AR - Proposed AR = $205,479

b.   Earnings on released funds = 205,479 x .20 = $41,096

c.   Proposed discounts = $5,000,000 x .80 x .02 = $80,000

Current discounts = $5,000,000 x .60 x .01 = $30,000

Increased cost of discounts = $80,000 - $30,000 = $50,000

d.   Earnings on released funds $41,096
     -Increased cost of discounts   -50,000
     Net pre-tax profit effect   ($ 8,904)

3.   The Loose Goose Egg Company is considering liberalizing its credit standards in order to increase sales. Under the proposed policy, credit will be liberally granted to more buyers. It is anticipated that annual sales of $5.2 million will increase by 25%. Bad debt losses will increase from 4% of sales to 5% of sales and the collection period will increase from 75 days to 110 days. Loose Goose's (or is it Loose Geese) profit contribution is 40% of sales and its required pre-tax return on receivables is 15%. Determine the net effect of this plan on the company's pre-tax profits.

Solution:

Additional sales   = (percent increase)(present sales)
                    = (.25)(5,200,000) = $1,300,000

Profit on additional sales
          =   (contribution)(additional sales)
          =   (.40)(1,300,000) = $520,000   (A)

(handwritten: "A)" and "copy")

Additional average receivables balance
     = New balance - old balance

New receivables balance
= (average daily sales)(collection period)
= (6,500,000/365)(110) = $1,958,904

Old receivables balance
= (5,200,000/365)(75) = $1,068,493

Additional average receivables balance = $890,411

Cost of additional receivables investment
= (additional investment)(required return)
= (890,411)(.15) = $133,562   (B)

Additional bad debt loss
= (new sales)(new ratio) - (old sales)(old ratio)
= (6,500,000)(.05) - (5,200,000)(.04) = 117,000   (C)

Net change in pre-tax profits
= A - (B + C) = $269,438

4. Leisure-Time Retirement World has asked you to perform an aging of their accounts receivable. It is now January 1. The aging is to be in categories of current, 1-30 days past due, 30-90 days past due, and more than 90 days past due. All bills are due net 30. You may assume that all months have 30 days. The accounts are as follows:

Account No.	Invoice Date	Amount Due
1131	Dec. 15	$1,225
3771	Nov. 14	765
7121	Nov. 25	522
9131	Dec. 14	1,204
4181	Aug. 10	469
3171	Dec. 5	1,707
3441	Sep. 8	295
4411	Oct. 28	417
6996	Sep. 5	983
1558	Jul. 5	1,945

Solution:

All accounts billed during December are current.

All accounts billed during November are 1-30 days past due.

All accounts billed during September and October are 30 to 90 days past due.

All accounts billed prior to September are more than 90 days past due.

From the above, we obtain the following schedule:

Current	$4,136
1 - 30 days past due	1,287
30 - 90 days past due	1,695
Over 90 days past due	2,414

5.   The Willard Company provides pest control services. They use 3,000 barrels of pesticide per year. It requires $2.59 worth of pesticide for the average household application. It costs $10 to place an order and $6 per barrel annual carrying cost. Determine the following:

a.   The economic order quantity
b.   The frequency of placing orders
c.   The total annual cost of ordering and holding inventory.

Solution:

a. $$EOQ = \sqrt{\frac{(2)(\text{order cost})(\text{annual demand})}{\text{annual carrying cost per unit}}} = \sqrt{\frac{2SD}{C}}$$ copy

$$\sqrt{\frac{(2)(3,000)(10)}{6}} = \sqrt{10,000} = 100$$

b.   Ordering in quantities of 100 barrels means placing 3,000/100 = 30 orders per year or an order about every 12 days.

c.   The total cost of the inventory policy is the cost of ordering plus carrying costs on the average level of inventory.

$$TC = \frac{D}{Q}(S) + \frac{Q}{2}(C)$$ place order   annual carrying cost   copy

$$\text{Total Cost} = \frac{3,000}{100} \times \$10 + \frac{100}{2} \times \$6 = \$600$$

6.   Suppose Willard faces a lead time of 6 days between placing an order and receiving it. What is the reorder point? What are the EOQ and annual inventory costs?

Solution:

The reorder point is

$$Q_r = n(D/365) = 6(3,000/365) = 49.3, \text{ or roughly 50 barrels}$$ copy

Introduction of a lead time does not affect the EOQ or the annual inventory costs. All that changes is the time the order is placed. The order will be placed

6 days sooner, but the inventory level will be zero when the shipment arrives so that the average level of inventory is not changed.

7. Suppose that Willard wishes to keep a safety stock of 20 barrels of pesticide. What are the EOQ and annual costs?

Solution:

Maintaining a safety stock does not affect the EOQ. The total cost is changed because the average inventory is increased by the amount of the safety stock.

Average inventory = EOQ/2 + safety stock = 100/2 + 20 = 70

Total cost = ordering costs + carrying costs
= 30 x $10 + $6 x 70 = $720

8. Georgia Business Services uses 10,000 boxes of computer paper per year at a uniform rate. The fixed cost per order is $100 and the carrying cost is $2 per box per year.

a. What is the economic order quantity and the resulting annual cost?

b. Georgia's supplier offers a $.15 per box discount if the order size is at least 2000 boxes. Should Georgia go for the discount?

Solution:

a.
$$Q^* = \sqrt{\frac{2SD}{C}} = \sqrt{\frac{2(100)(10,000)}{2}} = 1,000 \text{ boxes}$$

$$TC = \frac{D}{Q}(S) + \frac{Q}{2}(C)$$

$$TC = \frac{10,000}{1,000}(100) + \frac{1,000}{2}(2)$$

$$TC = 1,000 + 1,000 = \$2,000 \text{ per year}$$

b. If Georgia takes the discount, the annual cost increases to

$$TC = \frac{10,000}{2,000}(100) + \frac{2,000}{2}(2)$$

$$TC = 500 + 2,000 = \$2,500$$

This is a $500 increase over the cost using the EOQ.

The annual savings from the discount on the 10,000 boxes would be

Savings = .15(10,000) = $1,500.

The savings from the discount exceed the increased total inventory (carrying and ordering) costs, so the discount should be taken.

1000

20

Obtaining Short-Term Funds

Firms usually seek a balance of short-term and long-term sources of funds. Short-term credit includes all debt obligations that were originally scheduled for repayment within 1 year. Short-term debt may be either secured or unsecured and can be obtained from a variety of sources. Some of these sources are spontaneous such as trade credit and accruals while others such as bank credit, commercial paper and loans obtained against receivables or inventories are negotiated.

I.   Short-term credit can come from several sources, all of which have cost.

    A.   The annual financing cost, AFC, annualizes the cost of short-term borrowing

$$AFC = \frac{Interest + Fees}{Usable\ Funds} \times \frac{365}{Number\ of\ days}$$

    This is a single interest rate.

    B.   The true annual percentage rate, APR, that does consider compounding is

$$APR = \left[1 + \frac{Interest + fees}{Usable\ funds}\right]^m - 1$$

    where m is the number of times per year the loan is compounded (m = 365/number of days).

II.   The most important source of short-term financing for business firms is trade credit.

   A.   Trade credit arises whenever a firm receives merchandise from a supplier and is permitted to wait a specified period of time before paying for it.

      1.   Most trade credit is extended on open account. Open account trade credit is recognized on the books of the firm as accounts payable. No formal debt instrument is created.

      2.   An alternative to open account credit involves issuance of a promissory note carried on the books under notes payable. ·

      3.   Trade credit is considered a spontaneous source of financing since it tends to expand naturally as the firm's business expands.

   B.   Trade credit is never free although it frequently appears so because no explicit interest payment is specified.

      1.   The cost of trade credit is contained in the purchase price of goods purchased.

      2.   When a cash discount is offered, an identifiable expense of trade credit arises in the form of lost discounts if payment is not made within the discount period.

      3.   If a firm foregoes taking the cash discount but pays on the last day of the credit period, the annual financing cost of missing the discount is given by:

$$AFC = \frac{\% \, Discount}{100 - \% \, Discount} \times \frac{365}{Credit \, Period - Discount \, Period}$$

      4.   The cost of lost cash discounts can be reduced by late payment. This is called stretching accounts payable. Intangible costs in terms of lowered credit rating and ability to obtain future credit may result. Tangible costs of late charges or specific interest may offset the savings.

III.   Accruals and deferred income are additional sources of spontaneous financing.

   A.   Accruals of wages, taxes, and interest increase the firm's short-term liabilities and hence provide short-term financing. Use of these is determined by legal and practical considerations regarding the timing of payment, however.

   B.   Deferred income consists of payments received for goods and services to be delivered at a future date. Until these advance payments are earned by the firm through fulfillment of its obligation, they represent a liability on the balance sheet.

IV.   Loans from commercial banks are an important source of negotiated short-term financing.

    A.   Bank loans may be secured or unsecured. Bank loans usually appear as notes payable on the balance sheet.

    B.   Bank credit is commonly available under three different arrangements: single loans, lines of credit, and revolving credit agreements.

        1.   Single loans are usually arranged for specific financing needs.

            a.   The interest rate charged on a single loan is usually related to the prime rate.

            b.   The effective annual percentage cost of a bank loan depends on the payment schedule and whether a compensating balance is required.

            c.   If the interest is payable at maturity, the effective cost is equal to the stated interest rate.

            d.   If the loan is discounted, the bank deducts the amount of interest from the loan proceeds. This increases the actual interest rate above the stated rate.

        2.   A line of credit is an agreement which permits the firm to borrow up to a predetermined limit at any time during the life of the agreement.

            a.   A line of credit is usually negotiated for a 1-year period.

            b.   The interest rate on a line of credit is usually stated in terms of the prime rate and varies as the prime rate changes during the year.

            c.   A line of credit may contain restrictive covenants on working capital, allowable debt, and so on.

            d.   A line of credit frequently requires that the firm have no loans outstanding under the agreement for a portion of the year.

            e.   A line of credit does not guarantee that the bank will lend the firm the requested funds. The bank is not legally obligated to make loans if the firm's financial position has deteriorated or the bank lacks sufficient loanable funds to honor all commitments.

3.   A revolving credit agreement legally commits the bank to making loans up to the credit limit specified in the agreement.

    a.   Revolving credit agreements are usually secured.

    b.   Revolving credit agreements usually require the firm to pay a commitment fee on the unused portion of the funds.

    c.   The effective annual interest cost on a revolving credit agreement contains both actual interest costs and the commitment fee.

V.   Commercial paper consists of short-term unsecured promissory notes issued by large well-known corporations.

    A.   Maturities of commercial paper range from a few days to a maximum of 9 months. Maturity longer than 9 months would require SEC registration.

    B.   Commercial paper is sold on a discount basis so that the firm receives less than the stated amount and repays the full amount. The annual financing cost is computed as follows:

$$AFC = \frac{\text{Interest costs + Placement fee}}{\text{Funds received}} \quad x \quad \frac{365}{\text{Maturity (days)}} \quad x \quad 100$$

    C.   Purchasers of commercial paper include corporations with idle cash, banks, insurance companies, pension funds, money market funds, and other financial institutions.

    D.   If a firm's financial position deteriorates, it may be difficult or impossible to sell commercial paper.

VI.   Accounts receivable are one of the most common forms of collateral for secured short-term borrowing.

    A.   Accounts receivable are fairly liquid and are easier to handle than physical assets in the event of default.

    B.   Accounts receivable financing is subject to fraud if the borrower pledges nonexistent accounts. Administrative costs to the lender may be high.

    C.   Accounts receivable financing takes two common forms--pledging and factoring.

        1.   When accounts receivable are pledged, the firm retains title to them and continues to carry them on its balance sheet.

        a.   The firm sends copies of invoices to the lender who determines the amount he will advance depending on the credit-worthiness of the receivable. The borrower signs a note for the amount advanced.

        b.   If the loan is on a non-notification basis, the borrower receives payment on the invoices and then pays the lender.

        c.   If the loan is on a notification basis, the customer is notified to send payment directly to the lender.

        d.   The annual percentage cost of a loan involving pledged receivables consists of both the interest expense on the loan and the service fees charged for processing the receivables.

   2.   Factoring receivables involves the outright sale of the receivables to a financial institution known as a factor.

        a.   When receivables are factored, title passes to the factor and they no longer appear on the balance sheet of the firm.

        b.   Most factoring is on a non-recourse basis; as a result, the factor assumes the risk of default.

        c.   The firm may receive proceeds from the receivables from the factor as they are received (which is called maturity factoring) or may obtain an advance which constitutes a loan against the future collections (which is called advance factoring).

        d.   Costs of factoring include the fees and charges for the services as well as explicit interest on advances.

        e.   The cost of factoring may be offset by a reduction in the firm's own costs of collection, credit administration, etc.

VII.   Inventories constitute another common source of collateral for secured loans.

   A.   The suitability of inventory for collateral depends on the nature of the inventory. Particularly important characteristics include perishability, identifiability, marketability, and price stability.

   B.   Inventory loans are available from commercial banks and finance companies.

   C.   A number of arrangements are available with regard to possession of the collateral by the borrower or by a third party.

     1.   A floating lien is a general claim on all the firm's inventory.

        a.   Floating liens offer the lender little security.

b.   The loan amount as a percentage of inventory value is usually small.

c.   Floating liens are used for large-volume, small-value, high-turnover inventory held by turnover.

2.   A trust receipt is another form of inventory loan with the inventory held by the borrower.

a.   As the inventory is sold, the proceeds are forwarded to the lender along with notification of the goods sold.

b.   Trust receipts require specifically identifiable units of inventory.

c.   Trust receipt arrangements are common for items such as automobiles and appliances. These arrangements are also known as floor planning.

3.   Terminal warehouse plans require that the inventory be held in a bonded warehouse operated by a public warehouse company.

a.   The warehouse issues a receipt for the merchandise which then becomes the collateral for the lender.

b.   As the loan is paid off, the lender authorizes the warehouse to release the inventory.

c.   In addition to specific interest on the amount advanced, warehouse fees must be paid. These may be offset by reductions in the firm's own handling and storage costs.

4.   Under field warehouse agreements, the goods are kept in a segregated portion of the firm's premises under the control of a warehouse company. Other portions of the operation are similar to those under terminal warehousing.

TRUE AND FALSE QUESTIONS

Agree with each of the statements or reject it and modify it so that it is acceptable.

1.   Long-term debt with less than 1 year to maturity is a source of short-term financing.

2.   The cost of lost cash discounts is reduced the longer the firm does not pay.

3.   Accruals are an easily managed source for short-term financing.

4.   A line of credit obligates a bank to make the funds available upon request.

5.   A revolving credit agreement obligates the bank to make the funds available upon request in accordance with the agreement.

6.   Commercial paper has a relatively high risk of inability to renew the loan if money becomes tight or the firm's financial position deteriorates.

7.   Factoring of accounts receivable always involves an interest charge as well as service fees.

8.   A floating lien is a means of financing goods at sea.

9.   Trust receipt inventory financing is also known as floor planning.

10.   The formula for the cost of short-term credit can be summarized as: Total fees and interest paid/Amount available for use.

Answers to True and False Questions

1.   Only debt with an initial maturity of less than 1 year is considered short-term financing although longer-term debt which will mature in less than a year is a current liability.

2.   True. (The apparent reduction may be offset by intangible costs in the form of a lowered credit rating, however.)

3.   Accruals are not generally susceptible to discretionary increase and hence are not easily managed.

4.   A line of credit does not obligate a bank to make the funds available.

5.   True.

6.   True.

7.   Factoring does not involve an interest charge unless an advance is drawn against the factored receivables.

8.   A floating lien is a general lien on all the inventory of the borrowing firm.

9.   True.

10.   False. The number of days credit is extended is relevant.

$$AFC = \frac{Interest + fees}{Usable\ funds} \times \frac{365}{Number\ of\ days}$$

CHAPTER 20 PROBLEMS

1. The Paysome-Day Co. purchases $5,000 per day in raw materials and pays on the 30th day.

    a.   What is their current level of accounts payable?

    b.   If payment is stretched to the 40th day, what would the level of trade credit be?

    Solution:

    a.   Their accounts receivable would contain 30 days worth of purchases at $5,000 per day for a total of $150,000.

    b.   If payment is delayed until the 40th day, the level of trade credit would be 40 x $5,000 = $200,000.

2. If credit terms are 3/15, net 60, what is the cost of foregoing cash discounts on an annual percentage basis?

    60 − 15 = 45

    Solution:

    100 − 3
    = 97

    The annual financing cost of foregoing cash discounts is given by:

    $$AFC = \left(\frac{\% \text{ Discount}}{100 - \% \text{ Discount}}\right) \left(\frac{365}{\text{Credit pd} - \text{discount pd}}\right) = \frac{(3)(365)}{97 \quad 45} = 25.9\%$$

    The true annual percentage rate (that accounts for compound interest) is:

    $$APR = \left[1 + \frac{\% \text{ discount}}{100 - \% \text{ discount}}\right]^{m} - 1$$

    $$APR = \left[1 + \frac{3}{97}\right]^{365/45} - 1 = (1.0309)^{8.111} - 1 = 28.0\%$$

3. Determine the annual financing cost of a discounted loan for 1 year at an interest rate of 10% requiring a 15% compensating balance. Assume the loan is for $100,000.

    Solution:

    The annual interest is 10% of $100,000 = $10,000.

    The compensating balance is 15% of $100,000 = $15,000.
    The available proceeds of the loan are given by:

Proceeds = loan amount - discount interest - compensating balance

$$= \$100,000 - \$10,000 - \$15,000 = \$75,000$$

The annual financing cost is given by annual interest/proceeds, so

$$AFC = (\$10,000/\$75,000)(365/365) = 13.3\%$$

(Note that if the firm already has deposits which it intends to keep in the bank and which will serve for some or all of the compensating balance, the proceeds would be greater and the cost reduced.)

4.   Your firm has a revolving credit agreement with the bank under which it can borrow up to $1 million for one year. Interest on the borrowed amount is at 10% per year. You must maintain a 15% compensating balance on outstanding loans and pay a commitment fee of 1% on the unused portion of the credit line. Find the annual percentage cost if each of the following amount is borrowed.

    a. $ 250,000
    b. $ 500,000
    c. $1,000,000

Solution:

The cost is given by interest plus fees divided by the proceeds of the loan.

    a.   Interest = 10% of $250,000 = $25,000

           Fee = 1% of ($1,000,000 - $250,000) = $7,500

           Proceeds = $250,000 - 15% of $250,000 = $212,500

           Annual financing cost = ($25,000 + $7,500)/$212,500 = 15.3%

    b. $\dfrac{(.10)(\$500,000) + (.01)(\$500,000)}{\$500,000 - (.15)(\$500,000)} = 12.9\%$

    c. $\dfrac{(.10)(\$1,000,000)}{\$1,000,000 - (.15)(\$1,000,000)} = 11.8\%$

5.   The Polynomial Company is considering factoring its receivables. Average annual credit sales are $3.6 million with a one month collection period. The factor charges a fee of 2.5% on all receivables purchased and requires a 10% reserve for returns and allowances. Interest on funds advanced is at 10%. If the firm factors its receivables, it will eliminate credit department costs of $500 per month and bad-debt losses of 2% of sales. Interest is discounted.

    a.   Determine the amount of funds that Polynomial can receive by factoring.

b.   Determine the annual cost in dollars of factoring the receivables and borrowing the maximum amount available.

c.   Determine the effective annual percentage cost of obtaining funds in this manner.

Solution:

a.

Annual credit sales	$3.6 million	
Receivables turnover	12 times	
Average level of receivables	3,600,000/12	$300,000
Less: Factoring commission	2.5% of 300,000	- 7,500
Less: Reserve for returns	10% of 300,000	- 30,000
Advance available before interest		$262,500
Less: Interest	262,500(.1)/12	- 2,188
Usable funds		$260,312

b.

Factoring commission per month	$7,500	
Interest expense per month	+ 2,188	
Gross cost per month	$9,688	
Gross cost per year	x 12	$116,256
Less: Annual credit dept. costs	500 x 12	- 6,000
Less: Annual bad-debt losses	.02 x 3,600,000	-72,000
Net annual cost of factoring		$ 38,256

c. $\text{Annual Financing Cost} = \dfrac{\text{Net annual cost}}{\text{Amount advanced}} = \dfrac{\$38,256}{\$260,312} = 14.7\%$

6.   Polynomial also wishes to investigate obtaining financing by obtaining a secured loan under a field warehousing agreement. They could borrow up to $200,000 under such an arrangement at an annual interest cost of 10%. The cost of maintaining the warehouse would be $10,000 per year. If they borrow $100,000, what would be the annual financing cost?

Solution:

$\text{Annual Financing Cost} = \dfrac{\text{Interest cost + Warehousing cost}}{\text{Proceeds of loan}}$

The interest cost is $(.10)(\$100,000) = \$10,000$.

Warehousing cost is $10,000.

Proceeds of the loan amount to $100,000.

$\text{Annual Financing Cost} = \dfrac{\$10,000 + \$10,000}{\$100,000} = 20\%$

21

International Financial Management

The chapter shows how exchange rate risk can be minimized in international financial management.

I. There is a secular trend of greater scope for international trade and investment and of increasing numbers of firms engaging in various types of international financial transactions.

   A. The complexity of international financial transactions varies widely.

      1. The simplest case would be firms that only import or export finished products or raw materials.

      2. At the other extreme are multinational corporations, which have direct investments in manufacturing and/or distribution facilities in more than one country.

      3. Between these extremes are firms that maintain foreign branch sales offices, that have licensing arrangements, or that have joint ventures with foreign firms.

   B. There are special problems and risks facing firms engaged in international financial transactions.

      1. First, firms doing business in different currencies are concerned with fluctuations in the exchange rates between currencies.

2.   Second, there are different governmental regulations, tax laws, business practices, and political environments in foreign countries.

C.   The exchange rate is the number of units of one currency which may be exchanged for another currency. (For example, the exchange rate could be 2.4080 dollars per pound, or reciprocally, .4153 pounds per dollar.)

1.   The spot rate is the exchange rate for currencies being bought and sold for immediate delivery.

2.   Forward exchange rates are exchange rates for currencies being bought and sold for delivery at some future date, usually 30, 90, or 180 days from today.

3.   If the forward rate is higher than the spot rate, the higher rates are termed premiums. Premiums arise when the spot rate is expected to rise in the future. Discounts (the forward rate is below the spot rate) occur when the spot rate is expected to decline in the future. The premium between the spot rate and the forward rate can be expressed on an annual percentage basis using this equation

$$\text{Premium} = \frac{(F - S)}{S}\frac{(12)}{n}(100)$$

where:

S = spot rate
F = forward rate, and
n = number of months forward.

D.   The theory of <u>interest rate parity</u> states that the annual percentage forward premium for a currency. Quoted in terms of another currency is equal to the approximate difference in interest rates prevailing between the two countries. For example, for the United States (US) and Britain (UK)

$$\frac{(F - S)}{S}\frac{(12)}{n} = \frac{i_{US} - i_{UK}}{1 + i_{UK}}$$

F and S are the forward and spot rates for British pounds (in dollars per pound), i_{US} is the U.S. interest rate, and i_{UK} is the comparable British rate. If interest rate parity does not hold, arbitrage opportunities exist.

E.   In general, exchange rates fluctuate over time in response to changing supply and demand. Economic and political conditions change the supply and demand for a country's currency. Differential inflation rates and interest rates affect both spot rates and forward rates.

II.   Exchange rate risk occurs when the value of a contract denominated in a foreign currency (either a future inflow or outflow) changes due to a change in the exchange rate. International companies can manage foreign exchange risk by hedging.

A.   In foreign trade, firms have transaction exposure. For example, a U.S. business may purchase goods from a Japanese supplier and the transaction is stated in Japanese Yen. The U.S. firm is exposed to exchange rate risk if the value of the Yen changes. For short-term contracts, the firm can protect itself in two ways:

   1.   Executing a contract in the forward exchange market or in the foreign exchange futures market is the first method to manage exchange rate risk. In the example, the U. S. business could buy Japanese Yen in the forward exchange market. In contrast to forward contracts, futures contracts are standardized with respect to size and delivery dates and traded on organized exchanges.

   2.   The second technique is called a money market hedge. The U.S. firm could borrow funds from its bank, exchange them for Japanese yen in the spot market, and invest the Yen in interest-bearing Japanese securities that mature on the date payment is due to the Japanese supplier.

B.   Firms with direct investments in foreign subsidiaries face exchange rate risk in the form of translation exposure.

   1.   Accounting procedures define how the balance sheets of foreign subsidiaries are translated into the parent company's balance sheet.

      a.   Current assets (unless covered by forward exchange contracts) and fixed assets are translated into dollars at the rate of exchange prevailing on the date of the balance sheet.

      b.   Current and long-term liabilities payable in a foreign currency are translated into dollars at the rate of exchange prevailing on the date of the balance sheet.

   2.   Present accounting rules require that these translation losses (or gains) be reported on the balance sheet as a separate adjustment to stockholders' equity and not on the income statement of the parent company.

   3.   If a foreign subsidiary's assets are greater than its liabilities, currency exchange losses will occur if the exchange rate decreases.

   4.   A company can hedge against translation exposure by financing its foreign assets with debt denominated in financing its foreign assets with debt denominated in the same currency.

III.   Firms engaged in foreign trade have a variety of sources of financing that may not be available to domestic firms.

   A.   Firms importing goods from another country often use an import letter of credit to finance the transaction.

      1.   A <u>letter of credit</u> is issued by the importer's bank and guarantees payment for a particular shipment of goods.

      2.   The exporter presents a draft for payment in 90 days to its bank when it ships the goods.

      3.   The draft is forwarded to the importing firm's bank for acceptance. When it is accepted, the draft becomes a <u>bankers' acceptance</u>, which is a marketable security that can be sold for a discount prior to maturity if desired.

   B.   United States firms frequently find it advantageous to finance a major portion of their foreign investments with funds they raise abroad.

      1.   The government occasionally imposes restrictions or quotas on foreign investment.

      2.   Foreign financing reduces exchange rate risk and potential losses if the foreign country imposes restrictions on outflows of funds.

      3.   The firms avoid SEC (Securities and Exchange Commission) regulation.

      4.   Different banking practices abroad often lead to advantageous borrowing arrangements for U.S. firms. Examples of superior terms are longer term and handling loans on an overdraft basis.

   C.   Several unique sources of international funds include borrowing from Eurodollar markets, the World Bank, the Inter-American Development Bank, and national banks that lend to promote domestic economic development.

      1.   Eurodollars are U.S. dollars that have been deposited in foreign (mostly European) banks or foreign branches of U.S. banks. The foreign bank can then lend these dollar deposits in the form of Eurodollar loans.

      2.   A Eurobond is a bond issued outside the country in whose currency the bonds are denominated. A foreign bond is denominated in the currency of the currency in which it is issued. In addition to bonds denominated in a single currency, some Eurobonds are denominated in European currency units (ECU's) which is a composite whose value is a weighted average of ten European currencies.

TRUE AND FALSE QUESTIONS

Agree with each of the statements or reject it and modify it so that it is acceptable.

1. The exchange rate of 4.0000 pralines per dollar is identical to .2500 dollars per praline.

2. Because of the time value of money, forward exchange rates are always higher than spot rates.

3. If the interest rate is greater in the United States than in Switzerland, this will reduce the spot rate relative to the forward rates (in dollars per Swiss franc).

4. If you owe a debt in a foreign currency (such as Canadian dollars) in three months, you can protect yourself from exchange rate risk by buying Canadian dollars in the forward exchange market.

5. Borrowing in a foreign country to help finance an investment in that country is one way a multinational company can reduce exchange rate risk.

6. Assume a U.S. company has a subsidiary in a foreign country. If the foreign subsidiary has more foreign denominated assets than liabilities, a decrease in the exchange rate (in dollars per unit of the foreign currency) will result in translation losses.

7. A letter of credit is issued by the exporter's bank and guarantees payment for a particular shipment of goods.

8. A banker's acceptance is a draft the exporter forwards to the importer's bank, and the draft becomes a marketable security when the importer's bank accepts it and agrees to pay it at some future date.

9. One advantage to a U.S. firm of financing a portion of its foreign investment with funds raised aboard is to avoid SEC regulation.

10. A Eurodollar is a dollar denominated deposit in a foreign bank or foreign branch of a U.S. bank.

Answers to True and False Questions

1. True.

2. Forward rates may have either premiums or discounts over the spot rate.

3. True.

4. True.

5. True.

6. True.

7. The letter of credit is issued by the <u>importer's</u> bank.

8. True.

9. True.

10. True.

CHAPTER 21 PROBLEMS

1. Calculate the premium between the forward rate and spot rate (on an annual basis) for the following currencies.

Currency	Spot Rate	90-Day Forward Rate
British Pound	1.4665	1.4510
Canadian Dollar	.7201	.7156
Japanese Yen	.006399	.006416
Swiss Franc	.5895	.5920
West German Mark	.4787	.4806

   All the exchange rates are given in U.S. dollars per unit of the foreign currency.

   Solution:

   Use this equation for each currency.

   $$\text{Premium} = \frac{(F - S)}{S}\frac{(12)}{n}(100\%)$$

   Ninety days is three months.

British Pound:

$$\text{Premium} = \frac{1.4510-1.4665}{1.4665}\left(\frac{12}{3}\right)(100\%) = -4.23\%$$

Canadian Dollar:

$$\text{Premium} = \frac{.7156-.7201}{.7201}(4)(100\%) = -2.50\%$$

Japanese Yen:

$$\text{Premium} = \frac{.006416-.006399}{.006399}(4)(100\%) = 1.06\%$$

Swiss Franc:

$$\text{Premium} = \frac{.5920-.5895}{.5895}(4)(100\%) = 1.70\%$$

West German Mark

$$\text{Premium} = \frac{.4806-.4787}{.4787}(4)(100\%) = 1.59\%$$

2. The interest rate in the U.S. is 10% and the interest rate in West Germany is 8%. The spot rate is \$.4545 per Mark. If interest rate parity holds, what should be the 90 day forward rate for Marks?

Solution:

Use the formula

$$\frac{(F-S)}{S}\left(\frac{12}{n}\right) = \frac{i_{US} - i_{WG}}{1 + i_{WG}}$$

Substitute the above values and n = 3 months to get

$$\frac{F-.4545}{.4545}\left(\frac{12}{3}\right) = \frac{.10-.08}{1+.08}$$

Solve this for F to get

F = \$.4566 per Mark.

The forward rate is above the spot rate because the U.S. interest rate exceeds the interest rate in West Germany.

3. Paul Reingold has sold some denim to a Japanese firm and will be paid 200,000,000

yen in 90 days. The spot rate is 214.00 yen per dollar and the 90-day forward rate is 215.30 yen per dollar.

a.   If Paul sells the yen in the forward exchange market, how many dollars will he receive?

b.   On the other hand, suppose Paul waits and sells the yen in the spot market 90 days from now. What will his receipt be worth in dollars if the spot rate increases 3%? Decreases 3%?

Solution:

a.   Receipt in dollars = 200,000,000 yen/215.30 yen per dollar = $928,936

b.   3% increase in spot rate: 214.00(1.03) = 220.42

Receipt in dollars = 200,000,000 yen/220.42 yen per dollar = $907,359

3% decrease in spot rate: 214.00(.97) = 207.58

Receipt in dollars = 200,000,000 yen/207.58 yen per dollar = $963,484

4.   The spot rate on Swiss Francs is 0.6073 dollars per franc and the 180-day futures exchange rate is 0.6280 dollars per franc. Suppose you can earn 5% in 180 days in the United States and 3% in 180 days in Switzerland. With $1,000,000, should you invest in the U.S. or in Switzerland (ignore taxes and any applicable laws)?

Solution:

In the U.S. in 180 days, your investment earns 5%.

Terminal wealth = 1,000,000(1 + .05) = $1,050,000

In Switzerland, sell your dollars for francs in the spot market, calculate your terminal wealth in francs at 3%, and sell your francs for dollars in the futures market.

In the spot market, the price per franc is .6073, so buy

1,000,000/.6073 = 1,646,633 francs

Terminal value (francs) = 1,646,633(1 + .03) = 1,696,032 francs

Convert to dollars in 180-day futures.

Terminal value ($) = 1,696,032(.6280) = $1,065,108

Even though the interest rate is lower in Switzerland, you earn more there because the Swiss Franc is expected to grow in value about 3.4% relative to the dollar, which more than offsets the 2% interest rate differential.

======== C H A P T E R ========

22

Corporate Restructuring

This chapter discusses two major forms of corporate restructuring: external expansion (mergers) and failure (bankruptcy). Mergers and acquisitions involve broader considerations than their financial aspects alone. Nevertheless, their financial considerations are significant. In an economic sense, a business failure could be a firm that is earning an inadequate return on investment or that has revenues insufficient to cover costs. In a financial context, a business failure occurs when the firm is unable to meet its obligations to creditors. This chapter defines business failure and discusses its causes. Alternatives available to failing firms are discussed, including procedures under Federal bankruptcy laws.

I.   Businesses may grow externally by acquiring or combining with other businesses. When two companies combine, the shares of the acquired company are purchased by the acquiring company.

   A.   There are several legal types of combinations.

      1.   A merger is a combination of two (or more) companies in which the surviving company continues to operate under its own name and the other company (or companies) legally ceases to exist.

      2.   A consolidation is a combination in which the combining companies are dissolved legally and a new company is formed.

      3.   The term acquisition is synonymous with merger.

B. Mergers can also be categorized as vertical, horizontal, or conglomerate mergers.

1. A vertical merger is between companies that may have a buyer-seller relationship with each other.

2. A horizontal merger is a combination between companies that compete directly with each other.

3. A conglomerate merger is a combination in which the companies neither compete with each other nor have a buyer-seller relationship.

4. The Federal Trade Commission breaks down the conglomerate mergers into geographic market extension mergers, product extension mergers, and pure conglomerate mergers. In geographic market extension mergers, the merging firms make the same product but sell it in different markets. In product extension mergers, the merging companies sell different but related products. In a pure conglomerate merger the firms are essentially unrelated.

C. A merger may be completed through a stock purchase or an asset purchase.

1. In a stock purchase, the acquiring company buys the stock of the target company and assumes its liabilities.

2. In an asset purchase, the acquiring company buys some (or all) of the assets of the target company and does not assume any of its liabilities.

D. One form of business combination is the holding company in which the acquiring company purchases all or a controlling block of another company's shares. The companies then become affiliated, with the acquiring company becoming the holding company in a parent-subsidiary relationship.

E. A joint venture is a business combination in which two unaffiliated companies contribute to a company formed to engage in some business activity.

F. In a leveraged buyout (LBO), a buyer borrows a large amount of the purchase price to buy a company or division of a company.

G. Divestitures and restructurings often accompany mergers.

1. In a divestiture, part of the company can be sold for cash. Or, part of the company can be divested through a spinoff (or an equity carve-out) where shares in the divested company are distributed on a pro rata basis to the shareholders of the parent company.

2.   In an operational restructuring, the company changes the asset side of the balance sheet. In a financial restructuring, the company changes its capital structure.

H.   There may be a friendly agreement between two merging companies. If not, the acquiring company may make a <u>tender offer</u> to purchase the common stock of the merger candidate. The tender offer price must offer a premium over the target's market price to induce the target's shareholders to sell.

I.   Many companies have undertaken anti-takeover measures to discourage unfriendly takeover attempts.

    1.   One such measure is staggering the terms of the board of directors so that it may take several years to replace the entire board.

    2.   Key executives may be given "golden parachutes" in which they receive expensive benefits in the event of a merger.

    3.   A supermajority rule requires a supermajority of the shares (e.g., 80%) to approve a takeover proposal.

    4.   A "poison put" can be exercised by security holders in the event of a takeover. One example is that the bonds would have to be redeemed for cash.

    5.   In an unfriendly takeover attempt, the management of the target company might attempt a friendly merger with another company (the "white knight").

J.   There are several reasons a company might seek external growth through mergers.

    1.   It may be less expensive to buy needed assets by acquiring a firm that has them than to purchase the assets directly.

    2.   Economies of scale sometimes result from a horizontal merger. Synergy exists if the net income of the combined firms exceeds the sum of the net incomes before merger.

    3.   The acquiring firm in a vertical merger may wish to assure the availability of raw materials or end-product markets.

    4.   More rapid growth is frequently possible through acquisitions than through internal growth.

    5.   The firm's management may desire greater diversification.

6. A firm which has suffered losses and has a tax-loss carryforward may wish to merge with a profitable firm to use the tax-loss carryforwards.

K. Two different methods of accounting for mergers are employed: the purchase method and the pooling-of- interests method.

1. In the purchase method, the total value paid or exchanged by the acquiring firm is recorded on the books. Tangible assets are recorded at their fair market value and any excess paid beyond this is recorded as goodwill.

2. In the pooling-of-interests, the acquired company's assets are recorded in the acquiring company's books at their former book value. Thus, no goodwill accounts are created.

3. Since goodwill must be amortized (like a depreciation charge), reported net income is higher using the pooling-of-interests method. Furthermore, since amortization of goodwill is not a tax-deductible expense, it is deducted from net income after taxes.

II. The valuation of a merger candidate is an application of capital budgeting principals.

A. Valuation of a merger candidate is necessary to determine the price to be paid. Three major methods are used.

1. The <u>comparative price-earnings ratio method</u> examines prices and associated price-earnings ratios in recent acquisitions of similar companies.

2. The <u>adjusted book value method</u> attempts to determine the market value of the company's assets.

3. The <u>discounted cash flow method</u> applies usual capital budgeting techniques by discounting expected future cash flows at an appropriate risk-adjusted rate.

B. The terms of a merger may involve almost any combination of cash, stock, or other financial instruments.

1. In a stock-for-stock exchange, the exchange ratio (ER) is the ratio of shares in the surviving company received to the number of shares surrendered in the acquired company.

2. The current earnings per share of the surviving company will increase (or decrease) if the price- earnings ratio of the surviving firm is greater than (or less than) the price-earnings ratio (using acquisition price) of the acquired firm. The post- merger price of the firm's

stock may go up or down depending on the post-merger price-earnings ratio determined in the marketplace. Normally, the post-merger price-earnings ratio determined in the marketplace. Normally, the post-merger price- earnings ratio is a weighted average of the pre- merger price-earnings ratios. Earnings per share growth through mergers may be more phantasmic than real.

The earnings per share for the combined companies, EPS_c, is

$$EPS_c = \frac{E_1 + E_2 + E_{12}}{NS_1 + NS(ER)}$$

where

E_1 = earnings of the acquiring company,
E_2 = earnings of the acquired,
E_{12} =synergistic earnings for the merger (if any),
NS_1 =number of outstanding shares for acquirer,
NS_2 =number of outstanding shares for acquired company, and
ER =exchange ratio

If an acquirer suffers immediate EPS dilution, EPS may eventually be increased if the target is predicted to have fairly rapid earnings growth.

3.   Similar considerations arise if the firms have dissimilar dividend yields.

4.   Tax considerations may also be involved. Stock-for-stock exchanges are tax-free. Receipt by the selling shareholders of cash or nonvoting securities is taxable at the time of merger. For installment sales with cash down payments less than 30 percent, the seller can spread the capital gains tax over the payment period.

III.   There are different legal types of failures.

A.   A firm is <u>technically insolvent</u> if it is unable to meet its current obligations as they come due, but the firm's assets have greater value than its liabilities.

B.   A firm is <u>legally insolvent</u> if the recorded value of its assets is less than the recorded value of its liabilities.

C.   A firm is not actually <u>bankrupt</u> unless it is unable to pay its debts and it files a bankruptcy petition in accordance with Federal bankruptcy laws.

IV.   There are a variety of reasons why businesses fail.

A. Business risk causes of failure include industry downturns, over-expansion, inadequate sales, increased competition, and technological change.

B. Possible financial risk causes of failure could be too much financial leverage, too much short-term debt relative to long-term debt, and poor management of accounts receivable or accounts payable.

C. Incompetent management is a major factor in most failures. In fact, some of the causes of failure listed above may not be causes of failure so much as symptoms of incompetent management.

V. A failing firm has two alternatives.

A. The failing company can (1) attempt to resolve its difficulties with its creditors on a _voluntary_ or _informal_ basis, or (2) petition the courts and formally declare _bankruptcy_. A company's creditors may also petition the courts to declare the company bankrupt.

B. Regardless of whether the firm deals with its difficulties informally or formally, the company must decide whether to reorganize or liquidate the business.

1. The company should reorganize if its _going-concern value_ exceeds its _liquidation value_ and the company should liquidate if its liquidation value is more than its going-concern value.

2. Liquidation value is the proceeds that would be received from the sale of the firm's assets minus its liabilities.

3. The going-concern value is the capitalized value of the company's operating earnings minus its liabilities.

VI. When a company has cash flow problems, there are informal alternatives besides formal bankruptcy.

A. One of the first things a troubled firm may do is to stretch its payables, which may buy a few weeks of time.

B. Debt restructuring is one alternative available to a failing firm in which it attempts to resolve its difficulties with creditors on a voluntary basis through an extension or a composition.

1. In an extension, the failing firm gets its creditors to agree to extend the time it has to pay its debts.

2. In a composition, the creditors agree to settle for less than 100% of the amount owed and accept this as full discharge of their original claims.

3. Before lenders agree to a debt restructuring, they may also require the firm's suppliers to make concessions. The lenders may demand warrants in return for their concessions.

C. A troubled company can sell off real estate or operating divisions to raise cash.

D. Another method of raising cash is a sale and leaseback of land and buildings.

E. A creditor's committee may be formed to represent the company's creditors. The creditors' committee meets and negotiates with the company's management on appropriate actions to take. If successful, the legal and administrative expenses associated with formal bankruptcy may be avoided.

F. An assignment is the process of liquidation outside of the bankruptcy courts. A trustee is assigned the assets, and then the trustee is responsible for selling the assets and distributing the proceeds in the best interests of the creditors.

VII. Formal U. S. bankruptcy procedures are codified in the Bankruptcy Reform Act of 1978.

A. Reorganization, which should be attempted when a company's going-concern value exceeds its liquidation value, is covered in Chapter 11 of the Bankruptcy Reform Act.

1. In a Chapter 11 proceeding, the failing company seeks protection from its creditors while it attempts to work out a plan of reorganization.

2. The court may appoint a trustee to run the business and protect the creditors' interests.

3. Chapter 11 bankruptcy proceedings may be initiated voluntarily by the company or by a group of three or more unsecured creditors with aggregate claims of at least $500.

4. After working out a plan of reorganization, the plan must be approved first by the bankruptcy court and then by the company's creditors. If the court and creditors approve, the company can leave Chapter 11.

5. The bankruptcy court and the Securities and Exchange Commission (SEC) review the plan of reorganization on the basis of its fairness and its feasibility. Fairness means that claims are settled in order of their priority. Feasibility means that the business has a good change of reestablishing successful operations.

6.   Following the SEC review for fairness and feasibility, the bankruptcy court submits the plan of reorganization to the company's security holders. Before the court can finally approve the plan, two-thirds of each group of debtholders and a simple majority of stockholders must vote in favor of the plan. Dissenters may appeal to a higher court.

VIII.   Liquidation, which should be attempted when the company's going-concern value is less than its liquidation value, is covered in Chapter 7 of the Bankruptcy Reform Act of 1978.

A.   The court selects a referee to handle the administrative procedures. The referee arranges a meeting of the creditors who, in turn, select a trustee to liquidate the business and distribute the proceeds according to the priorities in Chapter 7 of the Bankruptcy Reform Act.

B.   Secured debts are satisfied first from the sale of the secured assets. Then the following order of priority is used to pay unsecured debts:

1.   expenses involved in administration of the bankruptcy;

2.   business expenses incurred after an involuntary petition is filed, but before a trustee is appointed;

3.   wages owed for services performed during the three months prior to bankruptcy proceedings, not to exceed $2,000 per employee;

4.   certain unpaid contributions to employee benefit plans (limited to $2,000);

5.   certain customer lay-away deposits, not to exceed $900 per individual;

6.   taxes owed to Federal, state, and local governments;

7.   claims of general or unsecured creditors;

8.   preferred stockholders; and

9.   common stockholders.

TRUE AND FALSE QUESTIONS

Agree with each of the statements or reject it and modify it so that it is acceptable.

1.   In a merger of two companies, the surviving company continues to operate under its own name and the other company legally ceases to exist.

2.   A consolidation is a form of business combination in which a company (the parent) purchases 100% or a controlling interest in another firm (the subsidiary). Both firms legally continue to exist.

3.   A horizontal merger is between two firms on the same floor in a building, a vertical merger is between two firms on different floors of the same building, and a conglomerate merger is between two firms in different buildings.

4.   One possible motive for mergers is to get assets cheaply when the acquired firm's securities are selling for substantially less than the value of its assets.

5.   When a high price-earnings ratio business acquires a low price-earnings ratio business, the earnings per share and market price per share of the surviving firm will increase.

6.   When a merger is accomplished by a pure exchange of shares (specified in the exchange ratio), the selling firm's stockholders are liable for capital gains taxes at the time of the merger.

7.   A leveraged buyout is a transaction in which the buyer of a company borrows a large portion of the purchase price, using the purchased asset as partial collateral for the loans.

8.   An acquiring firm is legally obligated to pay book value for any company it wishes to buy.

9.   In the purchase method of accounting for mergers, acquired assets are recorded at their fair market values, and any additional amount paid is listed as goodwill, which must then be amortized.

10.   A tender offer is a public announcement by a company (or individual) indicating that it will pay a price above the current market price for the shares "tendered" of a company it wishes to acquire.

11.   A firm is technically insolvent when it is unable to meet its current obligations as they come due, but the firm's assets are worth more than its liabilities.

12.   One thing a firm with cash flow problems may do to buy time is to stretch its accounts receivable.

13.   In an extension, the failing company gets its creditors to extend the time it has to pay its debts.

14.   In a composition, the creditors agree to accept less than 100 percent of the amount owed and discharge the balance of their claims.

15.   When the going-concern value of a bankrupt business exceeds the liquidation value, the firm should be liquidated and the proceeds distributed to various creditors.

16. An assignment is the process of informally liquidating a business outside of the jurisdiction of the bankruptcy court.

17. In a bankruptcy, secured creditors (such as mortgage holders) have top priority in liquidation.

18. When the SEC evaluates a plan or reorganization for fairness, the SEC tries to predict whether the business has a good chance for reestablishing successful operations.

19. Frequently, failing firms have too much financial leverage, too much short-term debt relative to long-term debt, and poor management of receivables and payables.

20. A business cannot be forced into bankruptcy involuntarily.

Answers to True and False Questions

1. True.

2. The statement applies to a holding company. In a consolidation, the combining companies are dissolved legally and another new company is formed.

3. Would you have the courage to write that for a finance or economics instructor? See the summary above for acceptable definitions.

4. True.

5. Earnings per share will increase, but the behavior of the share price is much more complicated (it may go in any direction).

6. Stock-for-stock exchanges are tax-free.

7. True.

8. There is no legal reason to pay book value for anything.

9. True.

10. True.

11. True.

12. This would make their cash flow problems worse. The company could stretch its payables.

13. True.

14. True.

15. In this situation, a reorganization should be attempted.

16. True.

17. Secured creditors have top priority in liquidation only to the extent that their claims are satisfied by the secured property. Any amount left over is considered a general claim, which is behind several categories on the priority for paying unsecured claims (ahead of preferred and common stockholders).

18. Fairness means that claims are settled in priority and feasibility means that the firm has some prospect of operating profitably.

19. True.

20. A company's creditors can petition the courts to have a company declared bankrupt.

CHAPTER 22 PROBLEMS

1. McConnell-Foster has negotiated the acquisition of Johnson Hydro-Pump. Under the terms of the merger, Johnson Hydro-Pump shareholders will receive 0.600 shares of McConnell-Foster for each of their old shares. The pre-merger data for the two firms is

	McConnell-Foster	Johnson Hydro-Pump
Sales	$120,000,000	$30,000,000
Net income	14,000,000	3,000,000
Common share outstanding	2,500,000	800,000
Earnings per share	5.60	3.75
Stock price	67.20	30.00
Price/earnings ratio	12x	8x

Assume there is no synergism.

a. What is the post-merger earnings per share?

b. If the post-merger price/earnings ratio drops to 11x, what is the premium received by Johnson shareholders (using the new price of McConnell-Foster)?

c. Was this a successful merger for McConnell-Foster shareholders?

Solution:

a. Net income = $14,000,000 + $3,000,000 = $17,000,000

   Outstanding shares = 2,500,000 + .6(800,000) = 2,980,000

Earnings per share = 17,0000,000/2,980,000 = $5.705

b.   Price = 5.705(11) = $62.755

Premium   =   [.6(62.755) - 30]/30 = (37.653 - 30)/30

           =   7.653/30 = .2551 or 25.51%

c.   No. Their shares dropped from $67.20 to $62.755, a decrease of $4.445 per share (about 6.6%). On the other hand, Johnson Hydro-Pump shareholders realized a 25.5 percent gain.

2.   The president of Ontario Business Products blindly seeks mergers without regard to anything except the effect on current earnings per share. Ontario's current net income and outstanding shares are $75,000,000 and 20,0000,000, respectively, the EPS is $3.75, and the price per share is $37.50. Old Bottom Line (the president's nickname) wants to buy out Welch Plumbing which has net income of $10,000,000, a price of $75.00, EPS of $10.00, and 1,000,000 outstanding shares.

a.   What is the maximum number of new shares Old Bottom Line can offer for Welch and keep his EPS at its current level?

b.   Old Bottom Line can float a bond paying 10% interest and use the proceeds to purchase Welch stock for cash. How much can he offer and maintain his EPS? The tax rate = .40.

Solution:

a.   3.75   =   net income/number of shares

             =   (75,000,000 + 10,000,000)/(20,000,000 + x)

       x   =   2,666,667 shares

b.   3.75   =   net income/number of shares

             =   [(75,000,000+10,000,000-.10(B)(1-.40)]/20,000,000

       B   = $166,666,667

Old Bottom Line could offer $166,666,667 total or $167 per share for Welch if he used a leveraged buyout and his EPS would still be $3.75.

3.   Princeton Products, Inc., is being liquidated following bankruptcy. The liabilities and capital of the firm prior to bankruptcy were

Accounts payable	$10,000,000
Short-term bank loan (secured by accounts receivable)	3,500,000
Accrued wages (all less than $2,000 per person and earned in the last three months)	1,500,000
Accrued taxes	2,000,000
Mortgage (secured by property)	10,000,000
Debenture	5,000,000
Subordinated debenture (subordinated to debenture)	3,000,000
Preferred stock	2,000,000
Common stock	8,000,000
Retained earnings	(4,500,000)
Total Liabilities and Capital	$40,500,000

The trustee has liquidated the firm's assets for $30,000,000, which includes $4,500,000 for the accounts receivable and $6,000,000 for the property which was security for the mortgage. Court costs and legal fees are $4,000,000. There are no customer lay-away deposits, no unpaid business expenses incurred after filing bankruptcy. Indicate the money each class of creditors or owners should receive from the liquidation proceeds. Following the priorities in Chapter 7 of the Bankruptcy Reform Act of 1978.

Solution:

Total liquidation proceeds	$30,000,000
Less distributions to secured creditors:	
Short-term bank loan	3,500,000
Mortgage bond	6,000,000
Funds available after secured claims	$20,500,000
Less priority claims:	
Bankruptcy administration costs	4,000,000
Wages due employees	1,500,000
Taxes	2,000,000
Funds available for general creditors	$13,000,000

Settlement percentage for
general and unsecured creditors $=$ $\dfrac{\text{Funds available for general and unsecured creditors}}{\text{Total claims of general and unsecured creditors}}$

$$= \frac{13,000,000}{22,000,000} = .590909$$

Claimant	Total Claim	Settlement (59%) Before Adjustment for Subordination	Settlement (59%) After Adjustment for Subordination
Accounts Payable	$10,000,000	$ 5,909,091	$ 5,909,091
Mortgage	4,000,000	2,363,636	2,363,636
Debenture	5,000,000	2,954,546	4,727,273
Subordinated debenture	3,000,000	1,772,727	0
	$22,000,000	$13,000,000	$13,000,000

Funds available for preferred and common shareholders: $0

After payment of secured claims, $20,500,000 remains. The short-term bank loan secured by accounts receivable is paid off 100% and the $6,000,000 proceeds of the sale of property are applied to the mortgage bonds, which leaves the mortgage bondholders as general creditors for the $4,000,000 unsatisfied balance of their bond. A total of $7,500,000 now is used for the priority claims for bankruptcy administration costs, wages payable, and taxes payable. Since only $13,000,000 are available for general creditor claims of $22,000,000, general creditors received approximately 59 cents on the dollar. The funds due to the subordinated debentures are transferred to the debenture holders, and, since the debentures were not fully paid, the subordinated debenture owners receive nothing. Preferred and common stockholders get nothing.